D.S. HARDIN

THE PARAGON

This novel is entirely a work of fiction. The names, characters and incidents portrayed in it are the work of the author's imagination. Any resemblance to actual persons, living or dead, events or localities is entirely coincidental.

First edition

*This book was professionally typeset on Reedsy.
Find out more at reedsy.com*

To my wife Lydia with all my love.
Which somehow, is enough.

Contents

Prologue

The new boiler was rigged to blow.

He had done his part. The inner walls were too thin. The whole abomination would rupture in less than ten minutes. They could stop this madness just by swaying public opinion. People would die. But that was the necessity. Workers died every day, cogs in the great machine. At least this time the lives lost would mean something. Sean Lute watched as a great vat of molten iron was winched across the ceiling and tipped forward, sending brilliant sparks of fiery metal dancing off a die. Slowly, the liquid metal filled every crevice. The other half of the die was forced down with a piston wider than a man, compressing the molten metal, and forcing it into the desired shape. Lute understood that feeling.

He had no choice in this. No, he did, and he was sure this was the right one. If the Chorus ever found out what treason he committed, he would be executed, his wife and children branded as Discordant, and banished from the city. His family's centuries-long legacy would be torn from history. Still, at least he could be relied on. Who knew what the boy would do? Rumor and hearsay would not lead to change. A grand and violent gesture might.

Sean took a pipe from the brushed steel case on his desk, loaded it with cured tobacco, and struck a match. He puffed for a few moments, as he listened to the shouts and machinations of the production floor below his office. The other plan was too hopeful by half. It felt like a betrayal. *We manipulate and deceive him, and for what? So we can save our own skins? So he would be innocent of the blood we put on his hands? We force him into the ultimate sacrifice so that we can sleep at night? And once the truth was known, perhaps he wouldn't even choose to go through with it. On top of that, we only know that one child is even alive! He could decide to walk away and doom us all.* The whole operation was flimsy and far better suited as a backup plan, if it even beggared consideration in the first place. That's why Sean had to sabotage the boiler. He would be in the front row of its unveiling. The blast would hit him before the rest of the crowd. He would bear the burden and put a stop to this madness, not a boy tricked into his own slaughter.

The piston whined as it retracted from the glowing red iron. Sean watched as the bottom die rotated and dumped the cast into a pool of cooling oil. The oil belched and bubbled at the iron's intense heat and slowly subsided. Pairs of tongs slid on ceiling rails as they were guided over the cast. A pair of Smelters donning leather coveralls stained black with oil secured them to the plate. Hot vapor poured off the delicate curves of the design. It was a flower, an iris. There was a knock on the door leading down to the refinery. He motioned for Muse, his daughter, inside.

She stepped through the doorway, her leathers covered in slag. "Pretty piece of siding," Muse said, admiring through the window.

"I think it will look fetching on the west-facing wall," he said, deep in thought, "odd lengths to go to in order to recreate something that you can pluck from the dirt."

Muse eyed her father for a moment. "Well, if you're done being enigmatic, some High-Collars from the Patron have come calling."

On the far side of the facility, Sean could just see two figures, flinching at the noise of the forges. "Oh good, more handshakes." He tapped out his pipe and stood to retrieve his hat. "Would you go be your delightful self and entertain them for a moment, dear? I won't be long."

She swept low with a thick-gloved hand and bowed. Muse stopped at the doorway. "Are you sure you're okay Dad?"

Sean smiled at her. "I will be after shooing this lot away."

Muse smirked at his deflection and went to greet the dignitaries.

Sean settled his hat on his head and watched his youngest daughter skip down the steel stairs to the workfloor. Sabotaging the boiler may not have been enough. Maybe that would only slow the Patron down for a little while. Perhaps that boy was the only solution to deal with the impending doom forever. Maybe he was always meant to pay the price for his forebearer's transgressions. Cursed with it, due to his own good nature. Sean walked down the stairs into the clamor of forges. It would be worth it, he decided ... if Jack had to die to save the rest of them.

Chapter 1

27 minutes, 12 seconds.

This could kill me.

Jack was going to miss his window. *Fourteen seconds behind.* The cool, wet air of the pre-dawn morning whipped across his face and carried the echo of his boots as he sprinted down the wide, worn, avenue of stone. Crumbling arches straddled the old boulevard, stretching skyward toward the fading light of the stars.

Jack had always hated how the cobblestone felt dead beneath his feet. It was too

permanent, too lasting. *Twenty-five minutes, fifty-seven seconds.* He turned onto a patchwork bridge that spanned a deep and quiet moat. Granite trusses on the near side of the bridge joined

haphazardly to patinated metal trusses. Haphazard could easily describe most of Cogrind's outer ring. Stonehall they called it - an engineering marvel of antiquity that over the centuries

had become the gutter to collect the city's unwanted and broken. Tenement shacks lined those

same stone streets, each precariously built atop the other, standing more out of habit than any

structural endurance.

Jack turned his back to Stonehall and rushed over the bridge. Living in Stonehall allowed

him to soak in the view of the city center each morning. Residents of Cogrind proper could

never fully appreciate the juxtaposition he witnessed every day. He stormed the bridge

at a breathless pace. When Jack felt the soft reverberation of his feet meeting the metal street,

he smiled. He may have slept in Stonehall, but Cogrind was home. He ran the dark alleys as swift and familiar as the cats that scattered at his charge, dodging exhaust vents and laundry lines with deft familiarity. The copper buildings stretched above him, muted red in the pre-dawn light. *Sixteen seconds behind.* Faster. He zigzagged across the intricate veins of the backstreets and picked up his pace. The sky turned gray with pre-dawn light as the blue Arc-lamps bore their light feebly against the coming day. Jack flicked his eyes to a street clock. He was eighteen seconds behind now, but his chance to make up time was coming.

Sixteen minutes, twenty-two seconds. Jack sprinted down a thin, rusting corridor as

copper shutters above him opened to the streets in rhythmic succession. Jack broke free of the

last alley and dashed across a wide thoroughfare made

entirely of bronze. The sun rose over rooftops and in a flash, the city of Cogrind was ablaze with shades of polished steel and

patinated brass.

Jack loved this time of the morning. 500,000 souls lived here, and right now the city was

his alone. It would stop being his if he happened to kill himself, which was becoming

more of a possibility at the moment. But if he could do it, he would be exact, precise. Perfect.

Forming a smaller ring within Stonehall, The Promenade girdled the entirety of the city

center, a two-mile diameter thoroughfare with a penthouse view of Cogrind's central district. Unlike Stonehall's forgotten and crumbling state, the Promenade was adorned with ornate plates and burnished tiles on the townhouses lining the street. Steel-pounded murals of his city's

achievements blurred past his view. Jack tore across the empty boulevard towards fourteen

floors worth of steep stairs and polished railing. This is where Jack would make up his time.

He leaped onto the railing and slid down towards the West Plaza. The flat metal expanse

of the West Plaza began to creak and clank underneath his feet as vending booths were

pushed up from the street and into position by the giant gears beneath the city.

One second ahead. The fifth-floor window of the Ironworks Conservatory, the structure that made up the very heart of the city, beckoned high above the streets. Conversely, this

was where the dying part also came into play.

With a trained stride, Jack jumped onto the first rising stall and then to the next, each

booth catapulting his steps. Their brass roofs launched him higher and higher until the time had

come. For the last three years, he had always pulled up short on top of the last roof. His eyes

locked onto the shuttered window, silently counting *three, two, one . . .* until they whipped open at precisely *zero.*

Jack sprang from the last roof, but the shutters hadn't whipped open. The shutters were still closed. He blinked, his brain pointlessly reviewing his inner clock. His body sensed the five

stories of air between him and the street. His eyes opened. So did the shutters. He tumbled

through the window, flailing and rolling across a lush carpet until he hit a very solid pair of gold

desk legs. Jack swept the hair from his face and looked up into the unswerving stare of Carrol

Crowley, a cup of tea in one hand, a silver fob watch in the other.

"Mr. Dowton. Right on time. You are aware that we have doors specifically made for

entering the Conservatory?" Crowley clicked his fob watch closed and slipped it into his vest

pocket.

Jack smiled as he picked himself up and squared to the middle-aged gentleman.

Crowley's salt and pepper hair was combed back in perfect little rows, revealing a drastic

widow's peak that further accented his pointed nose and thin, square chin. He wore his typical brown linen suit, perfectly pressed and slightly threadbare and impeccable white gloves.

The overall look gave the impression of a man constantly in motion, even when standing still.

Crowley's office was everything Jack was not, spotless and ornate. Glass floors framed by steel were lined with thick crimson rugs. Save for the curved glass windows at the back of the

office, artistic renderings of different schematics lined every other inch of the space, a blend of form and function. A chandelier lit by three dozen Arc-lights encased in amber haloed the room, its warm light dancing on silver, gold, and red. At the very center of the room, a console bloomed from the floor, a bouquet of brass levers waiting to be used.

"Apologies, but you must admit the window is a much more exciting entrance. Besides, my unique approach is why I've become so invaluable to you, isn't it?"

Crowley's face hardened. "You are not so invaluable as to be irreplaceable, Mouse."

Despite the reprimanding tone in Crowley's voice, Jack liked his nickname. It was pinned on him as an insult, but he wore it like a cape. It was given to him by the other apprentices, who bristled at the idea that a scrawny kid, newly hauled in from the street, would be chosen over ready apprentices still waiting for a Master. But after the first year of his apprenticeship, the Brassieres and Luthiers began to call on Mouse for his ability to squeeze into the smallest of spaces to weld broken gears or patch pipes that ran like veins through the Ironworks Conservatory. It also helped that Jack had long, white hair. Not platinum, but pure white, pulled back in a sweat-stained silk band that had slowly moldered to gray. The hair color was a rare trait that led to frequent tugging at his ponytail, thanks to an ages-old wives' tale. It was said the Paragon himself had curls of white, and those who shared this trait were destined to give a great gift to the City. His hair framed his bright eyes that could never decide if they were green or grey, so they settled on one of each.

Now, three years under the tutelage of Barin, Mouse had taken a more ironic tinge. If there was ever a dangerous situation, a burst pipe or broken main valve, Jack was the first one to volunteer. Jack figured on the logic that if anyone was going to be injured, it may as well be him, he could at least control that. Necessity above emotion. Duty above fear. Cogs for the greatest machine.

It was also a little selfish. It was at those moments that Jack felt most like himself. No time to think, only to fix what was broken. He could feel the problem in the back of his head. His hands would fly to the problem before his conscious self had time to think. He understood the mechanisms of the Conservatory as he understood his own breath. It was for these reasons that most of the age-toughened laborers had begrudgingly taken a shine to him. Besides, risking his life was how he got the job in the first place, and he would happily risk it again to keep it.

Crowley checked his polished silver fob watch, quickly returned it to his pocket, and began walking in the direction of the access lift. "We do not have time for pleasant banter at the moment, Mr. Dowton. The Number thirteen Arc-boiler has been losing pressure since last night. We've checked all the main valves to no avail, which leaves either the four spill valves or the Arc-points of the boiler itself."

Jack didn't dislike Carrol Crowley. In fact, he quite

respected him for his tireless dedication to his occupation. Crowley kept a city based upon the philosophy of unity running in perfect synchronicity. He was the Clockwork Maestro, Cogrind's hands of time. He knew as much about the inner machinations of the Ironworks Conservatory as anyone could. And he was not an unkind man. If an Oreman was sick, he allowed a half day for recovery. If a Tuner was pregnant, he conceded a week for birth and to reorganize their house accordingly. That being said, Jack thought that most times Crowley behaved more like the watch in his pocket than a man.

"I assume I'm to check the spill valves first?" Jack quickly followed the Maestro onto the open platform.

"First? You won't be touching the Arc-boiler. It's highly specialized work. An experienced hand is required. I've assigned Barin to the task. Finish *your* task and you will be able to observe."

Figured as much. He stepped onto the platform as Crowley adjusted the burnished levers to the proper coordinates, each movement ending in a satisfying *CLICK*. Jack smirked at the satin gloves wrapped around The Maestro's hands. He would abhor fingerprints on a piece of equipment so highly polished. Still, considering the amount of pressure he was under, Crowley's eccentricities could be understood. The access platform began to pneumatically slide down a claustrophobic shaft that emptied into the center of Jack's heart and the heart of Cogrind, The Proscenium.

The space had a distorting effect on Jack's vision. The Proscenium was so cavernous that the distance felt flat and compact. Each wall was clad in behemoth steel plates the size of a city block hanging two wide and two high. Four massive iron support beams rose along the length of the walls, arching to meet each other at the apex. Suspended from each arch were gold pendulums,one for each wall, the height of the structure itself, gliding silently back and forth in perfect unison. The morning light poured from the high-hung windows into the very center of the Shining City of Cogrind. Jack loved this place. He surmised this was the closest a person could come to being inside a living thing without actually being eaten. Jack even spied Crowley allowing himself a small grin when entering The Proscenium. After all, this was his orchestra.

In the center of the metal cavern, suspended amidst a spider's web of catwalks laced with workers and braided pipes, stood a circle of twelve copper cylinders, each twenty feet high. A pair of tubes protruded from the top of each cylinder swerving up like bull horns. Glass balls sixteen inches in diameter set upon the end of each tube. From between each glass orb swam a ripple of indigo energy, each ripple connected to the orb on the other side of the cylinder and to the orbs on each adjacent cylinder, a perfectly tuned lattice of Arc. The thin wisps of pure energy undulated in a single direction like a breeze atop a pond. Jack spotted the malfunctioning boiler immediately. The Arc on the number thirteen boiler was different. The Arc stretched and cracked against the shape of the wave, disrupting the tranquil weave. What was more disconcerting was how the body of the boiler itself was behaving to the imbalance. It wasn't so much vibrating as it was . . . shifting in space. It was as if it wasn't even connected to the myriad pipes that laced its carapace. The joints on the cylinder dislocated and reconnected like severed and reattached limbs in the blink of an eye.

11

Jack felt ill. "Is it really doing that?" His gaze affixed on the boiler. His stomach churned in response before he forced himself to look away.

"We utilize only a fraction of the power the Arc-boilers are capable of. Even I do not know the network's full capacity. That's the very reason we must keep every mechanism in this facility running in time." Crowley glared at the imbalanced Arc as if he could fix it with his eyes.

"I thought we kept everything in time in order to power the city," said Jack, still unable to tear his eyes away from the shifting cylinder.

"Mr. Dowton, If something were to go seriously awry within this facility, there wouldn't be a city to power."

The platform descended below the circle of boilers into a mesh of pipes. The sunlight from the windows above didn't illuminate much of the Proscenium under the catwalks. Instead, Arc-lamps sprouted on copper wires from wide, main feed tubes, casting a shimmering, cool light.

It gave Jack the impression of moonlight. "Where do I start?" He breathed in the damp air. The lift had slipped below ground now. He didn't not know much about the workings of the catwalks above, but he was quickly becoming an expert on the Proscenium's underbelly.

"I've brought the schematics for you," Crowley said, reaching into his pocket. Jack tore the folded papers from Crowley's hand. "You should look over them." He finished in his usual, chafed cadence.

Jack couldn't remember the last time Crowley spoke to him without a sarcastic tone and he planned on figuring out why, right after he sorted these valves. The lift landed at a catwalk amidst the blue-lit lamps, the sound of industry muffled by distance and depth.

"I would prefer you to have a spotter, Mr. Dowton. Even if you are only an apprentice, loss of labor is a burden to everyone else."

"And I would appreciate the company, but you and I both know they couldn't keep up with me." Jack knew it to be true and frankly, so did Crowley.

"Very well. I will see you at the Arc-chain within three hours, and nineteen minutes. And remember, to be early is to be on time, Mr. Dowton." Crowley crisply closed the watch and shifted the various levers of the lift.

"With bells on my toes." Jack smiled.

"Good hunting, Mr. Dowton." And with that, Crowley was lifted toward the morning light.

Jack closed his eyes in ritual and allowed his other senses to absorb his surroundings. It was almost completely silent. Jack figured at this point he was fifteen stories below the Proscenium, far away from the clamoring of hammers pelting bronze, and raucous shouts of Tuners. Jack could pick out only two sounds now; the soft plinking of the Arc-lamp's energy bouncing off its glass bulb and the intermittent sound of the giant metronome displacing the air above him. The smell was damp earth tinged with metal. His skin felt only the occasional breeze from the massive metronome above.

His hands moved to his tool belt, gliding along the smooth black leather and white stitching, with each holster occupied by the proper tool; gloves, vice grips, Arc-welder, a spool of welding wire, screwdriver, rubber mallet, a clutch of phosphorous torches and his beloved wrench. He relaxed and let his breath leave his body. If he had his tools he could fix most anything, at least anything he would find down here.

Jack opened his eyes, looked down either direction of the catwalk, and began running in the direction of the first spill valve.

The first valve was only a short distance away, located on a service platform twenty-five feet below the catwalk. There was a ladder reaching down to the platform but Jack wasn't interested in that. He had apprenticed for three years at the Conservatory, almost exclusively in the Orchestra Pit where he now stood. In that time, he estimated he studied about forty percent of the schematics of what he lovingly dubbed the Orchestra Pit. The reason for the placement and route of the innumerable pipes and platforms made no apparent sense, not even to the hungry eye of a prodigy. But Jack got the sense of some greater logic in the madness. Not anything he could pinpoint specifically, just that from what he could piece together, the sum of the pipeworks seemed right, logical, but only in the most roundabout way possible. He imagined it like a riddle, just between him and the Paragon. Jack pored over the first schematic to find a way down other than the obvious and frankly boring route of the ladder. Jack found it soon enough and decided that thinking about the risk of a jump from the catwalk into utter nothingness would only lead to him being late for the Arc-boiler replacement. Death would make him considerably later. Jack took a running leap into the pit.

His outstretched hand grasped the pipe of an Arc-lamp suspended over a three-foot wide pipe. He dropped down onto it and began walking towards his next acrobatic feat. His boots tapped against the top of the pipe in confident rhythm. He quickened his pace and jumped again. He ricocheted from the elbow of one pipe to an adjacent lower pipe. At least that was the plan. And it would've worked, too, had Jack not overshot his landing. If he tried to land on the lower, adjacent pipe, his feet would slip out from under him. On instinct, he angled his body into a dive and used the passing pipe as a springboard to propel himself toward the access platform. He made good contact with the pipe and managed to change his trajectory squarely towards the access platform.

This is going to hurt. His back bounced against the perch. He could feel his momentum carrying him past the platform. Twisting his body, Jack clutched the edge. He swung for a moment before pulling himself up.

Jack lay on the platform for a moment and reviewed what he had learned from this exercise: that as with every other area of the Orchestra Pit, he could navigate his way practically anywhere worth going by using nothing but the pipeworks. Second, he must have been incredibly stupid to attempt to do so. He now had some ideas as to why Crowley addressed him in such a sarcastic tone.

Well, it could have gone worse. So, I might as well get on with the job. He checked every inch of the valve for leaks without results. He tapped the fitting to check for rust to no avail. He made sure the bolts were cinched tight and scrambled up the access ladder onto the catwalk to locate the next spill valve. The second and third valves were also in pristine condition, which left the final valve. This part of the Conservatory was part of the Paragon's original build, and it was built to last. Rarely were there breakdowns in the Orchestra Pit. Most problems occurred above. Naturally, the last valve was located on the opposite side of the Proscenium.

The Paragon was a genius and a madman. Jack jogged his way across the catwalk, the sound of his boots for accompaniment.

Pools of light periodically illuminated his frame as he strode toward the final spill valve. His build was slight in the same way copper wire is thin; strong yet malleable. His body could be described as lanky, without the benefit of height. However, Jack's outward appearance of frailty belied his pound-for-pound strength. If a bolt existed in the Proscenium, he could turn it. Jack wore the standard gear for an apprentice: thick-soled leather boots, cotton trousers wrapped in leather chaps, and a loose-fitting tunic with a wide leather bib bearing a red X painted across the front. The X is what denoted him as an apprentice. If a fire broke out or a pipe burst, all hands flooded to that area. The X was meant to delineate who could help and who was useless in that situation. Jack, as with many things in the Conservatory, proved an exception to this rule. Every leather garment he wore had to be specially outfitted for him due to his thin build and age. Even at seventeen, Jack was still waiting for a very patient growth spurt. The standard age for admittance into apprenticeship was seventeen. Jack was fourteen when he started learning his craft under Barin, and now three months past his seventeenth birthday, Crowley assigned him solo tasks that would have other Masters bolted to the sides of their apprentices.

Jack was thankful he didn't have to spend much time in the Academy, the school for apprentices located in the Conservatory. It wasn't as though he felt above learning in a classroom, he just preferred to learn by scurrying around the quiet shadows of the Orchestra Pit. Besides, the other apprentices glared at him as he passed by their rows of chairs and tables lined with scale replicas of what he put his hands on everyday. The catwalk turned down into a flight of stairs leading deeper into the orchestra pit.

Jack leaped down the steps three at a time. Swollen return tubes slick with condensation ran parallel to the passageway on both sides, creating a canyon about the catwalk. A short distance farther it turned to the left and was abruptly blocked by interweaving lengths and widths of pipe. Jack peered in between the knot of tubes and assessed the situation. The Arc-lamps had grown sparse here and what light was present cast deep shadows. He could see that the catwalk continued along toward the safety valve but was repeatedly intersected with various pipes and tubes like vines strewn across a trail. A smile rose on his face.

Time for Mouse to earn his pay. He slipped in between two feed pipes and moved farther along the catwalk.

Jack weaved through the obstructions as he navigated the walkway in almost absolute darkness. His mind kept track of the distance he had moved and correlated it to the schematics he had memorized.

Should be along here somewhere. The darkness became total. Even with his eyes long settled to the lightless Orchestra Pit, Jack admitted defeat and lit a phosphorous torch. It blazed into life, throwing dancing white light across the claustrophobic space. Everything that he had learned by feel and dim light was now thrown into garish illumination. He felt that it disrespected the cool, dark dignity of the Pit, working tirelessly and hidden. Jack tossed the torch onto the catwalk and began searching among the pockets of light for the access ladder. He found it a short distance from where the torch lay and despite the incalculable amount of fun he would've had finding an alternate route to this platform, he decided the ladder would have to suffice. He made his way down to the platform to find the final spill valve in perfect running order. The threading was pristine and sealed. The flanges were spotless.

Figures. From the way that Arc-boiler was moving, it's a wonder why Crowley had me come down here in the first place. Jack finished his maintenance routine on the spill valve just as the light from the torch began to flicker and wilt. Grateful to return to the solitude of darkness, he climbed back onto the catwalk from the ladder. Jack stopped. There was a new sound. The Arc-lamp's soft plinking of energy striking glass could no longer be heard. The gold pendulum was still displacing air on its downswing like wind over a cliff. But now there was another sound underneath. Something was trying to mask the sound of breathing, with the pendulum swings. Jack peered through the darkness all around him. He saw them a good distance away— two small yellow orbs floating freely in the darkness. They continued to move closer to him. Jack stared at them for a moment Then he saw the black, vertical slits in both orbs. *Funny, they appear to be staring back.* Jack began to run in the opposite direction.

He flew through the mesh of pipes as quickly as he ever had, allowing his movements to be dictated by the schematics in his mind. Jack afforded a glance back. The eyes were thirty yards away.

How can it move that fast? Jack cracked his head against metal as he turned back to his escape. *I can't worry about that thing. If it gets me then it will be because it was faster, not because I'm stupid.* Jack escaped the nest of pipes and sprinted down the unobstructed catwalk. He heard the thing moving now to his right. Stealing through the canyon of gears and pipes above him slithered a limbless, metal body.

That explains his speed. It was then he realized he was in real trouble; the stairs to his salvation turned up and to the right, intersecting the creature's path. *It has the inside corner on me . . . doesn't matter. I can't stop now.* Jack looked up to see the creature just a few yards behind and above him. This was going to be close. He bounded up the steps two at a time, directly into the path of the monster. In the moment before his death, time slowed. The metal head of the snake lunged from a gap in the pipes, its lifeless yellow eyes trained on Jack's face. Lobstered bands made up its neck and body which allowed for such fluid movement through the Pit. Jack saw its metal jaws snap open, baring fangs the size of his leg.

This is going to hurt as well.

The serpent struck. Jack closed his eyes and spun his body outwards. He felt its fangs caress his torso as he was slammed against a pipe. The sound was horrible. Metallic screeching met furious white noise. Jack felt the snake's breath across his body, a blacksmith's mix of stale sweat and burnt ore. There was something else. It reeked of the retching saccharine of death.

He opened his eyes. The brass serpent had him wholly in its mouth, but it hadn't clamped down. Jack twisted to the right to see that both sets of fangs had penetrated a feed pipe. The serpent's body thrashed about violently in an attempt to free itself. Each time it did, showers of glowing steam flared from the fang holes in the pipe, scarring and burning the serpent, and Jack's apron. The heat felt like it was boring a hole through his chest. Jack started thrashing as well. He wrenched his right shoulder away from the pipe behind him.

The snake could feel his prey slipping away, its writhing became more violent, more desperate. Jack's left arm wriggled out of the snake's jaw and grabbing a railing, began to pull away from the monstrosity's grasp, the smaller teeth ripping at his skin. His upper body was almost free until he felt something snag. His tool belt. Jack hesitated only for a moment before plunging his hand back into the mouth of the beast, unbuckling his belt. The snake stopped moving its body. The hiss of steam grew louder and the shearing metal screamed. The snake was grinding its fangs through the pipe. He kicked with all his strength against the inside of the serpent's jaw. Jack sprang free just as the beast's jaws began to close, steam pouring into its unblinking eyes. Jack wanted to run, instead he turned to face his executioner. He reached his hand into the monster's closing maw and slipped back out with only his wrench before its jaws clamped shut. Jack sprinted up the remaining steps as the serpent whipped its head back and forth, maddened by blindness. Steam flooded the air obscuring the serpent as Jack flew down the catwalk towards the landing platform. His lungs burned as he took flights of stairs three at a time. He glanced back to see if he was being followed and immediately ran into a very solid pipe he didn't remember being there before.

"What's lit your tail on fire, Mouse?" rumbled a familiar voice.

Jack tilted his head forward, his body still prone and saw that it wasn't a thick pipe but a thick man. It was Barin, the Master Tuner of Cogrind.

"Has anyone ever told you you feel like metal when they run into you?"

Barin's cracked lips tightened around his jaw. Jack learned this was the closest thing Barin could muster for a smile. "More than once," Barin said, as he lifted Jack from the catwalk. "Although most who look where they are going make it a habit not to run into me. By cogs, you're soaked in sweat, boy."

Jack snapped to in an instant. "We've got to get out of here now!"

Barin assessed his apprentice for a moment. "You're in tatters, boy. Where's your belt?"

"It was eaten."

"It was what?"

"It was eaten by . . . by a gigantic metal serpent. He lodged himself into a feed pipe down three floors below me."

Barin examined his apprentice. Jack stared right back into his eyes. Barin's eyes were emotionless and observing, the eyes of a predator. They were light blue, set under a constantly furrowed brow. They were terrifying to look into, turning even a simple question into an interrogation. His body was made of hard-packed sinew from decades of twisting, turning and torquing the Proscenium to his will. If Carrol Crowley was the pendulum for Cogrind, Barin was most certainly the mainspring. He saw no lie in Jack's eyes. Barin knew that if it came from Mouse's lips, it was the truth, to Jack anyway.

"All right Mouse, show me." Barin stomped towards the direction of the stairs.

"Are you insane?"

Barin glanced back at him, a maze of scars across the old man's face. Considering the things Jack had seen Barin do in the three years he had been his apprentice, he should probably have rephrased the question. Barin turned and carried on.

"Its mouth is as big as I am." He followed behind Barin.

"How do you know that, Mouse?"

"Because I was inside it and I fit quite comfortably." Barin looked back at him again. "I meant in terms of size, not emotionally." Barin growled and turned the corner towards the stairs. "Barin, wait!" Jack sprinted around the corner.

"So where is this foul abomination?" asked Barin.

Jack gaped at the sight. There was no serpent. No glowing steam, no gaping holes in the return tube.

"So, where's your belt, boy?" demanded Barin.

Jack was too bewildered to speak.

"I asked you a question, apprentice." Barin squared himself to Jack.

"I . . . I swear it was here. It had me pinned against that pipe," whispered Jack, " I had to release my belt to get out. I only managed to save my wrench." He held out the polished instrument. His head swam in disbelief.

Barin paused for a moment before releasing a tired breath. "You'll earn a new belt Mouse, the hard way. For now, we must get to the Arc-chain. Number thirteen has taken a turn for the worse." Barin clomped his way back to the landing platform.

In silent bewilderment, Jack followed his master to the waiting lift.

Chapter 2

I might die today. The grey horizon betrayed no sign of the coming sun. The forest stretched before Sallah va Hawthorne, a motionless ocean of green peaks and dells, frosted with mist.

"Mistress, it is time," said Karra. Sallah's Consort stood at the base of the branch, her head bowed in reverence. Sallah returned her eyes to the Greensea.

She stood on a high, thin branch in the silence of the pre-dawn morning. The towering Hawthorne tree on which she stood was tall enough for Sallah to view the curve of the horizon, the pregnant belly of the earth, swollen with all of life. "Thank you, Karra. You may go."

Silently, the Consort retreated to the hollow trunk of the Hawthorne. Sallah stood for a moment longer and watched the sun break over the forest line and bathe the treetops in every hue of fire and viridescence. She whispered an old prayer to herself and stepped off the branch into the open air.

Her foot was met by an up-reaching limb. She stepped

gracefully down the exterior of the tree, each step supported by a waiting branch, like a servant's hand, which carried her down to the next outstretched branch. *Make it look effortless.* It took a good deal of concentration to bend the Mother Tree to her will, but she needed to show her strength. Her people were watching, specks beneath her feet. She didn't look down, but she knew they were there. Upturned faces looking at their salvation or damnation. Sallah stopped on a white-flowered limb as it swung inward to an arched opening in the trunk of the towering tree. She stepped into a foyer, wooden braids of age rings lining the floor and ceiling that opened to the hollowed interior of the Mother Tree. Waiting at the archway laid a white and silver serval.

"Ready, Tosi?"

The long cat blinked lazily at her, his oversized ears twitching at the slightest sound of the waking world. He stretched his claws across the wooden flesh of the floor.

"You'll be excited soon enough. Time to *hunt.*"

At that word, Tosi's eyes snapped into focus. Sallah allowed herself a grin as she strode towards an archway on the opposite side of the landing. Tosi swept quickly around to follow her. The opening led to a slow ramp of wooden sinew that corkscrewed down the interior of the massive tree. Sallah followed the spiraling path down towards the ground and to the breathless crush of her kin.

They were the people of the House of Hawthorne, her people. Each one appeared grave and anxious. Sallah walked through them. She met as many eyes as she could, her gaze practiced and stoic. They moved from her path, each head bowed as she passed.

She walked down a well-worn path through a grove of

white-petal Hawthornes, dancing with the morning breeze. Her gait slowed. *Will this be the last time I hear you?* she asked the trees as she passed. Sallah wished this walk would last forever, or better still, time would just stop. But she could already see her first destination.

The forested hill sloped to a glade along a thorny hedgerow where two others stood, awaiting their fate. The crowd halted a short distance away from the trio. Sallah bowed to her mentors.

"Oh stop it, child," said Agneth lifting her chin with a wink. "One of us will be dead by sundown, I have no need for honorifics."

Agneth was the name for 'mother' in the heart of Sallah. She was the first face Sallah loved and was the one who trained Sallah in her greatest gift. Agneth wore the customary huntress outfit of leather leggings and vambraces with a cinched leather vest over a simple blouse. Agneth was short and lithe, with the decades of hunting etched into her frame and a long braid tucked beneath her cloak. But she looked old now, older than yesterday. Sallah smiled for Agneth's sake.

"You have proven yourself before Dharra and the Mother Tree. You are Druida. You bow to no one," rumbled Terran.

The words felt soothing coming from Terran's lips. Sallah always felt Terran was appropriately named. He was as silent and steady as stone. He listened constantly and only spoke when asked a direct question or when absolutely necessary. And for this, she knew him to be wise. He knew the politics of the other Houses as well as any outsider could and had ushered in an alliance with the Houses of Rowan, Ash, and Reed. Terran brought honor to the House of Hawthorne and

25

he did so in a manner that no other House could manage quite so well; he did it quietly. Sallah studied the eyes of her fellow Druida. Neither showed the slightest sign of sadness.

Make it look effortless. These were Agneth's words. The first lesson she had taught Sallah in becoming a Druida. You could not simply do something, you had to demonstrate total mastery over the action. At first, Sallah took it to mean politically, but she learned over the years Agneth's lessons had many meanings. The eyes of the other Houses were everywhere and the slightest showing of weakness meant plots and schemes would hatch too plentiful to prevent.

Sallah mustered the same look as her mentors and a flicker of indignation rose in her chest at her weakness. "We shouldn't be late to our own Rite." She began walking into the hedge opening. Agneth smiled proudly and Terran gave a slow nod as they followed behind her, Tosi bringing up the rear.

The hedgerow was an ever-changing testimony to the House of Hawthorne's own dark history. Its twists and dead ends were rearranged every lunar cycle as a defense line against the other Houses during the Time of Fire, an age long since passed. Some paths led to dead ends, some to unmapped regions of the Greensea. Only those born under the shade of the Hawthorne were safe to navigate the hedgerow without fear. It guided them to whatever destination they wished. Sallah let her fingers glide across the smooth, dark leaves of the maze, the thorns retreating from her touch. Presently, no House would dare attack another outright. The barbaric days of daggers and arrows had given way to political maneuvering and sabotage. Conflicts were perhaps just as deadly, the Houses just got better at hiding the bodies.

She closed her eyes as she walked. Sallah could always feel the energy; the life force of all living things around her. Like hearing a whisper at the back of her mind, but when she closed her eyes, she could *see* the life force. Where there was no life was total void, total darkness, but plants and animals were faint outlines that glowed in infinite hue, soft ribbons of mist trailing from the leaves, moving to and fro on an unfelt breeze.

Sallah liked to think that only when her eyes were closed could she truly see. "What happens during the Rite?" Sallah's eyes were still closed. The Rite of Diodorus Siculus was an uncommon event. Sallah had never experienced one in her lifetime of nineteen years.

"You will see when the time comes," said Agneth.

Something terrible then.

No more than two Druida were allowed from each House, that much Sallah did know. Three Hawthorne Druida were walking through the hedgerow now. One would not walk back. Fear began to leak into Sallah's mind.

"Fear is a creature's first reaction to the unknown," said Agneth, intuitively aware of her pupil. "It is a weapon that can be used against others as well as yourself. Know that you are prepared for anything that the Greensea may reveal."

Sallah had heard these words many times before and each time they had the same soothing effect.

I am strong. I am feared. I am Druida.

For a while Sallah, Terran, and Agneth walked in silence. Sallah followed the faint outlines of the hedgerow behind closed eyes, hearing the robin and bluejays call. Perhaps she could get them lost, perhaps she could get the maze to take them far away.

The hedgerow turned one last time and formed a long corridor to the place Sallah was dreading when she opened her eyes.

The Grove of Ancients, the meeting place of the Twelve Houses. A circle of twelve trees: Alder, Ash, Birch, Elder, Hawthorne, Hazel, Holly, Ivy, Oak, Reed, Vine, and Willow. The trees encircled a meadow of foot-worn grass and daylilies two acres wide and four long. Each massive tree twisted and braided itself with another as they rose to form a domed canopy taller than the Hawthorne Mother Tree Sallah had stood on earlier that morning. The twelve stood uniform in height, thanks first to the power of the goddess and the upkeep of generations of her worshippers.

Sallah examined the massive trunks as she passed. Intricate carvings wove themselves almost imperceptibly around each trunk, The runes of ancient Druida, their meanings lost to time and conflict. Each time, it seemed as if the lines had moved. But this wasn't Sallah's favorite part of this ancient Artistry. It was the silver light that seeped from the lines. She couldn't see it if she looked directly at the runes, only out of the corner of her eye did the lines glow. She never felt alone in this place. She stared straight ahead and let the silver light play on the edge of her vision. She needed the company at the moment, even if it was the writings of long-dead Druida.

The morning sun pierced the leafy roof of the Grove and shimmered in a thousand spots along the ground. To one end of the meadow rose a massive Vine tree, the roots had been formed into a raised stage. The happiest and saddest of rituals were performed on that stage, all overseen by the ruling Matriarch.

I suppose this ritual will be both, depending on the House. Vine was the reigning House and had been for as long as she had been alive. A crowd of the other eleven Houses had gathered, a few were sad, some bore hungry eyes for the spectacle, and most wore triumphant smiles.

Without hesitation the three Druida of the Hawthorne strode towards the stage, the crowd parting at their approach. Sallah surveyed the crowd. She found who she was looking for without much effort. There stood Nissa directly within her path, a young Druida of the House of the Vine, her pointed face stretched out to a gleeful grin.

Sallah locked eyes with her. *I will survive if only to destroy you.* She brushed hard against Nissa as she passed as if to seal the pact.

Nissa's expression never changed. The flicker of indignation inside Sallah swelled to the beginning of rage. Sallah let it seep down to her feet and fingers. She breathed slowly. She needed to keep the flame kindled for her survival. But neither she nor her House could afford an outburst at such a pivotal moment. Sallah, Agneth, and Terran stopped in front of the stage.

Flanked by two Consorts stood Matriarch Sorren. She was the head of Vine and by right, leader of all twelve Houses of the Children of Dharra. She was nearing fifty years but her lean, angular body said otherwise. Her shallow, brown eyes had long been trained to a malicious point from years of settling squabbles and stamping out attempts at claiming her authority. She was Druida, as was one of the requirements for selection, but she was not made Matriarch by appointment or moot. She killed the previous Matriarch by proclaiming the Rite of Dux Contentio. Sorren killed a woman of seventy to lay claim to the title of Matriarch. This was not frowned

29

upon, but was a bit sudden. What was more impressive was her suppressing any revolt from loyalists within the House of the Vine.

But that was the rule of Nature; strength conquered weakness, new consumed old. Sallah had spent her entire life under Sorren's thumb. She couldn't help but wonder sometimes how different life would be if Agneth was Matriarch or even Terran if he wasn't a man.

Sorren gazed down and addressed the three Druida in a cold, business-like fashion. "As Matriarch of the Children of Dharra and ruler of the Twelve Houses, it is my duty to enact the Rite of Diodorus Siculus on the House of Hawthorne. No House may possess more than two Druida, lest the balance of the Houses be destroyed."

What an easy thing for you to say. Much of Sallah's training pertained to things like this. Circumventing the rules without actually breaking them. If the House of Hawthorne, or any House for that matter, had defied the law of two Druida, it would be tantamount to declaring open warfare on the other eleven Houses and sacrilege against Dharra. Technically, the Rite of Diodorus Siculus should have been conducted when Sallah was discovered to be a Druida thirteen years ago, but Terran politely and publicly reminded the House of the Vine that they had set a precedent with their own young Druida, Nissa. She was found to be Druida at the age of three, but the old Matriarch ordered Nissa be protected until she grew fully into her powers and was able to lead their House. The Vine would have been subject to the Rite Sallah was about to undergo, had Matriarch Sorren not killed her predecessor and taken the mantle of Matriarch.

"Your lives will be decided in the traditional manner. You

are to be sent to the Old Growth and there Dharra will reclaim one of your lives. You may return when only two remain."

Sallah was speechless. No one ventured there. The songs said it was the birthplace of Dharra and all her scions. To go there was to face the primal force of Nature itself. Some aging huntresses chose to travel there when they felt their time had become short and they wished to bestow honor onto their Houses. Their spears would fall in the cradle of their goddess. Sallah saw Sorren's jaw tighten ever so slightly.

Relish your control while you can. Sallah's rage had started to cloud her mind. Her fingertips twitched. She wanted to hurt something, anything.

"This trek may not be a total loss for your House," Sorren continued. "Whatever totems you can recover from the beasts you will surely face will bring great honor to Hawthorne. If there are those who wish to speak to the Druida before their venture, you may do so. You have until mid-morning. *Celereitate et Astu.*"

Sallah's mind blurred and twisted. Her breathing became erratic. She began looking for a target, as numerous Dharrans gathered around Sallah, Agneth, and Terran. Sallah was flush with malice. She wanted Nissa's blood, or Sorren's. Sallah began to search the crowd again for Nissa's almond-shaped eyes but before she could, someone touched her arm. Sallah twitched her head and saw Karra. Her Consort's deep blue eyes immediately quenched the heat of violence. Consorts were forbidden to look upon their masters. It was a rule Sallah had been made painfully aware of, in a different life.

Consorts were slaves. Orphans, whose parents had died by the chaos of the Greensea or the calculated hand of a rival House. The lucky ones were stripped of their Houses and their name and given to the Druida as Consorts. The unfortunate ones were called Nameless, cast into the wild to struggle and die. Consorts were trained, or more often, beaten into complete submission. The result was that Consorts became an absolute vessel of the Druida they served. They were no longer Children of Dharra. They were barely considered human.

Karra's lips parted to speak. "Mistress Sallah—"

"Remove your hand from your Master, Consort!" A dark-haired Rowan by the name of Dunlow witnessed Karra's transgression. Karra's cool eyes filled with terror. She began to flee.

Sallah turned herself squarely to Dunlow. "You will stand down, House of Rowan!" Her voice rang with righteous indignation. "Consort, return now."

Karra stopped dead in her tracks and turned with a bowed head, leading her back to her master. The gathered crowd was silent, waiting for the next move that would lead to a restoration of order or a glaring weakness in the House of Hawthorne.

Sallah noticed the silence. "I have final instructions for you Consort. You will remain by my side until ordered otherwise. And as for you, House of Rowan." Sallah turned a penetrating glare to Dunlow. "Just because Terran has graciously bestowed your fragile House with the gift of an alliance, do not think that I will be so gracious. If you attempt to meddle in my affairs again, your name will be sung as the destroyer of House Rowan. If that is your wish, then by all means continue to waggle your jaw. If not, then return to your House and pray to Dharra that I do not survive this Rite, because if I do, there will be no respite from the pain I will bear against all you hold dear. Quit my sight."

Dunlow stood dumbfounded for a moment under Sallah's glare. Without a word, he turned and left. Out of the corner of Sallah's eye, she could see Agneth shake in silent laughter. Karra had returned to her master, kneeling, forehead placed on the ground.

"You will stand behind me until I have finished speaking with the others."

Karra's head twitched in surprise. Sallah could have just as easily banished her at that moment, even slit her throat, like mercy killing a deer. The Consort dutifully moved behind Sallah just as Nissa approached.

"Give the people a show before you give them a show, Druida Sallah?" said Nissa, amongst a nest of tittering sycophants.

Sallah's rage reignited, but she felt more calm this time, more lucid. "I did not realize you could see hiding behind the Matriarch's hem, Nissa Va Vine." Sallah's response had to be calculated.

The House of Hawthorne was not strong enough to withstand vehement sabotage from The House of the Vine. Vine held the seat of the Matriarch and as a result, had plenty of other Houses for deeds that required insulation from any particular action. House Holly was one such lapdog and had been for many years. In turn, Holly could carry out their own agenda without any fear of true reprisal, just so long as it didn't affect the Vine. This made threats, let alone action, more difficult against the House Vine, but not impossible. But this was a very public place and Sallah knew Nissa was vying for a very public display.

"I will pray for your safe return. It is always a sad day when

33

one might lose a fellow Druida. We Daughters of Dharra are so rare." Nissa was an impressive Druida, showing her skills at a very early age. As a right of being Druida, she was one of the two ruling elders of the House of the Vine, even though Nissa was just twenty-three.

Nissa was the first face Sallah could remember and it was the one that taught her hate. Tosi, who had been weaving through Sallah's legs, silently jumped onto her shoulder. Two sets of green eyes bore down on Nissa Va Vine.

Sallah spoke in level tones, with Tosi on her shoulder. "If I die then it is the will of Dharra and I was not worthy to lead my House. But you of all the Children should know I do not die easily."

"What a poetic thing to say on the verge of your demise, Consort."

Agneth interrupted quickly. "Unless you have well wishes or some other matter of importance, I suggest you move on, little Nis, lest I am not here to protect you from Sallah this time."

To use a familiar name without consent was bad enough. To not address a Druida with their title was grounds for a fight. But to add 'little' was beyond forgivable. Yet Nissa could do nothing to Agneth. If she tried to challenge Agneth, she would go against the Rite enacted by Sorren and the House of the Vine, essentially an act of open warfare. Besides, who would begrudge a respected and dangerous Druida one final insult on the eve of her possible death?

Nissa bristled. "It matters little who rules the House of Hawthorne. What waits for the survivors will be the same." Nissa stormed away from the crowd with a gaggle of followers in her wake.

Tosi watched her stomp off as Agneth brushed Sallah's face with her own.

"Well done, Druida," whispered Agneth "You will be a fine elder."

Sallah's cheeks felt flush. "Never as good as you."

"Certainly not. Better." Agneth winked.

Sallah saw the edge of weariness in her. *You definitely look older than yesterday.* "We could last for many more years in the wild, Agneth. We have been bred and trained for it."

"And who would guide our people for those years?" said Agneth, assuming her mentorial tone. "Our enemies are everywhere and becoming bolder by the day. If our House is to endure, what must happen today must be done quickly."

Sallah's head fell slightly.

"Head up, Druida," said Agneth. "As you said, we have been trained for this."

Sallah straightened to her full height bordering on six feet. *I can put on a good show for those who want to destroy us, but can't lead like you.*

Tosi dropped from her shoulder, shaking her back to reality.

"Consort, come with me." Sallah whipped her head to where Karra stood. "We will speak in private of your actions." Sallah strode out from the midst of the crowd of allies and conspirators alike.

Karra dutifully followed her master down a leaf-strewn trail leading out of the Grove.

Sure that they were now alone, Sallah turned to her Consort. "Walk beside me, Karra." She dropped the pretense like a mask. Sallah despised the word Consort. She was intimately familiar with the venom, the subservience in that word.

Karra's eyes darted around for onlookers, before raising her head, straightening her shoulders, and quickening her pace. "Well, that was certainly interesting from the Rowan boy." She caught up to Sallah's strides. "I didn't mean to make trouble for you, but you seemed . . . off." She smiled apologetically at Sallah. "Which makes sense considering all of this."

Sallah studied Karra for a long moment, marveling at how well she played the role of Consort. How long had she known her? Twelve years at least. Karra was given to her not long after Sallah had been rescued from her own plight.

Sallah's parents had disappeared when she was only five and for the Children of Dharra disappearing was as good as dead. Sallah was branded Consort and given to a Druida three years older than she was—Nissa Va Vine. For a year she was ordered around, beaten, and humiliated, not unheard of for the life of a Consort even at that young age.

—

It was Agneth who saved her twelve years ago. During a savage and public beating in the middle of the Grove, Sallah revealed the first sign of both her gift and her curse. It was the first hunt of Earrach for the House of the Vine, blossoms on the trees had budded but not yet bloomed. Sallah had forgotten Nissa's gloves just before her master was to set off. Nissa needed no excuse to beat her Consort, but this stood as a very public chance to display her cruelty.

She methodically beat Sallah with both club and words relentlessly. Sallah lay heaped on the ground against the base of the great Hawthorne that stood in the Grove of Ancients, broken and bloody. Nissa swung her club down towards Sallah's head, intent on killing her Consort, but her club met only earth. Nissa blinked and was awestruck at what she saw. The Hawthorne tree was holding her Consort's limp body to its trunk, enfolding her entirely in its branches. There was only one possibility. She was a Daughter of Dharra, she was Druida of the House of Hawthorne.

Sallah's eyes popped open, but they were no longer the eyes of a child. They were the blood-red eyes of a starving wolf. Her slight frame was lost to rage. She saw Nissa's dumbstruck face and released a feral roar that no child, no human could make. Every blossom on the Hawthorne opened at the sound of her voice. She was beautiful and terrifying in that moment; the child-goddess surrounded by snowy petals preparing to exact her vengeance. This was Sanguinem Furor, the Blood Rage. Centuries-old songs told of ancient Druida being able to summon the absolute power of Dharra the moment before death, and now this child before them had brought legends to reality. Branches whipped towards Nissa from every angle.

In an instant, Agneth appeared and wrapped her entire body around little Nissa. The branches struck Agneth's back but sheared off, cleanly cut. Agneth waited for a second barrage but heard only silence. She turned to see Sallah, bloody and unconscious, lying against the great tree's trunk.

Sallah could recall none of this, of course. All she could remember afterward was waking to a cool cloth across her brow and Agneth's sweet voice whispering in her ear, "Rest now Druida, for you have much to learn when you rise."

—

37

Sallah snapped back to the present to see Karra looking at her, confused.

"You were right. I was off, angry. I'm glad you were there with me."

Karra was her only friend. Being sequestered away from the Children of Dharra during a Druida's training was common, often used as a political ploy to keep both allies and enemies uncertain of a House's future leadership. A child capable of the Blood Rage only catalyzed that strategy. Only fellow Druida of the House and perhaps a Consort would have regular contact.

"Though perhaps attempt a little more subtlety next time?" Sallah's last two words weighed the air down around them.

Karra was quiet for a time. "I wish you strength, Mistress Sallah. You are loyal and kind. You are destined to be the greatest of elders." Her voice was sincere, throttled by small sobs.

"You give me far too much credit. Terran and Agneth know how to navigate all of this better than I do. Besides, you're just worried I won't come back and you'll be given to another Druida." It was meant as a joke but Sallah realized her mistake immediately. She saw the quickly-hidden fear in her friend. If Sallah survived today, she would have the full weight of the House of Hawthorne ready to die for her whim. But the only thing Karra would ever have is Sallah. Sallah bristled at the injustice of it. This could have been Sallah, if not for blind chance.

"Karra, I'm sorry, that was a stupid thing to say." Karra quickly assumed her head-down posture, as if putting on a mask.

"That is an eventuality I do not wish to prepare for."

"Karra." Sallah rested her hand on her shoulder. "Look at me."

The Consort did as she was told. Sallah moved both hands behind her neck and unclasped her necklace. It was Sallah's second greatest treasure; three razor-sharp claws she took as totems from her first hunt. Agneth had made it for her. She told Sallah that as close as these claws were to her neck, death was closer.

Sallah smiled at Karra as she wrapped her arms around the Consort's neck. Tying the necklace, Sallah gently rearranged the totems as she spoke. "If I die during this Rite, you are to live among the House of Hawthorne as a true Child of Dharra. You will become Karra Va Hawthorne and you will no longer be subject to the rules of the Nameless or Consorts. You will live freely as any woman and you are to work daily towards the honor of Hawthorne. You are to present this necklace to any who oppose this command and you will draw blood if they do not listen. I will inform Terran and Agneth of my decision. These are my final instructions."

Karra stared back at Sallah in disbelief. "Sallah, I can't —"

"Are you disobeying the wishes of your Druida?" If Sallah were to die, then this would be her final act. She was satisfied with that prospect.

"Never," Karra whispered, caressing the trophies at her neck.

Sallah lifted her chin to stare into her eyes again.

Their practiced looks and trained gazes fell away.

"Besides," said Sallah, "What can Sorren do if she does not like my decision? Kill me?" Karra grinned into the mid-morning light.

"Sallah, let's begin." Agneth stood a good distance away.

"Time to be done with it."

"Coming," Sallah called back.

The pair walked back slowly, side-by-side.

Chapter 3

Jack just couldn't make sense of it. That thing was there, impossible but true. He was trying to piece it together as the platform whisked the two up into the mid-morning light.

Seven superior, three lateral, and four ventral to the Arc-chain. The access platform rode an ingenious design. No matter what dock it was boarded from, the coordinates to any other given dock were the same, like veins through the body. Jack attempted to relax and rode up towards the sunlight from the arched windows high above him. No good. His hands shook and his breathing was still ragged. Having been nearly eaten had put him a bit on edge.

And there was no hole in the pipe it had torn into. Did the serpent somehow repair the pipe? No, not repaired. That pipe was untouched. Like it never happened. But it had happened.

Even if he hadn't seen or felt it, that smell that still lingered in his nose assured Jack it was real. Sweat and burning metal. It wasn't like the blacksmith's forge though, Jack quite enjoyed that smell. The scent of a forge was the byproduct of imagination being shaped into reality. The stench of the

41

serpent possessed another quality— decay. As if a blacksmith ripped his flesh apart and grafted himself with metal.

So many questions ran through Jack's mind.

How did that thing get in here? The only entrances are guarded and it's not like it could get in through a window without someone noticing. And what in Paragon's name is it doing down there anyway? Did it come up from the earth? Who would create such a monstrosity? Why? More disturbing than the questions were the answers. That creature did not appear a creation of nature. Not that Jack was an expert in animals. The closest he got to wildlife was sparrows darting to pick up crumbs from a sidewalk cafe, or the rats slinking down gutters into the Undercroft. Even so, Jack would have heard of a titanous serpent made of metal that roamed beneath the city.

And it *was* metal, right down to the fangs. Someone had designed it, built it. It was a machine, yet it could think and move independently, so it wasn't a machine. Jack glanced over the edge of the ascending platform to the shadows below. Jack had always thought of the Orchestra Pit as his own. But now, he felt he was the mouse, scurrying inside someone else's walls. Regardless of how it got in, the fact remained it was there, lurking somewhere in the Orchestra Pit and someone had put it there. Barin was watching Jack out of the corner of his eye.

"Care to tell me what actually happened to your belt, Mouse?" Barin's voice was less brusque than usual.

"I told you, sir."

"No, you told me a big metal snake ate it."

"It did sir."

"No one lies to me, boy."

"I don't lie. You know that sir."

"I know you don't, which is why I find it odd you would start now."

"It was there. I can't explain why there aren't holes in the pipe and why he didn't continue to chase me, but it was there. I swear it on my wrench."

Barin sighed. Jack would happily die a lingering death if it meant his wrench was safe. It was Jack's only link to his parents, to what his life could have been.

"You'll earn your belt back by spending a week at the Academy. And no, you will not be allowed into The Proscenium during that time."

"It's so boring there," Jack muttered, admitting defeat. There was truly no point in trying to argue the Master Tuner's orders.

The lift swept the pair up to the access dock of the Arc-chain. This place was the melody, the harmony, the beat, and the rhythm for the orchestration of Cogrind. The centuries-old original design for the Chain possessed twelve Arc-boilers. The technology was thought to have been lost during the Age of Flames. But just a decade ago, Cogrind Composers announced they rediscovered the process for the creation of Arc-boilers. The Patron pronounced an order of massive expansion to the Arc-chain and every able citizen in the Shining City set to the task. 'Cogs for the Greatest Machine' was the cry that rang from Balcony Row to Bass Run. The order was to bring illumination to even the wretches, widows, and abandoned of Stonehall. This promise had not yet come to fruition but most within the city were too busy working towards the greater good to notice.

A throng of Tuners bustled about the catwalks as the access lift met the dock leading to the Arc-boiler. Barin stomped off with Jack in his wake. Tuners and Metalists jumped aside for the Master Tuner as he wound his way toward the number thirteen boiler, the first of the new installations. Its condition had become worse. The brass body was still shifting impossibly through space but now it had started a new, stomach-churning phenomenon. Jack couldn't tell at first but it seemed that the twenty-foot-tall boiler was coming in and out of existence. As if he were blinking too fast and all the pieces of reality had yet to return to their place. Not a soul was near the shifting boiler. Barin stopped just at the edge of the boiler's fit. Every laborer on the catwalk stopped dead in their tracks to gawk at Barin and his white-haired apprentice. A thousand held breaths hanging in the cavernous space of the Conservatory.

The Master Tuner turned his head. "Where's my replacement orb?"

The boiler seemed to sense his presence. It began to blink quicker back and forth as if something inside the huge brass belly was struggling to break free.

A thin, balding man on the edge of the crowd spoke up. "The Metalists just have finished constructing it. It will be down shortly," whispered the man.

"This thing is on the verge of collapse, Mr. Petty. Which means if you or anyone else here plans on seeing their loved ones tonight, we need that orb up here now." Barin's jaw tightened as the boiler's erratic movements swept it to and fro.

"Chain orbs are extremely expensive to produce, Mr. Barin. The man-hours alone wou—" Barin was staring over his shoulder at the balding James Petty.

"It . . . it's being delivered right now."

Jack envied Barin's presence. Barin had earned that presence through decades of toil, injury, and knowledge. But Jack didn't think it was those attributes that demanded such respect. They played a part of course. There was one aspect of Barin that rose above the others; passion. Barin loved machines. On calmer days, Jack would spot him on the observation deck by the high-hung windows, simply watching the Proscenium continue its endless task. Never a smile mind you, but his eyes were filled with love for the place and people.

Shouts rang out behind Jack as a Metalist bustled through the crowd, delicately holding a brass chest, secured with four clasps. After unhooking the latches, Jack pulled away a silk wrapping to reveal a glass ball.

Barin returned his eyes to the boiler. "Take the orb, Mouse. Hold it only by the cloth. Do not touch the surface."

The Metalist placed the delicate sphere into Jack's cradled hands. Jack sucked in his breath. There was no weight to the orb. It was like holding an idea in his hands. Only its shape gave it any definition at all. Turning his body around, Jack approached his Master with calculated steps.

Barin stripped off his gloves. He reached his naked hand behind his back, never taking his eyes from the impossible movements of the Arc-boiler. "In my hand boy," Barin's voice rumbled in a calm bass. "Take off a portion of the cloth and place the exposed portion in my hand. Got it?"

Jack did exactly as he was told and carefully moved the sphere into Barin's calloused grip. Barin took the slightest hold of the fragile implement. It hummed a single clarion chime as it made contact with his exposed skin. A pattern weaved up the crystal from his fingertips, like frost on a window. The Arc-boiler was shifting more now, emitting a nauseating screech each time it jumped. The Master Tuner held up his free hand, slowly, methodically moving it towards the Boiler. The boiler blinked again and met Barin's unmoving hand. The boiler stopped moving instantly. It vibrated with a low hum underneath his grizzled touch, but it did not move. Barin exhaled deeply as he ascended the stairs that wound up the boiler. He slid his hand along the cool, metal surface as he made his way towards the Arc-chain, his hand never breaking contact. The Boiler seemed to pull away from his touch, like a wounded animal too weak to move.

Rung by rung, Barin's boots stamped up the ladder until he had reached the top. Barin retreated to his hands and knees, still carrying the fragile salvation of Cogrind in hand. He could see the problem from the arm-length distance that stood between him and the broken boiler. As he approached the intersecting wisps of the Arc-chain, a spiderweb crack laced itself around the broken orb, splaying the languid stroke of the Arc-chain in scattered directions. As Barin's body disappeared over the top of the Boiler, Jack couldn't handle the anticipation. On impulse, he ran up the ladder on the boiler marked *No. 14* in print as big as his body to watch his master at work. He reached the top just as Barin had reached the edge of the Arc-chain.

Jack watched him slide from his knees to his back and wriggle underneath the wafting trails of energy. The old man's predatory eyes were fixed on the broken sphere, his free hand dutifully sliding along the boiler. Barin was in position to make the switch.

He kicked off his right boot and put his bare foot down

onto the humming vessel as he lifted his free hand away. Beads of sweat ran down Barin's forehead into his unkempt beard. He was mumbling something, though Jack could not decipher it. A prayer perhaps, or Jack could even imagine an atonement being uttered by his master. Five hundred thousand Cogrind souls rested in the old man's hand. Barin palmed the broken orb as he lifted it up and towards its replacement and slipped its replacement in front of the Arc-chain. The energy bounced and strained to and from the new sphere. The cracked orb glowed a dull orange upon contact with his hand as if refusing Barin's touch. Jack could hear the hiss of burning skin as Barin began to slip the broken sphere off its footing. In one fluid movement, he slipped off the faulty piece and set the new orb in its place. The boiler no longer strained against itself, barely contained by Barin's touch. The Boiler lay quiet, the beast quelled.

Jack hadn't realized how loud that humming had been until his ears met the returning silence. The old orb disintegrated in glowing wisps, leaving Barin's burned hands empty. The old man laid on his back and watched the now lazy trail of the Arc-chain swim silently to and fro above him, his pink-blistered palms turned up. This was not the unblinking, unwavering institution of a man who kept the Proscenium running. This was just a man, burned and exhausted and missing a boot, just trying to do his job the best way he knew.

Jack didn't know how long he stayed on top of that boiler watching his master breathe raggedly. The cheering below snapped Jack out of his trance. Whatever the cost was to his body, The Master Tuner yet again finished a job no other was willing or capable to take. Barin took a deep breath and turned himself around on his elbows as he slid from underneath the Arc-chain. Barin stood and clomped unevenly back to the ladder. Jack raced down the *No. 14* boiler to meet Barin at the bottom. Ravenous applause and shouts greeted Barin at the bottom of the stairs. Gone was the face of a tired man, exhaling the last dregs of fear and inhaling the relief of a dangerous job done. In its place the stoic look of a hawk returned. He walked calmly through the crowd. No one noticed his shaking hands.

"Now that your entertainment for the day is over I believe you all have tasks to accomplish."

Without another word, every man and woman hurried off to their appointed rounds.

Barin found Jack in the dissipating group. "Finish your tasks Mouse. Then meet me in the infirmary."

Jack hung around the Arc-chain for a while. He had already finished and could've simply rode with Barin up to the infirmary. He thought against it. If Barin had wanted to speak with him while he was being bandaged, he would have said so.

Instead, Jack traced the circular catwalk that wound around the Arc-boilers. Three of the new Boilers were installed. Two other Boilers marked *16* and *17* hung in the air by wenches like bronze clouds, waiting for their turn. The Conservatory returned to its usual buzz of energy and echoing shouts.

We all could have died just a few minutes ago. Now it's just another day.

After a few minutes more had passed, Jack called for the access platform, pushed and pulled the right levers, and let the platform carry him out of the Proscenium and to the encircling halls of the Ironworks Conservatory.

Jack walked through the door of the Infirmary. He loved

how powerful his steps sounded on the thick marble slabs. Wall-length arched windows framed in bright red drapes gave a view of the West Plaza and soaked the room in the golden light of the falling sun. White linen beds lined the walls. A few were occupied by careless apprentices or broken Luthiers from the quarry. On the opposite side of the room stood Barin, the last of the thick bandages being wrapped around his hands.

Of course, he's standing.

Barin spotted him and beckoned Jack over. "Apparently all this is necessary," said Barin, waving his bandages about, "and the good doctors have yet to determine how I'll set about working like this."

Jack stifled a chuckle. Barin looked like his arms had sprouted cotton balls in place of his powerful hands.

"You may have to rely on your inferiors for a few weeks sir. If you can stand it."

Barin grumbled out a sigh and inspected Jack for a moment. "No Mouse, I'm afraid it's even worse than that. I may have to rely on you."

Jack flinched at the news. "That's a horrible idea, sir."

"I think so too, boy."

"Then why do you want to use that idea, sir?"

"You saw how that lot acted down there. Not one of 'em went near number thirteen. They were afraid. I can't afford fear in my work, Mouse. Only you were willing to go near it. By cogs, you were the only one who chose to spot me while I was up there. Yes, I saw you boy."

Jack stared at his boots. This is what he had coveted ever since he could remember—the work of the Master Tuner. Still, his knowledge was rudimentary in comparison to Barin.

"Are you sure I'm the right choice?"

Barin grunted. "Absolutely not. But you're the only one willing to die for our pursuits, which makes you the most able candidate. Take the offer or spend the next week at the Academy earning back your belt. Should make for an easy decision."

"It certainly does sir."

For a moment, both remained silent.

Jack seized his opportunity to ask the question that had been needling him. "Barin, why didn't you wear your gloves? You could've avoided all this."

Barin grunted again. "I suppose I owe you some answers if you're going to be my hands. Very well then, those orbs are not typical glass. They are made from one of the few materials that can withstand constant exposure to Arc. In fact, it's capable of harnessing and directing the flow of Arc. It does, however, come with drawbacks. It imprints itself to the first touch of something organic, but it must be living, otherwise it will shatter the moment it comes into contact with Arc, hence why the gloves were out of the question."

Jack thought on this for a moment. "How did you know to touch the Boiler with your bare hand?"

The old man's face became grave. "I didn't. In all my years I had never seen a Boiler act like that. No documentation for such a phenomenon in any of our histories. So I guessed."

Jack stood in shocked silence.

"Jack," Barin's voice rumbled low and sincere, "the Age of Flames took most of our history and with it the knowledge for our technology. Despite what the Composers have discovered, much of what we do is still guesswork, not that the average citizen would know. It takes those willing to sacrifice themselves so that our people may move forward. There is no room for hesitation. That's why I picked you for an apprenticeship. Had you not acted on that day, many of our people could have died. But that's the price of greatness Jack, of legacy."

Jack recalled the day three years ago that changed his life forever. The grand reveal of the new Boilers on the steps of the Conservatory, the celebrations in the streets, the two hundred piece orchestra, the choir, three hundred strong. Then came the pop and hiss from the new Boiler on display for the city to see. Jack couldn't remember anything after that, until he was being pulled from underneath it, tossed onto shoulders, and praised as a hero of Cogrind. That was the day he met Barin

"On that day you moved towards the danger," continued Barin. "You are willing to die for this city. That is why you are my apprentice and that is why you will be my hands.

Jack was humbled by Barin's words.

"You're dismissed, boy. I will see you in the morning."

—

As Jack stepped out into the West Plaza, he watched the citizens of Cogrind scurry about, eager to finish the day's labor. The late summer sun had drifted to rest on the rooftops of the Townhouses and shops that lined the Promenade. What was a silent city this morning now rang with the lives of thousands. The miller's front wall was lowered down to form a ramp for a cart of wheat grown just outside of the walls of Stonehall. The Skytrain streaked overhead, the boxcars weaving through the rooftops laden with goods. The West

Plaza market stalls were sinking down into the metal street. Mr. Alfred Cork haggled with a woman wearing a trumpet-shaped hat over a bulk order of copper bolts, while a giggling girl chased after her hat as it rolled down the street with the wind.

Pieces of the machine.

He stopped at the baker and bought a day-old loaf of sourdough. Then he stopped at Cork's to purchase three sheets of thin bronze and two refurbished valves. An Apprentice's wage was not something to envy, since most Apprentices didn't require much in the way of money. Most boarded at the Academy, with meals provided. Any others who were unwilling to leave the affluent lifestyle their families provided, simply commuted to the Academy. Jack was neither dependent nor wealthy, but what he had was his own, and that suited him just fine.

Some people gave him a slight nod as he passed. His Tuner's garb was immediately recognizable and garnered respect from most citizens. Jack stepped from the warm light of the city into the dark alleyway that led to his home.

The warmth of the sun slipped behind a row of apartment buildings as the shadow recalled the morning's events. What bothered Jack more than being inches from death was that Barin thought he had lied. For whatever reason that monstrosity lurked within the dark maze of pipes, Jack knew it was not a good one. Perhaps it was commissioned and placed there by the Patron for security. That didn't seem likely. Entrances guarded by the Steel Watch kept anyone too curious or mischievous enough to do any real harm away from the Conservatory. Besides, no announcement was made to the workers of the Proscenium that a mechanical serpent the length of four grown men would be prowling beneath their feet.

Perhaps it was an inscrutable machination of the Paragon himself, designed to effortlessly weave through the Orchestra Pit to guard some great secret. But the Pit echoed down to unknowable depths, the plans long since lost to the Age of Flames. So if the serpent was guarding something down there, why would it be so close to the surface?

And then there was the feed pipe, unscratched, let alone torn open in four places. No, something wrong was happening in the abyss below the Proscenium and Jack intended to find out just what it was for the sake of his honor and the welfare of Cogrind.

The cost of legacy. The thought made his foot falter a moment, before continuing home.

As he crossed the half-stone half-metal bridge, the sound of playing children greeted him. The orphans had been let out of the Workhouse for a spot of play before curfew. He looked at his feet as he crossed the middle of the bridge. One step modernity, one step history. He walked down the cobblestone street of Stonehall as one of the urchins raced towards him. His name was Geoffrey but everyone called him Widget. He had wild, staring brown eyes, typically covered by his mess of curly blonde hair that hadn't been cut in the seven years of his life.

Widget pointed a grubby finger at the bread in Jack's hands. "That's for me right?" Widget's body bounced with anticipation. "It isn't that day-old stuff right?"

Jack snorted at the impetuous boy. "Since when did you start getting picky over what people give you?" Jack spun around in place as Widget chased after the bread.

"Since you started doing it every day."

Jack raised the bread high over Widget's mop of a head. Without hesitation, The boy jumped at Jack, grabbed him by his leather bib with one hand, and his up-held arm with the other. Widget expected his weight to bring down the bread-bearing arm. Instead, his feet dangled in space supported by the thin, tensed arm of Jack.

"So what's the next step in your master plan?" said Jack.

The suspended Widget thought about it for a moment. "May I have the bread?" asked the boy.

Jack put Widget down. "Only if you stick to our deal."

Widget ripped the loaf from Jack's hand and sprinted toward the other children, already breaking off sections for other hungry mouths. Jack turned the opposite way of the children and walked beside the south-curving moat to home.

His shack was built on top of three others and leaned drunkenly to the left. He could manage some semblance of repair on the timber, but recently his evenings had been filled with a more pressing project.

Jack stopped in front of the ramshackle tenements. "Charlie," he called at his house. "Rise and shine layabout. Time to put all six fingers to the task."

No one answered. With a heavy sigh, Jack stepped up the rotted plank stairs to his friend's hovel and opened the door. As he expected, Charlie was hunched over his desk.

"All right Charlie," said Jack.

"All right Jack," Said Charlie. The tall, dark-skinned man of twenty didn't look up, still staring intently at the trinkets on his desk, a bottle of clear liquor next to his left hand.

"An infinite power source at our fingertips and here you are mucking about with hot water."

"Steam," Charlie corrected, opening a valve that made one of his trinkets spin like a windmill. "You have the infinite power source, not me."

"Which is why we need to get work. Come on."

Charlie leaned back with a stretch and grabbed a well-worn tool belt with the thumb of his right hand and the bottle with his left.

"Leave it." said Jack.

"But this is my infinite power source." Charlie grinned.

"Leave it."

Charlie grunted as he left the bottle and headed out the door.

In his youth, Charlie Diamont had shown the makings of a great Luthier. An accident during his apprenticeship removed four of his right fingers and made him unemployable in his chosen profession. His dependence on drink took care of the rest. Perhaps it would have been different with another disability, but hands determined worth as a Luthier. With his injury pension, he could no longer afford to live inside the Shining City, so he found himself a stone's throw from the Workhouse where he grew up.

Jack had known Charlie his entire life and he was as good of a friend as any man could hope for. Jack was delighted to have a Luthier living beneath him and felt quite guilty for feeling such joy. Charlie was just what Jack needed and Jack hoped he was just what Charlie needed as well. The inexhaustible patience and strength that are the hallmarks of Charlie's former trade were not lost with his fingers. All that he was lacking was a purpose to drive him forward.

"Took you long enough to get back. Figured you either died or Cork was trying to get you to work for free. You bring the stuff?"

"No, I just thought we would construct it with songs and dreams. Of course I did, you sprung valve."

Charlie took a flight of make-shift stairs down the side of the shacks two at a time. He knocked on the door of a base-level shack as he passed. "Moira, stop lazing about," goaded the grinning Charlie. "We have work to do lovely."

The shack door Charlie had beaten burst open, and through it stepped a sweaty girl of eighteen, her short, brunette hair clung across her forehead and neck. Light and steam rolled through the open door and into the new-formed night, a burning look of indignation igniting her hazel eyes.

"If you ever want to actually help with the laundry business, drop by you lazy git," Moira replied.

Charlie winked at her. "Sorry love, fabric isn't my calling. I prefer something with a little more resistance."

Moira grinned slyly. "You'll find plenty of resistance to get air to your lungs after I punch you in the throat."

Jack chuckled. Moira always made Jack laugh and not because she made hollow threats. In fact, she tended to make good on her word and Jack suspected Charlie would be getting a light jab to the windpipe at some point tonight. Jack liked to joke that what Moira lacked in tact, she made up for in pure aggression.

Poverty was so often the starvation of one's soul; Moira Wingate used it as fuel. She left the Workhouse when she was twelve out of pride and spite. Hunger attempted to persuade her back, but Moira refused to return. Then she got an idea. She wagered with the Headmistress of the Workhouse that she could launder the same amount seven children did in one day. If Moira could do it then she would be compensated a portion of the money the Workhouse saved. The Headmistress accepted out of her love of frugality, and the desperate girl. Moira scrubbed, soaked, and dried for twenty straight hours using the pristine water of the upstream moat and a washboard she stole from the Workhouse. She won her wager.

With some food in her stomach, Moira began offering her services to some of the businesses on the outskirts of Cogrind, offering rates her competitors couldn't match. She dropped the Workhouse from her clientele and went into business for herself. Jack pointed out to her she had made enough to manage a small apartment inside the city but she had higher aspirations.

"I will enter the city on my terms," was always her reply. "Enough to buy a business and the apartment above it, on Balcony Row I should think." She was tireless in her task. And if they could finish this pipeline to bring power to her operation, she would triumphantly enter Cogrind that much sooner.

"Good evening Ms. Wingate," Jack said bowing slightly. "You're looking ravishing as ever."

Moira smirked. "Stow it Mr. Mouse or you'll be wheezing as hard as Charlie will be in a bit."

Charlie reflexively tucked in his chin. The Laundress and the Luthier gathered to where a kneeling Jack was positioning the materials.

"Not exactly a lot to work with," said Charlie. " We can get maybe twelve feet out of it." He rolled out his belt in front of the copper sheets and picked a heavy cylindrical pin, a small Arc-welder and a curved forming plate. He began rolling the sheet back and forth between the plate and the pin, slowly shaping a section of pipe.

"If Moira's estimations from last night are right, then twelve feet will be more than enough to get the pipe above the waterline. Then the hard part will be over," said Jack.

Moira scoffed. "Hard for who precisely? I'm the one who's been diving down there fitting the stuff." She peered over the edge of the moat, observing the reflection on the still surface.

"If I'm not mistaken, you volunteered for that job, Ms. Wingate." Jack scored the metal tubing to thread into what had already been laid before. "I could do it but you and I both know it would take twice as long. It must be tough being so talented a swimmer."

"With you two about, it most certainly is," Moira responded.

And that was how the three worked; One to guide, one to form, and one to place. They worked late into the night.

Chapter 4

Sallah cinched up her braided leather belt as she walked towards the Old Growth Gate. Streaks of late morning sunlight swayed across the forest floor. Two sheathed bone daggers tapped her hips in rhythm to her steps. Matriarch Sorren stood framed in front of the gate consisting of two thick branches for the frame with a multitude of interweaving vines blocking the path. Terran and Agneth were conversing quietly as Sallah approached. Sallah watched the lips of her mentors.

Terran's lips said "Decision" but Sallah couldn't decipher anything else.

Whatever they were discussing it was intense and Terran was losing. Agneth caught sight of Sallah and broke off the argument. Sallah took her place between the two.

"Have you finished your remaining affairs?" asked Sorren.

Sallah thought Sorren's tone sounded almost apologetic. Sallah looked to Terran and then Agneth before giving a small nod.

"Then I will open the gate. May Dharra strengthen you." The Matriarch turned to the blocked path and took a wide stance. She placed both her hands together and in a wide flowing circle, swept her hands across her chest to the left, then to the right. the impenetrable branches slid away from the path under the command of her movements. She turned again to the three Druida of the Hawthorne. Sorren took time to stare each one square in the eye. "Whatever happens in this Rite, your House is for the moment, vulnerable. My authority is unquestioned, but even my decree will not guarantee protection forever. Finish the Rite quickly. For the sake of your House." With that Matriarch Sorren turned and was lifted from the soft grass by a Vine branch and high into the canopy of the Grove of Ancients.

For a moment, the three remained silent and still. Terran glanced at Agneth over Sallah's head and nodded quickly. Tosi began to walk down the shaded path, the only one eager for what lay ahead. The other three followed.

The morning had well passed to Sallah's figuring and the trail still had not strayed from its perfectly straight path. Sallah knew from her training they could just be walking in a giant circle. Spread across miles, the curve of a circle can look straight to the naked eye. It certainly didn't help that each tree skirting the path was an identical Vine, its jagged leaves intertwining with the one beside it. Sallah had to guess on the passage of time because the dense branches above her covered her sight, save for the path ahead. Perhaps they weren't going to the Old Growth. Perhaps this is what the Rite really was, a death march. A slow execution as you watched your companions fall away from exhaustion. The thought only angered her. If that were the case, she would survive if only to exact revenge. She felt outside of her body. Sounds muted as she fell into her fear.

"Calm yourself," said Agneth, her voice several steps behind Sallah. "No need to rush. We will be there soon enough."

Sallah hadn't noticed her pace had quickened. Turning back, Sallah watched Terran and Agneth walking hand in hand. Agneth was smiling. Terran's hand enveloped hers and pulled tight to his side. They had always loved each other and it had always been secret. All Druida were forbidden from any sort of relationship, besides political. Agneth and Terran could have any number of concubines but they could not mate with, nor marry, each other. Agneth once told Sallah that was the only reason she had married him. Terran would have been too boring if it wasn't forbidden.

Sallah started walking again, trying to remain present. She felt the pores of her skin open and breathe as she resumed her walk. She focused on the earth beneath her feet and the air filling her nostrils. She tried to remain aware of herself and her surroundings, but as she continued to walk, the same uneasiness set in. The wind felt the same, birds sounded the same. The path was the same. But her world would look very different by the time the sun had set on this day.

After an impatient eternity, Sallah started noticing a difference. The path was becoming more narrow. Slowly, the Vines encroached on the trail until eventually, they had to progress single file, their shoulders stained with outreaching blood-red berries. Soon they were crouching down, pushing past the branches blocking the trail. Suddenly, the trail widened and they were free, stepping into an ancient forest.

The ground was perfectly level, a mat of brown needles blanketed the damp, dark earth. A thick fog wove between the enormous trunks of redwoods, stealing the sky from their view. Sallah couldn't help but feel as if this place was intentional somehow. More cultivated than wild. There was something else that bothered her. The silence.

No chirping from the branches above or chittering squirrels broke the ringing in her ears. Her breath even sounded too loud for this place. Sallah instinctively reached for the familiar leather-wrapped handles of her two daggers. She was accomplished in others, but these were the only hunting weapons she ever needed. Agneth gave them to her when she was twelve and trained her in the Cerintha, the hunting style of the House of Hawthorne. Most Houses preferred distance from their quarry, the House of Hawthorne did not believe in that philosophy.

The huntress should know the weight of each death they cause. Terran's words rumbled through Sallah's mind. Tosi sprang to her shoulder in search of a better view. She relaxed a little, feeling the weight of her hunting partner on her shoulder. Sallah knew the sun had to be near midday at this point but the mist stuck stubbornly to the ground. It felt unnatural to her.

"Sallah, scout ahead." Agneth watched her. "Terran will move east and I will head west."

"Absolutely not," Sallah's voice surprised her. "We stand a better chance surviving this together."

Agneth walked toward her, placing her hand under her chin. "Sallah my dear, this Rite is not meant to be survived. We will each test our fates and let Dharra decide who lives."

"If one of us does die, how do we ensure the other two live?" said Sallah. Agneth smiled wholeheartedly up at her.

"Dharra is not a distant goddess. She is a living force that

62

surrounds us, even now, especially now. The Rites are not a construction of our devising. They are commandments handed down by her divinity. She is with us always," Tosi rubbed against Sallah's boot as Agneth continued, "The evidence is all around us. Know in your heart that when one of us dies today, the others will be protected under her dominion. The Greensea is hers, as are all who shelter under her boughs."

Sallah fought back tears, struggling to maintain a neutral expression.

Effortless. Sallah knew Agneth was right. If she was near either Terran or Agneth she would drop everything to protect them, prolonging the Rite and exposing her House to foreign conspirators. Still, Sallah was unwilling to give up entirely.

"Fine, then we use the calls. Until we are out of earshot." It was a childish thing to suggest but Sallah didn't care.

Agneth opened her mouth to speak.

"I think that is an agreeable arrangement," said Terran. His eyes were clear looking at Sallah, the same stoic look etched permanently on his face. "It will ensure a sizable distance between us all so that we may hunt separately."

Agneth nodded at his words. "Then let us be off." Agneth turned from the other two without another word and walked into the blinding mist.

"Goodbye Sallah, I have no doubt you will survive this day." Terran bowed deeply, more than he would have in public, but what did that matter now?

When death was the only outcome, sincerity became the only language worth speaking. He opened his mouth to speak again but remained silent. Terran turned in the opposite direction of Agneth and let the fog envelop him as well.

Sallah let the silence seep through her. Tosi bunted her softly. He was ready to hunt. Sallah stepped slowly into the waiting arms of the Old Growth. She whistled the morning song of the lark to her mentors. An interminable moment passed until she heard Agneth from her right, then Terran to her left. Calm passed over her if only for an instant. The deep trenches of the Redwoods seemed identical. For the first time in all her years of hunting in the forest, Sallah felt lost. She whistled again and again and both calls returned to her. A swell of panic rose in her chest.

Even if I do survive, how will I manage my way back? Her thoughts gave her no sanctuary. *Damn fog.* She whistled again, but she heard only one directionless reply. It was Terran's call. She didn't hear Agneth. She began to run in the vague direction of Agneth, but Sallah froze. There was another sound, a soft sniffle.

She pulled her bone daggers, turning in the direction of the sound. She heard footsteps, muffled by the blanket of fallen needles. It wasn't human. It had four legs. Then she saw it. A wild boar stepped from the curtain of fog. It stood no higher than Sallah's calf, tusks just peeking past its jowls. They stood still for a moment, each regarding the other. Small pointed spines rose from the boar's back, it raised its pink snout and released a squeal that shattered the silence. Tosi raced from Sallah's side and bit through the tiny boar's throat. The strangled cry wilted in the thick air and hung in Sallah's ears as it kicked at the serval before collapsing. A beaming Tosi dragged the lifeless boar back to the feet of his partner, proud of such a kill so early in the morning.

"Good boy."

Another squeal rang from somewhere in the mist, then

another. It grew into a feral choir. Then came the footsteps, directionless and in droves. From the fog emerged three more farrows, then five, then a dozen, most bigger than the first. Sallah tightened her grip on her daggers. She knew their real numbers were hidden by the mist and the twelve that she saw were just the vanguard. These were Razorboar, and they moved in large families. Alone, they were small and slow-witted. In the full strength of their family, however, they would overrun and make most anything their prey.

But she was not prey. She was a Druida.

Her breath quickened, not from fear, but anticipation. The slavering pack squealed and rutted the damp earth. Sallah shrieked back, high and wild. They charged at her, baring razor-sharp tusks. Sallah didn't move from her wide stance, blades held at the ready. The first charged at her legs, jaws opened wide. Sallah swept to the side, slicing the beast's throat in a flash. Two more leaped forward, trying to gut her. Sallah arched her back violently, sticking both beasts in the sides as they passed over her body. Three more followed in an instant. She stabbed two in the eye and ducked below the third which Tosi tackled in mid-air. Still more came, a river of yellowed tusks bent on destroying the Huntress. She had no time to think. Instinct and training guided her hands now. Sallah's feet slid effortlessly along the ground, spinning and dodging. Her blades moved in long loops and staccato angles, each strike precise and lethal. It was her hunting technique, her dance, *Cerintha*. She flowed with the movements of her attackers, positioning herself for balance and counter-attack regardless of the angle from which they struck.

There's something wrong here. I killed the vanguard, that's how Razorboar gauge the strength of prey. They should have scattered by now. They don't care how many of their own die? Sallah's mind quickened, *It's like they are ants.* They began to swarm from all directions now. She closed her eyes. Her vision could not penetrate the mist, but with her eyes closed she could sense the life force in every direction. The boars were everywhere, and more were coming.

She had never heard of a pack so large. Sallah was losing position quickly. She retreated to the wide trunk of a Redwood. They couldn't surround her entirely this way. She could split the pack, then move back to the next Redwood. She had felled more than a dozen. Tosi, though bloodied, was handling more than a few himself. The boars were smaller now, barely bigger than the farrow the pack usually protected. They charged for her legs. The boar may have been adolescents, but their hooves were sharp and their tusks sharper.

I can't kill them all.

"Tosi, to me!" Sallah sprinted away from the swarm headlong into the thick fog. She needed to create distance to continue this fight. But Sallah sensed the Razorboar's auras fading away. *Something's wrong. They aren't pursuing.*

The forest had grown silent again, and the Huntress' breath filled her ears. Then, there was another sound, swimming beneath her gasping breath. A hum, low and primal, moved from her feet, up her legs, and pressed like a weight upon her chest. The hum raised in volume and intensity to an air-filling bellow.

I found the queen. The earth began to tremble in the rhythm of a gallop, growing stronger by the instant. Sallah closed her eyes to feel for the beast's presence and found it too late. The queen's life force was massive against the blackness of Sallah's perception as it galloped towards her. She tried to spin away from the charge, but the boar's massive tusk slipped through the side of the huntress' leather tunic and gashed her ribcage. The beast disappeared behind the curtain of fog, the ground shaking beneath its force.

Sallah opened her eyes. A scarlet ribbon of blood dripped down her side.

Could be worse. I can't be in the open though. It knows how to find me through the fog.

With her hand pressed hard against the wound, she took cover against the nearest redwood. That would at least cut down on the number of directions it could charge from. The ever-present rumbling again intensified. She needed to know the form of the beast. The queen broke from the fog to her right, bulging eyes set squarely on its target. It was a colossal creature, standing eight feet at its shoulder. A short, bristled coat reflected the dull brown of the forest floor and two pointed tusks the size of Sallah's arms protruded from blackened lips. Its sharp hooves dug deep troughs into the dirt. Spines circled her shoulders like a wreath; a rampaging vision of Nature.

Sallah fought her shock to spin to the other side of the trunk for cover as the behemoth sheared off a thick section of where Sallah had leaned a moment before. The queen vanished into the mist again. Sallah didn't hesitate. Stabbing her daggers one by one into the trunk, she began to climb. The gash in her ribs sent shooting pains down her leg as she pulled herself up the tree.

Find me now, pig.

The beast was returning. Sallah's arms began to shake from the exhaustion of battle and the loss of blood, but her hands kept hold. No matter how deeply she inhaled, Sallah couldn't catch her breath. Adrenaline was the only thing keeping her perched. She had reached her breaking point.

Hurry up. Sallah surveyed below her. *She has only one lane of attack now.*

The slavering boar emerged and heaved its full force into the tree trunk. The entire tree rocked violently beneath Sallah. Her grip betrayed her as she lost the grasp on one dagger and the other slipped away from the trunk. Sallah was falling, twisting herself in the air, her head pointing down. She grasped her single blade with both hands as her body fell towards the open jaws of the beast. She stabbed downwards with what little strength she still possessed. The queen boar and Sallah locked eyes as she fell. An infinite moment passed as the blade sunk deep into the Razorboar's eye. Time snapped back into pace as Sallah clung to her dagger. The beast flailed its massive head, sending Sallah flying limply to the earth. She bounced and rolled along the ground, her eyes unable to focus on the fast-spinning world.

Sallah blinked as she tried to refocus. She needed to get to her feet, but the adrenaline had left her, leaving her body bone-stiff with exhaustion. She only managed to curl her arm around the gash on her side, her forearm applying what little pressure Sallah could muster. Sallah turned to where her quarry lay. Each faltering death throe from the behemoth bounced Sallah's limp head off the ground. The last thing she felt was the queen breathing its last as Sallah's vision gave way to utter darkness.

—

It was the sun that woke her. The light of early afternoon

fought its way through the thinning fog as Sallah tried to open her eyes. They burned as she blinked to regain her focus. Sallah tilted her head. Her neck ached. Everything ached. Shapes took form in her burning eyes. The queen boar's body lay beside her, its snout a foot from her face. Its remaining eye stared vacantly at Sallah. The oppressive silence of the Old Growth was replaced by the soft breeze playing along the lofted branches of the Redwoods. She breathed as deeply as she could. A shooting pain cut its way across the right side of her body. The gash.

Sallah gently probed the wound with swollen fingers. It was a surprisingly clean cut and by the grace of the goddess, not mortally deep. Sallah sighed in frustration as she gingerly removed her boiled leather jerkin, exposing the wetness of her wound inside. Ripping off the right sleeve of her tunic, Sallah cut it in half, tying the two pieces together, and bound her torso as tightly as she could.

That should hold. Just avoid more acrobatics. And deep breaths.

She managed to work her way to stand on weary feet before having to lean against the now-still chest of her kill. The heft of the beast didn't budge under her weight. Sallah's breathing came short and stinging, but she was slowly regaining her constitution. Sallah worked her way around the front of the creature, examining her kill. The queen was a boulder of tightly drawn muscle. There was only one queen per sounder and queens were the most vicious of their kind, often killing and eating their siblings to reach this size and dominance. Patches of stiff fur were missing from well-worn scars on the queen's shoulders. Pale yellow quills the size of spearheads hung loosely on the skin of her neck. The boar's tusks came to an unnatural point, explaining the clean incision in Sallah's side. Relief washed over her when she spotted the hilt of her bone dagger sticking out from a bulging eye.

Not dead and not unarmed. Dharra blesses me. Sallah climbed onto one of the tusks and tugged on the blood-soaked grip. With a scrape, the blade begrudgingly released itself. Sallah puzzled over the impaled eye. That wasn't the sound she was expecting. The iris was thin and yellow, metallic really. Sallah tapped the dagger's tip against the iris and the sound of bone striking metal reached her ears.

Impossible. Metal was a rare material to the Children of Dharra. Besides, metal was found in ore deep in mountains and caves. Not an animal's eye.

But there it was.

She climbed down from its neck and began to probe along the rest of the boar's body for more signs of the unnatural. The ribs were bone and the sagging belly pure flesh. But her tusks were made of a pitted, yellowing metal.

This creature has been changed. Could even explain the number of her farrows as well . . . or perhaps it's this grove being undisturbed for so long that there is a new species? Or just a very old one? Sallah walked to the other side of the beast and removed its one good eye.

A completely unique trophy. It will look intimidating on my belt. Perhaps Terran will know how this happened. Terror flooded her body. Agneth. Her eyes swept across the forest. She let out her call. No one responded. Her mind spiraled to the worst, images of Agneth and Terran's bodies sprawled and broken on the forest floor.

Calm yourself. Agneth's refrain soothed the torrent in her mind. Breathing through the burning in her side, she leaned back on years of training for this precise moment. She needed to reorganize. She needed a plan.

Surveying the ground from the fight, Sallah had ranged a great deal. From the scattered needles of the forest floor, she surmised which direction from which she had originally run. Now that the fog had broken, Sallah was able to orientate herself using the sun peaking through the canopy. She spotted her other dagger fourteen feet above the ground, still stubbornly burrowed into the bark. *I can't make it up there with just one blade. I don't exactly have the strength either.* She decided one would have to do at this point and if any more savage beasts were lurking, then the gutted bodies of boars would be a much easier meal than her.

Sallah limped back in the direction she had run, moving in the vague direction of the Vine Gate. A pitiful mewling reached her ears.

Tosi! Numb feet carried her to the clearing of her morning battle.

"Tosi!" her head darted about. She called again, tears filling her eyes.

There was movement to her left. Crawling from a pile of four dead farrows, Tosi emerged, blood caked across his face. His left arm was clung to his chest, his paw hanging limply. Sallah ran to him. Blood had sealed his right eye closed, Tosi's or the boar's she couldn't tell. The top half of his right ear had been chewed off as well. He was alive though.

"*Síocháin*, Hunter," her voice caught in her throat. "Let's get you patched up."

Tosi did as he was told and let familiar hands perform a familiar act. Half of her sleeve became a bandage for the serval's ear, the other half secured a splint of thick bark bracing his arm. She cleaned what blood she could from

71

his face and was grateful to find both of Tosi's green eyes looking back at her. She didn't pet or hug him. That was not their agreement. That wasn't to say they didn't care or even love each other. They loved each other the way an archer loves her bow; one designed to hunt, the other to draw the string. She cleaned and dressed him as best she could, stood up, and sighed.

The bodies of their prey lay sprawled about the roots of the Redwoods. Studying the fallen beasts revealed no clues about their queen's metallic eyes or tusks. Each vacant stare showed a brown, natural iris, each belly limp flesh. Tosi began helping himself to a thigh. There was something wrong with the whole situation. She had never witnessed such selfless orchestration in all her years of hunting. The very idea of such devotion to the collective made her uneasy. Had the queen not attacked, she would have been overrun by her spawn.

What else lurks in this wretched forest that would force such adaptation?

Tosi chomped down on a boar leg. Sallah scooped down to pick him up. Tosi hissed and swiped at her hands. Sitting on his partner's shoulder was one thing. He could strike from a vertical vantage. But to be carried was an indignity he would not bear.

"You have a broken leg and we have miles to walk in possibly several wrong directions." said Sallah, extending her hands again. "Either you let me carry you or you walk the rest of the way."

Tosi inspected the never-ending grove and mewed pitifully as he approached Sallah's outstretched hands.

Sallah smiled. "We'll compromise." She lifted the wounded

serval to her shoulder, her hand secured below his broken arm.

Tosi leaned his blood-caked ribs against her neck.

Regaining her composure from the day's events, Sallah found she was at a loss for what to do next. "Going back doesn't do us any good yet until we find either Agneth or Terran." Their names stung her lips. "If we leave, we might be attacked again by who knows what monstrosity, and if we stay, every creature that enjoys meat will find us waiting." She sighed and surveyed aimlessly, patting her hip. Her waterskin was gone, flung or destroyed from the hunt.

"At the very least we need to find water."

But the ground was perfectly flat, so she couldn't just head downhill to find it. Animal tracks were pointless as the only prints she could find were from her now-dead quarry. The Redwoods proved there was groundwater, but her strength and injury would not allow her to dig. Her mind wasn't coming up with the answer.

"I suppose I'll let you decide. Which way Tosi?"

The silver cat surveyed and called softly in the direction to Sallah's left. Through four years of hunting and surviving within the eternal Greensea, Sallah knew that Tosi could be depended on for more than fighting.

"Then east is the way we go."

And with that, the two hunters limped towards the unknown.

The late afternoon sun warmed the pair's backs as they drank their fill from a shallow stream which weaved through the ancient trunks.

"Good boy," Sallah grinned at her exhausted partner.

Between the fighting, blood loss, full stomach, and broken

73

limb, Tosi had resigned himself to laying on his side and lapping lazily at the gentle stream. He seemed satisfied with his hunting display, even if he was a little worse for wear. Sallah began to notice a peculiar placement within the formation of the trees. When she had entered the ancient forest this morning she was facing south and all the trees seemed uniform in distance to one another, But as Tosi guided her east, the trees grew random, natural. She turned her head north; perfectly symmetrical, to the west wild and erratic. Hope filled her. She could find her way back to the gap in the tree line. The stream flowed from the north.

Perfect. Her cupped hands dipped into the water, her eyes searching north. In an instant Tosi swiped at her hands, drawing tiny drops of blood that dripped into the shimmering water.

"Damn it!"

Tosi didn't notice her. He hissed and spat at the stream, hobbling his way backward. She looked at the stream and gasped. Through the babbling current, she could make out a thin black ribbon. Her keen eyes gazed over the length of the substance. It writhed and wriggled in concert with the waves as its mass expanded and contracted as if it were breathing. She leaned closer. Each time the Ichor contracted, languid little fingers protruded from its side, sweeping with and against the current.

It's looking for something. The scratch on her hand released one more tear of blood, slid down her hand, and fell into the water. The tiny fingers absorbed it in an instant. The Ichor began to swell and twist, hungrily searching for more blood. Very slowly Sallah backed away from the writhing rivulet.

"Good boy," sighed Sallah.

Tosi paid no attention to her, still busy spitting his discontent at the newly found danger. She closed her eyes and turned her face to the infested brook. Its aura wasn't like the wafting glow of the trees or animals. It was an inhaling darkness, constantly pulling into itself. Even Tosi's aura was being pulled towards this ooze.

Death isn't the opposite of life. This Ichor is. Her eyes opened to the falling sun. The partners were running out of time.

"We're bloody, lost, and now some sort of liquid that drinks blood." Her single blade twirled slowly in Sallah's fingers. Thoughts of Agneth and Terran flicked across her mind, but she suppressed them immediately. "We need to find our way back. If for no other reason than to warn the Houses of this Ichor. Looks like all our hope lies upstream. Pray we don't find another fight." She stood on renewed legs, set Tosi back on her shoulder, and began the walk north in search of home and hope.

—

The Redwoods cast long shadows along the ground, striping the earth in rose gold and darkness. They hadn't been walking long before a peculiar noise teased her ear. Her body reflexively swept into a fighting stance. Whatever was making the sound hadn't taken notice of Sallah. She slowly prowled towards the source. It wasn't coming from a living thing, at least nothing that Sallah had ever heard. It was a song, like the elders performed at Festival, regaling the battles and hunts of the Children of Dharra. Sallah found the source, but could not make sense of it.

Alone among the trees and fallen needles stood a worn,

wooden table. It would have been ornate and beautifully carved at one time, but nature and the elements eroded its once-grand design. A peculiar wooden box sat on top and from the box sprouted a large blossoming metal flower. Sallah approached with waning caution. Crumbling rust caked most of its surface, but the sound poured from its throat unfettered. Tosi hopped from her shoulder to sniff among the mysterious box. It was filled with intricate metal wheels each turning in perfect rhythm with the next. A black cylinder rotated slowly against the point of a delicate needle. The song was beautiful and terribly sad. Sallah's eyes grew heavy as if she hadn't slept in days. Her arms felt limp and useless. Even Tosi's head began to bob in resistance to the sudden tiredness. She propped herself against the table and let the music wash over her. The madness of the queen boar's eye came first to her mind. It was not the eye of a living animal.

Was it the Ichor that cursed you? No creature should endure such atrocity.

Then came Karra's desperate face. She was much more than a servant to her, she was a friend. She was . . . Agneth and Terran forced themselves into her mind. Sallah wept silently.

Where are you? I pray for your strength. Loneliness. No one cared what would happen to the lost Druida, save the two who may already have died and another who was not allowed to have an opinion. Her consciousness spiraled into morose darkness, deeper and deeper.

Sallah snapped awake. The music had stopped. Just the clockwork ticking of the curious machine as the needle searched for more of the cylinder to play. Brushing the deadened needles from her legs, she found her body was no longer sore. Even the searing gash from Queen-boar's tusk had subdued to a dull throb. The sun had not lowered itself in the slightest, as if no time had passed at all. Tosi's back arched deeply, as he stretched the sleep from his body. He seemed in better spirits as well.

Thank you, Dharra, for returning my strength. Fear crept into her gratitude as Sallah realized a crimson light against darkening shadows. Wolves, boars, and bears bore no terror for her. Darkness was her only true fear. It was a necessary affliction born of her society.

Only fools and the dead rest easy at night, Agneth was fond of telling her.

Even the auras she saw behind the closed eyes became muddled and scattered by the night. With dagger in hand, she turned to trek north along the stream when a leather pouch behind the rust-covered bloom caught her eye. On top of the pouch set a slim piece of paper turned brown and brittle by the wind and rain. On its center a wax seal stamped red with an insignia of a wheel with symmetrical teeth laced along the outside. How long it had sat there Sallah could not fathom, but the note was written in the words of her people.

What is contained within is meant for you and only you. No other may bear them as no other may bear your soul. The Flame once quenched has begun to smolder and rise again. The Greensea will bathe in its destruction and few may stand against it. What you hold are the tools necessary to hold back the coming Flame. Know that you are never alone Daughter of Dharra, and others will rise to your aid. Take the cylinder in the machine with you as well and carry it with you always. Never let the cylinder out of your sight. Music is the language of the soul and another soul will hear its song just as you did.

—M

Sallah uncinched the worn string on the bag. Two pommels in the shape of Hawthorne blossoms shone steel-red in the failing light. They were attached to a thin metal ring that circled a white leather grip. Counter-set from the pommels, two shining steel blades curved towards razor points as if shaped by the wind itself. They were wide and delicately thin but kept a comfortable heft in her hands. The edges were honed to such wicked sharpness that the blades disappeared when viewed head-on. Her chipped bone dagger appeared laughably decrepit in comparison. Blood-stained fingers slipped around the pure white leather of each grip. Sallah's blood began to rush through her arms to her hands. The daggers felt warm and familiar.

These would move through flesh like a spirit through the forest. Sallah's lips twitched into a crooked grin though it didn't feel natural. Her breath quickened to a fevered pace and her eyes clouded with red haze.

Hunt something, anything, a voice whispered in her head. It was hers but crueler, merciless. Her mind swirled in a sea of heat and the hunt. As if in a different body, she felt Tosi's paw padding against her arm. The twin blade's trance broke only for a moment, and in that moment, she shoved both daggers into their sheathes. Night had claimed the Greensea, and terror had claimed Sallah. Tosi made a three-legged leap for his partner's shoulder and landed awkwardly on her neck and head. The far-away call of a blue jay spurred Sallah's feet towards the song. *Why does Terran call out alone?* She fretted, boots pounding the soft earth, weaving through pools of whitewashed moonlight. *Dharra, grant me speed.*

Chapter 5

Jack's boots beat a quick circuit in front of the Conservatory entryway. A white light seeped through the streets, thickening the morning fog. Leather gloves stretched against his sorely worked fingers. The top of the feed pipe had finally breached the Stonehall side of the moat. Moira and Charlie had given in to sleep at 2:07 am, leaving Jack to execute all three stages of construction for another three hours. That suited him well enough. Sleep never came easily for him. There were too many tasks, too many things to fix. Jack looked north, peering up at the Metronome Tower. Its massive clock face was pointing at 5:58 am. Soon, daylight would punctuate its gold and silver tracings, framing the glass eye that kept time and watch on the city.

"So you can be early," Said Barin as he stomped towards Jack, sipping coffee from a tin cup. "Time to put this machine to the task."

Jack scanned the silent streets. "Where's Crowley?"

Barin grunted as he clanged up the steps to the brass double doors. "He's been here earlier than me for a week now." The Master Tuner fumbled for his key ring with tightly bandaged fingers. "Boy. Keys. Now."

Jack's jaw clenched back a laugh. *I'll be lucky to get through this day alive.* He plucked the key ring from the old man's belt and found the one shaped like a quarter note. The double doors swung open.

"My guess is our Maestro hasn't left the Conservatory since yesterday," said Barin.

Haggard cooks hauled wheels of cheddar, baskets of wheat bread, and trays of sausages into the dining hall for the Academy's breakfast. Barin snatched a mitt full of sausage links and half a loaf of bread from a leery-eyed cook.

"You'd best grab some food, boy," Barin mouthed through a half-full maw, "I don't imagine you'll have the time for the rest of the day."

Jack gave his best commiserating smile to the cook as he took a couple of links and a few slices.

"Crowley doesn't have a partner, so no need for him to go home in the first place." Barin stepped up to a landing platform set in an alcove.

A quiet pneumatic whistle announced an iron elevator as it whisked down to the landing.

"Well, he does," said Jack, leaping onto the descending elevator. "But she's huge and requires a lot of upkeep."

With his usual grunt towards Jack's jokes, Barin stepped on and flipped the only lever on the control panel. They rose to Crowley's office.

The lift slid to a stop in front of a silent corridor. The doorway to his office opened, immaculate as its owner. Crushed velvet covered the entryway hall.

Crowley was sitting behind his desk of polished gold, set towards the back wall. "Good morning, gentleman, ready for the day's agenda?"

Jack saw the distant Metronome Tower staring into the office. He followed the giant eye's gaze down to his feet, where he could see the Arc-chain far below rippling peacefully.

From his suites in the distant Metronome Tower, the Patron could look down on the Conservatory and watch his brilliant machine at work. In particular, his Maestro. Jack felt both exposed and watched over. He stopped alongside Barin, who stood alien in this pristine and sterile environment.

"First off is you, Mr. Dowton. Barin has recommended you as his proxy until his hands have mended." Crowley's face hardened in scrutiny. "Your thoughts?"

A tingle streaked up Jack's spine. "I don't know . . ." His sight remained planted on the Arc-chain below his boots. "I don't know if I'm the most qualified candidate."

"I am inclined to agree, Mr.—" Barin stomped forward in interjection, cutting off Crowley.

"You have no say in this, Carroll," said Barin, "I am well aware James Petty is your personal choice, but his two outstanding qualities of cowardice and fawning over those in power will not serve in my duties." A long, exasperated sigh was Crowley's reply. "Now, if we have invested enough of the morning's time on a decision I've already made, perhaps we can move on to the more urgent issues of keeping the city running." Barin's tone brooked no further discussion.

"Very well, Barin," Said Crowley, " I will allow your apprentice to be your proxy for the time being. But bear in mind that if anything should go wrong, it is your responsibility."

"Isn't it always?"

Crowley slid two pieces of parchment across his desk. His pursed lips betrayed his frustration with the Master Tuner.

"A list of procurements required for the Tuners work today, routine pressure checkpoints at The Stacks . . . " A final parchment hung in Crowley's hand, "and an order to appear in front of The Patron."

Jack's head jerked up.

The Patron? What does the Patron want with Barin?

Barin met Crowley's eyes and grunted his understanding. There was a significance in that sound that made Jack uneasy. Looking back at his desk, Crowley flicked his fingers in dismissal with obvious indignation. Jack turned to retreat towards the hallway.

"Oh, and one more thing, Mr. Dowton," the Maestro's voice was cool and acidic. "I strongly advise you to keep any fairy tales you have imagined to yourself."

A moment hung in silence.

"Gossip travels quickly, and I will not allow any unnecessary disruptions in my workforce."

Rough hands shoved Jack out the door before he had time to respond.

"Why did you have to tell him that?" said Jack, his face hot in annoyance.

Barin was already moving away from the question and briskly down the hall. "Are you questioning my decisions too, boy?" Barin's tone was acutely rhetorical. "Or questioning who I told?"

Winding around the soft curve of the hallway, Jack was at a bit of a loss as to why he felt as he did.

Crowley had a right to know. Was it so foolish to think he would believe me?

"Stop consoling yourself, boy. Stand by what you saw if that is how it happened," said Barin.

"Starting to believe?" said Jack, the words dryer than dust.

Barin pulled down the only lever on the lift. "I should've stuck you in the Academy."

Down slid the platform, carrying Jack and Barin into the open space of the Proscenium.

—

Fresh morning light beamed off the polished patina stories, reaching into the sky of the northernmost district, Balcony Row. Tinkerers scurried about their booths, fidgeting with their displays of toys and tools on the street level. The autumn wind played its song amongst the ornamental trinkets and hand-blown baubles, waiting for buyers in the cool shade of the tiers above. Vendors with beards tucked into their bibs hauled wide racks burdened with roast chickens and smoke-cured beef, calling out their prices up and down the bustling thoroughfares of Balcony Row. Salons and boutiques flicked on their incandescence on the third level, ready for trade with the wealthy. Up and up the balconies rose, like perfect striations of wealth, corralled by the brass tubing of the Skytrain, weaving above and between them. Thin alleys trailed away from the Esplanade, the main artery of Balcony Row, and the high street of the Patron's Chorus, where Jack now found himself.

Holding four tightly wrapped boxes in bowed arms, Jack nudged his way through the crowd of powdered wigs as they traipsed down the Esplanade. Stiff-necked matrons bobbed by in starched gowns, their wrists held limply by bachelors in silk cravats and satin socks. Disdainful looks came easily to their upturned faces. Jack got the impression that his passing caused an offensive odor. They would not move out of the way.

"Patron's business," said Jack, far louder than was polite.

The wigs eyed him as they made a path. This was quickly becoming his favorite part of being a proxy. He weaved his way through the Esplanade, took a left, and backed his way into a Courier's office.

The Postman rolled on the *High Care* stamp on each box and sent them to the Singing Stacks. As Jack left, a gyro-balanced cart hummed down an alley to deliver the parcels. Back on the Esplanade, he walked down the clockwise turn towards The Stacks on the eastern side of the city. It was rare for him to walk about Cogrind during a workday. Watching the city he helped power as they used Arc without a second thought provided a lift to his boots he hadn't anticipated.

—

It was 11:32 am by the time Jack walked towards the steel gateway that marked the Singing Stacks District. A gear fifteen feet in diameter hung braced by beams as thick as Barin over the wide gate. The teeth of the gear were shaped like tongues of flame, twisting out and up. The gate itself was made of several doors inset into each other, designed to allow precisely the carrier passage and nothing else. Jack could already hear the hums rising from the exhaust stack's smelters and refineries as he approached the gate.

The guard inspected Crowley's parchment momentarily before hitting the gate release. The road among the Tin-clad refineries and smelters was wide and well-worn from

85

the constant pilgrimage of ore-laden wagons. Tall, airy warehouses stood shoulder-to-shoulder as exhaust stacks sprouted from their tops, blowing a hundred note harmony into a breezy sky. Sparkling steam rolled out the stacks, bobbing and twisting into ethereal cords. Gruff tradesmen with bushy mustaches and thick forearms moved down the rows with a workman's gait, weary and sure. Jack flicked up the collar of his peacoat against the blowing autumn wind and weaved his way through the wagons to Lute and Sons Smelters.

It was down the far-east end of the district, near the gate closest to the Prism Mines. The rumor was that Sean Lute's prime location and first pick of the ore were responsible for the Smelter's legendary quality. Jack knew better. He knocked on a door that was laughably small compared to the wall in which it hung. A rust-spotted wagon pulled up to where a service entrance met the featureless wall. Individual tin plates spun and lifted, forming an entrance small enough to clip the driver's hat as he pulled through. Jack banged on the door more fervently this time. It was wrenched open by a shag of sweat-clumped hair with two bright hazel eyes just underneath. The man looked to be in the mood to bark until he saw Jack.

Cracked, brown teeth revealed themselves under the mop of hair as Sean Lute warmed into a wide smile. "Well, get in here, Jack. It's been too long."

Sean's office was as cozy as Jack could expect for a smelting foreman. Daguerreotypes ringed the shelves, a visual history of Lute's family. Jack smiled at the story. There was Lute, his wife, and a very conspicuous bump in her belly. The next showed an infant and another bump, then two children and a bump, three and another bump, and eventually four children and a tired but smiling Mrs. Lute.

"Not bad, eh Jack?" He propped a pair of slag-covered boots on his desk and leaned back in his chair. Sean was in his late fifties now; his face was leather where it wasn't bearded. Slivers of silver and gold slag had burned permanently into his forearms. Smelter's Bracelets, they were called, a badge of his trade proudly worn.

"This was taken a month after the Boiler commencement." Sean tossed the metal plate into Jack's sure hands.

Lute's oldest son, Timbre, was a man in his early twenties, handsome and broad. Next was his daughter Muse, nineteen, with her mother's slender face and her father's smiling hazel eyes. His two youngest boys, Drummond and Sean Jr., hung from the older sibling's necks, all smiles and mischief.

"Would've been missing more than one if not for what you did, my boy."

Jack tossed the portrait back and watched Lute smile at his other empire, scores of men and women working the forge floor below.

"Most didn't know the danger they were in that day, but I do." He cracked another tobacco stained grin. "Still don't know how you made it without half your body peeled off."

Jack couldn't remember all the specifics of that day either. Everything blurred in panic and necessity. He just remembered the innocent ping of a bolt popping free and the terrible rush of that glowing steam. He remembered seeing the problem. The Arc-Boilers themselves were simple enough machines to understand. The inner wall had just started to rupture leading to extreme pressure on the return conduit. Why it had even been pressurized with Arc in the first place, Paragon only knew. Jack remembered the screams, too but he pushed that sound away as quickly as he could. It was that day he proved his worth to Cogrind. That he was more than an orphan at a workhouse. That he was a musician for the grand performance, a well-crafted cog for the Greatest Machine. Absent-mindedly, Jack stroked his wrench.

"Or is it that little beauty I owe my life to?" Lute pointed at the wrench. "May I?"

Jack flicked it at him. Lute caught with a curious look.

"Hm. Heavy. Much heavier than would be useful," his voice a mix of awe and consternation.

Jack had never thought his wrench was heavy. In fact, he could remember Barin's steel wrench of the same size being much heavier. Without warning, he rapped it against a shiny bronze ingot on his desk with a violent clang. A wrench-sized divot was laid in the block of pure alloy, the wrench didn't bear a scratch. Lute grunted in concentration, flicking his fingers periodically against the length of the wrench. "My father started this forge seventy-five years ago, and since I was ten, I've worked here. Every kind of metal the mine can give us has passed under my nose, and in all my decades, I have never seen this kind of material, alloy or pure." Lute's gray eyes stared longingly for a moment and a half before throwing it back to Jack.

He caught it without ever taking his eyes off of Lute.

"I suppose you wouldn't be willing to tell me where you found such a tool? We could make a fortune," said Lute with another brown, broken smile. "Well, another one anyway."

Jack moved his thumb down the unknown metal. In Lutes' hand, it had the ruddy brown tinge it always had when not in

Jack's hand. Now, there was warmth, a rose of life to its color. It was his as much as his nose. It was the only perfect thing about him. He may be short and thin, with mismatched eyes and bizarre white hair, but he was the guardian of a perfect instrument.

"I couldn't tell you. Headmistress told me it was in my basket when they found me. She told me I was holding onto it for everything I was worth."

Sean burst out with a wheezing cackle that sounded like it might kill him. "It is so hard to tell truth from fiction sometimes." He wiped joy from his eyes. "But that sounds like the truest thing I am ever like to hear."

Jack returned a smile of his own. "Perhaps I was born to the craft." He flicked his neck to remove the hair from his eyes.

Lute leaned forward on his desk, his hair quite comfortably strewn across his face. "Born and bred. You're the best. The best that I can remember and I hope I live long enough to see you don the Tuner's watch. You've got the touch of The Paragon to be sure."

Jack smiled again at this proclamation from Lute, a full, unabashed smile. He would never admit it out loud, but that's exactly what Jack wanted. He hoped Lute was right. But first came the work. "I'm afraid I'm already going to be late for my next appointment if we don't hurry on Mr. Lute."

"Sean, my dear boy. Friends and saviors call me Sean."

They settled the particulars for the four-thousand steel ingots needed for structural reinforcements at the Conservatory's foundation. At the doorway, they shook hands.

"If there is ever anything you need, Jack, just call on me."

Jack turned to walk away. "I can't wait to make you a poor

man, Sean."

Lute's laughter was borne away on the hum of the stacks as Jack stepped outside.

The Metronome Tower clock showed *3:12 pm* as he raced up its gilded steps. Two attendants barred the entrance as soon as they saw him.

"May we help you?" said the attendant on the right, although he was clearly saying, 'Go away.' The attendant's face was mostly hidden by the high-arched collar of his white overcoat.

Jack squared up to the man. "Master Tuner's business." He enjoyed every succulent syllable.

He was led wordlessly to an ornate lobby of gold and crimson.

Barin was padding a slow beat on the crushed velvet floor when he spotted his apprentice. "Cutting it a little too close, boy." He paced towards a gilded double door "The Patron does not wait."

The doors swung open silently from the other side. Jack had never been in the Metronome Tower. He never had reason to. It took considerable willpower not to gawk at the lavish fineries. What wasn't ceiling-to-floor windows were hung with tapestries, thick and vibrant. The floor was lined with red carpets that muffled their boot steps. As far as Jack could tell, everything else was set in gold and silver tracings. The room was a ring that girded the Tower. They came upon a second pair of gold doors which effortlessly swept open to reveal a second ringed room identical to the first, if not for being just slightly smaller. Barin never broke stride as he stomped towards a third set of identical doors. The next ring-room had a row of doors lined on the interior wall.

"Chorus member chambers," the old man said, " the Vox Populi."

Each door was closed and no movement could be heard.

"It must be hard to hear them from all the way in here," said Jack.

Barin gave a noncommittal grunt as they approached a fourth set of gold doors. These opened outwardly. The pair walked through a wide hallway and passed into the most interior of the ring-rooms. A stiff man sat behind a silver claw-foot desk.

"Master Tuner Barin and . . . apprentice?" asked the man.

Barin nodded curtly.

"Very good sirs," as he pressed a gold button on his desk.

The entire room stirred and Jack watched through the windows as the room lifted up to the highest level of the tower.

They left the attendant primping his pocket square and began to walk outwards from the innermost room. Where the ground floor was fairly lifeless, the top floor buzzed with the comings and goings of the Patron's Chorus and various attendants, a gold treble clef signet hung by their hearts. As they walked from ring to ring, Jack noticed the closer to the Patron's office he saw more valets and attendants and less of the Chorus. The city guard known as the Steel Watch began to increase in number as well, loitering in hallways that curved away from the gilded hall that the pair walked. Jack could not for the world think of why the Patron needed guards in the Metronome Tower in the first place. In the streets of Cogrind, it was only natural to have a presence to address illegal incidents. After all, not everyone worked for the glory of the Machine. But here, at the foot of the

Highseat?

Perhaps it's all for presentation. The Watchmen did indeed cut an impressive figure. The armor was brushed gray and standing seven feet tall, hemmed by angular welds, and powered by a small Arc-tank.

Silver and gold plates taller than Barin lined the walls depicting Luthiers, Maestros, and Tuners. Each one held inventions of their own design in the palm of their hands, each a link back to the previous. The Sky Train, the Slip Differential, the Arc-tank.

Moving down the hall, the designs became simpler yet more fundamental to Cogrind. As they reached the end of the hallway, the Patron's doors were gilded with the first plate, the original inspiration. It showed a faceless man holding a gear over his head. The gear teeth stretched like sunlight and in the center of the gear was a whole note. Music notes bloomed from both hands as rows of faceless others stood behind him in a unified ensemble.

No one knew the name of the faceless man, or indeed most of the other names at this end of the hall. But he was the originator of Cogrind's way of life and its philosophy. The man was known as The Paragon.

The final set of doors were also lined with four Steel Watch to a side and an attendant whose shirt was more rigid than his posture sitting behind a gold claw-foot desk.

"Just one moment sirs," said the attendant.

Jack examined the line of Steel Watch. Considering the imposing armor, it was hard to imagine there were just men inside.

Eight guards?

The attendant pressed a button and rose from his chair.

"Right this way, sirs." The attendant led them to a dim antechamber and bowed away with a flourish.

The room had no door save the one they entered from which now clicked shut behind the two. Silence hung heavier than the tapestries. Jack coughed into the quiet. A low whir started to his right and the wall they faced slid slowly into the floor.

A blast door?

They stepped into the Highseat of the Patron.

The first thing Jack noticed was the clock. The exterior wall held the giant and intricate mechanisms of the Metronome Tower clock. Jack felt the sure tick of seconds from the machine in his chest. He then noticed what was outside the clock. Almost the whole of Cogrind could be seen from this vantage, including Carroll Crowley's office in the Conservatory as it stood below. The chamber mimicked the curve of the clock, stretching up at least thirty feet into the air. Sunlight streamed at an angle through the stained glass. A well-oiled cranking announced the Patron's arrival.

Three silver plates slid back from the floor, as a polished gold throne sat atop a dias descended into the chamber. Etchings of music notes and clefs played on swirling music staffs up the length of the dias. The music bars continued their sway up the throne, meeting at the apex and connected by a large whole note. The Patron beheld the pair from where he sat. Jack could not see his eyes but felt the weight of his gaze.

"The tireless Barin, the hand that builds the Machine. It is always a pleasure to see such a dedicated servant to Cogrind in the Tower. We chant for your speedy convalescence." The Patron's voice felt soothing and baritone. "And his young apprentice, Jack Dowton." The Patron's throne lowered to the floor, his profile outlined in seraphic light and the inner workings of the clocktower, but casting deep shadows across his face.

Jack and Barin bowed in response. Jack's eyes stared at the floor as he felt the Patron approach.

"Protector of our lost technology. To think we would rediscover the Paragon's greatest invention only to lose it after our first attempt."

Jack felt a gentle hand lift his chin.

"No words nor song can truly attest what you have done for the city, Jack, and for me."

Jack dared to look. The face was gentle, aged softly to a man in his fifties. Light blue eyes gazed at him sincerely in gratitude, framed by white hair that matched Jack's own. A Palladium necklace in the shape of a whole note bobbed against his cream and crimson robes.

"Please, rise."

The pair found their feet as the Patron returned to his throne.

"I thank such hard-working gears for arriving with short notice. Good Barin I heard reports of your valiant repair at the Arc-chain. How fares your recovery?"

"Yes Patron, I'm on the mend and will be ready for duty soon enough. I've chosen Jack as my proxy."

"Oh, I am aware good Barin, and a prescient decision I believe," his voice amiable, "I summoned you to inquire of any assistance the Highseat may offer you."

Barin squinted towards the throne. "Thank you my Patron. I'm afraid the only assistance that I require is time to heal and the patience to trust my subordinates."

The Patron chuckled softly at this. "The curse of many leaders I am afraid."

"My Patron is wise. But for the time being, Mr. Dowton takes orders well enough,"

"Just the same," Replied the Patron, "I will have my personal physicians see to your hands. It is the very least your dedication deserves."

A breath caught in the Master Tuner's throat. "My Patron is too kind. Come, Jack—"

"Actually, I would like a word with Jack Dowton as well."

The bottom of Jack's stomach dropped out.

Barin stared gape-mouthed at his apprentice, the Patron and back again. "I'm afraid I don't understand my Patron. He is only my apprentice. My proxy, to be sure, but my Patron need not waste his precious time with one still learning."

The Patron's voice was calm and filled with effortless authority. "I believe that your apprentice needs to understand the weight of his current responsibilities and my voice may aid in this endeavor."

Jack could feel The Patron's eyes on the top of his head.

"My physicians are waiting for you, good Barin. I will not keep your apprentice long."

Jack's mind was empty save for the images of his hovel in Stonehall, a threadbare cot looking out an open air window. Now he kneeled in the most powerful room in the city. The wall slid down to reveal the antechamber. Barin stomped from the office, a hesitance to his gait Jack could hear.

The wall slid back up as the Patron addressed Mouse. "Tell me Jack, how are you faring with your new burden?" His voice grew warmer.

"This is only my first day my Patron, but I have accomplished the goals set before me well enough that Barin has yet to yell at me." Jack felt lightheaded as he spoke, his toes tingled.

The Patron chuckled softly. "I have no doubt you will perform your duties admirably. You work hard for those around you, an admirable and necessary trait for a gear of the Great Machine. But I do worry that all the effort you put in projects outside of your work in the Conservatory may be a detriment to Cogrind."

"My Patron?" Jack barely recognized his own voice.

The Patron stood from his throne and walked to the window that framed the Tower's clock, the whole of Cogrind displayed before him. "Come Jack, stand beside me."

Jack did as he was bid, though it felt closer to floating than walking. The city spilled out before him in a hectic display of industry and life. Balcony Row just below them, The Singing Stacks to his left and the West Plaza to his right. Bass Run to the south was all but hidden.

"I am aware of your project to bring the Arc to Stonehall. I admire your tenacity, but it is an unnecessary labor. Do you think I have forgotten the broken of Stonehall? My dear boy they, just like every other citizen, are vital to Cogrind's opus."

Jack felt a warm hand on his shoulder.

"Soon, we will bring every citizen into the power of the Arc-chain and their burdens will be lightened. That is your vision Jack, and an honorable one that we share. But first, we must install the new Boilers. That is my vision, Jack. A vision I ask you share with me."

"But..I live in Stonehall my Patron." Jack's tongue stuck to the roof of his mouth. He had never been this close to all his wants being answered with a whim.

"Yet another thing we might hope to correct Jack." The Patron's voice was calm and soothing. "Tell me, why do you not lodge at the Academy?"

"Money, my Patron. To lodge there would take almost all of my wages." Jack was not about to tell him he felt ostracized by others for his talents. That was well beneath the Patron's concern.

"You are the Master Tuner's proxy are you not? I will order Crowley to place additional bonuses onto your wages while you go about good Barin's work. That should more than suffice for any financial shortcomings."

Jack froze for want of what he should say. A week of Barin's wages would put Moira up in an apartment in West Plaza for the next six months. But that's not what Moira wanted.

"I . . . Just the same my Patron, I would prefer to live in Stonehall."

The wide smile slid into a pained expression. "And why is that Jack Dowton?"

The Patron's words were an open wound. Jack hesitated again before he spoke.

"Because that is where my friends live."

"Such loyalty to one's friends. I hope they are worth such sacrifices." The Patron sighed before returning to his throne. "Do I have your word Jack? You will stop this project and focus on the Boilers?"

Jack's tongue felt numb in his throat. He lamely managed to nod his head.

"I find that most assuring, Mr. Dowton." The Patron swept from the window. He sat upon his throne as he began rising to the ceiling. "We look forward to what other gifts you may give our city."

As Jack tried to speak up, something peculiar caught his attention. For a moment he could have sworn the whole note that was inlaid upon the top of the Highseat, blinked at him.

Chapter 6

Sallah's heart beat a frantic drum in her ears as she raced through the waxing darkness of the Greensea. She didn't know how long she had been running, she didn't care. The sound of the blue jay was the sound of home through the wilderness and she wouldn't stop until she found him.

Idiot. We never should have split up. My voice means just as much as Agneth or Terran's. She could already hear Terran's quiet, sure answer to that.

The point of the Rite wasn't for us all to survive, but for one to die.

Despite the burning exhaustion in her legs, she spurred herself faster. Tosi clung to her shoulder with three good paws, his claws digging in through leather and skin. Sallah couldn't feel it. Sweet, stupid hope was all she knew at that moment. After reorienting herself, her sense of direction kicked in. Plotting her course, she began to return toward the Vine Gate. The call came again, this time much closer.

One last mile Dharra that's all I ask, then you can have my legs for all I care.

Her body threatened to betray her but on she pushed until she saw them, both of them. Terran's hulking frame was on his knees and Agneth . . . Agneth lay on Terran's lap, her eyes closed.

Sallah fell over herself as she raced to their side. "Agneth, Agneth I'm here!" She wheezed over gasping breaths, "What happened?"

Agneth's eyes fluttered open, watery and weak. "There you are my child." She touched Sallah's cheek with cold fingers. "Listen now. When you return they will think you are mourning. Don't . . . don't let them," Her breaths came in ragged and shallow twitches. "This is what I wanted. Know that—" A cough sent a trickle of blood down the side of her face "Know that you are always my child, even if you aren't my daughter," Agneth's eyes began to flutter again.

Sallah lurched back from her frozen silence. "Agneth, don't leave me . . . please," begged Sallah.

Agneth gave a glazed glance at the leather pouch on Sallah's hip. "Oh good. You found them." Agneth's breath went slack, her eyes unfocused. Agneth Va Hawthorne was gone.

To the east, the dawn bloomed grey and cold. For a moment the world stood in silent mourning. Sallah's body shook in revolt.

This is impossible. I love you. Please don't leave me. It was only then that she saw Terran's bone-hewn blade thrown a short distance away, covered in blood.

"You?" Sallah gasped.

Terran kissed Agneth's forehead and closed her eyes. He nodded slowly, with the full weight of his act weighing down his head.

Sallah grabbed his blood-stained blade and lunged at him. "Why, why damn it!"

Agneth's blood streaked across his neck.

He would not look at his pupil. "She said she would kill herself if I did not." His head bobbed in dismay. "No Huntress should die by her own hand, especially not Agneth. She was perfect. In every way she was perfect."

That hushed argument before they entered the grove popped into Sallah's mind. She dropped the blade and examined Terran. He was a boulder broken, cracked never to be mended. She had had her fill of death today. She wanted to cry, to scream, to mourn the mentor she loved, but not yet. There was still one last test to pass. Agneth's final words would be obeyed. She picked up Agneth's body, Sallah's legs wobbling in exhausted protest. Terran tried to help but she wrenched the body free of his hands.

I may forgive you one day, but not today. She followed Terran's steps back to the gate.

She did not remember the walk back through the alley of trees, rain dripping fat drops on Agneth's limp frame, or the branched Vine Gate being pulled back. The murmuring of a crowd snapped her from her waking nightmare. They backed away from the gate's threshold as Terran stepped through, Sallah a few steps behind. She flung Agneth's corpse on the wet ground. The onlookers gasped. Sallah wanted nothing more than to fling herself on the ground as well and to curse anyone who didn't mourn with her. She couldn't though, not yet. She had to put on this farce first.

"Where is Matriarch Sorren?" Her voice sounded flat and empty in her head, but she was thankful no tears came.

The crowd parted as Matriarch Sorren stepped methodically towards the body. Her jaw clenched at the sight.

"She was not attacked by an animal." The Matriarch's piercing eyes studied the body intently. "At least you didn't stab her in the back. You had the strength to gut her face to face."

Sallah burned with anger.

Then Agneth's laugh chimed at the back of her mind. *Listen with the right ears child, you will find more gifts in your enemies' voice than curses.*

"Would you of all people fault me for strengthening my house through youth, Matriarch?" Her eyes had not left the crumpled corpse.

"Indeed. The Rite is complete. You have proven your strength to the Houses and your worth to your people." Her eyes flicked towards Sallah who was soaked with blood and rain. "Congratulations Sallah Va Hawthorne."

Sorren's words twisted her stomach. Nodding quickly, she limped through the crowd, the weightless emptiness of grief moving her numb legs.

"It was high time for the old bitch to go."

That venomous voice rang as familiar as Sallah's own.

"And what irony that it was the little girl's life she saved that gutted her like a fish."

Sallah's feet turned absently towards Nissa's words. She stood beaming in triumph among a group of Vines, savoring the view of Agneth's body.

"It looks like my prayers were answered."

Sallah regarded her with lifeless eyes set in sockets dark with exhaustion. The other Vines backed away as she stepped toward Nissa. Her grin melted as Sallah stopped an inch from her nose. She could feel Nissa's body tense as she wrapped a blood-stained hand behind her neck, holding her head in her grasp, gentle and unmoving. Sallah's lips brushed against Nissa's ear as she whispered through a hoarse breath, "Now there is no one to protect you from me, little Nissa." She let go of her neck without a hint of violence and turned away. She watched Terran pick up Agneth, a fragility in his strength only she could see, as he carried his precious burden. A sob caught in her throat and her eyes began to burn with tears.

The hedgerow, just let me get to the hedgerow.

—

"Mistress." Karra's voice was even gentler than usual. "They are almost finished with preparations."

A weary sigh was the only response she received.

Karra nodded to herself and turned to leave Sallah's bedroom.

"I didn't kill her," croaked her voice from the bed. "Don't tell anyone. We need the lie."

Karra paused at the entryway. "I know Mistress. I already knew." Karra sounded as if she were holding back tears of her own. "I will be outside if you need me."

For a while, Sallah listened to the breeze trip along the blossoms of the giant Hawthorne while birds chirped their calls and replies through staccato drops of autumn rain. It made Sallah angry. The world itself should stop in remembrance. She had known death, seen death, imparted death, but she had never felt such loss. She blinked away dried tears and a few hours sleep. Before she realized it, the day had passed behind an unbroken curtain of rain. It was almost sunset and she would be expected at the Root Tree. She hadn't bathed or even changed. Her hair wound in knots and tangles across her head. She didn't care. No one else would either. She was home now, among her own.

The evening air breathed sweet and chilly as the sun broke free of the clouds to cast vibrant waves of pinks, reds, and oranges behind the Root Tree. The rest of House Hawthorne had gathered beneath its countless wide branches as Sallah limped with bare feet along the wet grass down to the base of the trunk. The crowd opened to receive her, thousands of eyes, wet and reddened, looked up to her in their pain and in search of her comfort. She touched a few she knew as Agneth's friends on the shoulder as she passed. Terran stood by the Root Tree, its trunk made of an innumerable braid of saplings, bulging with life ancient and new. Beside him lay Agneth washed and prepared in her huntress garb, each hand held a bone blade across her chest. The knife hole in her jerkin had been meticulously repaired. Death had made Agneth unrecognizable. She had prepared for that, but it was still a shock to see what once was and will never be again.

Agneth has been reclaimed by Dharra. This body shall return to her.

Terran still would not look at her. She was too hollow to be angry with him now. She knew they would talk soon enough, but tonight they would mourn their loss together.

"I would like to say a few words if you would allow me Sallah." His voice was as strong as ever, but quieter.

Sallah kneeled next to Agneth's body. "You may."

Terran raised his eyes to the gathered House. Sallah could see the course his tears had made down his cheeks.

He lifted his palms to the sky as the Root Tree lifted him a few feet into the air. "House of Hawthorne."

The crowd fell silent at the sound of his voice.

"Agneth Va Hawthorne has returned to the goddess." His voice carried across the expanse of the grove. "She gave us wisdom, she gave us cunning, she gave us strength." Tears began to roll down his cheeks but his voice did not waiver. "She gave us all the gifts Dharra had wished for in an elder and a Druida," He was silent for a moment of grief but continued. "But she also gave us all that she was and taught us what we may be. She gave us trust and taught loyalty, she gave us her time and taught patience, she . . . she gave herself and taught us selflessness." He looked at Sallah then.

It was she who could not look at him.

"She gave her life and taught Sallah."

Sallah lifted her face to the sky and finally felt free to grieve.

"Agneth's body will be given to the Root Tree," Terran continued, "But her gifts and her lessons strengthen Hawthorne forever." He turned towards Sallah as the House screamed and shouted in loss.

Her eyes blinded by tears, she felt Terran place a hand on her shoulder and the other pressed a small object into one of her hands.

"Do you want to say something to your people?" he whispered.

Sallah thought for a moment. *What would Agneth say?* She shook her head wearily. "I have no words. Not tonight. I doubt anything I say tonight will help. Let us honor our Druida. Tomorrow, I will speak."

He nodded solemnly. She inspected what Terran had placed in her palm. A bright red hawthorne seed glowed warmly in the dying light. She knew the ritual. She slipped a blade from Agneth's cold fingers. The grip felt foreign in her hand as if her fingers had never held a dagger before. With tears still clouding her eyes, she slit open Agneth's leather jerkin in one clean cut. The next cut eased open her thin tunic. Finally she made a small cut in Agneth's chest, right where her heart had beat. She tucked the seed into the cut and gently replaced the tunic and jerkin. She turned to the Root Wall. Its trunk was a wall of woven bark, spanning a mile, with branches stretching beyond sight, a testament to the fallen generations before them. Each Huntress returned to guard the Hawthorne Grove in death as they did in life. Sallah willed its tangled cords open to welcome one of its kindred to join the braid of the Root Wall. The roots parted under her will and branches bent low to carry the body of Agneth Va Hawthorne deep beneath the tree. The roots closed around her and she was gone from Sallah's sight. She remained kneeling. She did not want to move.

Doubts of her ability to lead her people were already ambushing her mind. All she wanted at that moment was to rest. Then she felt someone kiss the top of her head and whisper "My Druida" into her ear. Sallah thought about looking up to see who it was, but she didn't. It made no difference to her who it was. It gave her peace for a moment and that was enough. She felt another kiss on the top of her head and someone else whispered "My Druida" in her ear. And so it continued. She didn't know how long she kneeled there. Hours maybe. But every few seconds came a kiss and a whisper of fealty. Each kiss was a drop of resolve that filled the void Agneth left. Each whisper, an ember that warmed her heart.

When she opened her eyes, she was no longer crying. The

rain had stopped. It was night, the full moon shone bright and blue across the grove. She wasn't afraid of her coming failures as Druida, not tonight. She was home. Her kindred had lit fires and begun to drink honey mead and tell stories of Agneth. Some had even begun a contests of skill to honor her. She saw a pair of knees enter her view and felt another press their lips softly on the top of her head.

She heard a familiar voice whisper "My Druida" in one ear and "My friend" in the other. It surprised Sallah how much she had wanted to hear those words from that voice alone.

"Thank you," said Sallah looking up at Karra.

Karra's eyes weighed down with worry. Sallah's talismans of claws hung tightly around her neck. She rose and together they walked towards the ever-growing clamor of mead-fueled boasts and toasts along the bonfires scattered about the grove. Glancing back to the Root Tree Sallah watched all its empty branches rattle in celebration at one new sapling in full white-petalled bloom, dancing happily in the moonlight.

"You'll cut yourself on those if you don't loosen the binding," said Sallah.

Karra stroked the necklace thoughtfully. "I didn't want to lose it. It's important."

Sallah wrapped an arm around her shoulder. It was the height of impropriety for a Druida to befriend a Nameless. But by Sallah's decree, Karra was no longer Nameless.

"So are you."

Karra smiled wide at Sallah's declaration.

"I've lived most of my life in seclusion while training. The only one I ever spent time with besides Terran and Agneth was you. I know every name in the House of Hawthorne but I do not know the person . . . and they do not know me."

Children weaved through their feet, playing whatever game that came to their mind. Watery eyes raised bowls of mead as they passed. Some glanced suspiciously at her but Sallah dismissed it as her imagination.

"Then let them know you," said Karra. "Show them who you are, and they will follow you into the teeth of the other Houses with a smile on their face."

Sallah's laugh surprised her. It felt good. Karra felt good. "I will try to avoid all-out war for a little while anyway," joked Sallah.

Karra stared at Sallah with that familiar, unmovable sincerity.

"There is much more to you than meets the eye, Karra va Hawthorne. I might be frightened if you weren't my friend."

Confusion replaced Karra's smile.

"But we have got to work on your sense of humor." Sallah smiled.

They had wandered towards the Killing-Trees. A boy and a girl around ten were shouting at each other. The boy saw Sallah and turned to run.

"Come here," Sallah commanded.

He stopped his retreat, head slung low.

"You too." Sallah pointed at the girl who had also tried to make a quick escape.

They stared at her with a child's fear, absolute and paralyzing. They were identical in every way; Roughspun green tunics that hid numerous grass stains, cotton breeches with the knees worn out and a bouquet of black textured hair sprouted from the top of their heads. Right down to how they shuffled their feet in shame.

"Timma and Tommin of the womb of Lassana. Yes, I

know who you are. Why do you squabble on a night of remembrance?"

The girl Timma, the braver of the two, spoke up first. "Tommin said my form was wrong but I did everything Teacher Soli taught me so Tommin has to be wrong, Druida."

Sallah turned to the boy. "Is this true?"

Tommin continued to study the ground intently before he whispered, "She keeps over-throwing her blade. So I told her to change her grip from the blade to the handle just like Teacher Pina taught me. Then she said my stance was too close together."

Sallah studied them both for a moment. "Let me see your throws."

The children stared up at her in surprise then quickly lined up. People nearby quieted as they watched the competition. Timma squared herself to one of the Killing Trees, its bark scarred from generations of training. The Druida would heal the trunks regularly but the scars would always remain. The girl squared herself to the tree and threw. Her form was good, but the handle gave a dull thud as it knocked against the trunk and fell harmlessly to the ground. Good-natured chuckles came from the crowd as Timma stood red-faced in the moonlight waiting for Tommin's throw. Tommin stood only four paces away from his mark. His stance was too close and the result was the same as Timma's.

Sallah smiled at them. "That makes it simple then," she said as the Hawthorne tree bent low under Sallah's will. "You were both right about each other and wrong about yourselves."

The tree wrapped a branch around each blade and placed them in Sallah's hand. The twins stood slack-jawed in identical awe. She had forgotten that children saw very few

109

displays of druidic power.

"Show me where you stood," said Sallah.

The children hurried toward their spots.

"The distance to your enemy is as important as your form." Sallah stepped behind Timma, placed her foot behind the child's and made her take a step forward. "How you grip your blade is determined by how many rotations you need to cover the distance." She then stepped in front of Tommin and placed a blade in his hand, grip-end up. "Once you have determined these two things you will be ready to use your form." She stepped back and nodded at the twins.

They threw in unison. Both blades sank satisfyingly deep into the bark. The gathered crowd laughed and cheered. The tree returned the blades from its belly and back into Sallah's hand.

She handed them back to the twins. "Have your teachers told you the most important lesson of blade-throwing?"

Their response was in unison. "To throw your knife is to lose your own hand. Do not throw unless you have no other choice."

"Good. Now there will be no more fighting from you two tonight. Is that understood?"

Both nodded their heads gravely.

"Then you may go." Sallah smiled.

But both stood where they were, kicking at the ground.

"Is there something else?" Sallah said.

"Yes Druida." Timma was the first to speak again. "We were hoping you might show us how you throw."

The crowd cheered at the idea.

Sallah sighed in mock impatience. "Very well, give them to me."

They did as they were bid, as a few more blades from onlookers were thrown at her feet. They wanted a demonstration of their new leader's skill. Sallah picked up six in all. The crowd hushed as she squared up to the tree, twelve paces away.

In a moment, she was seven again, Agneth's hands clasped over hers as she learned to grip a dagger. The gentleness and skill of her teaching, Moving Sallah's arm to mimic a throw. Sallah stared down at the dagger in her palm.

A different hand but the same grip. Closing her eyes, Sallah breathed in deeply. In three steps she loosed every blade. She threw two blades over-hand with her first step, two more under-hand with her second. She leaped spinning through the air with her final step, throwing the last two blades in split-second succession. The knives formed five points with the final blade buried to the grip in the center. The crowd unhinged in elation. She was powerful. She could hunt. She was theirs. The tree tugged each blade free as Sallah closed its wounds. Her House bowed respectfully as they made way for her path with Karra beside her.

"Into the very teeth of the other Houses," Karra repeated, "with a smile on their face."

Sallah couldn't help but smile at herself in satisfaction. She spied Timma and Tommin whispering excitedly as they chased each other back to their mother.

"Do they always fight like that?" Sallah said a little worried.

Karra watched them race away into the night. "Oh yes. They scream and kick. I've even seen them bloody each other more than once. But I have also seen them huddled next to each other on the grass, tracing constellations and trying to scare each other with stories of the ghosts of traitors that lurk

111

about the Killing-Trees, falling asleep side-by-side to keep the spirits away. Perhaps it is the nature of being around someone so similar to you. Or perhaps it's just the nature of siblings."

Sallah wondered what that would be like but dismissed it. *I wouldn't be who I am right now. It would've changed everything.* If she had any family of age she never would never have been dubbed Nameless as a child, would never have served Nissa, would never be in the position she is now. *Pointless.* It looked like Karra might be wondering the same. She let Karra have her daydream.

They wandered back to the Mother Tree, the Hawthorne that dominated the valley. Sallah was exhausted, but she knew she would not sleep. Agneth still weighed on her mind and the solitude of her bed would only make the memory heavier.

Karra hugged Sallah tightly and turned to go. "Oh I almost forgot." She untied the necklace around her neck. "Returned as promised."

"You've earned your name and freedom. Keep it. You wear it well." said Sallah.

Karra gave another full smile. "I thought you would say that. I will wake you at sunrise, Druida."

Sallah laughed softly. "You are named now, Karra. You are not obligated to serve

anyone now, including me."

"I am Karra Va Hawthorne, and I serve whomever I please." Karra's customary sincerity felt like a salve, "And I choose to serve you until Dharra reclaims me."

"Is that truly what you want?"

"It is."

"Then I will see you at sunrise."

Karra bowed and entered through the hollow of the tree. Many mourners were dispersing, wandering back home or sleeping on the soft grass. Some die-hards were still about, singing drunken songs in the old tongue, sloshing mead from their bowls as they meandered under the boughs of Hawthornes.

They are mine now. To protect or expose, they are mine. Dharra . . . Agneth give me wisdom. She willed a limb to lower next to her feet. She stepped up and was carried into the night sky and to the archway of her chambers.

Stepping into her chambers she smelled something wrong. Something reeked of alcohol. "Step out now."

Something moved on the floor. She was there in an instant, fists raised and ready.

"Calm yourself child. I'm not the one you need to fight." Terran struggled to his feet, his knees wobbling in drunken strain. His eyes were puffy and small and both hands clutched empty skins of mead.

"What are you doing here Terran?"

"I said we needed to talk. The sooner the better, for all of our sakes."

"Since when do you drink?"

"Since today."

Shouldering his bulk, Sallah helped him on to the bed. He sat slouched, drawing the last few drops from each skin. "You need to sleep. We can talk tomorrow."

He considered her with pain and frustration carved on every inch of his face. "No. Tomorrow will be too late. You must leave tonight."

Sallah huffed in exasperation. "I am not going anywhere."

"Then the House of Hawthorne—No, the Children of Dharra will die,"

Sallah was getting irritated quickly. She was not about to coddle the man who killed her mentor. "Stop your drunk babbling and sleep it off."

He flung the skins across the room and stood up. "You saw it didn't you? You saw what it could do to living creatures? The Ichor will kill us all."

Her mind plunged into ice. "You knew about that? Why wasn't I told?"

He sighed and hiccuped before answering. "We didn't know. Agneth . . . Agneth had heard some rumors of it and what it was doing to the beasts. Then, more reports came in, each time closer to the Children of Dharra. During the Rite, we found it as well, much closer than we had thought. Horrible abominations now roam The Greensea, and soon enough chaos will consume our people. The source must be found and destroyed." His head drooped from side to side. "And you must be the one to do it. That was Agneth's final order to me." Terran's drunken breathing was the only sound in the room. Sallah thought back to the massive boar in the Old Grove and the metal tusks that almost gored her. So the Ichor was an infection of some sort. One that mutates the host. Sallah though of how close she was to touching it at the stream and shuddered.

Finally, Sallah whispered, "Why only me?"

Terran boomed a sloppy chuckle. "Because the woman who gave you a name and gave her life for you ordered it. Do you of all people, Sallah Va Hawthorne, need any more reason than that?"

"But there *is* another reason."

"I'm sure there is but she didn't tell me what it was. She was one of the few that could keep a secret. Even from me." He rose and hobbled towards the inner archway.

"Why did you do it Terran? I deserve to know that much," Sallah whispered.

He leaned against the archway, his face in a deep shadow. "Because I loved her. More than all of my House, I loved her. I told her I would kill myself instead but she would have none of it. She threatened to take her own life as well and I knew her long enough to know she meant it. No one as fierce, wise, and beautiful as Agneth should die by her own hand. So I killed my love and now I will bear the burden. She loved you. She would've sacrificed everything for you, her House, the Children, everything."

"Why would she do that? That's stupid," Sallah spat in rejection.

Terran slammed his fist against the wall in response. Sallah started. This was not the Terran she had learned from.

"Not stupid Sallah. Compassionate. You are her daughter, in practice if not by blood. She couldn't have children . . . We couldn't have children. Then as a child you almost killed a Druida with the power of Hawthorne and a blood rage not seen in five centuries. As I said, you are her daughter." Terran heaved himself off the archway. "I'll spread rumors that you are putting the House's affairs in order. That should get you a few weeks before the other Houses get suspicious."

"The gateway to the Old Growth is sealed but for the Matriarch. How will I get in?"

"I spoke with the Matriarch while you were resting. Other Houses have reported the same from their hunting grounds. Each House has volunteered a hunting group to search for

115

the source in their own lands. She will be waiting at the gate until sunrise." Terran heaved one last sigh as he turned away. "Good luck, Sallah Va Hawthorne. May Dharra give you strength."

He left, leaving only the stale stench of alcohol behind him. Tosi appeared in the archway, his belly still bulging from his kills. He still had a slight hobble in his gait but the gash on his face had scabbed over, his ear was healing nicely and in all other ways he was as healthy as a serval could be. He plodded to Sallah's feet as she relaced her leather jerkin.

"What a lucky Tosi. Two hunts in one day."

What was left of his two ears perked up at the word 'hunt' and he vaulted onto her shoulder. She slung a few water skins around her waist. Those were the only preparations she would need. Anything else Sallah could find in the Greensea. Turning to the doorway that looked over the valley Sallah couldn't help but chuckle in utter frustration.

I had a home for less than a night. It's just one more thing taken from me. She picked up the leather bag containing the two peculiar blades and opened it. Even in the cool moonlight, the pair reflected a dull red. She heard Agneth's voice again, the last thing she would ever say.

Oh good, you found them . . .

Chapter 7

Requests, invoices, and audits dominated most of Jack's mornings for the last two weeks, including this one. Sitting behind Barin's desk, Jack could feel his hand start to cramp around the pen in his left hand. Barin had already sorted the paperwork to what he needed to sign. The late morning light sifted through an overcast sky and landed on approvals for new apprentice commissions, a budget audit for protective equipment, even a request from the Steel Watch for ore wagons that were being converted to prison transports. Jack figured Barin must take this kind of work home, as he had never seen him fill out any kind of paperwork. The old man was far too busy with his primary duties to be hobbled with this kind of pablum. If Barin was enjoying the reprieve from paperwork, he certainly wasn't showing it. Currently he moved in and out of Jack's periphery, staring at his fob watch, threatening the second hand to go faster. The only instance he took his eyes off the time was to make sure Jack had forged his signature correctly.

Today at 12:11 p.m., all other work in the Conservatory

would stop. All except for the new Arc-chain bracings. It was an all-hands endeavor. Sean Lute's steel had arrived this week. Luthiers toiled in double shifts to modify and prep the new beams while Tuners welded brace platforms at the more troublesome points. Once formed, the beams were then dangled laboriously between each platform along the base, before finally being welded into place, adding to the grand spiderweb of catwalks across the Proscenium.

"It's time," said Barin, snapping closed his smudged fob watch.

Jack blinked up from his stack of parchment. Barin's hands were still meant to be in heavy wraps, but he had harangued Jack long enough to cut away the bindings from the length of his fingers, leaving only the palms and fingertips. Jack imagined Barin was wearing the saddest approximation of Crowley's pristine white gloves.

Jack looked back down to hide his grin. "I'm almost finished."

"It'll keep 'til tomorrow Mouse. I won't have those buffoons go unsupervised for even a minute longer." He was already stepping out the door.

Jack gratefully plopped the pen back into the inkwell, and followed the already exiting Barin from his office.

Their platform slid along a glass-floored hallway. Jack watched Apprentices hard at work on the practice work-stations of the Academy a few floors below. Looking at them, Jack felt a pang of guilt at the bottom of his stomach, but he couldn't figure why. The apprentices disappeared underneath a steel floor as double doors opened to the Proscenium in front of them. In his new capacity, Jack had been all over the Conservatory's bright upper reaches. He hadn't been to his Orchestra Pit since the day he was almost eaten.

Two weeks and a lifetime ago. He peered down into the darkness as they slid along the railing of the access platform. He wanted to forget. He almost could, save that smell. The wretchedly sweet stench of death mixed with scorched iron. A gag tugged at the back of Jack's throat just from the thought. All of that was bad enough, but it was the silence that followed that was killing him now. Rumors of the incident had never gotten back to him, which made the pit in his stomach yawn deeper. Like everyone but Jack had an understanding not to speak of the incident. Actually no one had really interacted with Jack at all unless it was on Barin's behalf.

Jack loved the job of Proxy. He did. But that was precisely what he was. Just a proxy. Even then, workers' eyes went vacant when they spoke with him, as if they were talking into a Voxphone, like Jack was merely a vessel to carry a message. He had toiled separately for most of his time at the Conservatory, but with the title of Proxy, now Jack felt completely isolated.

He watched the shadows envelop his clenched hands as they slipped beneath the hypnotizing wave of the Arc-chain. Number thirteen was no longer blinking to and fro, but what was just below was a far worse sight. What should have been a perfectly symmetrical geometric lattice of steel beams reaching into the inky depths of the Conservatory, wasn't. The foundation of the Arc-chain was bowing outwards, like the top coat of an overly indulgent diner. Trusses had just begun to shift and bend under the strain of weight that was no different a month ago than it was today.

Jack looked up to see the same new Boilers suspended in

119

the air, unmoved for the last two weeks. *The only thing that changed was the number 13 boiler.* The unease Jack felt just kept filling his chest. All of this formed something greater, but it wouldn't come into focus. Perhaps he didn't want it to. He pushed those thoughts from his mind. His instructions from Crowley, and The Patron himself were clear; ignore what you saw.

A slight case of vertigo forced Jack to blink away from the depths. Barin was watching him.

"Not going to imagine any monsters today boy?" said Barin.

Jack felt equal parts relief and indignation. "What poetic last words those would be."

Barin huffed at the insolence but Jack would not be swayed.

"I shouldn't have said anything to start with. At least then I wouldn't be looked at like I was crazy."

The lift slid into the dock of the Arc-chain. What should have been a satisfying click was instead a groaning shudder. It seemed that the damage to the supports was throwing everything out of alignment.

Barin stepped onto the listing platform, Jack closely in tow. "You're different Jack. Get used to people looking at you. And if you do eventually take my job, people will most certainly be looking at you, mostly for answers. And they will have any number of opinions on your choices. Better to weather your skin now while you're young. Now, are you done fattening up on self-pity or should I hold our work until you've had enough sulking?"

Jack peered through the crowd of laborers securing beams to wenches and cranes that lined the edge of the landing. It wasn't just Jack on edge, everyone was feeling the strain of this operation. "I'll be keeping an eye out just the same." Jack assumed his typical position of walking behind his master.

Mr. Petty shimmied through the throng and slid alongside Barin. Jack could just make out his wheezing prattle.

"All of the damage sustained is above this landing," said Petty. "We are bracing the most problematic spots as we speak but we will have to replace each beam one at a time. The process will be slow. At least four weeks."

"Four weeks? Are you trying to test my patience?" said Barin, "The foundation has suffered near catastrophic damage in less than two weeks, and you propose to repair it in twice that time?"

"The Maestro himself designed this plan, Surely you do not intend to be insubordinate in such a crucial task?"

"Look at me Petty," said Barin, far louder than was necessary. "Crowley may be responsible for the planning of this great machine, but I'm responsible for that plan's execution."

The shouts and calls of work faded in the face of Barin's words.

"If these are the orders of Maestro Crowley, then he has proven insubordinate to the City and its people."

The old man's voice had risen from a growl to a roar. It took a moment for Jack to realize all movement on the platform had stopped. "Worm your way back to Crowley now Petty and tell him everything I said, when you're done licking his boots."

Jack could see the droplets of sweat collecting at the back of Petty's neck.

Barin turned on the frozen workers fresh with fury. "Full capacity! You have twenty-four hours for the repairs to be completed. Six hour shifts. Move it!"

The first of the steel beams began rising on wenches in a

weightless waltz.

Cranes whined as cables strained under load, but the laboriously measured clicks signaled the sure ascent of their burden. Welders hung like spiders from the catwalks by harnesses, waiting to perform the delicate operation of precisely installing several tons of steel. Jack watched as Barin stomped through the crowd to the middle of the platform.

He had never seen his master behave like that, at least when it came to Carroll Crowley. Barin and Crowley worked hand in glove. Sure they had disputes, even heated ones, but the issue would be resolved and the work would continue on. That was different. That felt . . . theatrical.

"What in the Paragon's name was that?" Jack was surprised to hear it was his voice asking the question.

So was Barin. He glared at Jack underneath grey, bushy eyebrows. "We are running out of time Jack. I won't be around forever. Don't forget who you do this for." Barin's hawkish eyes bore into Jack, before turning to secure a harness for one of the Tuners.

There was something else behind Barin's usual predatory stare. It was foreign to the features Jack was used to in his master's face. Was it fear?

Is he scared to fail the Patron? To fail his vision?

Then Jack heard the worst sound one could ever hear in the Conservatory; the ping of a sheared rivet. The bustling workers froze in their tracks as the sound rang across the cavernous space. The sound echoed from every wall, making it impossible to determine its origin. Another ping and Jack caught movement out of the corner of his eye. One of the cranes was bowing away from the platform. Jack could see the terror grow in the man's eyes as he scrambled in vain to get free. With an ear-piercing screech, the crane and its operator fell from Jack's view. He heard another scream of metal to his left, then his right. The cranes were falling. They were all falling.

The shouts of workers and sheared metal mixed into a cacophony of terror. Jack didn't hear it. He couldn't. He was too focused on the one crane that hadn't fallen from view yet. Jack raced towards the operator as she reached out in nauseous desperation. She began to shudder and tilt in the control chair of the crane.

Ten paces. Then what? The crane lurched away from the platform. Jack ripped his wrench from his belt as he leaped into open air. He jumped towards the operator. He saw the terror in the woman's face, her hand grasping at air. He grabbed her wrist as they began to fall into the darkness. Jack gripped her with all his strength. He didn't know how long they had fallen. He felt his wrench catch on something, followed by a sickeningly loud pop from inside his shoulder. They had stopped falling and a rush of stinging heat filled Jack's left shoulder. The crane banged and tumbled from platform to catwalk as it plunged into the blackest depths of the Proscenium. The woman clung to Jack's forearm, a slight sway as they hung in the air.

"By the Paragon," said the woman, "Thank you Mouse." Her eyes grew wider. "Your arm."

With a grunt Jack tilted his neck upward to see his arm had been ripped from its socket and dangled by nothing but sinew. Adrenaline pumped through his body. His hand wasn't even holding the wrench. Instead the wrench was holding his arm, coiled tightly like a vine, from wrist to elbow. Jack noticed something else strange as well. The wrench had clamped itself to a catwalk twenty feet above him. Somehow, some way, the wrench had grown and clamped itself to a catwalk. Jack felt himself exhale. He wished he hadn't. The pain was immense. His body throbbed in rhythm to his heartbeat. Even the operator's ragged breathing washed his body in waves of anguish. His body begged to go limp under the strain but his hand would not move from the woman's wrist. It certainly helped that her hands were locked to his.

Heads peeked over from the catwalk and hands began hoisting the two slowly and excruciatingly upward. Jack groaned with every pull. They pulled on his dislocated arm over and over. He felt hands underneath his arms. Jack tried not to scream. He did anyway. The pain was just too much. He felt his wrench uncoil from his arm. It felt more like flesh than metal, familiar and warm. He heard the gasps of disbelief as his eyes fluttered closed, succumbing to the pain.

—

She is there, above me. Curly, auburn hair tickles my nose. It smells like earth and honeysuckle and home. I can't see her face. It's too dark. But I know she is sad. She is crying. She kisses my brow and whispers into my ear. I don't know what she says but her voice is soft and sweet. There is another hand, not hers, calloused and gentle. His palm covers my chest. He kisses my brow too. His stubble scratches my skin. He smells like leather and lamp oil and safety. He puts something next to me. It's as big as I am and warm. They are gone now and all I see is a lamp above a doorway.

—

The intense light blurred Jack's vision; first in his left eye, then the right. Muffled sounds swam drunkenly through his ears. Someone was speaking to him.

"Mr. Dowton, Mr. Dowton can you hear me?"

Jack blinked back into focus. He was in the infirmary. Shades had been pulled back from the arched windows. It was night. He could make out the Stacks still billowing their eternal glowing mist into the night air. The infirmary glowed rosy with the light of the Arc-lamps on gilded sconces. A medic was leaning over him and to say he had bad breath was to be overly kind.

"Welcome back Mr. Dowton," said the medic.

Jack grimaced. His left arm was a methodic, dull throb of pain that would never go away.

"Just Jack." He managed to wince out.

The medic straightened himself. "Do you make it a habit of trying to kill yourself?"

Jack tried to swallow back a dry throat but only managed a racking cough. "Only if it looks spectacular." Jack turned to find his left arm bound and bandaged from fingertips up to his neck. "What's the damage?"

"four broken bones, a dislocated shoulder and elbow and extensive ligament and muscle damage. It's a small miracle that we saved the arm at all."

Jack tried to move it and stifled a scream. "I can't feel two fingers."

The medic froze in place. "Which two fingers lad?"

Jack swallowed again. "My index finger and my thumb."

The medic took a small pin and gingerly pricked the tip of Jack's thumb. Jack winced slightly to the visible relief of the medic.

"We better add nerve damage to the list of your injuries. The good news is if you can still feel pain there's a chance you will regain typical feeling."

"A chance?" the question caught in his throat.

Before the medic could answer Barin stepped through the doorway of the infirmary. He glared at the Medic. "Get out."

The Medic nodded and exited in the manner of a man not wishing to show how scared he truly was. A cold dread seeped into Jack. Barin had taken off his bandages in the time he was out. Miniscule shards of glass were still embedded in his hand, too deep or too small to remove. His hand threw pinpoints of light across the darkened room. He dragged a stool across the copper floor, screeching along the way. He leveled his eyes at Jack but did not speak. Jack's bandages started to itch but he was too afraid of the pain and those eyes to move. The only sound was the old man's heavy breathing.

"Are you going to say something or just enjoy the scenery?" Jack hoped to break the tension.

Barin's hand moved quicker than Jack had time to think. He backhanded the bandaged shoulder with the flick of his wrist. Jack yowled in pain.

"Stupid child." Barin's growl wasn't angry, but desperate. "Too stupid to think before you act?"

Jack was still too focused on the pain to respond.

Barin wouldn't have stopped anyway. "Twenty-three. Twenty-three operators died today. Their bodies fell so deep into the pit it will take weeks to find their bodies, if we ever do at all. Not to mention the damage done to the infrastructure. Now the Arc-chain's foundation has become critical." Jack could not evade the images of those that fell, the details especially. Their fingers grasping at air, the shape of their mouths as they sucked in their last breath. Danger was a constant companion when in pursuit of greatness, but this felt. . . unnecessary.

"What is the current status?" asked Jack.

Barin sighed. "What do you care, boy? You would rather kill yourself playing the hero than be around for the real problems what need fixing." Barin stood, turning away from Jack.

The pinpricks of reflected light shuttered as he picked at the embedded glass shards.

"I saved a woman's life!"

Barin reared around. "At what cost you fool? Your life? Mine? The City's?"

Jack was silent for a long moment before speaking. "Why get in the shouting match with Petty? You could have simply changed the plan. Crowley would be too late to stop you." The pain gnawed at the back of his mind.

The old man stood and began to pace along the foot of the bed. His eyes darted along the walls before leaning over Jack and whispering. "Why did you find a metal serpent? How did we rediscover the Paragon's lost technology?"

Jack could feel Barin's breath shallow and rapid.

"Why did we need to start building the Arc-boilers again? And why are you really my apprentice?" Barin straightened before continuing. "Good questions all, and worth asking. I hope someone stays alive long enough to start answering them."

Jack's confusion was replaced by the uncomfortable weight of equal parts responsibility and curiosity. "Well, why me then? You can answer that at least."

Barin's tone went from desperate to melancholy. "No. I

can't. And when you do find out, you'll understand why." Barin stopped his pacing and gazed at Jack.

The melancholy melting into something Jack would never have imagined seeing from the Master Tuner, helplessness.

"I'm not saying it's fair Jack, but what is?" The old man pulled Jack's wrench from his belt and studied it with tired eyes before tossing it on the bed. "I haven't the foggiest of how you did what you did with that thing and frankly I don't want to. The workers are already spreading the tale, so if I were you, I would refrain from those kinds of tricks in such public spaces."

Jack took the wrench and studied it. It was the same size, same weight as before. He knew this wrench like his own hand. It shouldn't have been possible for it to telescope like that. For it to wrap itself around his arm. But without it, he would not be in the infirmary now.

Barin put on his coat and donned his cap before heading for the door. He stopped before peering over his shoulder. "Rest up, heal and pray that your arm doesn't become useless. With any luck, I will still be here when you return."

Jack sat up these words. "What do you mean?"

Barin stopped at the doorway. "I have been called to a Coda for blatant insubordination and the death of twenty-three workers under my watch. Odd isn't it? The moment I disobeyed, something terrible happened. Goodbye Mouse."

The Coda was the highest court. A jury of chosen Chorus members would decide Barin's fate. Jack was left alone with only his thoughts and the rhythmic pain of his arm.

Chapter 8

Sallah stood at the edge of the Greensea entirely unsure of what she was seeing. She had been born and raised beneath the canopy of the great forest. She never imagined she would see its end. But after two weeks of hunting and following the trail of the Ichor, she stood at the last tree line, stretching north to south as far as she could see. A clear demarcation of her home and everything that lay beyond.

Leaving in the dead of night, Sallah didn't know how she would even track something so alien. It was not as if it were an elk. But much to her concern, the evidence of its wake was apparent. She need only follow the trail of desiccated wildlife leading to the east. Minks, badgers, spiders, all twisted farces of what they were, all hollowed of their lifeblood. Sallah surmised that would have been the eventuality of the Razorboar as well, had they not ran into her. Then there was the smell, a mix of death and something she couldn't quite place.

In her time tracking it, she had learned only two habits and nothing of the Ichor's origin. The first, and much to her relief, it didn't seem able to climb vertical services, so sleeping in trees became a much safer endeavor. The second trait was more confirmation of the one she already knew. It could sense and would seek out nearby fauna. Which was fine in the relative safety of the Greensea where she could keep a constant eye on the ground and keep a safe distance on the wriggling ribbons. Even then, she found herself on more than one occasion hemmed in from most sides by the web of Ichor.

Now here she stood at the edge of everything she knew staring at a wide, flat plain. An ocean of golden grass taller than her head swayed and danced with the wind. The only break in the scenery was a fist of foothills peaking above the horizon. Tosi stood upon her shoulder nervously looking back and forth. He was a creature of the Greensea as well and this alien land clearly unsettled him. The Ichor's trail disappeared beneath the dense, waving grass.

As soon as I step in, I won't be able to see or even navigate . . . and I won't be able to track that damn ooze. She closed her eyes and tilted her head to the sun. The wind cooled her face from the bright sun. Autumn was almost here and there was a storm coming. She could wait out the weather, but the pang of being away from home and the unknown of what was happening to the House of Hawthorne removed that option.

Turning her head down towards the plain she noticed something odd about the grass. No, not the grass, how the wind moved the grass. The breeze was a constant, gentle force, plying the grass in perfectly constant waves. She began to walk south, farther away from where she spied the Ichor disappearing into the grass. She would aim for the foothills, and try to pick up the trail from there.

Sallah stepped into the impenetrable field. Her steps were slow and measured. The wind revealed alleys as wide as her foot among the waves but only for half moments.

Dharra, I pray you keep the wind constant. For the moment, her prayer was answered.

For hours, she maintained her excruciatingly slow pace. The first time the wind stopped, so did her heart. Her feet froze in place, afraid of losing what little bearing she had. But the breeze kicked up again and she put one foot after the other. Tosi had taken to propping himself on top of her head, vainly searching for a way out of the grass. Sallah had no idea how long she could keep this up. Physically she was fine but for each time the wind changed, so did the openings. She opened her eyes for the first time in what seemed like days. The sun was beginning to fall. By her estimation she had a half day of daylight left. Then the darkness would come. She closed her eyes again and breathed deeply.

Just keep putting one foot in front of the other. Just keep facing east. I still don't know where the Ichor is so I can't risk going faster. Dharra, give me patience.

The day grew colder on her skin. Every instinct in her body told her not to open her eyes but her fear got the better of logic. The sun had dipped below the golden waves. Rolling clouds filled with falling rain were sweeping in from the west. She had one hour of light before a wet and absolute darkness would take her. Her heart began to flutter into her throat. The wind was becoming fierce on the back of the storm. The alleys for her steps had all but disappeared but thankfully the wind bowed the grass enough for Sallah to catch sight of the

Foothills she was aiming for. They were close. Sallah took three more calculated steps before she heard movement to her left, then her right. It was not the wind. She closed her eyes. The swallowing black of the Ichor surrounded her.

"Hold on Tosi!" She darted forward and leaped over the closing circle.

The Ichor flailed and caught her boot. Sallah tripped, rolling forward. Tosi landed on his feet just above her head. The substance was incredibly strong. She kicked at it with all her strength but even now its grip was growing tighter, wrapping itself around her boot.

"Tosi run!"

He hesitated for only a moment before disappearing into the cast-about stems. She kicked off her boot and watched the substance crush and swallow it. Sallah began to run in the direction of Tosi, at least she hoped so. The rain fell in drenching sheets as the grasses became whips under the violent winds, lashing her face and arms. She glanced back. The lightning illuminated flashes of movement. It was chasing her, moving faster than she had thought possible. Another lightning strike lanced the sky, blinding Sallah in flashes of green and purple. Concussive thunder rumbled through her body. She stole another glance back. The Ichor was gaining ground. This wasn't a trickle. This was a flood.

She spurned herself forward as a bolt of lightning crashed to the earth. Through the wind, thunder, and rain she raced. Then she heard the familiar mewing of her hunting partner. Another flash revealed him leaping into the air. He was holding something in his mouth. The spear of light was gone before she could make it out. At least she knew where to run now. The ground began to slope downwards. Her footing was treacherous with slick mud. Tosi continued his cries and Sallah navigated towards the sound between peals of thunder and whipping winds. In an instant, he pounced on her shoulder almost sliding her feet from beneath her. She turned to see what was in his mouth, but she already knew. It was a petal, a Hawthorne petal.

"Lead me!" Sallah could barely hear her own voice over the deafening roar of the storm.

He jumped away and took off beneath the underbrush. His tail whipped back and forth, leading Sallah as best as he could. Even so she would lose him from time to time until his mewing reached her ears. She couldn't afford a glance back at their pursuer but she knew it was there, inching ever closer. She felt it. That presence as familiar as her own heartbeat. She didn't need to see it. She knew where it was.

"Tosi," Sallah cried, "to me!"

In a flash, he was on her shoulder. They escaped the grassland and onto a rock-strewn patch of mud. Two hundred yards away stood the Hawthorne, tilting wearily on a mound of rocks. Unabashed joy swallowed her whole. She glanced back to find the Ichor reaching for her bare heel. All she had to do was to make it there and they would be safe.

The jagged rocks bit into her feet as she raced the final hundred yards, but it was a round pebble beneath her heel that betrayed her balance. She was only ten yards away now. The lightning was almost constant now, emitting piercing, scattered light. There was the Ichor sweeping across the ground and already at her feet. It latched onto her other boot as Sallah whipped her hand around, calling to the Hawthorne. A thousand thorns flew through the air and into the Ichor below her foot. The Ichor recoiled for only a moment; that was all she needed. She closed her fist and the thorns shattered in reply, severing the black finger from its host. Sallah scrambled to her feet and leapt into the awaiting embrace of the branches. They lifted her away from the rocks, mud, and death placing her gently on a high, thick branch. Tosi was already there, spitting his anger at their pursuer. Sallah ripped off her other boot and threw it to the ground below. The Ichor slithered hungrily around the tree but could not climb. She leaned her head against the tree and breathed deeply. Tosi was doing his best to lick himself dry, shivering all the while.

Sallah suddenly realized how cold it had become. "Tosi, come," she gulped air. She removed her leather jerkin and unbuttoned her soaked blouse.

Tosi crawled up against her body and balled up as tightly as he could. She refastened the buttons and curled her feet beneath her. With a thought, she closed the branches around them for protection from the rain and the wind. It would do nothing for the cold.

Thank you for your blessings Dharra. Keep us warm enough to survive the night.

She felt Tosi's measured breathing. He was already asleep. The heat of his belly on hers was the only warmth she felt.

As with most nights, she did not sleep well.

—

Sunlight peeked through the deadening leaves of the tightly woven branches. Sallah's eyes snapped open. Her ears strained to hear for danger for several moments, but was greeted by the distant call of a meadowlark. With a sigh she leaned her head back against the trunk. Tosi began to stir. She undid a few buttons to let him out. He stretched deeply and clawed the branch a few times for good measure. Sallah spread her arms out wide and parted the net of branches she had created last night. A gasp escaped her lips. Sallah couldn't decide whether to classify it as a single rock or a foothill.

Morning mist clung to the base of a spherical boulder three hundred feet tall and just as wide. Their perch sat at the base of a crevice within the great stone. Peering through the mist, Sallah could make out the outlines of at least three others in a perfect row, like the knuckles of a great giant clawing to escape the earth. Sallah reflected at the beauty of them for a long while. The fog burned away beneath the rising sun and Tosi began to hiss and spit at the ground. She peered down to find their nemesis had formed itself into a web along the earth, weaving wider than the reach of the Hawthorne's branches and disappearing into the fields of tall grass.

They would not be climbing down. The substance undulated with a sickening hunger. She again laid her head back against the trunk, breathing deeply. If she couldn't kill it, maybe at least she could annoy it. The Ichor had some form of intelligence she surmised, otherwise it would never set that snare in the plains, not to mention the web that sat and waited beneath her feet at this moment. The real question was how intelligent.

Does it realize I'm a specific threat and not just a meal? The other thing she realized was that it was growing, or at the very least, was making more of itself visible. As she surveyed the plains that she escaped, slight breezes revealed the web of Ichor that laid just beneath. Her stomach gurgled in famished protest. She hadn't eaten since yesterday morning; Robin eggs, roasted squirrel and wild strawberries. Tosi had the lion's share of the eggs and squirrel. Sallah didn't mind. In fact, she insisted. Last night was proof of how important a strong and healthy partner could be to a Huntress. Tosi was busy climbing to the tallest vantage point in hopes of finding a route for escape. Sallah smiled at him. Only five years ago he could have killed her and almost did.

—

Sallah was fourteen and eager to start her first trophy hunt. She had tracked an elk for the better part of the morning until it had become trapped against a cliff line. Her dagger mortally struck the elk, but a burst of the elk's adrenaline carried her prey out of sight. She tracked the blood to a small clearing. She waited for a while at the edge of the treeline studying the fallen beast. It wasn't moving. Eventually she approached, pulled the blade from her prey's side, and tapped its eye. It didn't move. She began preparations to field dress her prey when the elk twitched. A wounded animal six times her size was the last thing Sallah wanted to be near. She waited for a moment until she heard a low satisfied growl coming from the elk's chest. Stepping around the body, she saw a serval, emaciated and dirt-caked, trying his best to swallow the elk's stomach in one bite. As soon as he caught sight of Sallah, his ears pinned back and he bared his bloody fangs. This animal may not have been six times Sallah's size, but it was a desperate predator and she was now threatening his first meal in what looked like a long time.

Instead, Sallah just waited, despite the increasing aggression from the serval, swiping and spitting. She sat, avoiding the serval's gaze. The meat was all but ruined, as the serval had torn into the elk's organs. With that possibility gone, all she could hope for was the antlers. Eventually her patience paid off as the serval became used to her presence and his hunger drew his attention back to the kill. She lost sight of him as he went back to his grisly meal. After a long while, she inched along the ground toward the antlers. The serval was on the other side of the beast, staring at her as he gnawed on a rib. Avoiding his eyes, she began to cut at the base of one antler. It was a fragile peace, yet neither made an aggression toward the other. Both took what they needed, Darrah would claim the rest.

"You are welcome for the meal." said Sallah as she harnessed the antlers to her back. The serval suddenly leaped back and spit at her. No not her, something behind her in the treeline. A mountain lion pounced into the clearing. It was trying to scare Sallah off the easy meal, but she could not move away fast enough. As she stepped back, she tripped over the carcass. It appeared she was protecting her kill. The mountain lion stepped to the challenge, swiping and scraping Sallah's chest. The claws should have dug deeper into her flesh, but the emaciated serval had pounced on the Mountain lion's face as it struck. Both cats toppled in a pile of fur and fangs before separating. Sallah could have run, but she faltered. The serval tried to make himself as large as possible as they squared to one another, but gave ground to each testing swipe from the larger cat. She still had her blades in her hands. Silently, she moved behind the mountain lion. Why wasn't she running? She could have taken to the underbrush at this very moment. But the truth was she was still alive because of that starving serval. For some reason, she felt a debt to the creature. So if he was still fighting, she would fight too. Besides, for every second the Serval held its own was one more second Sallah was still alive.

Separate they would both be killed, but together... She lunged for the mountain lion's shoulders hoping to immobilize its arms. The serval took the cue and pounced from the front in distraction. Sallah's blade dug into her target's back, her other arm swung around and plunged the other into its throat. The mountain lion yowled and rolled in panic and pain. It crushed Sallah beneath its heft, forcing her to release her grip on the blades, but she had struck true. The Mountain Lion faltered, yowled and fell. Sallah waited until the cat no longer breathed before beginning to remove its claws. The serval returned to its meal, tearing into the elk. She finished retrieving her trophies and stood before the serval.

"May Dharra bless you hunter. You have helped me earn great trophies today." The serval only afforded her a side glance as it continued to gorge on ribs. She left the clearing and began to walk back to the game trail that led to Hawthorne territory. But after her first few steps she knew she wasn't alone. The serval stood behind her by twenty paces, his head slightly cocked. She took a step then he took a step. They continued this dance for a dozen steps until Sallah pulled a cured chunk of meat from her rations and held it out. The serval paced back and forth before slowly stalking forward and snatching the meat and retreating a few paces away. Sallah did her best to remember the old-tongue word for hunter.

"Tosi," the Serval's ears perked up and Sallah smiled.

—

"I think it's going to try and starve us out Tosi." Sallah pulled away from her reverie, absent-mindedly tracing the scars beneath her tunic. She pulled out her waterskin and concentrated on the tree where she sat, while folding her arms together. The Hawthorne mimicked her movements funneling and collecting dew from its leaves and collecting in the waterskin spout. She flicked her fingers and blossoms grew from the branches and spun lazily down into her hand. With an absent mind she chewed on the petals. It was better than nothing and Sallah liked the soft sweetness of the pollen. Her thoughts were with their escape.

She felt a bizarre calm about their predicament. Then she realized it was because in most of her near-death experiences she hadn't the time to think. Now however, she felt she had all the time in the world. She didn't of course. Finding a Hawthorne felt like providence from Dharra herself. It smelled like home.

Curious how it would sprout here unless . . . Sallah willed the branch she sat on towards the top of the tree to join Tosi. She focused on the massive boulder worn smooth by time and weather. A red leaf drifted lazily to and fro from the open sky. Tosi swiped at it playfully. It seemed he had lived among the blossoms of the Hawthornes so long they lifted his spirits as well. The falling leaf was the only proof that Sallah needed.

"Since we can't go down and we can't go across, our only option is up. Climb on and hold tight." Sallah lightly hopped onto the tallest branch of the tree, as if she weighed nothing.

Tosi jumped to her shoulder and carefully flexed his claws into her leather jerkin. She readied her bone blades before looking at them. If she tried to use them to dig into stone, they would shatter. She pulled at the cinch string of the leather pouch at her waist that held the three objects she found during that terrible Rite; a black cylinder from the odd flower playing music, and the two metal blades. Still weary of the voice she heard the last time she hesitated before touching one. Silence. No voice in her head beside her own. She placed the blades in her hip sheaths before gingerly placing her bone blades in the bag.

The tree began to bend lower and lower towards the earth. Sallah squatted low as well, closed her eyes and exhaled. The tree snapped straight, catapulting them into the air. The feeling was exhilarating and terrifying. They sped past the perfectly rounded belly of the great boulder so close she was tempted to brush her fingers across it. Sallah's stomach dropped. She couldn't feel the presence of the tree she was so sure was at the top. Their ascent began to slow until she stopped entirely. For a pregnant moment she floated, light as the clouds. Then they began to fall.

She pulled the metal blades from her belt and struck towards her only chance. That voice was in her mind again, her own, yet alien.

You need me Sallah, you would have died as a child without me, rang the voice, *you need my strength.* Hunger and fear were replaced by a burning strength. She stabbed out with both blades into the meat of the boulder. They slipped through hardened stone like a breeze through leaves. Slowly, she ground to a halt. Her feet dangled in empty space as the voice resounded in her mind again.

I will give you my strength Sallah. The voice sounded as if it were smiling, *Just let the rage take you.* She tried her best to block out the voice's calls, but the voice was hers. How could she? She pulled herself inch by inch along the stone's face. Her arms should've ached. Instead they felt inflamed with unknown strength and vigor. She felt angry, she felt alive. Each stab of the stone became easier. The burden of her body became lighter.

All the while that voice whispered to her. *Don't you enjoy this feeling? Absolute strength is yours. Just give in to me.*

The words tasted like honey across her lips. Wasn't that what she prayed to Dharra for? The strength to achieve the task set before her? She had already climbed half the length of the stone on tireless arms. Her feet began to find purchase on the upward slope. This was becoming easy. She stabbed into the rock quicker and quicker. Even the motion brought her a drunken joy.

You are a killer Sallah, a Huntress. The voice was practically screaming with elation, *No different than the wolves, tigers or the Ichor you seek to destroy.*

Sallah's frenzied joy halted.

Come Huntress, the voice soothed, *Isn't your very mission to destroy the source of the Ichor proof of that? To destroy the life of one that destroys life?* But it was for the greater good wasn't it? *Of course it is. It's why Terran sent you. We cannot deny our nature. We hunt. We kill.* Sallah's hands froze in place. Another blossom drifted by her face and grazed her cheek. It smelled like Agneth. It felt like Agneth. The memory of her mentor with the trickle of blood down her cheek came in a flash. The way Agneth touched her cheek, the pain of a

141

single death that weighed so heavily upon her now. In a fit, she threw one of the blades as hard as she could to the top of the stone.

The voice rang harsh and venomous. *You cannot deny us little Sallah. We are you.*

Sallah began searching for the presence of the Hawthorne with all her quickly draining strength *We cannot deny our nature.* Her body weakened under the full strain of the climb. *You will reach for us. It is only a question of when.*

There! With a final pull of her remaining strength she reached out to call for the Hawthorne to aid her. She scrambled up with all her might, throwing the other blade to the top. A long thin root peered over the edge of the stone and raced along the surface of the rock. She began to fall back as the young root wrapped around her wrist and dragged her up the face of the rock.

Sallah released the Hawthorne from her control as Tosi jumped from her back, the hair on his neck still raised with fear. Sitting up, she surveyed her new surroundings. A small pool of clear water stood still as glass in the crook of the trunk, gathered from the previous day's rain. Tufts of grass grew along the edges of the tree's roots. The Hawthorne was larger and older than what was within its nature. This was planted and cultivated. It was a Hawthorne grown giant by the hands of a Druida. Just like those in her own far-away grove.

Sallah kneeled beneath the boughs and whispered a prayer to Dharra. She drank greedily from the pool before Tosi took his fill. As she stood, her head banged against something unyielding. It was the handle of one of the blades she had thrown, the other stuck slightly above it, each buried to the hilt in the side of the tree.

She wrapped her hand in the sleeve of her blouse and pulled one of the blades away and dropped it on the ground. No voices, no gleeful rage. The voice was terrifying, but she was more afraid of its words. Pulling and dropping the second dagger, she placed a hand over each gash in the tree, closing the wounds she inflicted.

Honeysuckle crept up the bark with blossoms of gold and white. Sallah plucked them, gratefully sucking the nectar from each stamen, then popping the flower into her completely smashed collection of raspberries. She stepped around the gnarled roots to the other side. There stood the other five stone globes on each side of her own, and each one had a Hawthorne, exactly like the one she now stood beside. The stones were not perfect spheres after all. Only their exteriors were rounded. On the other side, the rock swept down at a precarious angle towards a lake at the center of a crater two miles wide. The far side of the crater from Sallah now stood was the opposite of the round stone Sallah found herself. Fingers of obsidian reached out in jagged points across the sky.

Looking down to the waving plain from where she escaped, Sallah saw the extent of what she was tasked to destroy. The Ichor laced around each of the stones, and threaded into the golden grass; a cancerous web, miles wide. She followed their trail until she lost sight at the far side of the stone. Sallah became light headed from such a vantage point. She had never been this high up before in her life. Then she noticed something by the edge of the lake. It was hard to see at first because it was the same color as the stone around it. But it was small and square and stood on stilts of wood out over the water. There was a thin, winding footpath cut into the stone that led from the hovel to where the Hawthorne stood. Sallah saw no signs of the Ichor anywhere. She finished another handful of honeysuckle.

"Ready, Tosi?"

He eyed her warily, the fur on his hackles already beginning to rise,

"Don't worry, our feet will be staying on the ground this time. Let us see if there's anyone home." Her feet picked the hewn-rock path with a practiced ease. Some portions had fallen away from lack of use and the march of time. Her progress did not suffer much for it. She was more hampered by the lack of boots.

—

The end of the path skirted the crystalline lake. Sallah had never heard such a silent place. Even her footsteps seemed to echo endlessly across the placid lake and along the obsidian crags. No birdsong whistled overhead, not even the plop of fish breaking the lake's surface to snag a bug. She closed her eyes to look for wisps of lifeforce. She was met with its total absence on land, water, or sky. The trail wandered as curiously as her mind, as she followed it to the shack on stilts.

The path led around the edge of the lake before stopping at a small dock in front of the hovel. The structure was squat and hewn from the same black glass as the surrounding mountains. The wooden stilts were petrified with age as they ran into the depths of the lake where even the light of the high, hot sun could not reach. Sallah approached silently, her hands an inch away from her bone blades. She rounded the shack to where the path stopped.

There sat a woman at the end of the dock. She sat cross-legged, looking out across the lake, without the slightest inkling that Sallah stood behind her. She was as still as the stone upon which she sat, breathing a rhythmic calm. Sallah didn't feel an immediate threat from the woman. In fact, Sallah's instincts told her the opposite. She was safe. Her hands fell away from the daggers. Cautiously she walked to the edge of the dock. Several minutes passed as she stared at the back of the woman's head. Her hair was jet black and shaved to the middle of her head, the rest collected in a large braid that ran down her back. Her palms lay open in her lap. She was unarmed. Another minute passed before Sallah unslung the blades from her belt and sat beside her.

She had a strong chin and sharp cheeks, creased with fine lines that seemed premature. Her robe was made of a simple rough canvas of long-aged white with a belt of the same material. It was her eyes that caught Sallah's attention; gray and tired but unflinching as they gazed over the sun-lit water. Sallah could not remember a moment in her life so still. She closed her eyes and turned away from the woman. For the first time she could remember, she saw no aura of life force, only darkness. She allowed herself to wallow in it.

"You should be going."

Sallah jumped at the sudden words. The sun had moved into the afternoon. Sallah studied the woman, yet she remained as still as ever. Sallah began to wonder whether she imagined the woman speaking.

"You know you cannot stay here." The woman turned to Sallah, her expression unmoving.

"You still have much to accomplish."

145

"How do you know that?" said Sallah.

A sad kindness spread across the woman's face. "Because I have eyes. You are travelling and this is no one's destination"

Sallah glanced down at her bare feet, cut and bloody, her leather jerkin stiff and cracked from the rain, her blouse stretched and torn. "Did you plant those Hawthornes at the top of those stones?"

The strange woman stared at her. "You are a Child of Dharra correct? A Druida I would guess?"

Sallah jumped up and backed away, wishing her blades were not off her hips.

The woman gave a silent chuckle. "Calm yourself, young one. There is no need to run away. I have seen my share of this world and her people."

Sallah stopped. "How did you know that?"

"I know that you came from the west, where the Greensea stretches beyond the horizon. Any other direction and I would have seen you approach my home."

"But how do you know I was a Druida or that we even exist?"

The woman turned her back on Sallah, her voice even and calm. "As I said, I have seen my fair share of people in this world, though your people in particular almost cost me my life."

Sallah walked cautiously back towards the end of the pier,

"You asked me if I had planted a Hawthorne on top of the foothills." The woman chuckled again. "That is how I guessed you were a Druida. If you were not, you would have asked how a tree could live, let alone grow, through pure stone. You may find that the ability to make a tree grow, despite where it may lie, is a singular gift among the Children of Dharra."

The woman grew silent again.

Sallah sat beside her again.

"Suspicion, another of your people's hallmarks," prodded the woman.

Sallah was annoyed that she felt her face blush. "What is this place?"

The woman remained still for a long time. Sallah sat and waited.

"It is an unnatural place," said the woman, "This was the site of a battle, lost to time and memory. Few remember it. I am one of them. It is my duty to remember."

Sallah surveyed the lake and mountains with fresh eyes.

"Your people call it the Time of Fire. A war five centuries ago where your people's history and heritage were all but lost."

Sallah nodded her head as she listened.

"It was a war, great and terrible. It brought mortals to the edge of oblivion."

This place made sense now, the stillness, the formations, the absence of life.

"Mortals? What do you mean?" Sallah's heart began to flutter, "Gods fought this war? There is another goddess besides Dharra?" *Why would I believe this stranger?*

The woman returned to silence yet again. Sallah huffed in frustration until she gave up entirely and sat and waited. It was late afternoon before the woman replied.

"What is a god, young one?"

Sallah remained still.

"Something that holds absolute dominion over a place? Someone who knows all things?" Asked the woman, "Perhaps I should ask you this question instead. Could something like

147

that ever truly die?"

This was a difficult question and one which Sallah took a good deal of time to think about. "No. Dharra is eternal, so if there are other gods, they would be as well."

"I would tend to agree, young one. But perhaps there is something else in the middle. What if a mortal endeavored to be the absolute example, the perfect representation of their beliefs and through that, gained their own kind of . . . divinity. Would that not be a god?"

Sallah's brow scrunched in confusion.

"Apologies. It has been quite some time since I last spoke with someone. I will rephrase this question as well. Who would you call the perfect Druida?"

Agneth. But no, she was empathetic and compassionate. Traits rarely seen in nature. Then she knew the answer. "Dharra. Dharra was the perfect Druida. She commanded the obedience of the animals. She knew every name and use for each leaf, flower and shrub. She was swift and strong and wise. She brought us from the warring savages we were, into the twelve Houses and she was the only Druida capable of bending all life to her will."

"I would agree with that choice as well. Yet all of these great accomplishments she achieved as a Druida. Not a goddess. And yet your people think of her daily, pray to her for guidance and strength. I would say she has achieved immortality through her teachings and divinity through your people's devotion to her beliefs. Thus, a goddess was made, not born."

Sallah's anger flared at the heretical idea, but she could not find the words to dispute the woman's claim. Besides, the woman was placid, she was not trying to argue. She merely spoke what she believed to be true. Sallah remained silent, thinking on the woman's words.

The sun rested on the tip of one of the jagged peaks to the east. Suddenly Sallah snapped into focus.

"There is an ooze that's feeding on living things. It's attacking the Greensea. I've tracked it here. What do you know?" Sallah felt less patient for an answer this time.

"I know what you seek lies farther east. The world can be a hard place, Druida. You will not be able to do this alone," The woman stood and walked towards her hovel. "I am afraid our time together is done. You must leave this place by nightfall. But wait here for a moment."

As the woman opened the door, Sallah spied only darkness within. She returned a short time later with small beads of sweat across her brow. She was holding a sack, a pair of well-worn boots and a waterskin. "Take these young one. You may eat only after you have left this place."

"But I have more questions." Sallah slung the sacks across her shoulders.

"Follow where the sun sets and you will have all the answers you seek."

They walked back to the edge of the lake where Sallah had dropped her blades.

"I don't even know your name." Sallah said, securing the belt across her waist.

That same sad smile came across the woman's face. "I have not had a name for many years and I do not have a use for one now, but perhaps with you I achieved my own little bit of immortality. Now go." Without another glance, the woman turned back, opened the door to her hovel, and closed it behind her.

Sallah felt the calm go with her and she was left with emptiness standing in a great scar on the world. With Tosi on her heels, she began to jog to the far side of the lake where the sun was setting.

The switchback trail led to a crevice between two sharp peaks and not a moment too soon. Sallah looked back to find a blanket of darkness sweeping across the lake. Even the full moon's light seemed weaker there. Sallah shivered and turned to pick her way across the treacherous path down the other side of the foothills. A sparkle of light caught her eye. It wasn't a star. There, on the horizon, played twinkling points of light. Sallah strained with sharp eyes.

Odd, it almost looks like the horizon is on fire.

Chapter 9

The pain was always there. Even in Jack's fitful sleep, the ache pulsing in his shoulder was his constant companion. fifteen unending days had passed since he saved that woman. He didn't even know her name but she very well may have cost him his livelihood, his passion. No, not her, he had made the choice. He was on injured leave now. The shoulder was mending, though there was a good deal of muscle, bone, and ligament to mend. What really worried him was the numbness in his hand. All he could do was sit and hope to get feeling back in his fingers. Otherwise . . .

His only solace was the work he, Charlie and Moira invested into the feed tube. Only two more nights of work and they would be able to run actual Arc into Moira's shack. A fully operating Arc-powered laundry in Stonehall. It was not like this created some utopia, but it was something they could hang their hat on. Then she would be able to compete with any laundress in the city proper. Her pace was feverish lately, with a stare to match.

Unfortunately, two problems had come up; a lack of money and the only two who could complete the installation, had only two good hands between them. There was another issue of course, the Patron's request to cease construction. Jack never mentioned the meeting to Charlie and Moira. Jack did not keep secrets from his best friends. Then again, Jack had never spoken to the leader of Cogrind before. Jack worried constantly that they would be found out, but they were so close to making Moira's dream a reality. Jack hung his hopes on the thin thread that the Patron was far too busy managing the city to punish a lowly (and quite possibly former) apprentice of the Conservatory.

With his injury, he was no longer Proxy and with the lack of title came the lack of wages. To make matters worse, and to Moira's growing frustration, Charlie had been drinking more. Jack rarely left his bed during the day. When he did, Jack couldn't glean any information about Barin's trial at the Coda. whether a Steel Watch guard or nosy seamstress, everyone was ignorant of any proceedings, are at least, feigned ignorance.

On the sixteenth morning sunlight beamed through Jack's window, catching him square in the face. Accosted by the morning, Jack turned over to block the light with his shoulder. Then he heard his bed rock with a familiar jolt.

"Get out of that bed this instant Jack Dowton," Moira sounded more feverish and commanding than usual, "This has become pathetic."

"Then let me sleep my pathetic-ness away." mumbled Jack through his lumpy pillow.

Moira kicked the bed with her heel again, jarring both Jack's arm and his sleep.

"Damn it woman, leave me be!"

Moira folded her arms. "As soon as you get up. I already

have to deal with one one-handed child, I will not have another."

Jack only sighed and slowly nodded his head in agreement.

Her tone softened immediately. "Go into the city." She sat softly on the bed. "Be around the silly contraptions that you love. This isn't permanent Jack."

A breath caught in his throat.

"Is it?" asked Moira.

Jack started to breathe again. It was the one fear that kept him in this damnable bed. "I don't know yet. I have no feeling in my thumb and finger. I didn't want to tell you both. I'm worried."

Softly, she combed his snow-white hair with her lye-stained fingers for a while. "All the more reason to get out of this bed," she said with a soothing softness in her voice. "I suppose the good news is that with my Arc-powered laundry service, I can make enough to take care of us all. At the very least we won't starve."

"All right, all right, I'm up," grumbled Jack, "The last thing I need is guilt from someone who is actually working."

Moira jumped up with a triumphant smile. "Excellent! Because you know I'm right and you do, in fact, stink. Go take a dip and I'll have your clothes laid out for you."

With a rueful smile Jack gingerly lifted himself from bed and headed out his front door.

The moat was cold and begrudgingly refreshing. Sunlight hopped and twinkled from one ripple to the next. It was only after bathing for a moment that he realized just how bad he had smelled. Jack sank his body up to his neck. His shoulder felt weightless and for a moment the pain subsided. He placed his good arm on the stone edge and tried to enjoy the bracing cold. Stonehall seemed quieter lately. Squeals of orphan's happily skipping out on the day's labor was scarce and farther off. He only spotted a handful of farmers on rickety horse-drawn carts rumbling across the stone-and-iron bridge where there should have been forty or fifty. The world itself seemed less populated. A chill went down Jack's spine and that familiar pit of wrongness wriggled its way back into his gut.

He decided it was time to get out. He lifted himself out of the water one-handed, with an ease of hard-earned strength. Despite everything else that was wrong, his strength had not betrayed him. Even so, wrapping himself in a towel with only one good hand was now a difficult task. His wrappings itched horribly but the medic assured him that they were necessary for the splints to set the bones properly. He also wasn't supposed to get them wet but he could only imagine the nagging Moira would produce if he still managed to stink after that chilly dip. Jack wrested the door open. True to her word, Jack's clothes were laid out on his bed, freshly pressed and smelling of starch. After a labor even more complex than wrapping a towel around his body, Jack was fully dressed and ready to go out.

But where? He had no desire to go to the Conservatory. Twenty-three voices were silenced from Cogrind's song. He was familiar with workers getting injured and leaving the Conservatory, but death at this scale was new and awful. It was stupid, but it felt like his fault. Perhaps this was worse than the gnawing pain in his arm; having no particular direction.

Jack decided to see Sean Lute. Sean was always kind and much more perceptive than he ever cared to show. Lute's future was not tied to the Conservatory as Jack's was. Maybe that was what he needed; some outside perspective. The sun caught a glint of metal from beneath his pillow. He sat on his bed and slipped his wrench from where it lay. Without so much as a thought, he spun it across his palms, flipped it through the air and caught it on end, perfectly balanced on his fingertip. He held it there for several seconds; so light and so incredibly strong.

The memory of the accident flashed across his mind. The wrench coiled in a life-saving hold around his wrist, stretching ten times its length.

How did you do that? For fifteen days Jack had tried extending the wrench, telescoping it or changing it in any way. He tried to command it. He tried to think it. He even tried to summon whatever feeling he had when he was falling into the pit, but nothing worked. He managed on his belt. Obviously there was nothing to do with his tools, but he felt naked without it. An old habit he hoped would never have to die.

Stomping feet rattled Jack's roof as Charlie made his way down the steps. He didn't even look into Jack's window, not a smile or a wave. The slam of Moira's door quickly followed.

"Lazy oaf! What good are you besides being a sponge for the nearest drop of booze!" With a huff and a final slam she went back into the steam and toil of the laundry.

Jack sighed and walked out his door. No matter what his problems might be, a friend in need was always a bigger one. He clambered up the clapboard landing and knocked softly on Moira's door.

"What?" she shouted.

He opened the door softly to find Moira bent over a hot

bath of diluted lye, abusing a tunic against a washboard.

"He barely works here and I still pay him as much as I can afford, and what does he do?" She slapped the other side of the tunic against the washboard and continued her beating. "Too drunk or hungover to be of any use to me, to us, to himself."

Jack placed a comforting hand on her shoulder. She slapped it away. He put it back. Moira wheeled around on him and hugged him with the incredible strength of a woman in pain.

"Why does he do it?"

Jack's broken arm was trapped between their bodies causing not a small amount of discomfort. He didn't move it. He just wrapped his other arm around her. "I'll go talk to him." Jack replied.

"Why? I've already talked to him 'til I was blue in the face," said Moira mumbling into Jack's shoulder between sobs, "He doesn't listen. He never listens."

Jack let her cry until her sobs began to subside. He couldn't help but smile. "This might be a talk where tutting and mothering may not be the trick." He said.

Moira sucked in a breath then burst out laughing, tears still running down her cheeks. "Damn it, why must you ruin a perfectly good cry?"

He wiped the tears away from each cheek. "One of my many gifts." He turned and opened the door before turning back around, "By the way, I'm almost positive that tunic will be clean for the next two months." He shut the door quickly before the tunic could hit him in the face.

Jack crossed the bridge and turned south, skirting the hagglers and sellers of the West Plaza market. Even here the stalls were practically deserted. Jack continued past street musicians and polished brass storefronts, past townhouses with unfolding steps like an elbow locking into place, until he hit Bass Run. Even in broad daylight, the southern district of Cogrind seemed covered in hazy shadow. Rust pocked the corners of abandoned trade shops and bootleg distilleries. Most of the buildings had long lost their mechanical functions from age and negligence. A layer of soot covered every window, terrace, and alley. They didn't use Arc-lamps down here in Bass Run. Barbaric braziers or mismatched kerosene lamps propped unlit on stripped screws. Here, the city seemed alive again. Seedy men with upturned collars pushed their way past the drunks and food vendors while residents of brothels hung their legs out of windows and called to their clients down below. It was a district apart from the rest of the city. Streets made for the conniving, the desperate or the castoff. Which is why Jack knew Charlie would be here. Jack figured Charlie thought of himself as two of those three.

The rusty metal sign for the Pin and Socket whined as it rocked in the wind. Jack took a deep breath and pushed the door open. The smell of cherry flavored tobacco and stale whiskey filled the low-ceilinged pub. The murmuring rumble quieted as he entered but soon resumed its secretive volume. Jack pushed passed the curtain of smoke until he heard the slurred voice of his oldest friend. Charlie's chin hung two inches from the bar. His hand clamped firmly on a tin cup. He was speaking bitterly to everyone and no one in particular. Jack saddled up on the stool next to him as the bartender approached.

"What'll it be?" coughed the bartender.

"Nothing for me," came Jack's reply.

Charlie's head bobbed up at the sound of his voice.

"Order something or bugger off." The bartender spit on the floor for emphasis.

Jack didn't much care for drinking.

"He'll have one of whatever it is I'm drinking," said Charlie. His watery eyes were fixed firmly on Jack, no matter where his head swooned.

The bartender grunted and moved towards one of the copper tanks that lined the back wall.

"How'd you figure I was here?" Charlie's tone was sour and needy.

Jack thought that perhaps Moira was more right than he wished to give her credit for. Charlie certainly was acting like a child. The bartender returned with a dented cup filled with a clear liquor. The wafting fumes made Jack's eyes water.

"This was the same place you came after losing your spot at the Conservatory. So this is how you spend the wages Moira gives you?" Jack needled in a half-joking tone.

Charlie slammed his cup down in response. "If that's why you're here, you can leave the way you came in." He sulked into silence.

Jack didn't move. He just pretended to take sips from his own cup. Slowly, Jack placed his hand on Charlie's shoulder. He didn't shrug it away.

"I wasn't made for doing laundry," Charlie's voice a confession, "I was made for building, for creating."

Jack nodded and remained silent.

"Now I can't. I can't do what I was made for. I'm useless."

A roar of laughter erupted from Jack. Charlie's face screwed up in all the rage a drunk could muster, which made Jack laugh all the harder.

"I'm sorry Charlie," Jack managed to wheeze out, "It's just that you are completely and entirely full of it."

This did not help Charlie's quickly souring disposition.

"What do you think we've been doing every night? We are bringing Arc power to Stonehall. Something even the Patron hasn't done." Jack caught himself as he said it. No one seemed to hear him, or at least seemed to care, but the worry returned.

"And once we install it into Moira's house, then what, Jack?" slurred Charlie.

Jack beamed back at him, stuffing the worry away.

"Then we continue on to my place, then yours, and then to the Workhouse. Paragon knows they could use some heat with winter coming," said Jack matter-of-factly.

Charlie nodded his head solemnly. He had spent enough nights fighting the chilling winds that blew through the thin clapboard walls of the Workhouse to know the truth in those words.

"We will just keep making Charlie. Just what you were meant for. You may be useless in the eyes of the Conservatory, but that doesn't make you useless to everyone." There was no consolement in Jack's voice, just the truth as far as he saw it.

They sat in silence for a while, Jack doing his best to avoid the fumes wafting from his cup.

Charlie pushed his tin cup away with the back of his hand. "It's not that I'm not grateful for Moira. My song would have ended years ago without her. I just . . . thought I would be more," he whispered.

"Well if it's any consolation, you're a considerably large pain in my ass."

Charlie's playful shove almost sent Jack off the barstool. It certainly sent Charlie off his.

"I don't know what you mean by more mate, but I know you mean a lot to at least a couple of people," said Jack.

Charlie twirled his cup around his finger as he thought on this. "Damn. I've been an idiot haven't I?"

"Well . . . yes. Speaking of making things, are you ready to make the best apology of your life to Moira?" Said Jack.

"I think I'll stay here and drink myself under the bar instead."

They laughed themselves hoarse and walked arms-over-shoulders out of The Pin and Sprocket and into the dingy streets of Bass Run.

Charlie winked at the girls that called to him from the brothels while Jack only blushed in envy at his friend's drunken confidence. By the time they had reached the West Plaza, Charlie had taken on a rather solemn face. Jack knew it was because he was about to face the unbridled ire of Moira.

"Where is everyone today?" Charlie said, looking in hopeful distraction.

Jack shrugged. Spending most of his time in bed for the past two weeks had cut him off from all the latest gossip. "Haven't the foggiest." He spied a vendor packing up her bushels of grain in defeat of a slow market day. "Excuse me miss, but where are all your customers?"

The gray-haired woman pushed back her hair with the back of her hand. "They got an execution today. Thought I might be able to sell a bit as everyone was headed up, but no such luck."

Jack's skin pricked up in goosebumps. "Who is to be executed?"

"A traitor of the city," she said. "Some higher up muckymuck. Thought his death would do a shine of good for my business. Supposedly he was trying to sabotage the whole of Cogrind."

Charlie shouted after him, but Jack was already running towards Metronome Tower.

The crush of the crowd made it hard to breathe, let alone move. Precarious throngs had even crowded the silver terraces of Balcony Row to steal a birdseye view of the execution. The gallows stood six steps higher than the street, squarely in front of the Metronome Tower. The Steel Watch lined the back of the gallows in crimson doublets and held steel halberds, each one wearing a gold embroidered gear soldered on the left breast. Jack looked about for familiar faces. Some stared on in shock, some in disbelief, but most wore masks of anger and vicarious indignation, the face of a mob hungry for violence.

It couldn't be, It couldn't be him. The double doors of Metronome Tower opened as a pair of Steel Watch in full mechanized armor brought out the damned man onto the gallows, in nothing but his under clothes. For a moment, Jack thought he was right. The man was old and his face was shaved. Weeping gashes across his legs and arms trickled blood. His ribcage stuck over his stomach in gaunt starvation. He didn't have half the muscle of Barin and couldn't even stand with the wide, proud bearing of his master.

Then Jack saw the eyes of a hawk nestled beneath bushy gray brows and he knew the truth of who stood there. The platform of the gallows began to rise so that most of the throng could see clearly. A pillory clicked and clanked as it snapped and assembled itself from the inner workings of the gallows. The Watch behind Barin threw the old man's head onto the bottom half of the pillory and slammed the top over his neck. The crowd cheered.

Jack only blinked dumbly. He felt a cold sweat bead between his shoulders as his breathing came quick and shallow. His feet were rooted to the ground. Impossible, this was all impossible. The Director of The Chorus, the hand-picked by the Patron, stood in a spotless cream silk robe. He stepped to the center of the gallows and raised his hands to quiet the crowd. A golden gear haloed his head.

Jack couldn't believe who was wearing it. It was Mr. Petty, his voice amplified by a Voxphone.

"My fellow citizens of the Shining City."

The crowd cheered to Petty's squeaking voice.

"The loss of any life is always a loss to our great city, but when a life can be so criminally vain, so horrifically egotistical to willfully endanger the lives of their fellow man, we have no choice but to put a stop to their threat."

The crowd cheered with a puppets' pliability.

"The idea of the self is the greatest danger to Cogrind. For we are cogs—"

—"FOR THE GREATEST MACHINE!" replied the jubilant throng.

Jack began pushing through the crowd, unsure of what his eyes were seeing. Barin's head hung low, braced between the slats of the pillory. He squeezed up to the base of the gallows.

"Barin!" Jack's voice drowned among the jeers and cries of the mob, "Barin!" His voice breaking in desperation.

The old man's eyes flickered towards Jack and then away. For a moment they were Barin's before they became the clouded, unfocused stare of an old man unsure of where he was.

"It's me, Jack."

Barin tilted his head to the left and then to the right. He peered at Jack and tried to spit on him. The spittle hit Jack square in the face. Jack looked back up in utter shock to find Barin as vacant and dumb as the moment before. Jack fumbled backwards into the crowd, drunk with confusion. Mr. Petty's words found their way back into his ears.

"—Despite his many years of toil for the city, this criminal forgot who he truly served. Not his own importance but the greater good of all. We as a society raise up the most capable among us so that they may be the humblest of servants. This criminal has been tried by Coda and found guilty of the most heinous crimes of Treason, Conspiracy to a Treasonous Act, and the wanton act of Ego. His song will end."

The crowd howled hungrily in response. The pillory sprang open and a guard pulled Barin onto his feet. The crowd hissed their discontent at the betrayer.

Petty squared his slim shoulders to Barin. "What last words does this broken cog have for the Machine he betrayed?" Petty's words slithered through his teeth in pious triumph.

Barin's head stopped rolling listlessly. He straightened himself to his full height and brushed past Petty to address the crowd. A silence blanketed the mob. Jack could sense the apprehension and even fear in the throng. It was a feeling Barin had given Jack many times.

The diamond-hard stare returned to Barin's eyes as he spoke. "You are convinced of my guilt. You are ready to believe the worst of me, yet how many of you truly know me or my heart? If Ego is my crime, have you not asked yourselves how I would benefit from the destruction of our city? The same city I have dedicated my life to? We work for each other, no man greater than the other. It is this philosophy of the Paragon that has built each wall and roof, each new invention and technology. But we are not the machines we create. We are people with minds to think for ourselves." Barin found Jack in the crowd. "I will not dispute my guilt. It was my decision and twenty-three souls bear the weight of my choice. That is my responsibility to bear. But there will come a time when you must decide for yourself where your responsibility lies. Is it with one man or is it with one another? And more importantly, will you have the courage to see your responsibility through to whatever end may befall you? Each and every man and woman must answer that question for themselves," he raised his hands, palms open and glittering with the embedded glass shards. "Do not look to your Patron for the answer, nor to the Paragon who's great melody we play. Destruction is coming and I hope you are prepared to band together. Not for the one above you. But for the ones beside you." Barin turned away from a now silent crowd, his boots stomping that familiar beat.

Mr. Petty's once triumphant smile had wilted to confusion. A murmur spread across the throng.

"Death to the traitor!" squealed Mr. Petty as he slipped past his prisoner and pulled a lever at the far side of the platform.

A few in the crowd still cheered but many people had seemed to lose the taste for this display. The pillory clicked and slid its way to the center of the platform. Then came the sound of a metronome, that symmetrical *tic-tock*, perfect and unyielding. The sound became louder and louder as a metronome six feet in height was raised through the platform. It was an exact imitation of the Metronome Tower that stood behind it, polished gold with a glass eye at its apex. The only difference was the imitation had a working arm and the weight at the end was a polished steel axe head. The arm swung back and forth as the guard pushed Barin into the pillory again. At least, he tried to. Instead Barin threw his head back, knocking the guard down. The crowd gasped. He did not attempt to escape. Instead, he placed his head into the pillory of his own will.

Barin eyed the much smaller Petty for exactly four beats of the metronome, then addressed the crowd one last time. "The whole note, my boy," His eyes fogged with tears as he shouted over the restless crowd. "The key is the whole note."

Petty pulled another lever and the Metronome began to slide closer to Barin's neck, keeping perfect time all the while. A numbing paralysis took hold of Jack. All of this was wrong. Barin was the greatest man he had ever known. Yet Petty's neck was hung with gold while Barin's waited for the axe.

What should I do? His body wouldn't budge as the axe slammed down a whisper away from Barin.

The old man looked up and found Jack in the crowd. It wasn't a difficult task with his long white hair. The axe tipped back and began its final swing forward. Barin saw Jack and smiled. The axe swung forward.

Jack went deaf to the crowd, muffled by grief and disbelief. He heard nothing but a far off voice shouting…

"No."

It sounded like his voice. He saw his hands clawing at the gallows, climbing to where his master once was. He couldn't feel his shoulder. Hands were grabbing at his arms and legs, pulling him backwards. He had no control. Everything was wrong and somehow it was all his fault. Jack's hands were behind his back now.

It took him several moments to realize he was in shackles. Sound came seeping back into his ears. The mass of people had burst into small skirmishes. A number of the Chorus cowered behind guards, welts around their necks where gold had been a moment before. It was a sea of flailing fists and running legs, except for one woman peering from the entrance of an alleyway.

She stood taller than he, with a tangle of matted auburn hair. She wore a leather jerkin, more cracks and stains than hide, with matching leggings. Her eyes were bright and wild, but what caught Jack's eye was what was strapped to her belt. They were blades, peculiar daggers that gleamed with a familiar metal.

Jack stumbled as two Steel Watch hauled him towards a holding wagon. He scanned the alley again but she was gone. Jack pushed back. The Watch's polearm cracked against the back of his legs, dropping him to his knees. They pulled him up by his shoulders, forcing a shout from Jack as they dragged him into the wagon. Just before they pulled a bag over his head he could have sworn he saw a large silver cat disappear from the barred window

The hood stank of sweat and old breath. The wagon puffed forward as the sounds of pandemonium died away. The smooth ride of metal wheels on metal ground gave way to the sound of fine gravel. The blinder made him relive the last swing of the metronome over and over. Jack lost track of time.

He was dead. Barin. All of his gristle and calluses and heart and knowledge and devotion. No one knew the Proscenium like he did. He cared for it like it was his child. He had no children of his own, no time to anyway. But the city was his legacy and its citizens roosted beneath his wing. And they killed him for it.

The wagon tilted forward. Jack could feel the air around him grow damp and chill and gravely silent. He had no idea what was about to happen to him and for the first time he could recall, Jack was afraid for his life. The engine hissed as the wagon chugged to a stop. Jack heard the door swing open. Metal-gloved hands grabbed him by the collar and dragged him out. It took Jack several moments to find his feet underneath him as the guards dragged him forward. The ground was wet and his footsteps echoed off of a low ceiling and stone walls. He couldn't see it, but this place felt very old.

Was this where they took Barin? Was this the same hood the Watch pulled over his head? Jack didn't want the answers but couldn't help asking the questions.

A door creaked open. More hands pushed him forward for a few dozen steps. Jack could hear rusted hinges, before being shoved onto a stone floor. The hood was pulled off of him as the door slammed behind the Steel Watch.

Jack found himself in a square cell no wider than his wingspan. Even the ceiling prevented Jack from standing up to his full, meager height. The guard's steps trailed away to the left of the cell. It was dark, at least it would have been to someone else. An Arc-lamp plinked somewhere to his right down the hallway.

If there is Arc-energy then I still must be inside the city. He began to feel along the walls and instantly found something etched into the stone. It was an eye. There was another right next to it and another below and above it. There were eyes scratched onto every surface of the cell, all identical and all familiar. Jack looked up to the ceiling. One large eye stared down on him.

He was alone and watched from all angles. The eye reminded him of how The Patron's office stared down into the Conservatory. Barin seemed to know this was coming. Despite his master's many faults, being unprepared wasn't one of them. He would have had a plan.

What was your plan, Barin?

The sound of footsteps shook Jack from his musing. From what little he could hear and see, there was no one else locked up here. These footsteps were for him. Jack sat on the bedrock and waited patiently as the pale blue light of an Arc-lamp bobbed and ebbed along the walls.

"Mr. Dowton," Came Carroll Crowley's voice from behind the lamp. "It is a shame I should have to meet with you down here, an unfortunate inevitability, considering your display."

A seething anger began to boil inside Jack but he remained silent. There was a tension in Crowley's voice. It was easy to recognize because it was rarely, if ever, there. Crowley was the man in charge. Stress was as familiar to him as his own breath. He had no reason to feel nervous unless . . .

"You almost destroyed your entire future with that display." The lamp was still in front of Crowley's face.

What are you hiding?

"Thankfully, the Watch detained you before the crowd could turn on you," said Crowley. Jack closed his eyes and tried to think back. Were they after him?

"Why? Why did it happen?" Jack's voice was hoarse and flat from screaming, his eyes still closed.

Crowley sighed. "The Coda found him guilty. The evidence was greatly against him. They had little choice." Crowley could not have been more matter-of-fact.

Jack opened his eyes. "What was Petty doing up there?" Jack saw the lamp bob slightly in response to his question.

"The Patron has bestowed the status of Chorus member to Mr. Petty for his many years of service. He is now the Director of the Chorus." Crowley was sounding less and less convincing.

"Odd that he would be given that status so quickly after Barin's Coda," said Jack. He could hear Crowley shifting his weight to his other foot before responding.

"Barin would have seen it as a boon to remove Petty from his Proscenium." Crowley's voice became higher. "And you should as well if you are to take Barin's place."

Jack sucked in his breath. The sound reverberated around his tiny cell. He said nothing, trying to ignore the guilt he felt for wanting it so badly.

Crowley's jaw tightened. "It is what you want, isn't it? No one who served as the Master Tuner's apprentice could resist such an offer. It is what you have trained for. By the Paragon's name, no one in all of Cogrind could say no to the opportunity to become one of the most powerful men in the City."

He was right of course. The title of Master Tuner was the culmination of all of Jack's work, his passion, his existence. Barin's face flashed into his mind the moment before he died, tears in his eyes and that beautiful, selfless smile on his face. Jack's throat felt dry.

"But, Barin was—"

"Barin was a self-admitted criminal who placed countless lives in danger," interrupted Crowley, "He is dead but the Shining City must continue. We have chosen you due to your prowess but you are not the only candidate. You may take the title of Master Tuner and become the greatest in our history or you can stay sitting in this oblivion until you starve and rot away. I will give you a day to decide." The lamp and Carroll Crowley swept from view.

Jack watched the light dance down the hallway to his right, leaving him with nothing but silence and the eyes that lined the cell watching him. He had the impulse to scream 'yes' through the bars. He was willing to do anything to get him out of this mess but the image of Barin stuck in the pillory stopped the words in his throat. This was not right. The only reason he had this opportunity was because Barin was dead. It would be a betrayal of someone who only sought to better his apprentice.

This isn't my time, not yet. Barin should have been the one to decide who bore the title of Master Tuner.

But then, what choice did he have? These were the most powerful men in the city. If he wanted to survive, he would take the deal. At least he knew that this wasn't Crowley's idea. Why else would he sound so agitated? He hated the idea of Jack taking over. Someone was forcing him to make this offer and the only one that had any power over Crowley was the Patron himself.

But why would the Patron want me? His arm began to throb, or maybe it had been hurting this entire time and he hadn't noticed yet. Laying in the infirmary flashed into his mind.

"Isn't it odd . . . "

Barin's words stung him. It was odd, Jack had to admit. Petty shriveled away from Barin that day yet proudly stood on the gallows to condemn the old man. They disagreed on the time table for the foundation repairs. No, not Petty and Barin, Crowley and Barin. Petty was just the messenger.

Barin was convinced the time table would lead to catastrophe. It did of course, except for Barin and the crane operators.

The Arc-boiler foundation, that's the start of all the trouble. Why was it so mangled in the first place?

"He killed your friend, threatens you with death, and leaves you in a hole in the earth,"

The phantom voice stopped Jack's heart. How could he have missed someone approaching in an echoing tunnel? It sounded more declarative than dangerous. He glanced up to see two pairs of green eyes peering in from the small barred window in the door.

It was the woman from the alleyway and a large silver cat on her shoulder. "Why listen to this man?"

Chapter 10

Sallah studied the boy. He was smaller up close, or perhaps it was the cell he was in. A pair of mismatched eyes peered out from behind a ragged curtain of pearl white hair, a look more of emptiness than fear. There was something disconcertingly familiar about it. He did not look like the one who would have the answers she was looking for, at least not on the outside. Perhaps her instincts had been wrong. No, he was the one that sparked the riot, the one that suffered the most loss at the death of that man. And that man seemed important. She needed someone motivated to give up this place's inner workings, or at least someone that could be manipulated.

What kind of barbaric people are these that hunger for a public execution? The Ichor led to the city, just like the woman by the lake said.

—

Sallah spent the better part of the previous night walking the rolling hills of grains and barley that sprawled out in wide strips around the city, like waving rays and the city was the sun. Low, fat clouds passed beneath a luminous moon, dipping the harvest in turns of light and shadow. Thankfully, this wheat didn't stretch above Sallah's head, making for considerably safer progress. When Sallah had first approached the outskirts of this strange city, it seemed deserted. She had traced the Ichor to where it seeped beneath the tall stone wall that girdled what appeared to be small buttes made of metal. Although just as tall as the featureless boulder she climbed yesterday, she easily scaled the crumbling stone wall with her hands. There was a large gate through which she could have entered, but she had no desire to be noticed by the small stream of carts and carriages entering the city.

She had mounted the wall, just as a man emerged from a structure made from dead wood far beneath her. A woman quickly followed, hurling insults in a lilting accent as he walked away. Sallah studied him as he walked across a bridge. He was tall, with a dark-complexion wearing a stained blue tunic, his right hand missing all his fingers except for his thumb. His steps were clumsy with drink. The woman had given up on yelling at him and instead took to pacing in front of her doorway, Her straw-colored hair blowing in the breeze. Quiet as the cat on her shoulder, Sallah slinked over the wall, picking her way down the other side, and on to the roof of a shack. The girl watched the one-handed man walk down the boulevard before disappearing back into her shack, punctuated with a slamming door. Sallah crawled along the shack roofs, stalking the man with one hand.

Her venture was to find the source of the Ichor. First she had to see who among these odd folk could be motivated to divulge information. A man missing a limb would be sure to have at least one good story of salvation or betrayal and if he was drunk, he might be more willing to tell it. Plus the benefit of not being observant enough to notice she was not from this place. She dropped onto the deserted stone street in silence. The woman was now yelling at some other sorry soul. The one-handed man had already stomped across the metal trellised half of the bridge, too distracted to notice the woman's shouts or his shadow.

He stole down an alley of tall, rectangular structures. These buildings were made of metal, not like the dead-wood shacks of the outlying farmers and the stone of the outer city. She darted towards the bridge, taking cover behind a stone pillar. Tosi hopped off her shoulder and onto a thin ledge of the bridge. He still walked with a slight limp but his leg was almost completely healed. The sun peeked over the wall as she slipped between the stone pillars and over the bridge.

The city was astonishing, like walking into a perfectly alien world. There was nothing but metal and glass and sky. No grass or trees or flowers as far as the eye can see. Well not natural ones anyway. She recognized metal flowers similar to the one she found in the Greensea, each playing a unique tune. Metal boxes slid about the sky on metal rails from building to building, disappearing as the buildings swallowed them whole before spitting them back out. Of course the Ichor would come from such an unnatural place. Street after street of metal blocks six, ten, and twenty times her height aligned in perfect, curving streets, laced with webs of alleyways threading around the buildings.

She darted from one shadow to the next with quickened silence until she reached a wide, open plain of metal. What seemed to be tradesfolk and farmers had a number of carts and pop-up stalls open for barter, but very few customers. The city for all its size and scale felt hollow. She was jarred to the ground by the sudden loud whistle that rang throughout the city. In a moment it was over and Sallah looked up to see a very confused old man staring down at her from a horseless cart.

"You all right, miss?" His accent was stiff and precise, but the language was thankfully the same.

Sallah straightened herself as Tosi leaped to his feet. "Yes," was all she managed to cough out as she hurried to catch up to her mark.

The farther south they walked, the more people began to emerge from the buildings around her. So, she attempted to blend in as best she could. The area of this strange city seemed abandoned by the builders, but not her people. So much so that she almost lost the one-armed man for a moment in the weave of people, but he was taller than most and Sallah had a Huntress' eyes. They were going against the flow of most of the crowd. The accents were thick and the voices were many, but it was not difficult for Sallah to pick out *"traitor"* and *"execution"* from the clamor of people heading north to some place called Balcony Row.

More than once Sallah was tempted to give up her quarry and to go find the spectacle these people talked about, but Agneth's voice repeated in her head:

The value in information lies in how few know it.

In the right situation what knowledge the one-armed man possessed could be useful to her mission, or just in controlling him. It never hurt to have a scapegoat. He stumbled through the crowd and down a dingy thoroughfare. It was jarring to see how grimy this part of the city, compared to where she had just walked. Perhaps these people were this city's version of the Nameless. Sallah watched pick-thieves and purse snatchers ply their trade. Nervous eyes peeked out from above upturned collars as quick hands exchanged trinkets or coins. Sallah felt safer here, or at least less conspicuous. Her mark pushed open a pair of rusted metal flaps and walked into what clearly smelled like a distillery. Sallah glanced around. She needed something to blend in. A woman was hanging her laundry out of her window from one of a web of lines that stretched to both sides of an alley.

"Tosi, give her something to worry about."

He bounced from her shoulder to an awning and up to the woman's window ledge. The woman shrieked as she turned around to find Tosi cleaning himself. Sallah ricocheted off a wall and onto the line, snatching a damp traveling cloak from the air. She whipped it around her shoulders and whistled for Tosi. He reluctantly stopped playing and followed his partner, leaving the woman entirely flustered and shy one traveling cloak. She pulled the hood far over her head and stepped through the creaky door flaps.

Sallah hated few smells more than the fume of wet tobacco smoke and this stuff weighed down the air like a heavy blanket. Swallowing back a retch, she kept her head down and walked towards an empty table at the back of the den. Peering out from under the hood, Sallah saw her target tilting back a cup and talking to no one in particular. The setting was certainly foreign, but she recognized a mead garden when she saw (and smelled) one. But where mead gardens would be a gathering for singing and trade and camaraderie, there was a desperation to this place. The minutes ticked by as the drunk man got drunker. Perhaps this lead was a dead end. Following him had led to this place, and this was a den rife with secrets hanging just between the whispering lips of conspirators in corners. Already Sallah had overheard the blackmailing of a lecherous Luthier, whatever that was. Sallah was busy listening to a group of teenage scam artists tell taller tales of conquest, when he walked in.

He was a strange boy. Rather short, but there was an easy strength to his walk. His eyes were aware and mismatched gray and green. Bright white hair flowed from his head and tied back in an attempt at a ponytail. He would have looked entirely out of place, no matter where he might be. There was something else to him. The boy seemed familiar. Sallah closed her eyes and studied his life force. She had never seen a pattern like his. Most of him glowed in oranges and reds. But his green eye was different. So was the top of his head. Instead of just a small range of hues that usually wafted from living things, his eye and hair shimmered with every tone under the sun. It was beautiful and jarring to see something so resplendent in life in a place so . . . manufactured.

Sallah's eyes flashed open. He walked towards the one-handed man and sat on the stool next to him revealing an odd-looking weapon on the side of his belt. Sallah's hood hid her smile while she prayed a quick thanks to Dharra. It was made of the same metal as those cursed metal blades at her hips. It was even made of the same peculiar design. This boy was the one to follow. Even if he didn't know of the Ichor, he would have knowledge about his own possessions and that in itself could shed light on her own venture. They talked for a while, the drunk man shed a tear or two, but Sallah mostly concentrated on the odd-looking boy. Jack was his name and he was attempting to console the drunk over his hand. The boy's arm was bandaged to the shoulder as well. Perhaps they shared a dangerous profession. Or this city was simply a dangerous place. In time, Jack and the man got up and left, laughing all the while, which was just as well because the bartender had taken notice of her.

Sallah stood and began to follow when a bald and impressively ugly man stepped in her way, bearing a yellow smile, a knife held at his side, and a network of scars sprouting from his chin. In an instant she appraised the man. He was strong, but unbalanced and had no idea how to handle a blade. Judging by his breath, he was deep in his cups as well. Whatever he was there for, it wasn't for her benefit.

The bald man raised a hand to her shoulder. "Excuse me Mis—" His bald head crashed through the table beside Sallah.

Her movement was so quick no one quite realized what had happened until it was already over. Sallah let go of the bald man's unconscious wrist with a flick and walked towards the exit. Tosi hopped on to the bar and eyed the bartender in disdain as he weaved through the glasses of stunned patrons. Sallah had to be ready to strike when the boy was alone.

Jack and his friend walked back the way they had come, with Sallah in tow. The boy called Jack didn't seem dangerous. He did seem troubled somehow. Something was weighing on him. The drunk man didn't notice it but Sallah could tell. Reading people was a necessary skill for a Druida. Gaining and protecting secrets kept a House strong and her people safe. Even by the way he held his shoulders, Sallah could tell the boy called Jack had more than one secret. They reached the wide metal plain, and to Sallah's astonishment, everything had changed. Hundreds of stalls stacked dozens of feet high had grown from nowhere. A handful of them were occupied, most were empty. Despite the sudden and perplexing appearance of the stalls, this made the task of tailing Jack considerably easier. She walked beside him a row to his left. He was such an odd boy, but Sallah couldn't shake the feeling that she knew him, like seeing a friend's face covered in greasepaint.

Impossible, I've never seen him before.

Why would a Huntress ignore her own instincts? Came Agneth's voice from the back of her mind. It gave Sallah a prisoner's resentment, but the blades on her waist and the object on his belt made it evident. She and Jack were connected in some way, even if it was coincidence. He stopped at one of the merchant stands occupied by an old woman. They were asking about all the empty stalls. Sallah turned away. She didn't want them seeing her face.

The boy screamed "No!" and was dashing down the street before Sallah could turn back around.

She followed in quick pursuit, dumping the bulky traveling cloak as she ran.

Finally, you are all alone now Jack. Sallah smiled. He was faster than she had given him credit for. It was a different kind of hunting, but she couldn't deny that this was becoming a little fun.

So this is where everyone was gathering.

Jack ran straight into a crush of people. Sallah stared in wonderment at the monolithic Tower that stretched into the sky before her. Massive was not a worthy word. Even The Grove of Ancients was dwarfed by this one structure alone. Sallah's distraction meant she lost sight of her quarry among the bobbing heads of the crowd that spilled into the side streets. The number of people seemed impossible to her. Merely looking at the expansive mob made her claustrophobic. She needed to get to higher ground. There were balconies lining every side of the street.

With ease, Sallah ricocheted off a wall and grabbed onto the balcony railing at the far side of the main street. Everyone was turned towards a large platform so she attracted little attention.

Sallah found Jack. In this innumerable crowd, he was the only one with pearl white hair. Towards the back of the platform stood four metal creatures shaped like men, holding axes attached to staves. Even by this distance Sallah could tell these monsters were designed for intimidation and martial ability.

They must be the ruling House's Guard. Considering how many people live here, these metal men may be necessary to keep the mob in line.

The murmur of the crowd died away as a small man in a billowy robe was raised from beneath the platform. The wind played with his halo of wispy hair and cream robe. Sallah recognized theatricality for the sake of flaunting power when she saw it.

"My fellow citizens of the Shining City," the robed man spoke into one of those large metal flowers. His tone was haughty and high-pitched but seemed to come from every corner of the square.

As he spoke, another man was raised from the platform, bound in chains and flanked by two unarmored guards in crimson and cream tunics with sashes bound tight across the chest. They shoved the prisoner onto his knees and forced his head and hands through a cruel looking contraption that assembled itself from the rising platform without a single person touching it. Sallah was more interested in Jack than the little clown's words. He had pushed his way towards the front of the platform at the sight of the prisoner whose head now hung over the platform. Jack was trying to get his attention.

"FOR THE GREATEST MACHINE!" erupted the crowd, startling her from her focus.

That seemed to have woken the mob from anticipation to bloodlust. A woman with a powdered face and wig wearing an unwieldy garment that must have hooped four feet around her hips stared at Sallah. She was attracting attention she didn't need. Sallah leaned backwards over the railing and landed on the street below.

There was an alley by the platform on the other side of the street. Sallah stole into it. She was close to Jack now, only thirty yards. He didn't notice her. He didn't notice anything. His eyes were fixated on the prisoner. The bound man's lips were moving and tears began to well in the boy's eyes. They cared for each other deeply. That was plain to see. Agneth's death flashed into her mind before she could catch it, but quickly pushed her cold face back into the shadows of her mind. They released the prisoner from his bindings. He stood more than a head taller than the robed man. He was at least given a chance to speak. He did not seem to need the metal flower for the crush people to hear him, as his voice rang out in practiced volume. Odd words like Patron and Paragon were given emphasis, though Sallah could not place their meaning.

"Destruction is coming . . . ," spoke the prisoner.

That got Sallah's attention. For a moment she worried the rulers of this place knew of her coming. But if they did, they clearly had any number of warriors to kill her.

Or perhaps he's talking about the Ichor. Clearly he disobeyed the ruling House and I can't think of anything more vile than that ooze. Is he dying to warn them?

Suddenly the boy called Jack was that much more important. If he was close to the prisoner, he must know something.

The platform began whirring and clanking as an echoic and measured ticking filled the square. Another device was raised into view . It was triangular in structure with a long stem swinging back and forth. And from the end of the stem was an axe head identical to the guard's halberds.

They are going to kill this man publicly? Sallah was beginning to despise these people. Death was a constant companion of the Children of Dharra, but to rejoice at the killing of an unarmed man smacked of the worst kind of barbarism. He wasn't even given a chance to fight for his innocence and here this crowd waited for his blood. A tear fell from Jack's eye, and his mouth hung open.

The condemned man whipped his head back, knocking over one of the metal men behind him. He didn't attempt to escape, however. He went to his knees and placed his own head inside the pillory. Sallah liked the condemned man.

That should emphasize his point.

As the axe head swung closer to the old man's neck, he tilted his head forward. His lips moved again in the direction of Jack. The boy stood frozen, unable or unwilling to move. Sallah hated him for it until a flash of a bleeding Agneth laying in her arms came into her mind's eye. Worse than anger or disgust, a new feeling crept in—empathy.

The axe came down on the old man's neck. A cheer of many rose up and was dwarfed by the scream of one. Jack vaulted through the metal guards and was climbing the platform. Confusion swept through the mob at the sight of the white-haired boy who now had scaled ten feet of the platform. People in the crowd seemed to recognize Jack.

That's when the hysteria broke out.

The crowd was dry kindling and that boy was the spark. Others had started climbing the platform as well, but only ones dressed like Jack. The ones with powdered wigs and lavish suits and gowns fled the crowd as calloused hands of the dirty and hungry ripped at their jewels and finery. There weren't enough guards to bring order. More of the metal guards came flooding from the huge building behind the platform, attempting in vain to quell the riot. The crowd may shout in unison, but this was a fractured people. They had finally managed to rip Jack from the platform and shackled his hands behind him. She couldn't lose him now. It seemed this society had no problems killing one of their own, so she would have to get what information she could before they killed Jack.

The guards shoved a bag over his head and hauled him to a dull grey wagon. In the struggle, the curious weapon fell from the boy's belt. Jack stared at her square in the face. It was like looking into a mirror that reflected not visage but emotion. He looked just as she felt the moment Agneth died. They managed the bag over his head as she shook herself from the stare and darted into the crowd, grabbing the boy's weapon along the way. With the pandemonium encircling her, it was not a difficult task to crawl beneath the wagon. her fingers dug into the undercarriage. Nothing was dragging it forward much to Sallah's amazement. It seemed to be moving of its own free will. The wagon took a right down a small street, then another right before heading down through a sliding portion of the wall in the base of the monolith. The shouts of the riot retreated with each turn.

The road led down and down and down. Sallah's heart was in her throat as the wall slid down behind her and the darkness became total. At night in the Greensea, Sallah at least had the life force of the forest around her to keep the fear of the dark at bay, but this place was made of lifeless metal. A darkness upon darkness. Well, there was one living thing. She focused on Tosi's lifeforce as he was hammocked on her stomach, counting out the distance travelled, in her mind. The wagon still rolled downward. Sallah's fingers burned and felt welded into place. The echoing of the wagon against metal walls dulled until the sound of the wheels met a quiet stone.

Gratefully, the wagon finally stopped in a low-hung cavern. Blue lights danced behind glass lanterns sprouting from the walls, granting small pools of light against the darkness. Sallah counted eleven different paths that led from the cave. She did her best to map the way she had come if a quick escape was necessary. But being blind and upside down for the journey made it guesswork at best.

She saw the boots of the two guards at the front of the wagon step off and open the back gate, dragging Jack down one of the pathways. She waited for them to disappear from view before releasing her grip from the undercarriage.

The lanterns caught her eye as she passed. It was like no fire Sallah had ever seen before. She closed her eyes and found out she was right. It was not fire, but life force, prismatic and calm. There was something more. It was the same pattern as the life force that came from Jack's green eye and hair.

This boy is more connected than perhaps even he knows.

She touched one. It didn't move or leap. The lamp didn't react at all. *These torches aren't alive, yet it's full of life force. How could this be possible? Just one more question to ask the boy.*

She peered down the path the guards had taken Jack. They were no more than thirty feet away. They threw the boy into a cell, locked the door, and turned back towards the wagon. Sallah stole around to the other side of the wagon as the guards climbed aboard. Sallah was a breath away from a guard's elbow as he sat. The earth itself began to spin slowly underneath her feet. It took all of Sallah's focus not to shout in surprise, as the circle of stone ground against stone and turned her and the wagon in a different direction. The wagon lurched forward and down a wider path than it had entered, leaving Sallah behind. Completely disoriented, Sallah had to look down six different passageways before she found the one which held Jack's cell. The place was deathly quiet. Even her breath felt loud here. This was a rarely visited place, which played into her favor perfectly.

She crept along the stone path towards Jack. A light emerged from one of the tunnels. With quiet feet, Sallah darted behind a thick pillar and held her breath. The light emerged into the pathway and down towards Jack. The footsteps were loud and hurried. Sallah risked a look and saw a tall, thin man dressed in a velvet coat. The man offered Jack a position, the dead man's position. She listened to him threaten Jack. The prisoner didn't respond. So the man turned and left the boy. He swept past Sallah. The lamp left him blinded to everything but the path in front of him. He ascended a different path from where he came, the sound of boots on stone as he ascended a set of stairs lost to the darkness. Sallah waited for a long time before heading towards Jack's cell again, certain each step would give her away to a guard in some dark alcove.

But nothing moved. Save for Jack and her, the place was deserted. Tosi took his place on her shoulder and together they poked their heads into the small window in the cell door.

—

The boy called Jack was dumb for words. He only managed to croak out a "Who . . . " before lapsing into a stupefied silence. Sallah recognized sorrow. He could be manipulated and time was of the essence.

"Who are you?" he asked.

"Someone who can get you out of here Jack."

Again, he responded with a mute stare.

She continued, "If you want to stop those that killed your friend, I can help." She needed to give him purpose. Get him out of this fugue state. Just enough to get him moving in the right direction.

"I'm Jack," the boy managed to sputter, "But you already knew that . . . somehow."

"I am Sallah and we need to leave this place." She began looking for a way to break the door.

His voice rang empty and lifeless. "Can I ask what you are doing here?" Sallah remained silent to his question, "Oh right." He continued, "You need my help. Sorry but I'm a little out of sorts today."

He was a far departure from the boy laughing and walking

with his one-handed friend only a few hours ago. Sallah surveyed up and down the passage before turning back to decipher the iron lock. She needed to get him out of here. They intended to use him or kill him, she didn't doubt that. And the longer he stayed in this damnable darkness, the more likely all of this would be useless to find the Ichor.

"We need to get you out of there," she repeated.

The low ceilings and tight walls amplified the tiniest of noises. She would have no chance of escape if she were caught like this.

"I can't," said the boy, "Crowley will be back tomorrow." Jack began rocking back and forth.

Crowley must have been the one in the velvet jacket.

"And if you do not do as he says, he will kill you or keep you imprisoned," Sallah declared, her voice harsher than she intended. "And you will be with your cowardly friend they killed today."

Jack sprang up and wrapped his hand around Sallah's neck before she had time to react. He pulled her face against the bars. The void was gone from his eyes, and was replaced with a venomous hatred. His hand squeezed the air from her throat. Try as she might, she couldn't pull free. This boy was much stronger than she.

"His name is Barin," he growled, "And no one will speak against him."

Her sight began to flutter and shrink.

"You wait for the man who killed him," she labored to wheeze out.

Jack let go instantly. With a rasping cough, air flooded back into her lungs. When she began to breathe again, Sallah found herself on the stone floor, with Jack looking over her from his cell window.

Thank Dharra I need you boy.

"I'm sorry." His voice sounded genuine.

"Stay here then and wait for others to decide your fate," Sallah said, turning and storming off.

"Wait please!" cried Jack.

She slowed her walk then stopped.

Well that worked perfectly. Sallah did need him. He just didn't know for what and how badly. He was her best chance to lead to the source of the Ichor. She turned and breathed deeply, her neck thumping in time to her heartbeat from the throttling. She walked back to the cell and glared at him.

"I'm sorry, I don't know what came over me. It's just Barin is a good man . . . was a good man and I had the honor of calling him friend, an honor few could boast. He was tireless in his work to the people," Jack took a deep breath, "and his work teaching me. And all he got for thanks was a public execution."

Sallah knew the earnestness in his voice to be true. It seemed her theory on the prisoner was right.

"I will help you escape if you answer all of my questions, all of them, completely. You will help me in everything that I require to ensure the success of my venture, and if I so much as even think you are going to attempt to attack me again, I swear on Dharra herself that you will join your friend Barin in death."

"So what makes you a better option than Crowley again?"

She put her hands around the cell window bars. "With me you have a chance to survive. With him he will imprison you for the rest of your life or kill you when it is expedient."

Jack took a moment to digest this, "Get me out of here."

Sallah took Jack's weapon from her belt. It was heavy, much heavier than her blades, but the metal seemed the same.

"Where did you get my wrench?" He quickly checked his empty belt.

She placed the wrench in between the bars and Jack grasped it greedily.

He held it with both hands clutched against his chest like a mother with her child. He looked up to see her studying him. "Back away from the door." He quickly steadied himself.

She did so. From behind the door came clanking and the whining of metal on metal. The door lurched once, then lurched again and fell forward as Jack shouldered through it, stumbling into the passageway.

"Apologies, that shouldn't have taken so long," he coughed through the risen dust. "Rust makes everything slower. Where are we?"

Sallah stood in amazement for a moment before answering. That door outweighed him ten to one.

He could have snapped my neck if he had wanted.

"We are underneath the monolith." She stared at the now-prone iron door. "How did you do that?"

"The hinge pins were on the inside. It would have been difficult to create enough leverage without the proper tool. But that is precisely what you provided. My thanks," said Jack. He peered down the stone passage. "The monolith . . . " he mumbled. For the first time he really looked at her. "You're not from Cogrind, are you?"

Sallah opened her palms, and swept them in front of her cracked leather armor. "Clearly not. We are underneath the big tower with the glass eye on top." She felt annoyed that she lacked a better description.

"We're underneath Metronome Tower? I didn't even know it had a dungeon, unless . . . oh..." He bit his lip as he glanced down one way of the passage, then the other.

Sallah gave him a moment before—"Oh what?" asked Sallah, equal parts annoyed and anxious.

"I believe we have found ourselves in the Undercroft," Jack said with a quiet reverence Sallah did not understand.

"And what does that mean?" asked Sallah, ignoring the awe that had overtaken her new companion.

Jack snapped back to her bewilderment before it dawned on him. "Right, you're not from here. The Paragon gave the city three gifts. The Undercroft was the second. It was the first iteration of the city you saw above. The legend says the Paragon had mastered lodestones to move and fit slabs of stone to form the skeleton of what would become Cogrind. The city had a different name then, but that has been lost to time and disaster. The outer ring of the city is the last bit of the Undercroft that's still above ground. The rest was built upon over generations until . . . " Jack pointed above his head, "It was simply no longer useful."

He was clearly distracted by where they found themselves and Sallah could feel the press of time.

"So how do we get out of this Undercroft?"

Jack chewed on his lip. "Do you remember which way you came in?"

Sallah pushed his shoulder in the direction of the wagon. "Of course I do. This way."

Jack rubbed his shoulder with a grimace on his face. "I hope you aren't going to make a habit out of that."

Sallah led him out of the passageway.

"I suppose that depends on how often you annoy me."

They emerged into the circular cavern. Jack began sucking on his teeth again. Sallah punched him in the same shoulder.

"I didn't say anything!" yelled Jack.

Sallah was busy studying each path. She pushed back the fear raised in her as she looked down each path enveloped in darkness. "Yes, but it annoyed me."

Jack huffed and gingerly rubbed his shoulder.

Sallah was sure to avoid the bandaged arm, so she considered it a courtesy. "The ground twisted me and the wagon around before it left, which got me turned around. Any ideas?"

"Are you going to hit me if I talk?" retorted Jack.

Sallah balled up her fist again and Jack flinched. "Not if it's useful talking." she said flatly.

Jack rolled his eyes before taking stock of the situation. "There's only four paths wide enough to allow a cart . . . " He studied the ground, "That's the way out." Jack pointed into one of the wide paths clothed in darkness and began to walk.

"How can you tell?" Sallah quickened her pace to follow him.

"There were only two pairs of fresh wheel tracks and this one was perpendicular to the other which would explain the turning you described. Besides, the path leads up a little ways in," Sallah squinted into the passage and saw only the dark.

Jack ducked from view for a moment before his head popped back out into the relative light of the cavern. "Are you coming? I'm not the slow one currently."

Her palms began to sweat. The less Jack knew, the better. "You can see in there?"

Jack smiled. "Sure can. I've always been able to see better in the dark than most. It certainly helps in my profession."

Breathing deeply, Sallah walked stone-faced into her one great fear.

—

It was excruciating. Every step was a snare waiting to close. Every breath was a beast stalking her. Something brushed against her leg, forcing a gasp from her lips. Tosi's green eyes stared up at her, reflecting what little light there was.

"Are you all right?" Jack's voice came from somewhere in front and above her.

She managed a curt, "Fine." She had the choice of closing her eyes to follow Jack and risking a stumble into stones or Dharra-knows-what, or eyes opened to glean what she could of the path and possibly lose Jack. She decided on a mix of the two.

"Jack?" Her eyes were open, straining for light.

"Yeah?"

She gasped again. He was right beside her now.

"Sorry, didn't mean to startle you," Jack chuckled.

Sallah swung a fist in his direction and connected firmly, "Damn it! I thought you couldn't see? Same spot too . . . "

Eyes closed from now on. The passage ramped up steeply now. Her boots struggled to find purchase on the thin layer of dust.

"I don't remember the way down being so steep," She needed to break the silence, anything that could distract her from the darkness. She could hear Jack having a difficult time of it as well.

"Well there were only two possibilities of where that wagon came in, so unless they turned the stone back after the wagon left . . . " Jack's footsteps stopped, which in turn froze Sallah in place.

Fear coiled around her chest. With closed eyes, she examined Jack in his ephemeral form, turning his head forward then behind them.

"Sallah? Do you happen to remember if a wall closed behind you when you came in?"

"Do walls normally do that here?" She watched Jack smirk at her.

"Yes they do, but those are typically metal, not stone. Actually I'm shocked to see how serviceable these tunnels are. They are centuries old, dating back before the Age of Flames."

The phrase ticked something in the Druida's mind, but fear and darkness left little room for thought,

"I think we are going to have to find another way out," said Jack.

From the silence below their feet rose a bass whistle. A hum of vibration rising from her boots and from no particular direction.

"And we need to do it fast." He grabbed her hand and with a jerk, they were slipping and running back down the tunnel.

Everything in Sallah wanted to resist. She was never helpless and now her only chance of escape rested on the shoulders of a boy she threatened to kill and in turn had almost killed her. The pitch and intensity of the path rose higher as they retreated downwards. All she could do for the moment was watch the prismatic life force of the boy and hope he didn't decide to abandon her. He turned to the right and sped down a passage where she thought there was only a wall.

Jack turned back to her as they ran. "Are your eyes closed?"

She opened them in response and found that there was some blue torchlight here but only farther down the path. On impulse, Sallah wrenched her hand away from his and took the lead.

"Do you know where you're going?" asked Jack between gulps of air.

Tosi sped ahead of her and into the lead.

"No more than you do. That's why I have Tosi." replied Sallah.

"The cat?"

Sallah eyed him over her shoulder. "No, the Hunter."

There were passageways to the left and right every ten feet but Tosi raced past them all, towards the end of the hall where an iron gate blocked the path. The vibration grew deafening now, unable to escape the stone that surrounded them.

"I got the gate," said Jack, his wrench already in his hand.

His hands were a blur of delicate and precise movements as he worked at the hinges. And then the vibration halted, echoing across stone.

"My guess is that was an escape alarm." Jack freed the pin from the middle hinge.

Sallah could hear a host of footsteps behind them.

"And I guess that would be the Steel Watch responding to the alarm." finished Jack. Guards poured through the passageways, their halberds scraping the stone ceiling.

Wrong weapon. Sallah gathered her hands into fists. She couldn't risk using her blades here. Though she reveled in the intoxicating power that voice gave her, she couldn't risk killing Jack in the grip of the blood rush.

The metal men were not made for the small confines of

these hallways, and neither were their halberds. They could only fit single file in the tunnel. The first guard ran towards Sallah, the halberd's spear tip aimed straight for Sallah's heart. They thrust, but met only air. In one fluid movement she spun away from his strike, forced the blade into the stone floor, and allowed his momentum for his own weapon to crack him across the helmet. The second Steel Watch jumped over his unconscious comrade, his halberd pointing forward just like the first. With a flick of her foot Sallah stuck the halberd into the stone ceiling.

The guard drove the base of the weapon into his own armor with an audible "Oohf". Sallah grabbed haft of the halberd where it was wedged and and drove it under the

Watches's chin, rattling his head inside his helmet.

"Got it!" said Jack, who was currently holding the now unhinged gate, "Get moving."

Sallah turned away from the pursuing guards and up a winding stone staircase. She glanced back to see Jack hurl the gate down the tunnel, stumbling their pursuers. Sallah hurtled up the staircase, three steps at a time, keeping an eye on Tosi's tail all the while. Jack was behind her, keeping pace. The spiral was so tight it felt like running in place. To the left, Tosi darted through a granite archway and on to a thin and worn bridge.

Sallah followed and held back a retch. Far below, wastewater flowed in from stone sewers and congealed into a single flowing muck, falling deeper below the Tower and lost to depth. The sound was a deafening wall of white noise. The smell rose up in waves, blurring her vision. The strip of granite that she was running on was no wider than her shoulders and split into five separate paths. Three led to the far side of the sluiceway, two crumbled into open air. Tosi was over the middle of the bridge and bounded down the path to the right. Sallah risked a look down. The pillars on which the bridge lay bowed drunkenly as they stretched to a bottomless end. The guards were on the bridge, ten paces from Jack's heels. Most had given up on their halberds, resorting to daggers.

Sallah leaned to the right and barreled towards a six-foot gap. Tosi cleared it with a feline nonchalance. Sallah leaped and landed surely. The bridge tremored and Sallah felt an instant of weightlessness as a chunk of the bridge gave way underneath her foot. Jack had two steps to react. With a grunt of surprise he flew towards the other side of the bridge. His boot scraped against the crumbled edge for purchase. Jack threw his other foot up as guards hurled their weapons at his exposed back. Most missed, one did not. Sallah halted to see the boy lift himself back onto the bridge with the hilt of a dagger sticking out of the meat of his left shoulder. He wasn't in pain, at least, he didn't look to be. His face was focused. His eyes bore no pain or even fear, only the necessity of survival. He didn't even seem aware of the dagger in his shoulder as he sped past Sallah. She pulled it out of his back and turned to follow. It was heavy and unbalanced, but it was serviceable. Three of the braver guards attempted to leap the gap, only to find open air and the wastewater far below. The third was able to grab the ledge before the stone crumbled in his hand.

Jack and Sallah raced into the stone archway and up another spiral staircase. Sallah could hear the constant whistle of steam all around them. The stone staircase around them began to change as well. Swirls of silver, gold, and copper metal swirled into the dull grey of the stone. She could hear the metallic tromping of another set of guards giving chase farther down the stairs. Jack had taken the lead from Tosi and turned his head over his shoulder.

"This way!" He turned into another archway.

The sound of hissing steam rose as they passed into an airy corridor made entirely of metal. Huge cylinders twice her height curved up and around each other in every possible direction. Where they stood was just one of a maze of tunnels that stretched beyond sight. His face remained unchanged, but his body now moved with purpose. In short order, he jumped onto the lip of two connecting pipes, swung his wrench onto a bracket, and landed softly on the top of one of the wide tubes.

Taking a moment to orient himself, he turned to Sallah. "We just need to keep on this pipe and we should come out somewhere in Stonehall." He offered his unbandaged hand which Sallah reluctantly took. Blood formed a pointed stain on the white bandages of his other arms. He didn't seem to notice.

"How do you know?" she asked as they resumed their run.

"This is close to where I work, Or used to, anyway. These are exhaust pipes and exhaust pipes run to the outskirts of Cogrind. "

The Steel Watch had reached the room now, but their bulky armor hampered their pursuit as their quarry climbed higher. Soon, they were out of sight as they made their way down another tunnel. The only sound they made was the clangor of their boots striking on metal.

There, in the distance, she spied a pinprick of light. Sallah had never felt such relief. All she had to do was keep running and she would be bathed in pure, perfect sunlight. Her ankle flexed and she fell. Cursing her own clumsiness, Sallah picked herself up and almost fell over again. The pipe was moving. Then came a stench that forced a second retch from Sallah that day. It was the sweet smell of death mixed with the smell of something burning. Jack had stopped too.

"Paragon save us," said Jack, "Get up!"

She didn't wait to question him. They were off. Sallah kept pace as best she could but the pipe buckled more violently. Jack was well in front of her now, Tosi just behind him. The smell was growing worse. She couldn't find enough air to breathe. She tripped forward as a new sound approached her ears. Louder than the steam, it sounded like the hissing of a snake but bigger. Sallah stole a look back. Metal snakes four times the length of her body slithered around the pipe and towards her with unnatural speed. She stuttered forward but she knew the truth; she wasn't going to make it to the sunlight. Fear flushed through her body.

Darrah, grant me speed.

"Sallah, this way!" said Jack a short distance ahead. He was beside a ladder that led into a metal lid high overhead.

She threw herself at him. He caught her and lifted her onto the first rung. She studied him as she climbed. He wore the mask of the fervent calm of a hunter, nothing more.

Verum Cordis, as Agneth would say. Tosi scrambled to her shoulder as she climbed as quickly as her hands would fly. Jack was just below them. She pulled herself up and toward a hatch. The ladder shook as a yellow-eyed serpent weaved its way up from the base of the ladder. She threw her weight into the hatch and it thankfully gave way. She threw herself out into the blinding sunlight of the paved street. Jack emerged quickly after. Then she heard the desperate cry of Tosi. He had fallen off her shoulder and held to a rung as a host of serpents snapped at his tail. Jack flung his upper body into the sewer, extending his arm into the darkness. "Get ready to close it!"

Sallah grabbed the lid and made a quick prayer. Tosi's claws bit into Jack's bandages as he crawled up his arm and towards daylight.

"Now!" Jack cried as he pulled his arm up, but something tugged it back down. He grunted painfully as he tried to wrench his arm free, his eyes bulging in panic.

With a horrible scream, his body rolled free of the hatch and Sallah slammed the lid down, throwing her body over it. The lid didn't buckle or move under her weight. The serpents were not pursuing them above ground.

"Thank Dharra we're alive. What were those things?" Sallah leaned back on her palms and began to breathe deeply of the fresh air.

Jack didn't respond. Sallah turned to see Jack's unconscious body lying among the stalls she had trailed him through earlier that morning. But where once there was a bandaged arm, there was nothing more than a bloody stump.

Chapter 11

She feels warm. Her arms hold me tightly against her body as she walks. I am safe here.

"How will they know?" she asks him.

He's there too, very close. I am safe here.

"We need to trust the others. If we do not play our part first, then his part in all of this will be forfeit. Besides, we owe a great debt and this is the only way to repay it." His voice is deep. He sounds sad. We are walking. We have been since I woke up. It is dark. I cannot see anything. I can feel her breath on my forehead. I am safe here.

We stop walking. She gently lowers me onto blankets. They are warm, but not her kind of warmth, and they don't smell like her either. She is still close, though. I am safe here.

I can see the outline of a building in the moonlight. It looks old. She is there, above me. I can see with only one eye. One is covered and the covering itches. Curly, auburn hair tickles my nose. It smells like earth and honeysuckle and home. I can't see her face. Her hair makes a veil over me. But I know she is sad. She kisses my brow and whispers into my ear. Her voice is soft and sweet. I don't hear everything she says.

" . . . not alone." There is another hand, not hers, calloused and gentle. His palm covers my chest. He kisses my brow too. His stubble prickles my skin. He smells like leather and lamp oil and warmth. He puts something next to me. It's as big as I am and warm. Not her kind of warmth but it is familiar. They are gone now and all I see is a lamp above a doorway. Someone that's not her is carrying me now, inside the building. It smells sour and clean. It does not smell like her. I am not safe here. I start to cry . . .

Jack's tongue snapped dryly against the roof of his mouth. He needed water. He tried to move but his strength was gone. It took all his concentration just to open his eyes. Not that he could see much. Halos of light blurred the already fuzzy objects in his vision. His eyes burned. Everything hurt. There was a weight on his chest. He groaned involuntarily as he tried to blink into focus. A bright pair of green eyes stared back at him. It was Tosi sitting on his chest with his twitching nose, an inch from Jack's. His purring was loud.

That explains the weight.

"Tosi." His lips barely moved.

"He's hardly left that spot. It seems you have a friend," said a voice to his left. It was a woman's voice, older.

With a concerted effort Jack tilted his head. It was the Headmistress of the Workhouse.

Claire . . . something, Jack tried to piece it together, *Claire Sonnet?* Jack couldn't remember. He had never called her anything but Headmistress. All of the orphans did. Then Jack knew where he was. It was the smell of lye and steam that gave it away. He was laying in the loft of the Workhouse. It was hard to forget a smell one had awoken to for most of his life.

"Water," said Jack.

Claire moved to the side of the bed and placed a cup against Jack's lips and tipped it forward slightly. The tin cup made the water taste metallic, but it felt amazing slipping down his throat. Claire righted the cup. Jack's eyes were coming back into focus. Her hair was greyer than it had been when he lived here, perhaps her jowls a little more defined, but she still wore the stiff high-collar dress and the same pursed lips.

"Thank you."

Claire sighed laboriously. She did that a lot, Jack recalled.

Of course, he could hardly argue that she didn't deserve to whenever the mood struck. She cared for castoff children of Cogrind, and there were many. She turned most into respectable citizens, apprentices, miners, and artisans. Some couldn't be helped and she let them go at the age of sixteen to become another shadow on the streets of Bass Run. But she tried, with all of them, she gave her everything. As such, most of her former charges credited her with being the true power behind the City and she did it all without a smile and without formal thanks. Jack didn't know why he was back here, but the cat was present, which meant that woman was here too. Jack thought of all of this as a wave of exhaustion led him back to sleep.

When he awoke the next time, Headmistress was gone but Moira was there.

Her hands were sweaty from all of the hand-wringing. She sat on a wooden chair to his right.

"Hey." said Jack.

In a flash Moira was up and leaning over him. He groaned when she jarred the bed. She had been crying, her eyes red and puffy.

"Sorry. Are you all right? How are you feeling? Oh Jack, I'm so sorry," she said softly.

It all was a little too much to bear at the moment, but he attempted a smile all the same.

"Fine, you?"

She almost scolded him, then threw her arms around his head in a clumsy, heartfelt, hug. She began a motherly sob before she straightened herself to look at him then wrapped his head in her arms again. "I was so worried when that woman carried you home. You were unconscious and bleeding and . . . "Another bout of tears overtook her. "And it was all so terrible and I didn't know if you were going to . . . to," she threw her head into Jack's chest and sobbed. "But you're okay now though, right? I mean you're feeling stronger, right?"

He lifted his right arm and laid it on the back of her neck. He didn't want to try to move his left. It felt like it was still there and as long as he didn't try to move it, that was the truth. "I'll be okay." He wondered if that was true. She didn't need to know that though. He asked for some water right before exhaustion overtook him again.

—

He woke this time in less fog and much more pain. His left arm ached horribly. He didn't want to look. He turned to his left. A white bandage cupped his shoulder where his arm should have been. It was over. The dream of Master Tuner ripped from him twice over; a broken tool and now escaped prisoner of the Shining City. By cogs, even a normal life was no longer possible. He would be useless now to even

Moira and Charlie building out the Arc access for the laundry. He was hopeless now, ready to be discarded with the other amputees scraping a life from Bass Run. He had everything and now —

"Still abed, lay about?" asked Charlie.

Jack coughed raspingly as Charlie handed him a cup of water. Jack didn't know how long he had been there.

"All right, Charlie," said Jack.

"All right, Jack," Said Charlie, sitting on the wooden chair next to Jack's bed, "Good to see you're still with us, even if there's less of you to be here with."

Jack's eyes moved to Charlie's missing fingers.

Charlie smiled. "You'll get used to it after a bit. The damn phantom pains go away after a while. If they don't, I'll show you a trick." He leaned back in the chair and sighed. "Care to talk about it?"

Jack raised one eyebrow in response.

"Yeah, maybe when you're feeling less peaked. Head-mistress has been keeping you on a steady dose of laudanum. Listen Jack, I need to get this outta the way. I wanted to thank you."

Jack did his best to furrow his brow in response.

"You're a good man Jack and you've been a better friend to me then I could ever be for you. I'm not drinking anymore and Moira's doing her damnable best to make sure I stick to it."

"You're screwed," said Jack.

Charlie chuckled, low and deep. Jack always liked that sound and he realized how few times he had heard it in the last few years.

Charlie stood up and took Jack's hand in his and squeezed.

"You saved my life. I would've offed myself a long time ago if you weren't such a good friend and I was more of a coward. By the Paragon, I was going to end my song that day you found me in Bass Run. So, I'm paying it back. Whatever you need, whenever you need it, I'll be there mate. You have the word of a good drunk and a bad friend, for whatever that is worth."

"A lot," whispered Jack. He fought back a tear and lost.

Charlie squeezed a little bit harder then turned to go down the ladder which served as access to the loft.

"She loves you." Jack raised his head from the pillow for the first time.

Charlie stopped, one foot on the ladder. A soft smile drew across his face. "Then there's someone else I need to talk to as well."

Charlie dropped from sight and Jack drifted back to sleep.

—

He didn't know how long he slept, but when he awoke, there was a different pair of green eyes staring back at him. Sallah was standing at the foot of the bed with her arms crossed. Her face was inscrutable. She was cleaner than before. Her hair was no longer in knots. She could even pass for a citizen, but there was something too wild in her eyes and her posture, like she was ready to pounce at any moment. They stared at each other for several silent moments.

"How long?" asked Jack.

"Three and a half days."

Tosi jumped onto the foot of the bed and sniffed at Jack's feet. The cat ticked a memory in his head. He tried to move his left arm. It felt like it was moving. Jack watched his shoulder give a twitch. "Damn,"

"Dumbest thing you could've done." Sallah said. She walked deliberately to his left hand side.

Jack just watched her.

"You should've left him back there. I wouldn't have faulted you, neither would Tosi."

Jack looked down. Tosi had moved up the bed, sniffing where his left arm should be, then stared back up at Sallah. "He just seemed scared to me."

Sallah flinched. Tosi walked onto Jack's chest and sniffed at his nose. Jack tried to pet him. Tosi hissed and batted his hand away.

"He likes you. Otherwise, he would've drawn blood," said Sallah.

Jack gave a weak smile.

"Sounds like someone else I know," Jack managed to quip.

Sallah swallowed and sighed through her nose. "You do not know me Jack."

Jack watched the cat slide over to Sallah and jump to her shoulder.

"Perhaps, but I know the kind of person you are." Jack felt another wave of sleep coming over him.

"And what kind of person am I?"

Jack exhaled deeply before speaking. "The kind of person like the one you saw executed." He closed his eyes and drifted off. Yet another thing that he lost. Perhaps in time he could learn to adjust to life with one arm, but he didn't know how he would make it without Barin.

—

The next time he awoke, raised voices sounded below him. The loft window showed it was the deep of night, the wind rattling and seeping with the cold of approaching winter.

" . . . and I will tell you again I haven't spoken to him since he left my care four years ago."

It was Headmistress's voice to be sure and she was using a tone Jack had heard many times. A man's voice replied.

"We know he lives in the area. Just let the Captain do a quick search and we'll be on our way." The man sounded humbled.

"And disturb the children's slumber? I think not. Really Jeffrey, I thought I taught you better than to disturb people at all hours of the night. Surely, there is actual crime and mischief happening across the city that requires your attention."

"I . . . Yes ma'am, sorry ma'am." conceded the other voice.

Jack heard the Workhouse door close as a shiver ran down his spine. He didn't sleep for the rest of the night. He waited for the next knock or the crack of the door being knocked down. But the only sound he heard for the rest of the night was the rattling wind against the clapboard walls, and the shuffling of the Headmistress.

Sunlight creeped through the triangle window above his head. He was feeling stronger today, strong enough to talk more at least, though even moving his head felt like a feat. Someone was climbing the ladder. It was Moira, with a pitcher slung around her wrist. Some of the water sloshed out as she topped the ladder.

"How's Charlie?" asked Jack.

Moira gave a squeak of surprise. "I thought you were still asleep." She walked to the small table at the side of his bed, pouring water into the tin cup.

"Didn't answer my question."

Moira hid a sheepish smile behind a veil of her brunette hair. "He's doing just fine, though he was deeper in the bottle than I had realized. His shakes have gone down though."

"Still didn't answer my question."

She screwed her face up in mock anger, then hugged him. "Thank you, Jack. It isn't easy. He gets angry when the shakes take him, but I think he's really trying now. He's even helping with the laundry."

Jack smiled and patted her on the back. Then a pressing thought came to mind. "How's our visitor? Is she still here?"

She offered Jack a cup of water. He tried to sit up and fell to his left.

This will take some getting used to. Leaning on his right hand, Jack managed to prop himself up on the wall.

Moira pretended not to notice. "She's about, though I could hardly tell you where exactly. She appears and disappears without so much as a whisper."

"What do you think of her?" asked Jack.

Moira was a sincere spirit and in Jack's experience, that sincerity made her an excellent judge of character. "She's . . . focused . . . determined and different to be sure. She isn't from here, so whatever she needs you for, she has come a long way because of it." She took Jack's cup and fretted at his pillows for a moment before continuing. "Scared is what I would say. She isn't a bad person and I certainly wouldn't call her good, just scared of something. And for whatever reason, she has decided she needs you. And that's what worries me. She will use whoever is convenient to get what she wants."

That's what Jack had thought as well. "I need you to find

her. Or send her here if she sneaks up on you."

Moira giggled, a light and dancing sound.

"No need," Sallah said flatly, "I'm here now," only her head was visible from where Jack sat. She climbed the last few rungs of the ladder as silently as the rest. "We need to talk."

"Yes we do." What surprised him most, was that he didn't feel surprised at her appearance. He had a feeling she was close, even if he couldn't see her.

Moira snapped up the pitcher and tripped over her dress in her rush to descend the ladder. She smiled meekly as she passed Sallah. Sallah gave a curt nod in reply, never looking away from Jack.

Focused indeed.

"Will you sit?" said Jack, offering the chair.

"No, I would rather stand."

"I figured as much. You helped me escape, so I will answer your questions just as I promised, but you will answer my questions as well."

Sallah's posture stiffened. "That wasn't a part of the deal."

"Neither was losing my arm. If you want answers at all, I suggest you answer my questions fully." Jack saw her jaw tighten in response, then relax.

"Fair, I'll start. What do you know of the Ichor?" Sallah folded her arms.

Jack raised his eyebrows. "Nothing."

Sallah's eyes filled with anger but she inhaled and exhaled deeply. "You haven't seen it? Anywhere in the city? A black ooze that moves on its own and seeks living flesh?"

Jack stared at her blankly for a few moments. "That sounds like something I would remember if I saw it," Jack couldn't keep the sarcasm from his voice. It came so naturally.

209

Without another word Sallah turned towards the ladder.

"You haven't answered one of my questions yet,," said Jack.

"And you didn't answer mine."

"Sure I did. You just didn't like the answer."

Why am I goading her like this? Jack chastised himself. Her head dipped from view right before Jack spoke again.

"Where did you get your daggers?"

A pregnant moment of silence passed before Sallah's head re-emerged into view. She glared at Jack. Her eyes flicked to and from his amputation.

She climbed back up the ladder. "In a place called the Old Growth at the heart of the Greensea,"

Jack burst with a gust of laughter. He held up his hand in conciliation, "I'm sorry I wasn't laughing at you. It just struck me how we don't seem to be very good at answering each other's questions." He wiped a tear from his eye. It felt good to laugh. "I was born with my wrench or near enough. Headmistress said it was in the basket with me the day she found me on her doorstep, this doorstep as a matter of fact. It's been with me ever since."

Sallah seemed to soften at this. Even now Jack could feel it pressing against his hip. Charlie or Moira must've slung his belt around him while he had slept.

"You are Nameless? You are an orphan?" asked Sallah.

"Among other things, yes. Do your blades . . . behave oddly?"

Sallah's big eyes were enough answer for Jack.

"They . . . talk to me." Sallah prepared for another quip, but Jack only chewed his lip in concentration.

"What do they say?" asked Jack.

Sallah stiffened again. "No, your turn to answer a question."

Jack pulled the wrench from his belt and inspected it. "The bandage on my arm, what was my arm, anyway . . . The day my arm got injured, my wrench grew. It changed shape too, like a rope. It even moved on its own. I would've died if it hadn't. Haven't been able to make it do that since though." He lost himself staring at the wrench but snapped back to reality when Sallah started talking.

"They tell me to do things. Things that I wouldn't normally do, violent things."

Jack snorted and whispered a quick 'sorry' underneath her glare. Then his head snapped up. "You held the wrench, did it say anything to you?"

"No."

They both lapsed into silence. The only sound was the hiss of pressed dresses and the murmur of children below them.

"What were those serpents down there?" asked Sallah

"Besides being the start of my troubles? Paragon only knows. They shouldn't be there. They shouldn't exist. I tried to alert Crowley and Barin . . . those in charge of running the city," Jack clarified at Sallah's puzzled look, "But I was told to forget about them. That I was just going to cause hysteria." Jack was surprised at the anger he felt.

"Who instructed you to forget about them?" Her eyes searched Jack for a lie.

"The Patron himself," said Jack.

Sallah tilted her head.

"The leader of the city."

"When did you first see these snakes?" Sallah asked

"Perhaps a month ago. A little longer."

She nodded her head and searched the floor for an answer. She had seemed to come to a conclusion. "The man who they

211

killed—"

"Barin is his name. Well, was his name." Jack corrected himself.

"Barin then. What did he do for your city?" She began to pace back and forth.

Jack snorted.

"What didn't he do? The man was a living legend. His title was Master Tuner. He was the one responsible for building or fixing any of Cogrind's machinery and the entirety of Cogrind is one giant machine. There are only two men more powerful than he; Crowley and the Patron. He was respected by anyone who knew him. He wasn't a kind man, but he was dedicated. No one in Cogrind knew more about mechanization and Arc . . . and I was his apprentice." Jack brushed his fingers across the burnished wrench, lost in thought.

"What's Arc?" She closed her eyes.

Jack noticed she did this quite a lot. "Do you remember what I said about the Paragon giving the City three gifts? Arc was his third, final, and greatest gift. Arc is pure energy that we have managed to harness. Everything in Cogrind runs on it, from windows and doors to wagons and even how we clean the streets. Everything, everything is connected to the Conservatory. Did you see that huge building in the very center of the city?"

Sallah nodded, eyes still closed.

"That's the Conservatory, and inside it is the Proscenium, where the Arc-boilers sit. We create, regulate, and recycle Arc that is generated by the Arc-boilers." Melancholy crept into Jack's voice. He gripped the wrench awkwardly in his right hand and squeezed until his knuckles turned white and ached.

"So those torches we saw underground are fed on this Arc?" asked Sallah. Her eyes were open again.

"We call it fueled here, but fed or fueled you are correct."

"How do you make Arc?" Sallah walked to the chair and sat down, her back as straight as the chair's.

"Would that I knew. The technology was lost during the Age of Flames five hundred years ago as well as the Paragon himself. That was until just over three years ago. The Patron's Artificers rediscovered how to reconstruct Arc-boilers and the Patron commissioned them to be built. But how they produce the Arc itself has been kept a secret, known only to the Patron and his circle. That's actually how I got my apprenticeship at the Conservatory."

Sallah leaned forward incrementally. "How exactly did you get your position?" She closed her eyes again.

Jack couldn't fight the feeling that she was still watching him somehow. "There was a festival to commemorate the first new Boilers completion. The whole city turned out for it. They unveiled them on the steps of the Conservatory. Somehow, one of them had activated before they were ever installed with the rest of the Boiler network. It shouldn't have been powered at all. Regardless, the inner tank wall ruptured, it was going to explode. Most of the city had turned up for the unveiling. The crowd started panicking and trampling. Then . . . well I don't exactly remember it all, I just remember seeing the emergency release valve and running towards the thing with my wrench in hand and the next thing I remember I was being pulled out from underneath it and people were cheering. That's when I met Barin and he offered me the apprenticeship on the spot."

213

Without so much as a nod, Sallah got up and walked toward the ladder.

"Where are you going?" asked Jack.

"I need to think on this."

"To think on what?" Jack was feeling dumber by the second.

"To think on the connection between the Arc, Barin's execution, the Ichor, the metal serpents, and your apprenticeship and arrest. This Patron is responsible, that much is obvious. He's the only one with enough authority to make the other puppets dance, but I don't know to what purpose. The Ichor is being made in your city, there are machine animals that reek of death beneath your feet and a prominent and respected man was publicly executed. Of course this is all connected and we need to find to what end. For the sake of my people." Sallah quickly added, "And yours."

Jack could tell that the people of Cogrind were clearly an afterthought for this strange woman. "You think the Patron is responsible? But he's responsible for the prosperity of all of Cogrind."

"And what have his actions harvested? I may be a stranger to this place, but I know corrupted power when I see it."

Jack wanted to argue but had a hard time finding logic to counter the evidence. Barin was gone. He was told to keep quiet about danger beneath Cogrind's streets. Petty even sat in a hallowed place of honor.

Have I been so blind? To what end would he do such a thing? What could possibly be the goal?

Sallah put a foot on the top rung before turning back. Tosi bunted Jack's foot before leaping onto Sallah's shoulders.

"I am sorry about your arm. I don't know if I would've done the same."

This drew a smile from Jack. Sallah either didn't notice or didn't care.

"But I do believe we can help each other and help our people. You're strong, you're quick, have good reflexes and you're not afraid of death. You would've made a good Hunter. If you could grow another arm, I would teach you how to truly hunt."

Jack gasped and bolted upright. A joy and fear filled his being he hadn't felt since the first day of becoming an apprentice. "Sallah, ask the Headmistress for parchment and a pencil and go find Charlie. He should be at Moira's. Now, please."

Sallah started in surprise by this sudden burst of excitement. "Why?"

Jack laughed from deep in his belly. So hard, his eyes began to water and his stomach cramped. This was insane. This was the epitome of desperate and maybe, just maybe could start to fix things.

Jack wheezed out between fits. "Because that's exactly what I'm going to do. I'm going to grow an arm."

Chapter 12

Her mind was a tumble of conjecture and possibilities as Sallah descended the ladder. That boy Jack didn't help much either.

What other kind of powers does he have if he could grow an arm? He couldn't possibly, could he? This was a strange place and the people stranger. Buildings bigger than the Mothertree would shift and morph at a whim. Why couldn't he grow an arm? She touched down on the worn, wooden floor of the Workhouse.

A handful of children sat at one of the scarred wooden tables that dominated the center of the low and wide interior, giggling into their bowl of oats over a secret joke. A few more worked clothes over washboards placed over a series of steaming tubs that lined three of the four walls. A small wing to the north side of the Workhouse held twenty bunk beds crammed together side by side, ten on each wall with a small corridor between. There were even more cots stored against the wall, their frames pocked with rust. Sallah counted seventeen children in all this morning. The Headmistress was busy walking between the children's table and the laundry at the back. She looked tired. It was still early.

"Headmistress," said Sallah. Her tone was stiffer than it would've been among her own people.

Home. Dharra keeps my House strong and vigilant. Our enemies surround us both near and far.

"Yes, Ms . . . Well, Ms. Sallah I suppose? I'm terribly sorry, I don't know your last name," said The Headmistress.

"Hawthorne." Even this felt like a betrayal of some sort to her people and her mission.

The Headmistress walked up closely to Sallah in case of sensitive information. Sallah liked her more than anyone she had met in Cogrind. She was very much like Agneth, but certainly lacked her sense of irreverence. Sallah gazed at the dark stain on the children's table that wasn't there a few days ago.

—

Sallah remembered how light Jack's body felt as she carried him to Moira's. She used her leather jerkin as an awkward tourniquet to staunch the blood flowing from his shoulder. Moira let out a shriek when she opened her door to see this strange woman holding a bleeding and unconscious Jack and quickly ushered her over to the Workhouse. When the Headmistress opened her door to see the same she didn't even pause.

"On the table," she commanded, "Children go play outside now!"

Sallah did so as Claire rolled up the sleeves of her faded

217

green dress and pulled out pristine surgical tools rolled into a leather clutch from a cupboard.

"Moira, I need you to leave. Not you." She pointed at Sallah.

"I will need your assistance." Moira ran out the door, still hysterical.

Sallah stood frozen on the spot. "I'm not trained to heal."

"Then consider this your first lesson. Wash up at the sink and be sure to get in between your fingers and up to your elbows." Claire unrolled the leather clutch and picked her first instrument.

Magnificent. There was no other word Sallah could describe the Headmistress, Claire Sonnet's ability in convalescence. Claire's movements were never wasted. She was quick but never hurried, precise and sure. Once during the operation, she told Sallah to clamp off a vein. A spout of blood sprayed Claire across her face and into her left eye. She shook her head once, blinked twice and continued her work, her expression unchanged. She pulled the skin over the wound and laced it with sutures before taking a step back and exhaled deeply.

"That's the best I can do for him," Claire confessed, "It's been too long since I last operated," She turned to Sallah and studied her for the first time. "You did very well Miss . . . "

"Sallah," she fumbled in dumbstruck wonder. "That was amazing. Who trained you?" Claire tittered softly, high and breathy. It was a sound that seemed out of practice.

"My father was a surgeon. Ever since I could stand tall enough to see over the operating table, I watched him work. He would instruct me while he went about the healing arts. I became his unofficial apprentice. I loved it but when he passed I had to give up the practice. Women are not allowed to be surgeons in Cogrind." There was a sadness there not visited in a long time.

Sallah piled shocked onto dumbstruck. "Then they are fools, the crop of them. Dharra is the female divine among my people. Women hold any title they are strong enough to take. You would be an honored healer in the Greensea."

Claire pumped a spout handle several times before sticking her hands beneath the running tap over a tub, turning the water a gruesome pink. She gave Sallah a weary smile. "I do needed work here. These children need someone to care for them and I do it gladly. Including this one," Claire said, nodding over to Jack, "Now we wait and see if he's strong enough."

There must have been a look of worry on Sallah's face. Claire patted her on the shoulder with damp hands. "I wouldn't worry dear. He's much, much stronger than he looks."

—

Now staring at the scrubbed and darkened stain, Sallah realized the truth of those words. "I am of the House of Hawthorne so you may call me that if you wish," said Sallah.

Headmistress cracked a prim and proper smile.

Claire handed Sallah a thick slice of toast, melted butter, seeping into the crumb. "Miss Hawthorne then, a lovely name." She turned her head over her shoulder. "Time to switch, children. Be sure to wash the soap off your hands before eating please. No grumbling, Norman. We all work for each other." She turned back to Sallah. "Now then, what do you need Ms. Hawthorne?"

Agneth's voice whispered to Sallah. *And quite frankly I would prefer to hear my familiar name right now, seeing as I'm about to die and all.*

"I would prefer if you called me by my familiar name, Headmistress," Sallah's tone was still business-like but Headmistress understood the point.

"Then I would prefer it if you called me Claire," she said with more than a hint of that prim smile.

Sallah risked one too before lowering her voice. "He needs something called parchment and pencil. He plans to grow an arm."

Claire's smile turned to horror. "Damn fool boy!" she exclaimed before turning on her heels. "Going to take my life-saving work and ruin it!" She continued her tirade the whole time she walked to a cupboard, pulled out a small stack of parchment and conic piece of charcoal, filed to a point, and walked to the base of the loft ladder, crumpling the parchment around the charcoal and angrily throwing them over the edge. " . . . risk of infection is tremendous and if he thinks I am going to open him back up again to attempt something so astonishingly stupid, he can forget it!" She stormed off toward the coal-fired stove, punishing the bubbling oatmeal with her ladle.

With even more confusion in tow then before, Sallah walked out of the Workhouse and on to Moira's shack.

The sky was a slate of grey uniformity. Gusts from the north swept in and carried away what was left of autumn.

Smells like snow, tomorrow or tonight. The hunt and harvest had been bountiful this last summer. Hawthorne would not have need of pelts or grain this winter. Another gust blew in and snapped at her cloak she had borrowed from Moira.

She was running out of time. The Ichor could have reached the Children by now, doing Dharra-knows-what to her House. The same Ichor that slid in the unseen shadows of Cogrind. Perhaps she should find her way back into the Undercroft. The Patron's secrets were just beneath her feet after all. but the darkness below and the memory of those monstrous serpents deterred her from that option. Not to mention if the Undercroft really was the footprint of all of Cogrind, it could take her months or years to make any sort of progress in her search. And according to Jack, they hadn't reached near the bottom of that place.

Perhaps the Ichor is a byproduct of growing those serpents? Perhaps it is the byproduct of these new Arc-boilers. If Arc is in fact life force, how could it be harnessed by machines? It would make sense something as vile as the Ichor would be made by such an unnatural process. She had learned some of what she could from Jack, save for a few questions on the city and the political situation. The greater problem seemed to be asking him the right questions.

There was a connection between her blades and Jack's wrench, but to what severity and to what end were still impossible to determine.

Oh good, you found them . . .

Agneth's last words drifted to her mind. It was no mistake these blades were meant for her. She felt stupid for not asking Terran about them, but to be fair, she hadn't really had the time or the mental wherewithal. They were meant for her, but they certainly did not feel like a boon. Not like Jack's wrench. Perhaps even more disturbing to her, was the implication that if the blades were hers and the wrench was Jack's, that there was a deeper connection between them, however impossible that may have been. They must have the same origin, but neither one knew what or who that was. Just the thought made her feel claustrophobic.

Sallah decided then that she needed to keep Jack close, at least until her hunt in Cogrind was complete. That boy was a quandary. As far as Sallah could tell, each person that knew Jack liked him. She would even say they respected him. But Sallah had always been distrustful of strangers, a trait that kept her alive among the leaves and daggers of The Children. She was more suspicious of people if they did a kind turn. A small sacrifice for the opportunity to stick a knife in her back. It was exactly what she would do.

But Jack's sacrifice of his arm was not small. It changed the course of his life. Especially considering how this city treated her wounded. With the Children, each member of your House was precious. Even those gravely wounded like Jack, would be honored for their sacrifice. Their stories would be shared and passed on as knowledge hard-won. Even the Nameless, whose parents returned to Dharra, were hidden by their former Houses for as long as possible. Some Houses like her own, recruited Nameless, even if they could not take on the House name. In Cogrind though, people were parts, replaceable when broken.

She watched horse-drawn wagons file across the bridge, filled with squash, pumpkins, grain, pelts, and apples. The horses drew some sympathy from Sallah but if they were too weak to resist, then they deserved their servitude. The same seemed to be true for the city itself.

Curious to witness the many serving the few. Their shackles are not felt, but they are secured. A dozen children screamed and shouted as they ran about the edges of western Stonehall, cheeks puffed and red from the cold, as they climbed crumbling stone and petrified wood. After a while, Sallah found the right set of clapboard hovels. The one with steam spilling from every gap in the shingles was Moira's. clambering up the makeshift stairs, Sallah knocked on Moira's door three times.

Moira answered and stifled a shock. "Oh, hello Sallah. Please come in."

Moira's house felt warm wafting out to the winter winds, but Sallah declined. "Actually, Jack asked me to get Charlie for him."

Moira opened up the door a little more.

Charlie was elbow-deep in a vat of frothing water, steam and sweat dripping from his brow.

"What's wrong with him?" asked Charlie, straightening to his full height.

"He needs your help, I think. He said he was going to grow an arm."

Charlie froze for several seconds, blinking back his confusion. Then with a boisterous laugh, "By the Paragon, I have to see this. Excuse me, love." He planted an affectionate kiss on Moira's forehead and walked passed Sallah.

She turned to follow.

"Excuse me Sallah." Moira's voice was halting but determined. "I would like to speak to you for a moment, if I could."

Sallah hesitated for only a moment before she ducked into the doorway without another word.

The air was thick and wet, heavy with the sting of lye and soap. The back half of her roof was a mesh screen, which allowed the steam to pour out. A tarred, wooden flap hung against the wall in case it needed to be closed against the weather. On a table against the front facing wall, wax candles guttered against the steamy air and mixed with the lifeless light of the grey skies above. It gave the impression of constant daybreak. On the walls, hung a handful of daguerreotypes, each beaded with moisture.

The first four depicted a giddy girl of eight or nine with straight hair that flowed to her waist, sitting on a woman's lap. The woman was beautiful and composed and had Moira's big, laughing eyes. There was another of the girl and a man with broad shoulders, a broad smile, and a thick, black beard. The next one had all three, the girl kissing the smiling man's cheek. The last one in the row however, was taken in front of the Workhouse. There were perhaps fifty children lined in three neat rows. A younger-looking Headmistress stood to the right, her mouth drawn into that familiar prim smile. In the first row towards the center, the girl sat with her knees beneath her. She was a couple of years older than the first few prints. She had her arms wrapped around a neck on either side of her. One neck belonged to a thin, handsome boy with mischievous mismatched eyes and a smile to match. The other neck was attached to a tall boy with dark skin and two developing arms wrapped around the girl's waist. Each one was smiling that smile of the absolute happiness of childhood. The girl wore the biggest of them all.

Sallah stood in the center of the hovel, unsure of what was to come next.

Moira closed the door softly and walked towards Sallah, stopping a few feet short. "I wanted to say thank you." Moira's eyes pointed to her feet. "For saving Jack. Charlie saw him get arrested."

Sallah was taken aback.

"He means a lot to me. He means a lot to a great many people, though he may not know it." She looked up to Sallah, the top of Moira's head at her chin.

"Uh, you're welcome," said Sallah, "though I don't think you should be thanking me. Tosi caused him severe injury. Besides, I have my own reasons for helping him," Sallah had no idea why she would be this honest.

Moira stared at her, a fragile strength in her eyes. "That's what I wanted to talk to you about. Jack's a good boy, trusting. At times too trusting, in my view." The fragility was gone from her and all that remained was a defiance against her own weakness. "When I saw him that day . . . You're a dangerous person Sallah."

"What I have been tasked to do is dangerous by its nature and Jack can help me finish it." Sallah's voice softened. "It was never my intention for Jack to get hurt and he wouldn't have if he hadn't been so foolish." The pang of guilt began to way heavier in her chest.

Why am I explaining myself to this woman?

"That's the kind of foolish Jack is, I'm afraid." Moira gave a tired smile. "When we were children some of the older boys threw my doll my mother made me onto the roof of the Workhouse. Jack told them to start climbing and got a bloody lip and a black eye as thanks. When they were through, he picked himself up and climbed on top of the roof to get my doll." Moira turned to glance at the last of the daguerreotypes. "He sprained his ankle on the jump down. When Headmistress asked him what had happened, he said he was climbing on the tenement shacks and fell. Headmistress didn't believe him but Jack wasn't willing to make the older boys go without supper for the next week, so that's the story he stuck with." She turned to Sallah. "That's the kind of foolish he is and I wouldn't have it any other way. He will give you everything he can, Sallah, and he will do it with a grin and a laugh and then ask if you need anything else. So this is what I ask Sallah; Protect him, even from himself."

The sound of churning water filled the silence left behind by her words. Moira studied her closely.

Sallah matched her gaze and inhaled deeply. "I cannot promise that," Sallah said, not unkind, "If he does not take his own safety into account, there is nothing I can do for him."

Moira took the news with a look of inevitable disappointment.

"But I will try," Sallah lied. The words came easily to her lips. She had a House to protect. That was far more important than a stranger with a death wish. "Actually, I would request something from you as well. Don't go back to the Workhouse while Jack is still there. I would ask Charlie the same when he returns from this visit. It is possible you are being watched by the Patron. I do not want to lead him to Jack." Sallah kept her voice level.

Moira's eyes widened in fear. "I . . . of course." Moira walked to her front door and opened it. "Just know this. You may view him as just a way of helping your own cause, but to me and Charlie, he's family."

Sallah nodded and walked out the door.

"Oh and Sallah? I know what it's like to be in a place you don't want to be, surrounded by people you don't know. So if you ever need to talk, you can come by, if you like."

Sallah nodded and allowed a small smile in the direction of the young laundress. She pulled on the hood of her traveling cloak and headed south.

The wind buffeted against her cloak, but the thick wool kept its warmth. A tune began to play in Sallah's head. It took her a moment to remember what it was. It was the song from the music cylinder. She decided to grab it from the bag she stashed behind some loose rocks in the towering wall of Stonehall. From underneath the shadow of her hood, Sallah counted three Steel Watch patrols total on her walk. She could hear them long before she saw them. Two-by-two, the imposing armors announced their presence with clanking echos off stone. She waited for a fourth patrol to pass in an alley before climbing the three-high shacks and pulling some of the crumbling stones free. She grabbed her leather satchel and dropped back to the street before a fifth patrol came around the bend.

She hadn't seen the Steel Watch outside of the city proper in the four days she had been here. But now, they were looking for Jack. Things were getting complicated and quickly. It wasn't just the metal men or the Patron. Sallah was starting to like these people, well, relate to them anyway. The public execution still left a bitter taste in her mouth.

Jack wouldn't have escaped with me if Barin was still alive. Of course he wouldn't have been arrested either. He would have been a moral tale of the orphan who became a leader . . . Sounds familiar.

—

She hid after another patrol passed, before ducking into the skylight of the Workhouse, quiet as her shadow. Already she could hear a spirited debate between Jack and Charlie. She was annoyed to find Tosi sitting on the window sill above

Jack's head, looking sideways at the drawings now strewn across the bed. They had not noticed her entering. These people were so busy and self-involved, they usually didn't.

"How could you possibly control that with any sense of precision?" said Charlie.

"It would have to be attached to a dedicated muscle group. By the Paragon, we could make it a specific muscle strand within a group that needs to be flexed to perform the function anyway. I'm not about to risk my life for just a replacement arm, Charlie boy. It needs to have a few new tricks." Jack had a wide-eyed manic look.

Charlie had pushed the chair right up to Jack's bed. Both had stacks of parchment, both had charcoals already worn to nubs.

"Keep adding all the functions you want," Charlie rebuffed. "But it has to fit within a frame no greater than your proposed dimensions *and* you have to be able to lift the damn thing!"

Jack flung another piece of parchment to the foot of the bed. Tosi pounced from the sill and caught it mid-flight. He batted at it for a moment before jumping back onto his perch and began cleaning the back of his paws.

"The frame is going to have to be aluminum alloy. Strong and light is the name of the game, I agree." Jack did a double take at Sallah before continuing his feverish work. "Hey, thanks for grabbing Charlie," He said, his head in the full flight of creation. "I may have to ask you to do something else for me in a little bit if that's alright?" He looked up with a beaming smile identical to the boy in the daguerreotype.

She was thinking of all manner of conspiracy and plot and here this boy sat in the middle of them all, shy an arm he had a few days ago, beaming at a stranger that almost got him killed.

Strange doesn't even begin to cover you.

"If it will speed your recovery and your ability to help me, then I will oblige," Sallah said diplomatically.

Jack's smile turned more mischievous. "And if it doesn't?"

Charlie tried his best to keep his eye on the sketch in front of him, but his eyes peered from the side of his sockets.

"Considering you're acting like a puppy with a new bone, I know it will, so there's no need to answer. Also, I wish to speak with you in private as soon as possible. Tosi, come." She turned to go.

The serval casually hopped from the window sill to his perch on Sallah's shoulder.

"Wait a minute Sallah. We are almost finished." Jack worked his thumb over his index finger in concentration, then began to scribble furiously.

Charlie stood up and offered his chair. Sallah declined.

"Yeah, she prefers to stand," Jack said, never taking his eyes away from the sketch. He tried his best to scrawl on the parchment wedged between his knees and elbow, "Charlie a little help please? I'm afraid I don't have the right tool for the job." He finally admitted defeat.

Sallah noted it did not seem out of a sense of pride, only a sense of haste. She recalled that Jack held his wrench in what was his left hand. He had lost his dominant hand. Sallah pushed out the empathy.

Boy with a deathwish.

Charlie bent over his bed and took the sheet of parchment Jack was working on. His eyes grew big, then squinty and finally a low-rumbling chuckle. "It technically does fit within the given dimensions," said Charlie.

"Technically correct is my favorite kind of correct," said Jack, grinning while he took the paper from Charlie and re-examined it carefully. With an emphatic nod, he grabbed three more pieces of parchment to his side, rolled them up, laced the whole package tight with a bit of parcel string, and tossed it to Sallah.

She snatched it out of the air and unrolled them. The first three were a jumble of shapes with annotations written on the margins. The last one she examined carefully. She noticed some of the previous shapes had been installed and stacked and connected together inside a three bar frame with a hinge in the middle.

Despite its mechanical nature even Sallah could see that it was an arm. "You're going to build it? You are going to make your arm?" Sallah hated being the dumbest one in the room, but this idea was too incredible for her to resist. "How are you going to attach it to yourself?"

"Painfully, I'm afraid," said Jack.

This seemed to dissolve some of his effervescence. "But it should work and, given a little practice, I should be able to do everything I did before. And if we have the Paragon's fortune, maybe, a few more tricks to boot."

Charlie grinned and shook his head slowly.

"What is the danger involved with it?" Sallah asked.

Jack breathed a labored sigh. "There is a possibility—"

"A very good possibility," interjected Charlie.

"There is **a** possibility," continued Jack, "that I may die from the operation. Well, not the operation itself, more of an infection during the operation, or blood loss, or my body rejecting the prosthesis entirely."

His face and his words were at complete odds. Sallah didn't

like this one bit and it must have shown.

"But it would be a while before an infection took hold, so you would be able to ask all the questions you would need before my clock ticks its last tock."

It was Sallah's turn to shake her head in consternation. "Who will be performing the operation?"

"Headmistress, once I've had enough time to talk to her," said Jack. It was clear Jack was not to be swayed in his plan.

If she refused to, he would have found someone else and would probably get himself arrested in the process.

"So what else do you need me to do?" asked Sallah.

"Well, the Steel Watch are looking for me," said Jack.

"So I've noticed."

"And if they are looking for me, then they will be looking for Charlie and Moira and in all likelihood, tailing them wherever they go. But you're an unknown. Not to mention your well-demonstrated skills of slipping in and out of places unseen. You can get through the city without being caught." He grabbed a scrap of parchment from the bed stand, folding it up and tossing it to Sallah. "So I need you to deliver this to a man by the name of Sean Lute in the Singing Stacks District. Tell him I am calling in the favor he owes me. This should help you get there."

She unfolded it to find a sketched map of Cogrind with simple landmarks, where the Workhouse was and on the far side of the city an X with Lute and Sons scrawled above it.

Sallah let the rough map fall to the floor. "And what am I receiving in return for all this? I've already fetched Charlie and now you want me to travel to the far side of the city and risk being spotted by the Steel Watch who will most certainly be on the look out for me after I broke you out of the Undercroft, in order to meet with a stranger, who could easily sell you out, to speak on your behalf in regards to an operation that might kill you. before you are of any actual use to me." This was the first time since his epiphany, Sallah watched Jack's enthusiasm wane, "Our deal has become one-sided."

Jack let the weight of her words settle. He seemed embarrassed.

"You're right." he said, finally relenting to the reality of his situation. There was a long pause. "You do this for me and I will smuggle you into the Orchestra Pit . . . The place below the Conservatory."

She furrowed her brow.

"It's the first place I saw those serpents, and I'd be willing to bet we'll find your Ichor."

"Before you attempt to attach your new arm. That's when we go. There's no guarantee you'll survive your surgery, and I would like to get my end of the bargain."

Jack's eyes darted between her face and the parchment parcel in her hand, chewing on his lip. "Deal," He said in a tone more serious than Sallah had ever heard him. "Deliver those schematics to Sean Lute without the Steel Watch crashing around our heads, and I will get you inside the Conservatory. Just don't be seen. The Steel Watch is on alert for anything suspicious or out of the ordinary and a strange girl checking a map for an area of town she has no business being in will make them ask questions they don't need to ask."

Sallah sniffed at this. "Your city's guards are laughable. They don't so much attack so much as wait to get hit." It was true, mostly. She had no idea how she would actually win an open fight against soldiers in metal suits, but hiding from and evading them should prove trivial.

"That almost sounded like a joke," said Jack

"I will still punch a one-armed man," said Sallah.

"Fair enough. Just the same, I wouldn't be afraid to use those disappearing skills, if I were you."

Sallah folded the map and put it in her bag, along with the rest of the schematics. "If I were you," she returned, descending the ladder, "I would still have two arms."

Sallah could hear Jack and Charlie's stifled chuckling as she descended the last few rungs, with Tosi bounding after. Despite his many shortcomings, Jack was at least incredibly resilient.

Claire was in the back with the rest of the children, tying up crisply folded linens into waxed paper with burlap string. Although the folding table was already stacked high and tilting with laundry, mountains more waited on the other side of the washing vats that the children worked over. Almost all stood on rusting foot stools to reach over the side, but many more stools were stacked underneath the folding table and a handful more stood empty around the washing tubs. Claire nodded as Sallah stepped out into the blustering afternoon.

So this is Cogrind on a normal day.

The air steamed with work from open-doored shops and street grates. Cries of the artisans and craftsmen hocking musical instruments and labor saving trinkets filled the chilly streets. A dog ran between her legs and jerked with a yelp as Tosi spit at him. A chasing child tackled the dog and both went sprawling. A young mother ran over and grabbed each by the ear. Her cheeks flushed an embarrassed red as passersby applauded her capture. A symphony of clicks, clanks, and buskers came from every direction. A trumpeter regaled a playful tune to everyone and no one in particular. It was a pleasant scene. One that Sallah did not trust.

Which is your true face? A smile and laugh today, but I have seen you cry for the blood of a man who served you.

She clutched her cloak about her shoulders and weaved through an aisle of brass stalls and into the northern section of the city.

She had to spy the map under her cloak more than a handful of times. Set her out in a forest and it would be a matter of hours before she could find suitable drinking water, shelter, and hunting grounds. That was easy to navigate. Each tree was an individual signature that denoted its position in context of the rest of the forest. But these buildings were identically haphazard. Like each building was part of a matching set with a misplaced piece that was used for another building. And there were rows upon rows upon rows of them. Despite this, Sallah decided to stick to the backstreets and alleyways to lower the chance for spying eyes.

The hairs on the nape of her neck stood. It wasn't a guard. There was no clumsy shuffling of metal greaves and gauntlets that announced their clumsy presence. These were light feet, with steps that dissipated into the hum of the city. Her path took her through the northern quarter of the city and her shadow dutifully followed. She had no advantage here. It was best to stay patient and find her moment.

The Balcony Row side streets still rattled and whispered with life. A pair of valets in white wigs and dusty pink trousers flanked those in the aristocracy, heading towards the highstreet. Wrapped in vibrant hues of purple and blue, they were the only color beyond a world of steels and bronzes. Sallah looked to her shoulder to see Tosi looking behind them.

He did not like to be stalked. Sallah smirked and whispered a whistle to get his attention.

"Go on."

Tosi ran off to double back on her pursuer. It had been too long since he had hunted, and this was not so different from the Greensea after all. The street dumped out to a small intersection. With a sudden THUNK, a strip of street behind Sallah ramped up, wrapping around the face of a tall textile factory. An Arc powered wagon puffed and chugged its way up the ramp to a gateway set in the middle of the wall. She stumbled away from it and over a juggler and his clockwork monkey. She apologized quickly and took down the street as fast as walking would allow.

After twenty minutes, Tosi sidled up beside her, a rat held proudly in his jaws. Which meant Tosi got distracted, or he scared their tail away. She wove into the high street and over to the sidestreets facing the interior. Turning a tight corner, she caught a glimpse of a mop dirty blonde hair disappearing into the crowds.

A child? They were short and vanished among a gaggle of women in hoop skirts. She wanted to pursue, but Steel Watch pairs towering over the processions of people stayed her advance. Sallah prayed that would be enough to discourage any further attention. One way or another, she decided the Workhouse was no longer safe for any of them.

Stealing past the primped and powdered wigs of Balcony Row, she wound her way to the east. The great, glass eye to the north watching her progress wherever she walked.

She passed underneath the iron gate that led to the Singing Stacks district. Looking back, she could still see the top of the Metronome Tower, its glass eye looking down over the whole of Cogrind. The tall, wide, windowless buildings of the Stacks were identical, save for the unique burnish of each exterior. Sallah imagined them as rows of teeth in a massive maw. An illusion aided by the harmonious hum that poured from the chimney stacks. She glanced at the map from underneath the folds of her cloak, took a left, and walked into the small door in the wall of Lute and Sons smelting and forging.

The place stunk of scorched metal slag and ink, though the small office was clean. Corners of parchment poked out from the tops of drawers and cabinets while five metal bricks of varying hues held down others on the polished desk at the center of the room. A door opened to her right, bringing with it a cacophony of the labor behind it. Sallah turned to see an old man, shorter than she was. His wispy white hair stuck out in different impossible angles from the crown of his head.

He stared at her with no small amount of surprise, looked back at the door to check the placard, and then back to her. "This is my office alright. Which means you either need something or are in fact lost. I hope it's the former because you are very pretty and I would appreciate having a nice conversation," He smiled a beige smile and plopped down into a swiveling chair behind the desk.

What an odd little man.

"Jack Dowton sent me with this." Sallah handed over the roll of parchment from her bag, "He said he wants to call in his favor."

The old man studied them with bright, if wizened, eyes. "And what is your name, Miss?"

She hesitated for a moment. "Sallah."

He winked at her knowingly. "They call me Sean Lute. At

least my mother started calling me that and everyone else decided she would be the one to know such things. It's a pleasure to meet you Sallah, although I must say that Sallah is a rather uncommon name for Cogrind."

"That is because I am not from here," said Sallah.

Sean laughed, loud, cackling, and wheezy. "As honest an answer you would ever like to hear." Sean wiped a tear from his eye. He slipped his spectacles onto his nose and peered down at the parchments. The smile dissolved from his face as he cocked his head. "Has something happened to our friend? I mean besides starting a riot, getting arrested, and escaping imprisonment, of course" He searched her eyes.

Sallah pushed down the impulse to run. "His left arm was bitten off by a metal serpent as I helped him escape from the Undercroft," Sallah said matter-of-factly. She didn't like divulging more information than needed, but this was the only way to get Jack moving towards her goal. Besides, everyone that knew Jack seemed more than willing to help him, even if it was against their better judgment.

Sean Lute leaned back in his chair and took the glasses from his face. "A tongue that honest might get you into trouble among certain company."

Sallah tensed, her eyes darting across the room.

"Certain company Sallah, not mine. I owe Jack far more than my life and I would sooner lose my business than betray him," He shuffled to the next sheet and examined it, "And if we are not very careful I may end up losing much more than that. Do we understand each other?"

This was not a threat Sallah knew, but a pact.

"I think it best if I undertook this project personally, to ensure the strictest standards of construction. Of course I'm not as sure-handed as I used to be."

"You lie Sean Lute."

The old man laughed so hard Sallah thought he might actually die from lack of breath.

"I joke, Sallah Va Hawthorne. By the Paragon, you are so very serious for someone so young, from a burden forced on you, no doubt. Why else would you be here? Just like Jack. Children should never be weighed down with the mistakes of their forebears, but I fear that is the way of it these days." Sean leaned forward and beckoned Sallah to do the same. "These are dangerous times to be that boy's friend, which is precisely why he needs friends right now. Two weeks. The arm will be done in two weeks. Some of these components have to be custom made and I don't need any eyes looking into what we are doing," He rolled up the parchment, produced a small, gold key from under his shirt, and unlocked the bottom right drawer of his desk. He shuffled the papers inside.

An odd question came to Sallah's mind. "What did Jack do for you that you would risk so much?"

Without a moment's hesitation Sean took a metal print from his desk and displayed it for her. It was a daguerreotype like Moira's, but this was in color. "He saved my family during the Arc-boiler commencement. He saved half the city including me, my wife, and my four children. My children almost died because of the Patron's damnable Arc-boilers. The city doesn't even require that much energy. It's all for that man's vanity."

Sallah felt like she got kicked in the head. Jack explaining Arc, the empty beds at the Workhouse, the folded cots, the unused footstools, Moira's daguerreotype with the fifty children and the new Arc-boilers all smashed together to form one unthinkable conclusion.

It couldn't be, could it? "I have to go. I will be back in two weeks to collect."

A bemused Sean tried to ask what was wrong but it was too late. She was out the door and down the chilly street.

She blundered through the packed city streets, weaving back to the side streets, past the Metronome Tower, through the West Plaza and across the bridge into Stonehall. She climbed up the side of the Workhouse out-of-breath and frantic. She slid down the roof and tripped through the skylight. Sallah saw Charlie and Jack, both mouths agape.

"Jack, it's the Nameless. The orphans! They are using the children for the Arc-boilers!"

Chapter 13

It took a moment for Jack to register exactly what Sallah was saying. The Arc-boilers? He listened for a moment to the children downstairs. He hadn't seen or heard Widget in the days he had stayed in the Workhouse. There were only about two dozen orphans at the moment when typically the walls were filled to bursting with forty or more.

But that's impossible. What's to gain by that? "That's ridiculous. It would bring the city down on the Patron. Did Sean get you drunk? Oh and when will my arm be done?"

Sallah punched him squarely in the sternum which sent him sprawling back into bed gasping for air.

"Okay, I'm willing to listen," Jack breathed out after taking a moment to recover.

Sallah started in. "What you call Arc, my people call life force. It is the essence of all living things. It's like a signature. Each plant and animal possesses its own unique life force according to its kin. Before you start laughing, the reason I know this is because I can see it."

Sallah's statement was met with furrowed brows, so she continued. "You wondered why I was able to see you underneath the Tower in darkness? Because I can see your life force Jack. Just like I'm looking at you right now,"

Jack's face was unmoved while his unfocused eyes scanned about the room for the truth of it. He thought back on the day Barin burned his hands on the new Number thirteen Arc-boiler. How it seemed to move and stretch against itself, like something clawing to get out. How Barin seemed to be whispering to it. This was beyond thinking. If this were a fact he would have labored for years for a ladder of monsters. After his imprisonment, his perspective of those in power certainly changed, but to use innocents to fuel the new Arc-boilers was far beyond a battle of egos or a power grab. It was evil.

What did Barin know? What did he do?

"Let's assume this is all true then. What is there to gain in doing this?" Jack asked.

Sallah's face screwed tightly in anger. Jack reflected on how well he could infuriate people without even trying.

"I don't know yet. but you must see everything is connected. I tracked the Ichor to your city. The Ichor is death itself. No, it's more than death. It is un-life. Why couldn't it be produced by something as vile as extracting the lifeforce of a child?"

Jack worked this all over in his head. "So you're saying it's a byproduct, like slag." He chewed on his lip. "There's another similarity as well. Those serpents down there smell like a dead body and from your description, so does this Ichor. There are fewer orphans here than I have ever seen. Maybe Barin found out and tried to stop it so they had to get him out of the way, which, I guess, is why they needed me. I can do

241

a majority of what Barin could, enough anyway to keep the Conservatory functioning long enough for them to achieve their ends. But what are they trying to achieve? Annihilation of the City? Their own deaths?"

Why am I even entertaining this? It couldn't possibly be true.

Sallah paced the length of the loft, which was only four steps across. "I had a mentor as well. She was fond of saying 'The only thing more dangerous than power is the want of power.'"

Jack leaned forward with a hushed voice. "Do you think Headmistress is involved? She gets funding directly from the city." He was too close to this. He couldn't think clearly. This was all too much to reconcile.

Sallah stopped to think. "No, I don't think so. If she was, there would have been a battalion of your Steel Watch beating down the door as soon as she saw you. Not to mention how she saved your life. Besides," Sallah looked down from the loft and watched Headmistress as she stooped over a steaming kettle of broth being cooked on an iron furnace. "She loves these children. She would have to in order to keep doing this for so long."

Jack nodded in agreement.

"Uh, should I be listening to this?" asked Charlie, his eyes blinking at the implications. Sallah caught him in a cold stare.

"I'm afraid it's a little too late for that Charlie-boy. You are in it as deep as we are." replied Jack.

"And Moira," added Charlie with a baritone solemnity.

Jack didn't care for that fact either but, a sober Charlie could protect Moira, which gave him some comfort. With one hand or two, Charlie had always been devastatingly strong, and, when given the proper motivation, dangerously driven.

Moira is most certainly the proper motivation.

"So you have a theory on what the Patron is doing. But what about them?" Jack pointed to the sound of children below them. The weight of the situation began to dawn on him, and for some reason, having Sallah near brought him some comfort.

Probably because she is terrifying and violent.

"We get the rest of the children out of here," Sallah said flatly. "Find them somewhere hidden until we can stop this. After that, we still don't know the end goal for the Patron, so we go for Petty and anyone who is associated with him."

Petty's weasel face popped into Jack's mind. There was an anger boiling inside of him, an unabashed hatred for that man. Petty, the man who betrayed both Jack and his master.

Someone has got to pay for what happened to Barin. I can start with him.

"I'm in," said Jack. "Petty has perverted the idea on which my home was founded. He has killed someone that served him in order to serve himself. He is a broken cog that no longer serves the machine. I will remove him."

Sallah looked on with a mix of mild surprise and satisfaction.

Jack threw the cover from the bed and stood on unsure legs. "If it helps you as well, then so much the better." He tested the tenderness of his shoulder. "If any of this is true, we can fix two leaks with one gasket. First, we are going to need to find a way to conceal and ferry a couple dozen children, unnoticed, through heavily patrolled streets." Jack chewed his lip again before making eye contact with Sallah.

They both had the same idea.

"We don't use the heavily patrolled streets," he said, vocalizing their shared idea, "But the cat's on his own this time."

"Fair enough," Sallah replied. "Obviously it's dangerous, but at least it gives them a chance. Better than what they have staying here. And one more thing." Sallah had a light in her eyes. "I need to teach you how to fight."

Jack did not care for that look.

"You have a legion of metal men, and who knows how many of those damn snakes between you and stopping the Patron. Smiling at them won't get you very far,"

Biting his lip, Jack relented. "But how? My left was my dominant hand and it will be two weeks until I can even get the surgery."

Sallah gleefully smiled back. "Actually that works out in your favor. My mentor trained me first exclusively on my off-hand until it was equal. It was so tempting to use my right hand but you won't have that problem."

A smile as dry as the desert spread across Jack's face. "Lucky me." He sat back down on the bed. "Well we've figured out how Sallah is going to hit me in the near future, so next we need to find someplace safe and hidden."

"I . . . think I might be able to help with that," replied Charlie, "There's plenty of quiet warehouses in the Singing Stacks."

"After that, Petty." Jack's jaw clenched around the sound of his name.

—

Jack had no idea how they were going to navigate the Undercroft, but he did have a good theory; they weren't going to. If the Undercroft was the footprint of Cogrind, all they had to do was stay on the uppermost and outermost edge of the ruins, and eventually they would make it to the eastern district of the Singing Stacks. Jack volunteered to make some scouting runs. Mostly to get his legs moving, but no small part of him needed to expose himself to the memory of what happened last time he travelled underneath the city. Being terrified would not be a good look when guiding children through underground ruins. Besides, this place wasn't evil. It was a gift from the Paragon. Men in power may have been using it for awful purposes, but it was first made for everyone.

During his forays, Jack marveled at the masonry of the Undercroft. Not a seam out of place in each run of curved stones that made the outer walls. The pinnings were imperceptible dots along the slope. The care of craft was obvious. Combine that with the scale of the Undercroft, and you had nothing short of a marvel. And as far as he could tell, his theory held true. They could trace the exterior wall of the Undercroft all the way to the Stacks. The only real problem was that the only access points to the Undercroft he could find were in the city proper, away from the relative safety of Stonehall.

So they would have to ferry eighteen children across the bridge and down a twenty foot ladder without being seen. Jack had marked a preferred manhole, tucked into a blind corner in a knot of back alleys on the exterior edge of the West Plaza. They had debated on escorting two or three at a time, but decided that just gave them more chance and time to get caught or a child to do something childish. They would go as one group. They would also move at night. As Jack had his considerable night vision, he would bring up the rear to ensure no child was lost during the sprint.

Charlie volunteered to run a distraction just in case. Jack and Sallah agreed that it was a decent, if dangerous backup plan. Their destination was an empty and little used warehouse owned by Sean Lute. Jack sent what he thought was a clever message to the old man in the form of a copied invoice and check for rent at that address. Lute replied with an envelope bearing a letter of occupancy for *Fragile Cargo Transport Co.* and a set of brass keys. No questions asked.

This would of course all be overkill if Sallah's theory wasn't true. It could just be a Bass Run gang like the Mezzo Mummers Society recruiting heavily. But still, just Jack's presence near the children already placed them at some level of risk. He couldn't bear it if something happened to them because of his own stupidity.

And if Sallah's theory is true then . . . Well either way, the Workhouse is no longer safe for anyone. Sallah had timed the guard patrols after learning how to use a clock to tell time. They would leave at 3:01 am. The Watch were late when changing the guard on the graveyard shift. The plan was set. There was nothing left to do, but the doing.

—

The children were groggy and confused when they awoke that chilly night. No one told them until that moment for fear of the plan accidentally or intentionally leaking. eighteen little ones bundled against the cold and told to be as quiet as they could. Sallah would lead the group, Headmistress in the middle, and Jack bringing up the rear. Sallah climbed out of the loft hatch. Before a minute passed, she was opening the front door. The coast was clear.

Out they moved into the quiet, frigid night. It was far too quiet for Jack's liking. Their jumbled footsteps echoed off the cobblestones, their breath fogging the air as they briskly walked. What he wouldn't give for a breeze to mask their passing.

As they approached the bridge to the city proper, Sallah suddenly stopped in the moonlight. She turned and began shepherding children to the shadows of the shacks off the road. The Steel Watch was on time tonight. The lantern light just peaked into view across the bridge. It now depended on which way they turned. If it was South, they would just have to wait for the Patrol's passing. If it was North, they would be sitting ducks. Jack felt useless, cursing his left stump still gnawing in pain. The mechanized steps rang steadily louder as the Watch in their Arc-powered armor crossed the bridge. Jack and Sallah wouldn't have the benefit of confined spaces like before in the Undercroft. Besides, they could threaten the children or Headmistress. Jack had a feeling Sallah would try to attack the Watch anyway, and he knew he would follow.

The Steel Watch crossed and turned North. Jack began to creep forward along the line of children as the lantern light grew steadily brighter. He froze when he heard a familiar baritone drunkenly singing in the distance.

Two hundred yards away, Charlie was urinating in the moat. For a moment, Jack actually thought he was tippled before remembering an absolute truth; Charlie was a sad drunk. He would never be singing. The Watch turned away from the group. Jack couldn't make out what the raised voices were saying over the distance, but he did see Charlie sprinting down Stonehall while there was still a good distance between him and the Watch. The patrol gave chase, their metal suits bounding with unnatural speed. Sallah was back on the road and moving toward the bridge immediately. Jack could see the Headmistress now had a pair of little ones on her hips.

"Here we go everyone," whispered Jack as he ushered the back of the line to keep up.

Please be okay Charlie. At best, he wouldn't know until morning. Jack eyed the Watch until they rounded the long bend of Stonehall. Quiet as they could, the group crossed the bridge into Cogrind. Jack preferred this Undercroft entrance for one reason. The access point was only used for maintenance, no apartments, corner stores, or windows within a city block.

Their steps grew louder now as they tamped against the metal alleyways. Or maybe it was because they were so close to being safe from prying eyes. He picked up a straggler on his back and one on his hip as they finally hit the last stretch. Jack spotted the small ring of light as Sallah opened up the manhole to the Undercroft. They made it.

Well that's the easy part done.

Sallah climbed down first, as Headmistress started putting order to the children's descent. Jack tried to breathe against how interminable this felt. He couldn't help but squint down the alley from where they had come. Still, they weren't going to risk injury by getting sloppy now. Finally, Headmistress stepped down with a child latched around her shoulders. It was more than a little awkward to manage the manhole cover over top of the access with one arm, but Jack eventually managed it. Climbing down, Sallah was already eyeing him. The space was dimly lit in silver. Jack began handing out phosphorous torches to Sallah and Headmistress and a few of the teenagers. Despite the relative warmth in the Undercroft, there was a damp fear running through the group. Jack could feel it.

"This is how we are going to keep you safe okay?" Jack said with a broad smile. "We can move across the entire city without being seen or heard. It's like the Paragon made it just for us. Follow Miss Sallah and we will be to our new place in no time. She is a fearless warrior from a far away land."

Sallah looked upon the children with the most kindness he had seen on her face in the short time knowing her. Perhaps they just needed to hear a voice from someone in charge, but the mood did seem to lighten.

Being in charge is a new feeling. An odd mixture of pride and nausea. Soon they were moving again. Jack made the rule that your right hand had to be on the outer wall.

An hour and thirty-three minutes later, they passed how far Jack had scouted. About halfway to the Stacks. They were underneath Bass Run now. The first of the flares began to gutter and Jack resupplied the carriers with three more each. He couldn't help but notice the relief on Sallah's face. She really did hate the dark.

"You alright?" Jack asked.

Sallah was about to say something cutting before looking in Jack's eyes, taking a long breath, and curtly nodding. "I'll be able to think more clearly once this is done. I don't know what I was anticipating when I was sent to this city, but this definitely wasn't it." There was a long pause as she looked at the children behind them. "Let's just get them there safely."

Another twenty-nine minutes passed until they encountered their next problem. A host of exhaust pipes ran vertically down and perpendicular across their path. They were blocked off. Huddling together, they decided Sallah would take the lead and climb across the ledge to the other side of the pipes with one end of a rope tied to her. They would harness a child and then tie off Jack at the end, leaving enough slack for the pair to ferry them across.

Some of the smaller children began to sniffle at the prospect of dangling over a chasm.

"I'm an orphan too, you know," Sallah whispered to the first girl they were going to harness. Eve was her name. "Though where I come from we are called Nameless. But do you know what's true of both Nameless and orphans? We are braver than any other children. We have to be. So dry your eyes and look at me."

Eve wiped at her face with the back of her hand.

"I will not let you fall."

Sliding down the wall, Sallah carried herself across the ledge hand-over-hand with swift assurance.

Jack paced out the slack and harnessed up the first child. "Just keep looking at me okay?" said Jack, "And when you can't see me anymore you look at Miss Sallah alright? Here we go." Even with one arm, Jack was surprised at how light the girl was as he allowed the slack to pass through his grip and Sallah pulled from the other side.

The girl vanished from view and a long moment passed. Then the rope went slack and Jack heard Sallah whisper across the stone.

"Next one."

And so they worked. Each one passed along the underside of the pipeworks. Considering the dress Headmistress was wearing, the harnessing technique drew giggles from one side of the obstacle before the hushed laughter followed her to the other side. Jack kept peering into the darkness to scout any serpents, but one by one, the operation passed without interference. Maybe they didn't usually travel this far out to the edge of the Undercroft or this close to the surface, preferring the depths of the Orchestra Pit in the Ironworks Conservatory.

Jack estimated another forty minutes had passed during this effort. Getting to the warehouse before daybreak would be ideal, to limit any eyes that might see their little caravan once they get back topside. Right now, they would be pushing it. Jack lowered himself down the ledge. Ignoring his own advice he peered down into depths swallowed by shadow. He was used to heights, however. This was reminiscent of any other day in his apprenticeship. His boot slipped slightly and he reached out with his left hand to steady himself.

Sallah's right. I **am** *an idiot.* Jack began to fall. He hadn't harnessed himself at all. A victim of his own overconfidence. The rope was loosely knotted around his waist, unraveling and spinning him. His vision was a twisted whirl of darkness and distant flare light before connecting flatly with a stone floor. Once he eventually wheezed his lungs into working again, the entirety of the right side of his body felt bruised. He thanked the rope for slowing his momentum. Now it dangled well out of reach, Sallah and the children were patches of white light well above that.

"Don't move, I'm coming down," echoed Sallah's voice.

Jack checked his body before replying. "Just stay quiet and get them moving. We're running out of time before sunrise." Jack rolled over to his stomach, before pressing himself up, "I'll find my way to you." He thankfully still had his bag. Inside he still had three torches. He could feel one was too damaged to be safely used. The other two were in decent repair. He popped one into life with a burst of white light. "I'll see you all soon." He could sense Sallah's hesitation, but she knew

251

the truth as well as he did.

The children were the priority. Her flare stalled over the edge for a few seconds before disappearing and illuminating the walkway so out of his reach. Actually, the walkway was moving farther away each moment. The stone slab on which he stood was silently descending into what could only be described as a barely-lit, labyrinth haunted by his own nightmares.

Well at least the outside is starting to match the inside. It seemed no matter what he did, particularly what he thought was the right thing, only seemed to make things worse.

Let's solve this problem. Then we will figure out the next, much bigger one.

At the very least the first problem could also be the first solution. If this slab went down, maybe he could make it go up. He searched the rock for any sort of switch, plate, or button, but the stone was uniform and featureless. He peered over the edge. The torch revealed layers upon layers of forgotten city. Even when he and Sallah escaped, they hadn't even scratched the surface of the Undercroft. He tried to imagine the cityscape baking in the summer sun or bracing against a winter storm. Eventually, even the pipeworks were swallowed by darkness as he continued to descend.

Open-air pavilions, switch-back stairs, trellised arboretums and wide balconies, swept in and out of view from the flare's light before retreating back into total darkness. Jack tried to imagine the years of people, work, and skill required for such an endeavor. Perhaps the Undercroft was the Paragon's vision, but it was most certainly not one person's work. Still he descended, a single point of light in a sea of shadow. If being in the Proscenium was like being inside someone's body, the Undercroft felt like being in someone's mind. The design was intimate somehow, like a poem carved of stone. There was more than care in its creation. There was affection.

Amazing what you can notice about a place when you aren't running for your life.

The bottom announced itself suddenly and silently. Jack re-examined the once floating slab, vainly searching for a mechanism that would lead to his ascent. But the stone, now nestled in its base, wouldn't budge. He calculated he had another hour on this flare before he would have to use his last one. He had no idea how far he had dropped. Maybe hundreds of feet, maybe miles.

Looks like I'm taking the stairs. He decided to continue heading east, the same as his group far above him. Hopefully there would be some way up without having to double back a different direction. He even traced his hand along the outer wall, like he instructed the children. He tried to push the thought of being hunted out of his mind, pretending to study the architecture more than peering through the darkness for yellow eyes.

After twenty-four minutes of walking the stoney quiet was finally broken by a high pitched *TING* that crept on the edge of his hearing. In regular rhythm the sound grew louder as Jack started to see the edges of warm light from an archway further to the east. Jack debated if he wanted to deal with whatever nightmare was down the hallway. Again, he checked his surroundings for some stairs along the city. This time he actually found a ramp that led up and out of range of his flare's light. He turned towards the wall, before stopping and taking a deep sigh.

Sallah would kill me if I didn't at least look. This could be the epicenter of all our troubles.

It felt better to blame her than admit he was more than a little morbidly curious himself. Besides, he could stop something terrible happening, all the better. His job is to fix things, after all. He turned around and crept along the wall before peering around the corner. The archway was actually the entrance to a wide avenue. It reminded him of Stonehall, as the street curved north. The lights and sound however came from a courtyard a hundred yards away. Even from this far, the space radiated brightness that rivaled the noonday sun. The *TING* rang down the hallway in regular beats. Jack knew the sound as a hammer hitting metal. He ghosted down the avenue in rhythm to the sound, dowsing his flare.

The light hurt his eyes as he approached the courtyard. He had to lower his vision as he hid behind a colonnade, but when he saw wild green grass creeping out from the cobblestones, he gave his eyes a moment longer to adjust. There were a handful of trees among the courtyard as well. A dilapidated windmill dominated the center of the space, the tattered blades barely rotating. A U-shaped stone footing reached up into the darkness, pocked with blinding spotlights illuminating the wide courtyard it girdled. Shading his sight, he finally saw the source of the noise. It was just a man, in a black apron, a hammer and chisel in his hands, shaping a dark stone that matched the rest of the Undercroft. Jack's eyes strained as he watched the man work. He finished hammering the chisel to the corner, before putting his face against the edge he carved. He must have been gauging his lines before his eyes moved past the stone and spied Jack.

"Oh Cogs!" he exclaimed, falling backwards. He clutched his chest as he studied Jack's outline. He turned his face towards the surface before looking back at Jack and blowing out a breath of relief. "Damn near wet meself." He picked himself up and showed a relieved grin. "It's all right, come in to the light young man. Considerably preferable to the alternative."

Jack almost bolted back down the avenue, but curiosity rooted him to the spot. The man didn't seem dangerous. Jack slowly walked into the courtyard. It felt like stepping from clouded night into a spring day. "What are you doing down here?" He guessed the man to be in his fifties. Creases of dustlined sweat ran across his face and arms. His salt and pepper beard was wide and wild, but his brown eyes were friendly and sane.

"Could be asking you the same m'lad," said the man, leaning against the stone, "Not as if this is a common route for constitutionals." He pulled a canteen from his belt and took a drink before handing it towards Jack.

Jack hadn't realized how parched he was. "I got lost."

"Well I should say." He studied Jack for a moment. "I know you. You were the Tuner's apprentice, Barin. Shame that. He was a good man."

Jack handed the canteen back to the man as he spoke. It was odd to hear anyone's opinion on Barin besides his own. It made him feel oddly territorial.

"Never seen the city act like that neither," continued the man. "Where are my manners? I'm Phillip Mason." He held his gloved hand.

"Jack Dowton," he replied, gliding his hand down the stone. "You are appropriately named." Philip chuckled and puffed up his chest.

"I should certainly hope so. My family was one of the first stonecutters in Songcradle, though now I suppose we call it the Undercroft don't we." said Philip. He surveyed the stone around him with a sigh, "My family has been maintaining her ever since."

"So you live down here?" asked Jack. "Do many people live down here?"

"By the Paragon, no. I prefer the company of my wife and two little ones up top, thank you very much." Philip stood up from the stone and stretched his back. "But I will spend up to a week down here depending on the job. And this one's just about reached its end. Would you mind helping me? Rare day when I have an extra pair of hands."

Jack nodded.

Philip walked to a large canvas bag resting on the base of the windmill and returned with a glove similar to what the Mason wore. He proffered it to Jack with a smile. "You'll be needing this." It was far heavier than it should have been. Perhaps being bed-ridden had taken his strength. "Don't mind the weight," said Philip, noticing Jack's concern. "There are lodestones stitched in, see? That's how we'll be moving this beast." He went back to the canvas bag and pulled out four identical mechanized steel rails with wheels at the bottom, which he placed on each side of the stone. They connected each of the railings together, forming a small pen.

"You see this is what the Paragon discovered," said Philip, "The farmland outside the city wasn't always there. Life used to be much harder here. Craggy soil made raising crops difficult. But the stones in the area were rich in ferrous deposits." He flicked a switch on the side of each railing.

Metal sheeting on the interior folded down and the stone grumbled as it lifted into the air a few feet from the ground.

Jack stared in dumb amazement.

"Once he figured that out, all he had to do was get to work." Philip nodded to Jack, who lifted his gloved hand. The pen and stone inched forward in response.

"Easy as," said Philip with a satisfied grin.

There was something so simple and satisfying with how it responded to his movement, as if it was sliding on ice. Philip directed him to the interior of the u-shaped stone footing. As he walked, Jack couldn't help but look at the windmill. Even compared to the Undercroft, the windmill felt much older still.

"No idea how it keeps turning, but turn it does," said Philip. "If my father was to be believed, it is the oldest structure in the Undercroft."

They found themselves at the base of the footing. Fifteen feet above his head there was a gap in the stone the same size as their slab.

Philip placed a curved handle into a socket on the railing and began to crank. "Hop on the stone would you? I'll need you to guide it in. All the footings have been damaged after that Arc-boiler collapse. Me and the other Mason's been working overtime to cut and replace."

Jack had no idea that this was even a profession, let alone their necessity. He jumped on the stone and felt it bob slightly under his weight. He began to ascend, and he realized how he had descended down there on that platform. It must have been the same general principle. Working together, they adjusted the height and width until they were precisely lined up. Stepping onto the railing, Jack guided the tons-heavy stone into its place. He could feel the slight resistance of the new stone sliding into place. Jack lowered his glove and assessed his handiwork. It looked like it had always been there.

"Well done lad." Philip called from below.

From his vantage, Jack stared out into the darkness. Now that he knew what to look for, he felt confident he could find a lift near his original route. How else would the Masons get down there to maintain the footings? Philip began to crank in the opposite direction, slowly lowering him down, when a pinpoint of light blinked into existence a few feet from Jack's face.

A quick *tic tic tic* quietly kept time as it floated in front of him. As Jack lowered into the light, he saw that it was a lightning bug. He reached out and lightly clasped it in his hands. It was heavy for its size. Jack rubbed his eyes at what he was seeing. It was made of copper patina. It was a clockwork creature, delicate in its engineering. The design was identical to its living counterpart. Jack had caught enough as a child to know, though the creature was double in size. It wandered about his hand for a moment. It certainly acted like a real bug. It didn't seem to possess any predetermined behavior either like a windup toy in the shop windows so far above. It flashed softly the familiar blue of Arc-lamps before flitting its wings and floated up into the darkness.

What you call Arc, my people call life force.

Pieces to the puzzle were clicking into place. Jack did not like the picture.

"What's got you so mesmerized?" asked Philip.

"A bug. A mechanical bug?" He watched as the prick of

flight flashed against the swallowing darkness.

The frame lowered to the ground.

"Ah a good omen then," said Philip. "They say the Paragon made a whole mechanical menagerie. A love letter to his long lost paramour if legends are to be believed. Could be that the creature you held was crafted by the Paragon's hands himself. All this was made before the Age of Flames, of course. One of the many things lost. Now it seems the only creatures left are the ones who can survive in darkness. Frankly, if rumor is to be believed, it's best to stay in the light. They say clockwork snakes are roaming about, twice the size of a man." Philip took a deep pull from his canteen. "Can't imagine the Paragon in all his wisdom would've built something like that."

Jack could hardly believe his ears. "Four times," said Jack.

Philip choked on his water before staring blankly at Jack. It took a moment before something dawned on Philip. "Right, you were his apprentice. Barin made an awful lot of noise about 'em before his . . . conviction."

It was Jack's turn to stare blankly.

"Did you not know lad? Oh yes. He was already under some scrutiny with his handling of the new Arc-boilers, but spreading that kind of information . . . well, all but sealed it I'm afraid. Hard enough to keep the peace and order as it is without gossiping about monsters beneath the citizenry's feet." Philip offered water with his words.

Jack took the canteen. *Barin didn't want me saying anything. He wanted to risk his own reputation. Hard not to take the warning seriously then.* "How well did you know him?"

"Only professionally, but I knew him in that particular capacity for two decades. To be

frank, I doubt anyone knew him beyond professionally.

Dedicated man he was." said Philip.

Jack returned the canteen. "I had no idea. . . that he was talking to so many about these serpents."

"That's why I'm down here. Couldn't risk one of my workers if the rumors were true. If there is risk involved, might as well be me doing the risking,"

"Who are you?" asked Jack.

"I told the You. Philip Mason. The Mason." Philip smiled with no small amount of pride. Jack gaped at him curiously. "You're responsible for the entire Undercroft?"

Philip chuckled. "Just the stone my boy, and even then, my Masons do plenty more work than I do or even could. But they come to me for their assignments."

"If you ever got to know Barin better, I'm sure you would have been friends," said Jack.

Philip dusted off his hands. "Well then, fair's fair. You help me, I help you. Let's get you out of here."

"I'm looking to go to the Stacks, as close to the eastern gate as possible. I don't wish to keep you from your family any longer than need be. Perhaps a map if you have one?"

"Well, I can certainly make one." Philip pulled some charcoal from his bag and a thick sheet of parchment. His precision in stone translated to parchment as Philip sketched an outline of the base floor of the Undercroft.

There were layers of untold history here and the Mason sketched through it. Thankfully it was not going to require much navigation.

"That way's east," said the Mason pointing into the darkness, "Stay along this boulevard, take the third right along the canal and you'll find the lift you need. Thanks again for the help Jack and best of luck to you. In all you do."

"I tried to activate one before but it didn't work," said Jack.

"Did you step off, and then back on?" asked Philip.

Jack could feel his face flush. "No. No I didn't."

They shook hands. Jack popped a flare as he began to round the ancient windmill in the center of the courtyard.

"One last question Mr. Mason. What is this windmill?"

Philip sighed deeply before answering. "Always bothered me as well. But all my father told me was what his father told him. We don't repair it. Just keep it as it is." Philip placed a calloused hand along the aged stone, looking at the slowly moving blades. "He told me It was where the Paragon was born."

Jack walked around it until he came to a collapsed section of the wall. The stones lay scattered inside its base. But the Spurn Wheel on the second floor still turned. He snapped back into focus. He needed to find the Children and Sallah. "Thank you again Mr. Mason," said Jack.

Philip chuckled. "If we ever meet again lad, just call me Philip."

Jack turned and began down the corridor, a pinpoint of light in the ocean of darkness.

If the Patron rediscovered how to make Arc-boilers, why couldn't he rediscover the Paragon's clockwork creatures as well? And just like the Boilers, he got it wrong. Horribly wrong.

As Jack walked, it was becoming more difficult not to believe Sallah's theory. But the end was still missing. What was the motivation for it? Legacy? If it ever came to light what it took to make the Boilers, The Patron would be demonized forever. Expansion? According to Crowley, Cogrind was only tapping a fraction of what was possible with the original Boiler Chain to begin with. There would be no point to their construction. There were still gaps but Jack felt something different now. He didn't want to just survive. He was determined to understand why anyone would do this. He still secretly hoped it would all make sense. He meant his work for the people of Cogrind, not those in charge of it.

He followed Philip's map and true to his directions, he found a similar stone platform set in its base. He stepped on and immediately the slab began to lift silently upward. He rose quickly through the Undercroft with a new appreciation for all that surrounded him, all the wonders above it held in its foundation.

Eventually, the platform came to a rest. He flipped through the parchments until he found the right one and began walking south in hopes of finding his crew. After eleven minutes, he heard his name from a distant voice.

"Jack?" came a whisper. It was Sallah from somewhere nearby.

His flare had blinded him. Twenty yards ahead Sallah stepped from the shadows, with Headmistress and the children in tow.

"Thank the Paragon," said Jack, "Everyone alright?"

Sallah nodded her head. "It's good to see you. We walked until we were unsure of how far we travelled. We were debating on next steps when we saw your flare."

Jack smiled in the white light. "No need for that now. Follow me."

Sallah took up the rear as Jack began to lead them. Previously, he was going to go by trial and error to find the right access but there was no need now thanks to the Mason. Another fourteen minutes passed until he found the access hatch they needed. Pulling down the ladder, he opened the hatch top to the early morning chill of the Singing Stacks. The access emptied into an alley facing the southside of the warehouse. After a few minutes of transporting the children up, he unlocked a small door.

The warehouse was massive and empty, save for the Southeast corner where partition walls had been put in place. Rounding the partitions, they found a comfortable space larger than the Workhouse. Cots with thick blankets lined three walls and a long galley kitchen had been installed against the fourth. Barrels of food lined a larder with no laundry equipment in sight. Headmistress began to tear up as she hurried herself about the children, getting them settled and trying in vain to keep them quiet.

"I didn't think I would see you again," said Sallah. "That would have made our partnership difficult."

"Was that a joke?" said Jack

"No. It was the truth." She turned and saw the little ones already playing improvised games in their new home. "Now that they are safe, I will begin tracking Petty properly. And you should get ready for your surgery."

He turned to her with the accomplished sigh of a bad plan poorly executed to undeserved success. "Indeed." He felt the gnawing pain of an arm that wasn't there. "He must be the weakest point in this conspiracy. Besides, my accidental foray into the Undercroft provided us some answers. I don't know if they will help us yet, but we are at least getting closer to seeing the whole picture."

Chapter 14

Sallah knew Petty was a coward. But he was smarter than either she or Jack had given him credit for. There were no less than two Steel Watch near his person at any given time he was in public. Despite how obviously he valued his life, Sallah got the inkling he enjoyed the vanity of it as well.

The tip of the Metronome Tower tickled the bellies of low rolling clouds that morning, gorged with snow. Petty was dressed in a milk white woolen cloak, the collar lined with fox. For two weeks Sallah had followed him and he never once wore the same cloak twice. He had two guards as he entered through the main golden doors of the tower. One opened the door, the other entered, Petty followed and the first closed the door behind all three. Sallah walked down a side street, dropped from an exhaust vent and scrambled onto a second floor awning before lifting herself onto the roof. She was learning the streets quickly. It proved a forest of a sort, though a lifeless substitute, except for the sparrows, raccoons, and pigeons she disturbed.

The city was more like a maze from some of the higher roofs. More than once, she dove for cover as the Sky Train hurled past the rooftops on pneumatic rails. That would be something she would never get used to.

No matter how far she climbed though, the Metronome Tower was higher. Heavy maroon curtains were pulled over many of the steep, thin windows. Petty could be behind any one of them, so Sallah had set about finding which one that would be. Jack was for the moment, mentally and physically unprepared for a kidnapping and the better she understood this place, its people, and especially Jack, the better. She trusted him, she did, but that didn't mean he was without weakness. If he could be manipulated, she would be exposed. His friends were the only liability Sallah had found so far, though one could argue their strengths could far outweigh the risks.

And Moira can certainly stitch a fine blouse.

After a few weeks, she looked like a citizen, as Moira slowly replaced her worn travelling garb for pieces far less conspicuous in much better repair.

The rooftops provided another perspective. The single-mindedness of Cogrind could have proved a boon or a plague. It depended to which side the mob swayed.

She picked her way lightly from tin chimneys to brass balustrades as she circled about the tower, ornate and uniform in decadent striations. The ground level was made of contoured arches that rippled out from the golden double doors onto the street. The second depicted workers clad in aprons, with arms stretched over their heads clasping a gear with both hands. The next level was wave upon wave of what Jack told her was written music. Bars swelled and crested as schools of notes rode the currents. The final portion of Metronome Tower was a flat disc, half gold half glass cut at a sharp angle. The towering eye wept with melted snowflakes.

The wide thoroughfare that skirted the Tower made it stand unassailable from the surrounding rooftops. To add sweat to the wound, the tower was precisely that. The other buildings shrank beneath its gaze. Sallah didn't like the idea of infiltrating The Tower to begin with. She had never been inside and Jack had only one account of it, an ever-shrinking echo of rooms moving towards the central elevator. She would much prefer to take Petty at his apartments but he never left by the front entrance on the High Road. Sallah had even cancelled one of Jack's training sessions three days prior just to observe the entrance.

Petty had walked in wearing a regal blue cloak and polished black boots that day, but he never came out. Sallah had set about to find another way that Petty had managed to sneak out unseen. So, she watched the gate she rode in underneath the Tower to no avail. She spied a few more underground gates and service entrances but Petty had never emerged from those either. There were simply too many, too well spaced out. To make tracking worse, he never approached the same way on consecutive days either. One time he would pop out from an alleyway. The following day from the west, down the highstreet of Balcony Row. Each time a new route and a new cloak.

The City was changing as well. Posters with Jack's face plastered many squares and public buildings with the word *DANGER* written in wide letters. It wasn't a daguerreotype image, which she learned through Jack's annoying enthusiasm, was a lifelike acid burn on tin of a moment in time. This was but a sketch of his face. The artist tried to make him look older, but it was an unconvincing execution. His eyes were beady instead of bright, his lips were pursed and serpent thin, but the rest was him. His face was framed with a gear broken in half. Cogrind letters were so blocky and commanding to her eyes. The smaller print on the poster said

the citizenry have the responsibility to alert the Steel Watch with any information regarding this dissonance to our great harmony

Sallah was unimpressed with the feebleness of this smear campaign. The mob may be a stupid, fickle herd, but an individual's thoughts were still their own. There were more guards making rounds as well, but marching in pairs through the blustering winter winds meant very few ever peered up to Sallah's perch along the roofs.

She watched the tops of heads braid among the city streets.

How many were a part of that riot? Now, walking around with your civilities intact?

Sallah studied the Tower from entrance to eye. But isn't that their strength? As a whole, they could achieve impossible things, that much was evident. They dominated their surroundings, bending it to their vision of perfection. And was it so wrong? They praised themselves for their own hard labors to make each other greater, a cyclically infectious sort of society where participation was praised for the sake of helping one's neighbor. At least that's Cogrind's history as Jack explained it. It was clear that these people were striated now. Instead of standing on each other's shoulders, the few sat with obese wants atop the many. It was an unbalanced proposition and one that is waiting to tumble. Barin's execution was proof of that.

She doubted she was going to have better luck tracking Petty today. Besides, she had other responsibilities. Jack was getting his arm attached and Claire had requested her assistance.

"You aren't squeamish at the sight of blood. That is a very good trait to possess as a surgeon," Claire said.

Though Moira meant well and was the first to volunteer, she was not well suited to help in this case. Though she had proven useful in other ways. Sallah's heart went out to Moira. She had to abandon her laundry for the sake of Jack and Charlie. Moira did so without a moment's hesitation.

Sallah raced across the rooftops, hurdling over alleyways and frozen laundry lines. For a moment she let herself be a Huntress chasing some phantom game. The frozen air clung to her throat. Her eyes stung with snowflakes and wind. Agneth's voice came playful and honest to her mind.

"No matter where you may find yourself sweet child, remember that you are always a Huntress and they are only your prey."

She closed her eyes and immediately tripped and rolled on an errant duct.

Different kind of forest.

Sallah laughed to herself. Tosi's face looked down on her judgmentally. She hobbled down three awnings and slipped through the wrought iron gate that marked the entrance to the Singing Stacks. A small side benefit to the increased patrols in Stonehall and Balcony Row meant less patrols in the Stacks. For the moment, Jack, Sallah, Moira, and Charlie were staying in the Warehouse as well. They would move elsewhere soon, probably Bass Run. Charlie was working some connections he had in the southern district, where there was no love lost for the Patron or the Steel Watch.

The Warehouse was warm and well lit when she announced her presence with a gust of snow from the side door. Jack sat on a steel table lined with linens, Claire was standing next to him. They were looking at four different schematics, lit from the back. A host of candles surrounded the table like a halo, each one placed in a polished tin candle holder with a high curved reflector, creating a bright stage of light around the pair.

Claire's clutch lay unraveled at the head of the table, her tools gleaming. "Hello dear," welcomed Claire, "Wash up won't you? Be thorough please, just like I showed you."

There was a looseness to the headmistress, a relaxed posture and demeanor foreign to her character, foreign but welcome.

"Of course Claire. Where are the children?" asked Sallah.

Claire smiled with confidence. "With Moira and Charlie safe and sound on the other side of the building. Now, if you would please wash up and if Tosi would be so kind as to retire."

Tosi weaved his lengthy body up a ladder and padded down a catwalk and lay down in a circle to watch the proceedings from above.

"We will begin shortly," said Clair.

At the far end of the table was a plain copper box about the width of the table, with no particular markings. Sallah felt her eyes being pulled toward it.

"Want to see it?" Jack smiled though his shoulders were tense.

A sudden weight lodged in her chest. She was responsible now.

He's the only one who can help me. Better for me to do this than anyone.

She nodded genuinely. Jack hopped off the table and over to the box. Two latches released crisply and he pushed open the top. It was shadowed away from the reflected candlelight. She turned the box towards the reflected light. It was in six parts; two sections for the upper and lower arm each, then the banded interlocking coverings polished and oiled to a brilliant sheen. The arm as a whole was roughly a third larger than his natural one.

"It's an aluminum alloy frame, precipitation-hardened," beamed Jack, a tone of reverence in his voice. "The cranks are tempered steel, the wire leads are high tensile, wound tungsten. Each movement is balanced by six gyroscopes in both the upper and lower arms and powered by this." He pulled a copper cylinder from underneath the table, the length and width of his forearm. "Muscle movement is amplified by the energy in the Arc-tank, meaning I should be able to do more things with this than I ever could with the arm I was born with." Jack flicked the Arc-tank at Sallah.

She snatched it from the air. It weighed a little more than the bronze it was made of. It hummed with energy in her grasp. Sallah spied him biting his lip and staring blankly at the space just above her head. "No fear in notching up another stupid choice in your ever-growing list?"

Sallah's words raised a worn smile to Jack's lips.

"Perhaps you are simply stupid after all."

"I've been told pain is inevitable," Jack said, looking out from eyes baggy and purple with lost sleep. Yet he seemed a little steadier, his breathing slowed. "We're in a fight, are we not?"

"We are. But If you go through with this operation, it could fail in a hundred different ways. Your words. It's very difficult to fight when you aren't breathing. Why put yourself at such risk?" Sallah's voice rang with sincerity. She remembered the weight of his limp body clinging to life and she began to feel it again.

He blinked twice then visibly registered the question. "All my life I wanted to be a part of it, the city, I mean." He reached for the wrench in its holster. He had switched it to his right side, "I tried to be an apprentice and was rejected. They didn't want me. That didn't stop me though. I taught myself how to build and repair. And then I fixed the new boiler and I became the Master Tuner's apprentice. It was exactly what I wanted, but it wasn't what I remember about that day. I remember the fear in peoples faces when they thought they were going to die and the relief when they realized they weren't going to because of what I did, the risk I took. And now it feels like the same thing. They don't just don't want me, they are hunting me. I saw the fear in the little ones' faces and their relief when we made it here." He raised his new arm and let the light bounce off the radiant metal, dancing with an inner fire of its own. "And if this arm works, I mean actually, really works, it could help a lot of people. So yes, it's worth the risk. We are broken, but I can fix it."

Jack delicately laid the wrench into the relaxed grasp of what was to be his left hand.

Sallah could see the grip of the fingers formed a perfect contour to the handle. The outside of the fingers were flat and wide, so that when clenched they formed a ball of plate metal. He started chewing on his lip again.

"Thank you for saving Tosi, Jack," said Sallah, her face remained emotionless, "He's very important to me and you

271

saved him and there is a great deal to be said for that in my eyes. Besides," her face straightened into a practiced stoicism, "it does seem that with all the stupid things you do, at least some good comes from them."

He glanced at Sallah from the corner of his eye as a lopsided grin grew on his face. "Then get to cutting. And please don't screw this up."

—

Sallah counted twelve of Jack's blinks before the sleeping agent took hold. Claire's gloved hands opened Jack's eyelids separately. Each eyeball had rolled back in his head. The patch of linen covering her mouth moved as she spoke a few silent words over Jack. A bleached cloth covered the table. Jack's arm lay toward the center of it. The stub still glistened with iodine and alcohol. Claire took the two sections that made the new upper arm and examined the back-lit schematics. This was the only piece of construction they were tasked with. Pending Jack's recovery, he would install the rest. The sections slid together on a rail-and-guide system and with a final push, a permanent wedge clicked into place behind the pinion. Where the arm met the amputation, the two halves formed a cone recess which would cradle the bone and sinew. She then tightened four latches, securing the guides together. Setting it aside and orienting it bicep up, she beckoned Sallah with a finger and brought her surgical tools between them. Sallah did her best to slow her breathing. She had faced death before, so why did this frighten her so much? It wasn't the blood. She was a Huntress. Blood was a part of her vocation. Perhaps that was it. She was now tasked with the opposite of all that she knew. Not to destroy, but to mend.

Claire studied her own diagrams of where and how she placed his muscles during the amputation. After she had finally given her consent for the surgery, her input had been invaluable in forming Jack's revised plans for his arm. She took the scalpel into her thin fingers and made the first incision. The work was minute, yet exhaustive. Sallah's hands were kept busy with clear and decisive commands from Claire, often for clearing blood or handing Claire new instruments. Jolts of static charge coaxed the muscles away from his bone. Claire's fingers entwined sinew to wire, muscle to cable, each strand and group of muscle in syncopation with another. She fed the wire and cable through specific holes in the upper arm chassis.

Every fiber of tendon had to be properly allocated and perfectly attached to a particular cable assembly. And Claire did it to an exacting copy of her diagrams. The candles melted half their life away before Claire called Sallah to set the four screws that secured the chassis to Jack's shoulder. She pulled the skin down inside the frame and around the interwoven muscle. The drill hissed as it drove the screw through bone, as the screw head nestled flush with the chassis. Three interlocking teeth clamped over his shoulder, further securing the overall assembly.

"I will say one thing about Jack," Claire panted after forcing the teeth to mesh, locking the arm assembly into place, "he's thorough in his designs."

Sallah studied his face. The sleeping agent was powerful. If not for the slight flush to his face, he could have been a corpse. The first of the candles dripped away the last of its life by the time Sallah removed her mask. She wiped away the ring of condensation around her mouth. She didn't think she could be so tired from doing so little. Claire's fingers gingerly turned the augmentation slightly right, then left, the seam between flesh and metal tightly bandaged. Straightening her spine, she sighed wearily and loosened her own mask.

"Thank you Sallah." Claire smiled. "You've got the healer's touch in you,"

Sallah wished that were true. She smiled in thanks and gazed at the augmentation. It proved a difficult task and all they had for proof was the nub of an arm. It was up to Jack now.

What will the pain be like? Will we have to sedate him?

"How long will he be asleep?" Sallah asked. It was hard not to keep the worry from her voice.

"No more than eight hours," assured Claire, after checking her fob watch, "Help me carry him to bed. I'll carry the rest of his arm."

The first hour felt interminable. Half of her wanted to look for Petty, though the other half knew it would be fruitless. She hated feeling restless. Sallah took one of the shirts from the mending stack and a sewing box and sat on the bench at the foot of the operating table. Her stitching was clumsy. The children made it look easy, their small fingers nimble and practiced, their stitching tight and precise.

The students of a surgeon.

She felt Claire as she sat at her side, a shirt in one hand, a threaded needle in the other. For a moment, Sallah let her hands rest on her lap and watched Claire work. The woman's hands were fatigued but sure. Sallah studied the movement closely then picked up her shirt. Slowly the stitching became tighter, the seams straighter. Hours were lost in the rhythmic pattern and movement. Without a word, Claire took to her feet and went to the pantry. She returned with wafers, a wedge of cheese and cured sausage. They ate in silence, with only the crunch of stale crackers as conversation. When Claire began folding her hands in ache, Sallah took the food and returned it to the pantry.

They took the sheet from the operating table and washed it together. Without the steaming vats of water and soap, they made due in a large basin. They draped it over a clothesline that circled above the cast iron stove to dry.

"Sit with me Sallah," Claire sat back down at the table, "We have operated on the same man twice, yet I know almost nothing about you." Her elbows rested uncharacteristically on the table. She looked tired and accomplished. For once, her smile came easy, her eyelids drooped with fatigue.

Sallah sat down across from her. She knew Claire wouldn't sleep until Jack woke. "What would you like to know?" There was more than a whisper of Agneth to this woman.

"Everything, dear. You come from a very different people and I suspect a very different place. Tell me about your home."

Sallah hesitated for a moment. "I do not think you will believe me if I told you about my home." But she was grateful for the time to recount her House, so far away now.

Her story jumped back and forth for context and her own tired mind. Claire's eyebrows raised when she told her of her home, the twelve Houses and Dharra, Goddess of nature. She smiled when Sallah told her she was Druida, elder of her House and a leader among the Children of Dharra. Sallah spoke of Karra, Timma and Tommin, of Nissa and Sorren. Sallah told her of Agneth and Terran and the Ichor and her venture here in a flood of confessions. The burden was heavier than she realized and sharing it was more needed than she knew. Claire did not flinch at her violent actions and smiled at her acts of kindness. The few questions Claire did ask dealt with how Sallah felt and not what she did.

The sun fell underneath the high set windows before darkness forced a break from conversation. They lit two kerosene lamps and placed them on either side of the table. The orange light revealed Jack lying on his back in the alcove of beds. His chest rose and fell in drugged sleep.

Claire's fob watch clicked shut. "Another ten minutes dear." She walked to the medicine cabinet and removed a small satchel. She sat on Jack's bed. Opening the satchel, she withdrew a syringe and a small vial filled with a golden liquid. "This should ease the pain when he wakes, which will be considerable." The needle pierced his arm and the liquid injected beneath his skin, "We may need to put him back under if the pain is too great."

He stirred immediately after the last of the painkiller was spent. They had taken the liberty of immobilizing his shoulder. Despite Jack's precautions, Claire didn't want his shoulder moving against the augmentation so soon after surgery. His breathing became irregular as his body fought against waking. But soon his eyes lazily fluttered open to slits.

Sallah climbed onto the other side of Jack's bed.

He swallowed dryly. His breath reset to a conscious rhythm. Mismatched eyes focused on Sallah. " . . . Good?"

"Yes."

He exhaled deeply. The left side of his face was drawn in a slight smile.

"The pain . . . "

"How bad is it?" asked Claire.

Jack waited a few moments before answering, his eyes unfocused again."Worse." Jack smiled a little more.

Sallah thought perhaps the sleeping agent was having an unexpected effect. "Are you alright?"

He nodded. His eyes gradually widened. "Water, please."

In half a blink, Claire pressed a cup onto his lips. Jack settled into a rhythm of shallow sips and long sighs. He still hadn't looked at his arm. He turned away from the cup and settled his head back into the musty pillow. After the first hour, he was awake but his mind was distant. Sallah closed her eyes and watched him. Most of his life force didn't radiate as brightly as it had before, a consequence of the sleeping agent, she surmised. What surprised her most was that life force foreign to the rest of his body; the top of his head and left eye. They blazed a chromatic fire swept up in a prairie wind, with all the dancing tongues reaching for Jack's new brace. They were bright and expectant, no colors of fear or pain or weakness.

It's as if those pieces of him are excited.

She opened her eyes and there lay only a boy, with a metal cone attached to his shoulder in place of his arm. He breathed through pursed lips and finally studied the result of his surgery.

"Good," he breathed. "Perfect." His eyes began to glisten as a smile creased his face. He fumbled at his eyes and hoisted himself to a sitting position.

Claire's hands instinctively reached out to stop him, but she allowed him some movement once he settled back on the pillow. He searched the room with hungry eyes until he found the metal box with the rest of the augmentation. He whipped the blanket off his body and almost made it to his feet until Claire put an adamant hand on his chest.

"You have already tested my patience and destroyed my better judgment with this operation. You will at least obey what I say now: Rest."

Jack clicked his teeth together and admitted defeat.

"Might a recovering patient ask for the company of his best friend as he rested?" Claire blinked slowly before bolting up to her feet. "What an absolutely insufferable child," she fumed, walking to the end of the partition wall. "Foolish, headstrong, practically asking for injury." She slammed the tin cup on a cupboard shelf and stormed off, insults still flowing from her mouth.

"What a lovely woman," said Jack, turning back to his metal bicep.

Sallah had to ask the question. "Once the dust has settled, do you think this arm is really going to work?"

The smile returned to his face. "I have absolutely no idea, but I do know that I've tried my damnedest. And so did you. Thank you. Besides, even if it doesn't work we may still be able to use it," Sallah's eyebrows furrowed before he continued, "Like for a door-knocker, or perhaps a paper weight." A laugh escaped her before she realized it. Jack beamed, thoroughly pleased with himself. "About time. I know it will work. It will do everything it is designed to do, that's not the question. The real question is will I be strong enough and smart enough to use it." Jack's shoulder twitched, but the machine did not react.

From around the partition Charlie walked in, carrying a worn toolbox and wearing a worried look. As soon as he saw an awake and smiling Jack, the worry was quickly replaced with a large, smug grin.

"All right Charlie," said Jack.

"All right Jack," said Charlie. He approached his friend in long strides. "Let's take a look at the damage." He walked to the foot of the bed, set down the toolbox and peered at Jack's arm. "Everything looks to spec. And it only makes you look twice as hideous as before."

"That still makes me twice as pretty as you," said Jack.

"Can you feel anything in your muscles? Pain, discomfort, tension?"

Jack snorted. "Considering I just came out of a surgery to attach wires to my flesh, yes there is a considerable amount of all three."

"Can it, smartass, I meant your muscles," Charlie said. "Can you feel them at all?" There was a hopeful twinge to his voice. Jack shook his head, "That was probably too much to hope for right out of the gate but that's what we planned for.."

Charlie went to the wide table, pinched the metal box between his hip and his hand and carried it back over to the bed. He unlocked the box. Sallah watched Charlie shiver like a grateful child as he opened it.

"Right then, my turn." Charlie set to work.

Quips flew back and forth as he slid the outer casings into place. As it came together Sallah realized the design was actually quite simple. It took less than an hour before Charlie was lifting the final piece from the box and fitting it around Jack's neck. His hand was calm as he slid the piece across Jack's shoulder and into place with a ringing *cling*.

Charlie took a few steps back and scratched the back of his neck. "What do you think?"

Sallah couldn't help but tilt her head. Jack looked off

balance but . . . regal, at least in the fashion of Cogrind. The bronze casing swam with the circular current of buff marks from numerous polishings. The upper forearm and outer bicep bore three matching slats that folded inside the casing. The inside was striped with bands like the muscle that should have been beneath it. The shoulder boasted a thick, three-quarter cog for a pauldron that swept down across the length of his shoulder and formed a high straight half collar, the top adorned with interlocking whole notes.

"Whole notes were always my favorite," said Jack, "Besides, I thought they give it a nice sense of completion."

She knew he couldn't help but gloat a little. And he deserved to. Sallah agreed the arm was beautiful in an alien sort of way, even if the whole of him was hopelessly mismatched.

"Just one last thing to do," said Charlie, lifting the Arc-tank from the case. With a practiced grace he slid the receiving collar down and popped it securely into the back of the arm with barely a puff of glowing steam.

Still Sallah couldn't help but wonder how many lives that might have been.

How many lives has the Ichor taken?

No, she could not worry about her House now; one suicidal task at a time. The arm began to stir almost immediately, small gears attempting to find rhythm with each other while pulleys whined as they tightened cords. Jack winced more than once but Sallah was sure he was hiding more pain than he let on. Then it sat in silence

"Here we go." Jack reached over and turned the Arc-tanc's knob to full open. He grabbed one of Charlie's screwdrivers and slotted into one of the small screws at the base of his wrist and turned. His arm hissed as he groaned in pain and concentration. Until finally he let off the screw. Jack panted in relief "This may turn out to be a bit of a process."

"But you felt something right?" said Charlie.

"Mostly just the excruciating pain."

"That's a good first step. Pain means blood is circulating and nerves are firing, said Charlie.

Sallah could see the muscle test took more out of Jack than even he first realized.

His head sagged unwillingly to his chest before Charlie took his leave. "Big first day mate, tomorrow should be twice as fun."

"Why do all my friends enjoy seeing me in pain?" Jack's eyes drooped.

"Because you can take it mate, and then some." Charlie stepped out of the partition and back to mind the children.

Sallah did her best to not outwardly react to being called his friend.

Jack closed his eyes soon after. Sallah decided to do the same. She wanted to understand what this did to him on more than a physical level. His aura had become a shimmering white folding in on himself. The aura closest to his body was exactly the opposite. A razor line of chromatic fire danced along his outline.

"You're looking at me aren't you?" asked Jack, his voice monotone with exhaustion.

"Yes."

"What do you see?" His voice drifted.

"I don't know. But whatever you turn out to be, you'll be a powerful one."

Jack snorted in reply, "Then why do all I feel is a lot of pain?"

Sallah opened her eyes as he watched him drift to sleep.
"Because pain is strength in its first form."

Chapter 15

The Oak tree on the hill just outside of Stonehall's stone walls rattled with bitter gusts. The sun squinted sickly from behind thin, grey clouds. Jack watched from his back the bare branches clatter their derision at his efforts as his eyes refocused. He heard her coming towards him again. She was screaming like she always did right before she attacked. He needed to move. With a jerk, Jack rolled to his stomach. He felt the thud of Sallah's knee strike the ground where he had been a moment before.

It's going to be one of those kind of days. He rolled onto his back and wrenched his new arm up just in time to block the back side of Sallah's fist.

The blow vibrated his teeth with an audible ring. But it knocked her off balance just long enough. With his back still on the ground, Jack swept his foot towards the side of Sallah's head. She rolled away, avoiding Jack's kick with a reluctant nonchalance and gaining her feet in one motion. Her face twitched as she stretched her fist, bright red from rapping it against cold metal. He used the moment to regain his feet and prepare for another onslaught.

In the seven weeks following the surgery, Jack had only gotten his arm to work in two directions, flexing and extending at the elbow, with an unpredictably strong amount of force each time he did so. There was no improvement on more refined movements like bending fingers or twisting his wrist, let alone the specialized mechanizations like the hydraulic punch and the wrist drill. Then, there was the ever-present pain in his shoulder and now in his back. It was getting worse by the day, but he would never tell anyone the extra weight on one side of his body strained his back, if he stood for too long, or how he hadn't slept soundly in weeks. Of course, Headmistress had told him it was nothing short of a miracle that he was even alive, let alone how such a half-screwed idea had even managed to work was nothing less than the Paragon himself helping the fool boy.

The new arm did have its benefits as well. It provided an element of unpredictability when sparring against Sallah, which flustered her more than she would ever admit. Jack felt that this was in itself a victory and to see her so annoyed was well worth this and another forty surgeries after.

She came rushing again. Jack braced himself for the bullrush. Instead Sallah slipped to the side at the last moment and lashed a round-house kick from an awkward angle. Jack managed to deflect only part of her force as her foot glanced off his head. Jack tried to counter-strike, but it was too late. Sallah planted her fist in the center of his chest. Falling backwards, Jack stuck his metal arm into the ground and spun away, gaining distance from his opponent and keeping his feet. Sallah's eyes narrowed.

She didn't expect that. Let's see if we can surprise her again.

Flexing his once dead muscles, Jack's metal elbow bent with an audible *clang*. This time it was Jack who sprinted forward,

His metal arm held up by his natural one. He watched his opponent smirk at the ridiculous sight of a man running at her, yelling, with both arms above his head.

Perfect.

Just outside the distance of Sallah's dangerous kicks, Jack let go of his arm and flexed again. His arm extended with violent power as it drove into the frozen earth. The force whipped Jack's body towards Sallah's face, feet first. She tried to sidestep but a boot caught her in the temple and the hip. She rolled and bounced down the hill. The fog of her breath plumed from her nostrils in thick streams as she staggered to her feet.

Venom was etched on her face as she glared at him from the bottom of the hill. "Good," said Sallah, "You're improving." Without another word she stomped off in the direction of Stonehall.

Jack watched her go, his own breath puffing white clouds. He tried to celebrate as best he could but two realizations put a damper on that; Training would now be that much tougher and that trick would not work again. Still, he had won a skirmish against a Huntress who had been trained all her life to fight. He sat beneath the bare tree and leaned gingerly against the trunk. The punch to his chest made it hard to breathe, his shoulder was aching and stinging more than ever but he was getting better at fighting. And if they were about to pull off this plan, he needed to be as prepared as possible.

Jack walked to the wall and turned south. Just as they thought, the Workhouse was no longer safe. Guards had been posted outside of the abandoned building and even more began to patrol Stonehall in force.

Thirty-seven minutes passed before Jack reached a crude

slit that had eroded in the stone wall over decades. He slid through the crack, mortar scraping his back and neck. Kerosene smoke filled his nose even before he reached the other side of the wall. Bass Run was busier than Jack had ever seen it. Frigid rain pelted cloaks and awnings alike. There were more than just the typical drunkards, gangsters, and cutpurses. Children clung to their mothers' hips. Merchants Jack recognized from the West Plaza had set up shop beneath the wet, rusted awnings of the streets. Bass Run was no longer the home of those not wishing to be found, it had now become home for those who were seeking refuge from other districts. And those that were observant enough to feel the change in Cogrind, like the traders whose goods could no longer be found in the West Plaza and now sold their wares in the southernmost district. News of an increasing number of guards disappearing on night patrols around the perimeter of Bass Run made this district an appealing home for many nowadays.

Cogrind had changed.

Or perhaps it has always been this way and I just now see it.

Fear ran through the crowded streets as cold as the ever-blowing winter wind. Jack pulled his hood far over his face, clutched the cloak over his left arm, and shouldered into the door of The Pin and Sprocket.

He had grown used to the thick smoke from tobacco pipes and tallow candles. His shoulder ached at the warmth of the tavern then stung as his metal arm slowly warmed. His teeth grated against the pain for a moment before he walked slowly into the dimmer depths of the tavern. Jack didn't look up. These were desperate times and he had no doubt if one hard up citizen recognized him, that would be the end of his freedom and his friends. He watched the seams of the floor plates as he walked, using them as a guide to lead him back to the private den. Only after the door was closed and locked behind him did Jack peel back his hood.

The den was much brighter than the rest of The Pin and Sprocket and cleaner too.

Moira is the queen of nesting.

She was fretting about the main room, fixing tea and a place setting to match. The sound of the lock clicking was enough to break her concentration. The main room was sparsely furnished with a couch and two simple chairs upholstered with what used to be a rich color of red.

"Jack, thank the Paragon." She hurried over to him and whipped off his soaking cloak. She had greeted Jack this way every day since they had moved here. She bustled over to a clothesline near the furnace and draped the dripping cloak.

Has Sallah returned yet?" Jack asked.

Moira let out a long sigh. "No. She sneaks about as she pleases. She very well could be and I just haven't noticed." Moira sighed again. "Is it really necessary to do this? What the Patron is doing is unspeakably awful, but why must you go? Why must . . . "

"I involve Charlie?" Jack smiled at her. His mouth felt heavy. Smiling didn't come as easy as it used to. "We only need him for a little while. He won't be there when we take Petty."

Moira searched for the truth in Jack's eyes. She found it, but not the comfort she hoped it would bring.

That's who she's worried about.

He couldn't help a pang of jealousy. Not because he fancied Moira, but he wanted someone to think of him in the same

287

way.

"But why must *you* do this?" asked Moira.

"If not us, then who? We know what's happening, but we have no evidence. Without it, we have no recourse. We need Petty. People are scared. This is not our Cogrind and we have to fix it."

Tears came to her eyes and she blinked them back. "Small comfort to their loved ones," Moira rebutted.

Jack wrapped his arms around her.

She sobbed silently for twenty-seven ticks on the clock. "Why am I so useless?" Her voice was muffled against his chest.

Jack breathed at a deep, constant pace. It took nineteen more ticks before she matched his rhythm.

In every room, in every building, in all of Cogrind, there hung a clock directly linked to the Proscenium. Some kept time silently. Others ticked every tock. Some were crafted of gold and platinum. Others were corroded tin and aluminum. But they all kept perfect sync with one another according to the metronomes in the Ironworks Conservatory.

"You've kept me clothed since you could sew. Do you remember the first shirt you made me? It was the worst stitched garment in the city and by far the smelliest and uncomfortable thing I have ever worn." He felt her jump with bits of reluctant laughter. "But without it I would've been naked . . . and it kept me warm. You have cared for me, protected me. My life would be forfeit without yours, as would Charlie's. It's for you we are doing this and all the ones like you."

The room shook with a sudden thud. Jack's arm threw him off balance, but Moira caught him. A fist was beating at the door. As Jack strode for the door, another shock sent tremors through the building. The room was still ringing as Jack reached for the door. The fist kept pounding the door at a panicked pace. Jack slammed open the shutter.

Sallah's green eyes stared back. "Get out. Now!" she exclaimed over the clamor of the tavern's patrons behind her.

Jack turned to grab Moira. The sound of tearing metal pierced his ears and the room shook violently. Jack watched Moira's eyes turn to look to the direction of the sound as her body lurched into the air. Jack tumbled towards her as best as his tired muscles could manage. He stole a look away from Moira to find the cause. A blunted cone the length of two grown men, stuck through the wall of the den. With another tearing screech it wrenched itself back.

A Tin Punch. The largest Tin Punch any man has ever built.

Crushed ceiling panels crashed down around him. Jack found his feet and made for Moira.

Two seconds.

There was a blur of metal and Jack felt his feet leave the ground. His back slammed against a wall as the Punch blocked his view from Moira. He attempted to clamber over the top of it. He froze. She wasn't there. Just heaps of wall panels, cogs, coils and sheared beams. Jack felt his body wrenched back by his collar.

"Get out of here now!" Said Sallah behind him.

Finding his feet, Jack made for the door as best he could. The punch wrenched itself free, the freezing rain rushing in. Sallah and Jack tripped towards the main room of the Pin and Sprocket. It was chaos. The whole building bucked, with everyone inside it. Drunks tried stumbling for the exit, but the combination of drink, noise, and the shifting floor left most rolling on the ground and clawing in vain for the exit.

A bronze panel slammed to the ground on Jack's right, scraping his shoulder. Sallah seemed more able to maintain her balance. She dragged Jack for the door.

Just a few more steps.

The punch tore through the backroom of the Tavern. The Barkeep's eyes filled with fear, right before he was buried in a pile of what was left of the wall. The shock shot a nest of cross beams across the room. They were trapped. Sallah froze for a moment. Fear crept into her eyes.

"Up!" Jack screamed, finding his feet and his voice.

They made for what was left of a staircase, scrambling on hands and feet. This time Sallah followed Jack.

There has to be a maintenance hatch for the roof.

Jack didn't have an answer for what came after making it onto the roof. At least they wouldn't have tons of metal over their heads.

Up the second flight of stairs they climbed and rounded for the third. Another shock threw them from their feet. Then came a groan that rattled his teeth. Jack had heard that noise before, when the supports for the Arc-boiler began to collapse. That nauseating sound of far too much weight with too little support. The building began to tilt. He clambered on to the next flight of stairs, Sallah at his heel. He began walking with one foot on the stair and one on the wall. Jack could feel the building irreparably twisting over itself, like someone punched in the gut.

There was the hatch. At the top of the stairs. Jack hauled himself up through the shaking to the last few stairs. He reached for the hatch. His hand found purchase and he wrenched on it with all that he had left. It flung open sending Jack crashing against a wall that was quickly becoming the floor. Sallah ran for him.

"Out now!" he heard himself say.

Sallah hesitated for only a heartbeat before crawling through the hatch. Jack rolled sideways as the building buckled further. Somehow he found his feet. The hatch was looking at the side of the neighboring building. Jack leaped through it. He felt the cold night breeze on his face and he saw the next building was a sheer metal wall. He was going to fall to his death.

I couldn't stop them. I'm sorry Sallah, Charlie . . . Moira.

His breath heaved from his chest with a jerk. His shirt was caught by something. He tilted his head and saw Sallah clenching his shirttail. He reached back and grabbed her forearm and with more than a few heaves, Jack rolled onto the roof of the next door Tannery. The cries from the street were horrible. Desperate wailing sang soprano to the rumbling bass of the crumbling tavern. The smoke began seeping from cracks of what was left. Arc steam hissed from every gouge. In the moments after, flames licked out from the edges of the rubble.

"Moira." He crawled to his knees.

The building had collapsed right on top of the gigantic metal punch.

"We need to get out of here," said Sallah looking down on him. "Someone must have spotted you."

By the light of the flames, he saw tears forming at the corners of her eyes.

Has she even spoken with Moira before? Jack kneeled, absently shaking off the soot from his pants. "Who would do this?

291

Who would bring this down on so many people." He blinked back his own tears.

"A leader who kills his own people," Sallah said, rubbing her shoulder. "My guess is someone looking for a reward. Or who had no idea what the Patron would do with the information."

Another jaw-ringing *CLANG* split through the clamor of the night. Three blocks to the south, another two-story tall Punch drew back to pummel a tenement building. Another cry of twisted metal rang out. He could see six of them now, each one drawing back in clanking rhythm, each one hurling forward in mechanical brutality. Fires sprouted around them across the night of Bass Run.

"He's bringing down Bass Run. All of it," Jack said. "Charlie . . ."

"Focus." Sallah grabbed him by the chin and turned his head. "Unless we do something now, Charlie is already dead. We keep with the plan." She took a few breaths through her nose, "That's all that's left." She helped him up.

"Do you think they would risk Petty now?"

"You still do not understand?" Sallah said. "The Patron views you as a threat. You are a danger. Dangerous enough to bring down a quarter of the city. But who would believe you, now that the city is littered with posters for your bounty? We may still not understand the Patron's end goal, but we know his methods."

There was an emptiness in Jack's chest. He wanted to move, to rise off his knees but he couldn't bring himself to stand. The loss was too heavy. His heart had been taken. He kept eyeing the smoking rubble that was the Pin and Sprocket. Maybe she had survived, maybe. Perhaps she was just stuck, he just needed to free her. He made for the edge of the roof before he felt the warmth of Sallah's hand on his shoulder. He looked up to see rare kindness. Not sympathy or pity, just a shared pain he was surprised to see. She gasped and Jack snapped from his stupor for a moment. She fumbled with the knot that secured the cylindrical parcel on her back. She rolled out the cloth to reveal a phonograph recording, but it was much larger and oddly shaped than any Jack had seen before. The Phonograph would have to be twice the size Jack could ever recall seeing. He hurried over to it. Across its length curved a thin crack.

"Damn fool," Sallah muttered. Her hands hovered over its surface twitching with frustration.

"Where did you get this?"

"My home, the Greensea, in a very old grove. One my people try to avoid. It was in a machine from your people. It helped me heal, I think. There was a note that said I should carry it with me."

Jack leaned in closer. It wasn't perfectly cylindrical. The fires of a fallen city cast more than enough light for Jack to see. Even with the warped imperfection, the grooves, from which the sound is replayed, were not warped at all. Cylinders were cast then pressed. This had not melted. It was designed to be this particular elliptical shape.

Jack gingerly picked it up and viewed it from one of its sides. He gently placed it back down. "It's too large for most any phonograph I've seen." He swore he had seen one that could fit this, he just couldn't place it. "May I hold on to it?"

"I think that is best. But it is broken." Sallah rolled it snuggly into the cloth. She wound the parcel onto Jack's back.

He blinked at her, the knot tight against his empty chest.

"We can fix it." The knot cinched as she pulled it tight over one shoulder and under the other. "With any luck they will think you are somewhere down there."

Bass Run was a sea of firelight. Some of the machines still rang out through the night. Three had toppled and one had been crushed by the building it destroyed. Metal walls and streets danced in reflection to the licking, spitting inferno. The wet cold, an hour past, burned beneath a smoke filled sky. There were no stars in Bass Run tonight. The screams had fallen away to the distance. A couple shouts rang above the alleys from good meaning people, banging on strangers' doors and checking for others.

"We go," Sallah said, adjusting her belt.

They made for the next rooftop. Before five steps there came a crackle across the network of Voxphones across the City. There came an inhale and then-

"We will find you Jack," hissed Petty's voice across Cogrind. "We are coming for you."

Chapter 16

I'm sorry Moira. Sallah felt the air freeze in her nostrils. She moved silently across the cloud-covered rooftops of early morning. This hadn't been a problem only an hour ago. The heat and fire of Bass Run drove away the freezing rain. But not here, towards the southern edge of the Singing Stacks. Rooftops were coated in a layer of ice. Sallah's eyes could only see the outlines of the vents and balustrades around her. *Picking the right path is always a dangerous prospect.*

She tried to push the thought of Moira out of her mind. It made her think of worse things, like home, like Agneth, like Karra.

One foot in front of the other. This hunt is how I get home. One way or another, I'm close now.

It was true. She had found the who and the what, though now, after the sacking of Bass Run, it felt moot. Regardless, this city was producing the Ichor. The smell, the serpents, the new Arc-boilers. Acts like these always came with a heavy price.

More than once that morning she thought about running out of the Eastern Gate and into the farms and pastures beyond. She could make it back home in twenty days, maybe fifteen if she didn't sleep much. She longed for that one evening as a Druida. in the warmth of her people's embrace. She could go home right now, but what would it matter? Her venture wasn't to come running back to The Grove. She was here to stop the destruction of her House and the Children of Dharra, no matter the cost. Sallah peered over at Jack. She could see his outline with the slowly swelling light. He was favoring his left side severely now. The arm was pulling him off balance. She could tell he was in constant pain.

But she couldn't let him rest, let him mourn, not yet. She had to keep him moving towards the Patron. No leader would jeopardize his power by wantonly killing his own people. The Patron was desperate enough to destroy his own legacy and legitimacy. He had an endgame in mind.

Which left Sallah with two possibilities. The Patron was completely insane, or his ends did not lie with the city. Jack needed to stay desperate too. She pushed out the guilt with another deep breath. Jack had earned her trust. That had not been the question for some time. Jack was strong and smart and adaptable and utterly impulsive. That was the part she didn't trust. He could react in any sort of unpredictable way that could get them both killed. She had been drilled on political maneuvering for a decade. It was a necessary skill for her position as Druida. She could get them both through this. Her heel skipped across a patch of ice. With an audible grunt, Jack caught her by the arm. She nodded a quick thanks in the dark before resuming their walk

I'm helping him, right? Sallah searched herself for the truth of this. *No. I am a Druida of the House of Hawthorne. My responsibility is to my people, my family. If it is necessary, Jack is expendable. I think he may want to be expendable.* She made a silent prayer to Dharra that sacrifice would not be necessary. For the moment though, Jack needed to stay alive. *I still need him to stop the Ichor.*

They stopped on the edge of a rooftop that skirted a wide and empty street that served as a major thoroughfare through the Singing Stacks. A sign on the corner read *TIMPANI AVENUE.*

The first goal was still the same; find Petty and make him talk. He would be their means of access to the Patron without taking on a battalion of Steel Watch. After that, they would confront the Patron and shut down whatever was creating the Ichor. The problem was they still didn't know where Petty was going to appear at the Metronome Tower in the morning.

"The Skytrain," Jack had mumbled an hour previous. "The main depot is in the Stacks. The Steel Watch will still inspect cargo being brought into the Tower, but there won't be nearly as many as there would be on the streets."

The voice was hollow and Sallah's heart ached for him. Since that time, he had lapsed back into silence, despite her voiced questions about the plan. She wanted to get angry at him, retaliate in some way at his silence. But then she remembered the day Agneth was taken from her. She had her whole House to soothe her pain. Jack had a stranger and frozen rain. All she could do was follow his outline into the night and away from the flames.

Sallah found purchase on some gutters and started her climb down to street level. The building shook with a dull thud. For a moment Sallah thought those damned machines had found them again. She looked about for Jack and found him on a balcony several feet below her. Jack had landed awkwardly, slamming his metal fist against the floor.

"Jack," Sallah hissed, pointing to her ear.

His head tilted toward her, but his face was hidden behind shadow and white hair. With silent compliance, he grabbed onto the same guttering Sallah was on and slid his way down. Sallah scanned for any life among the shadows and pre-dawn light. Nothing stirred. She closed her eyes and prepared for her descent. Jack was waiting for her, leaned against the wall, his chin at his chest. His head tilted towards her at the sound of her footsteps.

"Quickly," Sallah whispered.

"There's no one here," he said in a low voice. "I can actually see in the dark." He stepped casually across the high street as if perusing for some apples.

The sound of his boot steps rang against the shuttered refineries. He made it to the other side and stood among the shadows. Sallah waited for another moment. Nothing moved toward Jack. With a stinging breath in her nose, Sallah sprinted towards the far end of the avenue.

They made their way through the secluded alleyways between the smelters and foundries. She hated being led blindly. The plan was brazen, left them vulnerable from all sides, and would leave little time for interrogation, but after the events of the night, it was the best option left to them. Feeling committed to a bad plan was oddly calming. Perhaps it was just having any plan that actually moved towards her goal.

The freezing rain had not coated the streets like it had the rooftops. Sallah vaguely remembered something Jack had said about coils of Arc lining the street plates, heating them to where snow and ice were never an issue. Fixing a problem you created in the first place seemed an odd thing to be proud of. Perhaps that was the point of these people. Failure was just as interesting as success to them.

She remembered his smile more than anything he said. He always had that same half-grin any time he talked about the workings of this city. As she ran to the next shadow that hid Jack, she realized how very far away that smile was now. As soon as she reached the other side, Jack moved for the nearest alley.

Sallah stopped him with a pull of the shoulder. "I will mourn her." She tried to find his eyes.

Jack's body shifted in her general direction.

"But we have to focus on our counterattack. Use the anger. Don't let it get you killed."

'Too many spots' said the Leopard to the Jaguar.

Still he said nothing. His eyes were hidden.

"Petty," she said.

His eyes met hers, wet with tears.

"Focus on him."

They darted into a crack between two massive smelters as the warm light of day tipped the frozen rooftops.

The alleyways were a drunken maze of corners and turns. Jack quickened his pace. Each time they passed an intersection, Sallah reflexively checked for trouble. Most were empty, a few held homeless, sleeping beneath ragged cloaks. One saw them passing.

They came to a six street intersection with a tall, hexagonal building at its center. Even in the relative quiet of the morning, this building was in constant motion. Rails stuck out at all angles, spinning and shifting to connect rails from other parts of the city. Entire floors rotated, lifted, and sunk as cargo boxes were eaten and spit out by the structure.

Her ears pricked up. Someone was talking. She grabbed Jack by the back of his shirt and backed themselves against a wall. They padded to the next corner. There were two voices now, but the rain patter and wind robbed them of their words. Sallah peered around the corner. Two Steel Watchmen in their metal armor stood amidst the cold.

" . . . Petty . . . "

She heard it clear as dawn. Sallah's neck whipped back. An impact from behind her. Her body sprawled to the ground as she saw Jack race around the corner. He had heard it too. His wrench was in his hand. By the time she found her feet, he had already tackled one. The second guard's shock turned to anger as he readied his halberd to come crashing down on Jack's neck.

"Above!" Said Sallah.

His metal arm raised above him out of reflex. The blade bit deep into the arm's lobstered plating. The downed guard grabbed at Jack while the second guard raised his blade over his head again.

Undisciplined. Sallah grimaced.

Already on a dead sprint, she quickly closed the distance. Vaulting against Jack's back with an extra hard stomp, she planted her knee underneath the standing guard's chin. rattling his head against the inside of his helmet, and falling to his knees. Sallah grabbed the halberd from his now slack hands and struck the back of his helmet. His body collapsed to the ground in a limp pile of metal. Her knee screamed in pain as she struck.

Please don't be dislocated.

Jack was swallowed in a bear hug on the ground before his metal arm extended violently, breaking the guard's grapple. Jack reared back to rain down a blow. Jack was going to kill him. With a swipe of her halberd, she deflected his punch and struck the downed guard cold with the back of the weapon. The ground cradled a sizable dent from where Jack's fist landed. He looked like he wanted to strike again. His arm was heavy enough to crush the helmet and the guard's head.

She kicked him off the unconscious watchman.

"This is Moira's legacy? This is what you choose? You will help me stop whatever abomination your people created then, then I will kill you myself if that is what you want, but do not throw your life away because Moira is gone." Still, she couldn't help but notice the considerable control he had over his arm with that strike.

The punch was almost . . . natural.

Jack got to his feet and eyed her as he turned over one of the guards. He pulled off the armor's back plate to reveal an Arc-tank slightly larger than his own. He pulled it from the fitting and repeated the process on the other watchman.

"They can't move their armor without them," said Jack. He walked to the Skytrain Depot, leaving Sallah to drag the two into an alley. He began scanning a wall until he opened a small panel. He fiddled with the gears inside until a piece of the wall split open and revealed the ground floor of the depot. Jack walked through the opening with Sallah limping behind him.

The inside was a deafening whirl of action, but much to Sallah's surprise, there didn't seem to be anyone inside. The interior of the building was almost completely open, as cargo boxes slid in from all angles above her on rails. Bristles the width of her finger rolled along the side of each container as they entered the building.

"It's a coordinate system," said Jack. "Each cargo box has indentations on the side. The wheel bristles 'read' the indentations and shift that cargo's destination to the correct Skytrain."

Sallah stared at the operation. Every cargo box was identical except for one that caught her eye on the second floor. It was sorted and stacked neatly like any other box around it. Except for the front. It was a door that belonged to the inside of a building, not the outside. The door itself was silver with a fogged glass window with the words *M. Petty, Chorus Director* written in gold filigree. Jack had thankfully become distracted by the constant action and ingenuity to retreat back into his anger. She began to climb to the second floor from an access ladder.

Only then did Jack pull himself away from his reverie to notice what she was climbing for. "This . . . does not belong here." Jack followed behind her.

He was more contemplative than confused, so Sallah assumed this was something possible. They both moved toward the door.

"This would explain how you were never able to catch him leaving the Tower," said Jack. "They haul him out with the rest of the cargo." He gasped and checked his fob watch. "Seven fifty-eight am. The whistle will sound soon. We need to get in there and quickly."

Sallah mouthed a silent prayer of thanks to Dharra. She had no doubt they would have found their way into the Tower, but this gave Jack a much-needed distraction and direction. Already he had slid a panel away from the wall and began to tinker with its inner workings.

"Jack, we are about to be in much more dangerous territory. We can't afford to do what you did back there. We have to be smart and patient. We are hunting, not going feral."

Jack only grunted in response, not looking away from his work. Sallah left it there. She needed him to attack the problem, not each other. With a long hiss, Petty's office door slid open a few inches.

He grabbed one side and extended his mechanical arm. "In we get," said Jack.

And not a moment too soon. As Sallah's heel lifted from the second floor, so too did the office. She felt the motions of the depot as it tilted, spun, and connected the office to a retinue of other boxes and slung itself into the wintry morning sky.

The inside was not a reflection of its polished exterior. Coats and gold chains hung rent and broken on bent racks. Silver dishes of half-eaten steaks and spoiled pie lay where they were thrown. A gilded partition left half the room still hidden. Piles of luxurious wardrobes mounded haphazardly against overturned tables. One of the walls was lined with a window that would match the Metronome Tower's exterior precisely, but was marred with greasy handprints and shallow scratches.

Like an animal.

Sallah turned to Jack, who had found a sheath of documents strewn about a gold desk. The office slammed to a halt, knocking them both off balance. Looking out the window, Sallah saw the end cargo box was now sitting on a raised platform on the top of a building before it was lowered and swallowed by the roof. With a Hiss from the pneumatics, they lurched forward again, sending her stumbling back. She did notice, however, that the up-right furniture didn't budge from the sudden acceleration. She surveyed the desk Jack was studying. It was bolted to the floor. She spied an upturned fainting couch. There were bolt holes at the feet but they were sheared off, like they were ripped from their fasteners.

Petty couldn't do this. He is weak and pampered

Sallah turned to Jack. "We should find somewhere to hide. No telling just how thorough his security escort is. We need him alone and silent." She began looking for a suitable replacement for rope. Deciding on some floral silk robes, she cut them into long strips and began to braid them together. Mostly she needed to distract herself from the windows.

The speed and height was nauseating. Mix that with the anticipation of riding into the lion's den and she needed to at least keep her hands busy.

There was something else in the back of her mind. Something was not right about this. She had scouted Petty for weeks. He wallowed in his excess, but his trappings and office were clearly held in disregard, even malice.

"We're here," said Jack.

Managing to look out the window, she saw the large glass eye of Metronome Tower glaring at them as the Skytrain rounded its side and began to decelerate. A segmented wall in the tower fell open and swallowed the containers. The sunrise gave way to total darkness. She could hear the machine outside shifting them to and fro. Losing her balance, she felt herself caught by Jack's metal arm.

"You head behind the divider and I'll go behind the desk," said Jack.

Sallah felt her way across the room. He seemed calmer now, or perhaps he had found his patience to get proper retribution on Petty. Thankfully for Sallah, sunlight slowly returned to the office as the container shifted down into its slot, the windows taking in the winter morning as if it was a room like any other. The office was padded in silence and anticipation. The door clicked and swung open silently. Sallah strained to hear someone entering the room. Peeking through a crack in the partition, she clenched her jaw against a wretch.

Petty's skin stretched over his bones. It looked like he hadn't slept in days or eaten for a month. He was huddled in a crusty white fur cloak, as he shuffled in. There was no sign of the Steel Watch escort. His eyes darted everywhere, but he focused on nothing. Petty's hunched body settled on a chair.

"Petty," said Jack as he stood up from where he hid.

Petty twitched before blinking into focus. He grinned at Jack before tilting his head back and choking out a laugh.

Jack walked toward Petty. Sallah's eyes darted back between them.

"What happened to you?" said Jack.

Petty's frail body had stopped shaking from laughter. "You did," said Petty, "They wanted information on what Barin was telling you and where you disappeared at night. Not an easy task, but worth it. I found you then and you come to me now. My loyalty to the Patron will be rewarded as always." A coughing fit left him gasping.

He pulled Petty upright. Sallah tensed in her hiding place.

Jack could only grunt against Petty's stench.

"What is he planning? What is the point of all of this? The Boilers? The Serpents?" His voice barely contained rage.

305

"Why would I tell a traitor? You are a dissonant voice in Cogrind's great song. My loyalty is to the Patron, his vision. He has made his own discoveries far beyond even the likes of the Paragon himself. His destiny lies beyond the control of a mere city. He holds the power to dominate everything, to become a god." Petty was trying to shout but his strength left him quickly limp against Jack's grip.

"What did he do to you?" Jack asked.

Some life had returned to Petty's face but not his sanity. He smiled wider than possible. His skin tightened around his skull. "He has made me a vessel. I have drank of Life itself. We have become greater than man little Mouse." Petty flung himself forward with a surprising quickness, knocking Jack against the far wall. He rounded the partition and found Sallah waiting. His frame was impossibly thin, like the weight of his head should have snapped his back in two. The way he moved was odd. His body was leading and his head dragged behind. His jaw cracked as his smile widened even more seeing Sallah. "And we know all about you Sallah va Hawthorne. Your home burns as we speak. You abandoned your people to ashes and death." He lunged forward.

Sallah managed to circle away from him. His punch came from nowhere and she felt her hands raise to block. The force from the blow still knocked her stumbling back. Jack came rushing in. Petty blocked Jack's wrench with his forearm with a sickening crack. He grabbed Jack by his wrist, spun him once and threw him, knocking the partition off its hinges. Jack rolled off a desk and landed behind it.

"Jack!" screamed Sallah.

"I'm fine," came a bruised voice from behind the desk. "Keep him busy for as long as you can," Jack said, suddenly excited.

"I found something!"

"That long?" Sallah said under her breath. She turned her attention back to the shambling body of Petty.

He cracked his arm back into place and lurched towards Sallah. She cursed herself every day for ever losing her bone blades. This would have been over quickly. Jack was too close to use the cursed blades at her hips right now.

Winter Form, Endure.

It was always her least favorite form in training. Avoid, deflect, receive every strike at a weak angle, then time your shot. She felt her body take the stance, bobbing on the balls of her feet. Two open palms, ready to engage. She back-stepped the tackle and shifted away to a better angle. But Petty was already sweeping for her legs. He caught her heel but she maintained her balance. His speed was impossible. He was already up and swinging, forcing Sallah back. She couldn't find the gap to sidestep a better angle. Her arms were numb from elbows to fingertips. Each punch sent a shock through her body no matter how she blocked. And still he didn't tire. His body moved like a marionette.

Her back hit the wall and she tried to spin away. Petty caught her by the throat. She kicked out for his leg and tripped him but his grasp remained tight, sending them both crashing down. Already Sallah was seeing spots. Her body wouldn't react. She was exhausted.

Petty regained his feet and slid her up the wall. "You will die here princess, no earth beneath your feet. Alone, away from the House you couldn't protect." His voice was joined by other sounds welling from his body.

She could barely hear his words. Darkness faded into her eyes. Her head was going to burst.

No, no, no were the only words she could find. *No . . . no,* Then the grip gave way, and she felt like she was falling. Air seeped back into her lungs. She blinked one last time to see Petty's smiling face wrapped tight around his skull. "NO!" She gripped her blade at her waist and thrust behind Petty's jaw. The blade stuck deep.

You cannot deny our nature, Sallah. Killing is a part of us. The voice seeped into her mind surrounding her in a rage like a warm cloak. The sensation of falling would not abate.

This was a good start. Now kill the boy.

With a screeching crunch, her body found the ground, knocking the blade from her grip. Tears streamed down her face as she coughed her way back into existence. Her right side ached from the impact, but she was alive. And there was no voice in her head. She could hear Jack running to her.

"Are you all right?" Jack propped her up as gently as he could.

Sallah wished he hadn't. Slowly, breath returned to her body in irregular intervals. "What did you do?"

"I dropped the room off a thirty-foot ledge, so to speak," said Jack, "It would have been a lot worse if you had not fallen into about three dozen coats."

Tenderly, Sallah began flexing her limbs. She could hear her heart pounding in her head with a murderous rhythm. Everything was bruised. Nothing was broken. "Impressive and painful," she said, flexing her ankle. "Petty!"

Jack placed a hand on her shoulder. "You do impressive work yourself." The anger was still in his throat, then softened. He pointed over to Petty.

Her blade was lodged behind his jaw.

"I'm glad you did it," said Jack.

Sallah stared at him quizzically.

"It doesn't fix any of this of course. But you're right. It would have been worse if I had killed him. I'm not saying I'm not capable of it . . . but the fewer things I have in common with Petty or the Patron, the better."

Sallah sat up. "Good," It still hurt her throat to breathe in.

"I'm sorry," said Jack, still staring at what was left of Petty. "You've saved my life more than once. I shut you out. That wasn't right. We are in this nightmare together. I will start acting like it. After all, Moira said I should look after you."

Of course Moira would tell him that.

"Even better." Sallah was glad she had ended Petty. She had killed before. That was something Jack did not need to experience, not yet anyway. Sallah gave a full smile against a chest full of guilt.

What if the time comes when your life stands in my way?

At least it would be easier to betray him then. He wouldn't see the switch coming. Sallah made another quick prayer. She had been making a lot more prayers lately. Her head was sent swimming at the slightest movement. "Actually I'm going to lay back down for a while."

"Good plan." He placed her gently back on the heap of cloaks.

Her body began to relax.

"I should get back to the control panel anyway. It seems to work on the same principle as the platform in the Conservatory. Now with any luck, I haven't completely wrecked the railing system and trapped us thirty feet below the streets."

Sallah was no longer relaxed.

"It should be fine." He half grinned.

Her throat was painful to the touch, but it was hard not to look around. The adrenaline was still coursing through her body. She looked over to the other body laying on the floor. Petty's lifeless eyes stared back at her. She had never been that close to death before.

How did you know so much about me? How powerful is this Patron? The power to become a god?

Petty was supposed to provide answers. He just left them with more questions. Perhaps her mind was too clouded in that moment. The adrenaline finally let go and Sallah had to fight the urge to sleep. They were right about one thing though. The Patron's goals were greater than Cogrind.

Of course, Moira's gloves. She cinched them out of a belt pouch and slipped them on. Normally she never wore gloves. even in the bitterest cold she preferred the tactile numbness of her fingers to the fumbling comfort of gloves. These were warm, worn leather, trimmed in wool and lined with flannel. Even by her own people's considerable leathercraft, these were respectable. She attempted to sit up again with much better results.

Slowly, she got to her feet. Her right ankle definitely took a knock, but she could walk it off. She kneeled down over Petty and poked the hilt of her blade. No voices or murderous impulses. She patted it a few more times with gloved hands before taking the grip. She pulled it out without trying to touch the corpse. The blade scraped against something metal in Petty's throat. She wrenched the rest of the blade out and cleaned it with the nearest coat. She studied Petty's mouth. A rusty brown liquid dripped from his lips. It moved like blood. It certainly did not smell like blood. It smelled closer to rust and decaying flesh.

Sallah found a scarf on a nearby pile and wrapped it around her nose to protect her from the sour tang. Then she grabbed a lamp that had the good luck to fall on a pile of robes and set the blinder to form a beam of light about the size of her fist. She pried open his mouth. Something shined back at her. She opened his dislocated jaw further. It was the head of a snake but made of metal.

Maybe you do have some more answers after all. The head was an identical, miniature version of those things that took Jack's arm. Its familiar yellow eyes stared back at her, unmoving. The back of its skull was split in half where Sallah's blade struck. She wanted to study it further. Unfortunately, only the head was visible.

Twice thankful for Moira's gloves, she reached into Petty's mouth and grasped the snake's head and pulled softly. It came unwillingly, but she made progress. That was until she noticed the corpse's arms lifting and flexing towards his chest.

How is that possible? Unless-

She let go of the creature and Petty's arms flopped back on the ground. The creature was grafted to the man. She flicked out her blade, pulled open the nearby lamp's aperture, and laid the corpse's left arm palm up. Years of experience field dressing kills tempered by Claire's training made it simple work for a clean incision. Besides Jack though, Sallah had never done this to a human before. Then again, she had a harder time classifying Petty as human by the minute.

Starting from the crook of his elbow she cut through his papery skin. The arm was so thin Sallah was afraid she would cut right through it. She traced the blade along the radius and peeled back the flesh. Coiled tightly around Petty's frail bones, was the metallic body of the snake. She could even see where Jack's wrench broke Petty's arm and the snake had compensated by coiling tighter around the wound. It would be safe to assume the same was true for the rest of his appendages. She opened his mouth again and examined the snake. Its head was positioned at the opening of the throat. the plates of food and Petty's emaciated state started making sense. The serpent was starving him from the inside. Petty was a cocoon for this abomination. A shiver trickled down her spine.

No one in their right mind would volunteer for this.

She started to pity the man she had killed. So desperate for power, he disregarded his own survival. there was an uncomfortable familiarity to that thought.

"That should do it," said Jack, climbing from under the desk, "I purged the broken pressure line and transferred pressure to an intersecting valve. We should have enough pressure to get us going again."

Sallah backed away from Petty and covered him with a nearby cloak. Not out of respect, just to hamper the stink. There were shouts from above them.

"Eight twenty-six. Someone has found the guards in the Stacks by now. we need to go," said Jack, pressing and switching the instruments on the desk.

"Can this thing take us to the Conservatory?" She needed to finish this venture and get back to her people.

The Patron could be only a few floors above them right now. The impulse to storm the Tower was tempting, But he would be well protected. These things could be living inside the Steel Watch that guarded him. Even with the help of Jack, she had barely survived one. How could she manage against a troop of these abominations clad in metal?

"I don't think we can take the Patron as we are right now," Sallah said. " Not if he's surrounded by these things. But if we can get to the Conservatory, we can at least start ruining his plans."

"I'm sure it can. The problem is I haven't a clue on how to pilot a Skytrain. I don't know the coordinates to get to the Conservatory. Let alone, where we would actually end up inside of the building. It could drop us off in the Steel Garrison for all we know." Besides, there might be more Petty's waiting for us there." He chewed his lip, staring blankly at the platform levers before he raised his eyebrows. "We can't fight this alone anymore. I have an idea."

For the first hour, Jack couldn't be bothered, muttering frustrations and taking notes while shifting levers and turning knobs. The control panel was twice the size Jack had used inside the Proscenium, which made navigating possible directions that much more difficult. One moment they would pop inside the facade of a derelict shop in Bass Run, the ruins of city blocks still smoldering from the previous night. Next, they were occupying a penthouse overlooking Balcony Row. Petty could have watched the entire city from his office. He could be all the eyes and ears the Patron would ever need. Jack stood gaping like a fish when The Skytrain dipped under the city and reappeared just three blocks away from the Workhouse. A chill rolled down her spine.

They knew where we slept. Why didn't they hunt us down right here? perhaps they thought weren't as much of a threat then?

Not a word passed between them as Jack shifted levers to new coordinates and they slid over the city. Jack began to find his bearings after the second hour. Slowly they were homing

313

in on the center of the city, The Ironworks Conservatory. Each street was more desolate, the people more stern, than when Sallah first entered Cogrind. It wasn't just Bass Run on edge. The whole city felt tense, waiting to burst.

"How's your arm?" Sallah asked, as the office slid silently over Cogrind. She had wanted to ask since Jack attacked the two guards outside of Petty's office.

"Fine." Jack said, still staring at the control console.

"You were using it perfectly against the two guards."

Jack blinked out of his concentration. "I guess I hadn't thought about it," Jack said with a sigh. "There's been quite a bit on my plate lately."

"Now would be the time to start thinking. You were using it back there, like it was your own. Can you?"

It was no use. Jack had slipped back into his concentration over the console. Through clenched teeth, Sallah let the question lapse into silence. She hated being ignored, but he was right. The last thing they needed was showing up in the wrong place. Another couple of hours passed and Sallah spent it watching Jack. She still had no idea what his mental state was and if he decided to have another outburst, it could cost both of them everything.

As time ticked by though, the anger released from his face. The lifeless look in his eyes was replaced by concentration. This was a challenge he understood and for the first time since meeting him months ago, Sallah watched Jack in his natural element. She remembered just how young he was. At seventeen, she was being groomed to lead a House of tens of thousands. She had wished countless times to be just another member of her House, another face, to be like Jack. Now this teenage boy had the fate of two societies in his hands. He

314

was not groomed for conspiracy and fighting and Politics. He was trained for fixing machines, and for the first time that day, Sallah was grateful Jack was in front of a large and complicated one. He was happy, even if he didn't know it.

While aware of it, he had only managed an open palm and closed fist, but now, his metal fingers twitched when he would mumble a combination to no one in particular. "Got it!" yelled Jack, both arms, raised in victory.

Sallah smiled at the shock on Jack's face as he studied his new arm. "You're right. Maybe you don't think about it."

Jack tried to bring his arm down slowly. Instead it collapsed limply to his side.

"So where have you decided to take us?" She needed to keep him focused on moving forward, not the difficulties and not the losses.

"Someplace where everyone can see us." He slammed three levers into different slots and they began to fly over the city once again.

Chapter 17

Everything was broken. He was broken. Jack was tired of it. Moreover, he was tired of everyone acting as if everything wasn't. That's why they were going to the Ironworks Conservatory. The City could not afford to ignore their reality any longer and he was going to show his people in the most drastic way he could devise. Sallah was right though, there was no way they could storm the Metronome Tower with just the two of them. They would need help.

The Skytrain rose to the top floor of the Conservatory, where Jack had passed underneath it every day for years. It was late afternoon by the time Jack had found the proper coordinates on the control panel. The sun glowed a dull orange as it started to dip below the horizon. Petty's body now lay under layers of his own coats to cover the stench.

Thankfully, Jack had become nose-blind to him at some point. That was preferred beyond the obvious reasons, especially if he was going to do what he was planning. The Tuners and Luthiers of first shift would be done soon. Jack could hear them leaving from beyond the door. He should have been hearing jokes and raucous laughter. Instead there was nothing but hushed whispers. Most everyone would be gone for the day. There was always a skeleton crew in place to watch over the Proscenium, but the majority of workers had gone home, tired and afraid of what tomorrow could bring.

Count me among them.

He had no idea if this was going to work. Even if the plan didn't work, Jack felt a sense of satisfaction at such a public act of defiance. They would wait a few more hours, in hopes of clearing out any stragglers. A wave of exhaustion hit him now that there's nothing to do but wait. His chin hit his chest more than once.

"Sleep," said Sallah, "I will be here to wake you." She had been staring at him since they left Bass Run. She tried to be discreet but it was impossible not to notice at times.

Admittedly, he did fly off the handle at the Skytrain depot. He was ashamed. The Watch was doing their job, just like he had done. They were complicit, but so was he, and much more directly. After all, he had helped repair and install the Patron's new Arc-boilers.

And no one was dead, well, besides Petty. Jack stared at the mound of garments covering his body. Jack wondered if Petty's previous state could be considered "alive". He tried to imagine being puppeteered by something inside of you. He shuddered.

I can't believe she survived that long against him.

Jack considered what he would be doing if Sallah had never found him, never exposed him to the truth. He shuddered again.

All of his work, his effort had been to the detriment of the people he meant to serve. Injury and even death in pursuit of one's vision was a part of his culture, his city, and that wasn't going to stop now. He had lost an arm running away. He was more than willing to lose everything charging forward. They were close to truly disrupting the Patron's conspiracy. He was actually going to help Cogrind for once. Although the Patron's end goal for all of this escaped them still, from what Sallah had gathered, he knew the Patron's ambitions lay beyond just Cogrind.

"Thanks." Jack pointed to the clock "Wake me when the little arrow points to eleven and when the big arrow points to twelve." With that, he fell instantly to sleep.

—

Her hair dangled over my face and tickled my nose. She smelled like home. His stubble scratched my forehead. He smelled like leather. He said he loved me and kissed my head. She leaned over me again.

"You can save them Jack. You can fix it."

—

"It's time," Sallah's voice snapped him out of sleep immediately.

Petty's office was dark, save the Arc-lamps outside the windows, casting long shadows with their cool, blue light. The hallway was dark and silent. They wrapped Petty up in a red and gold cloak, the Patron's colors. Together they began dragging him out of the office, and down the twelfth floor hall of the Conservatory. The polished floors made it easier but the body was unnaturally heavy.

Luckily, the service platform wasn't far away. Jack almost

didn't see it as he passed by, but muscle memory stopped him at Barin's office. His name wasn't on the door any longer. The gold filigree scraped off the frosted glass. as if they could just erase the old man. Jack tried the handle. Just as it was in Barin's time, the door was unlocked. Jack opened it slowly.

"What are you doing?" said Sallah.

"I need some things." which was true. He also just missed Barin.

The office was the same as the last time he was there. Barin was a highly respected man among the laborers of the Conservatory. On the rare occasions he couldn't be found in the Proscenium, they were always welcome to open his office. It was sparsely decorated, except for the shelves of phonograph recordings and trick puzzles that lined the workbench and desk. It was like looking at the inside of his mind. Jack counted himself lucky to have spent hours here. He grazed his hands across the suede record covers. Barin knew each song in his library by heart. He would hum them when he wasn't paying attention. Usually with his fingers moving along a puzzle. A few of those puzzles still laid on his desk. Barin was unfairly good at trick puzzles. So good that he had solved all the ones he could find from shops and had taken to commissioning them from the finest Trinketeers in the city. It was one of his few expenditures and fewer personal joys. Barin had told Jack he should try his hand at it. Jack had never found the time. Each one on the desk was solved, save one. It was the same puzzle Barin had been working on before Jack took medical leave. It was like a ball of entwined gears hopelessly knotted. Barin had told him that the goal was to form a perfect cube by pressing at precise points and twisting just so.

Fat lot of good that does me now. The phantom pains still had not abated. He was beginning to hate his new arm. Still, Jack took the puzzle and tucked it into his pocket.

Who knows? Maybe it will be good practice for coordination. If I can ever get my fingers to work. Just behind the desk stood a work rack with piled-on leather aprons, worn tools, and sweat-stained tunics. Jack caught a glimpse of what he didn't know he was looking for, just beneath them. It was Barin's tool belt.

He remembered the first time he saw it. It was a ritual for an apprentice to carry their master's belt for the first week of apprenticeship. Barin made him carry it for four. Most apprentices carried the belts in whatever comfortable way they could find, so long as they were careful not to drop tools.

Barin made Jack carry it palms up, draped flat over both forearms as he chased his master up and down the Proscenium. One day, a lead puck fell from Barin's belt. Jack asked him what it was for.

"For you boy," Barin said, "Now, I believe you've carried that belt long enough." Barin took the belt from Jack's arms, dumped out another seven lead pucks, strapped the belt around his waist and carried on without another word.

He wanted me to be strong. No, not just strong, inquisitive.

Jack shoved the clothes to the ground and picked up the toolbelt. It was so light in comparison to those first four weeks, even with one hand. It still held all of his master's tools. Jack slung the belt across his shoulder. It was far too large for his waist, probably always would be. But he needed the tools for what he planned for Petty. He had lost all of his own tools, save for his wrench. And more than that, perhaps he needed to feel his Master close to him, as he tried for the

320

first time in his life to intentionally break something. He then turned to a large closet. Heaps of fasteners, stained canvas, brushes and paint stacked against the walls. There were suitable storage spaces for such sundries throughout the Conservatory, but Barin hated wasted steps. Jack grabbed four tins of paint they used on the apprentices' aprons and two wide brushes. He stepped out into the hall and closed the door behind him.

"Did you find what you were looking for?" asked Sallah. Shockingly, she didn't seem annoyed at the detour.

Jack let out a deep breath. "I believe I did." Without another word, he grabbed the tail of the coat Petty was wrapped in and dragged him down the hall to the elevator platform.

Sallah looked at him curiously.

"Going up?" asked Jack.

"For lack of a better option," said Sallah, stepping onto the platform. "I hope you know what you're doing."

"I haven't the faintest idea." said Jack as he flashed a very wide smile.

Sallah smirked in return. They ascended to the top of the Ironworks Conservatory to enact the start of their plan.

—

They waited on the roof of the Conservatory. Jack couldn't take his eyes from the Metronome tower that gazed down on them half a mile away.

The Patron could have seen us at any time. He could be looking at us right now. I hope he is.

He peered over the edge to the empty streets below. Typically there would be at least a few citizens tracing the streets before the whistle blew at eight a.m., but after what happened last night in Bass Run, no one would be caught in the streets alone. But the sun would rise, the whistle would blow, and all the people below would leave the supposed safety of their houses and see Jack and Sallah's handiwork.

"This was a good plan Jack." Her eyes surveying the city below them.

"It's only a good plan if it works," Jack replied, letting out a sigh of steaming breath.

"It will." She turned her gaze to him. "Even if it doesn't work today, you have planted the seed of truth in their minds. Your people are balanced by their trust of one another. It's admirable, if naive. It has enabled your people to build all of this and it allowed your people to be manipulated by a monster. It is the same with all things in nature. A creature's greatest strength masks its greatest weakness."

"Are we not just manipulating them into doing what we think is right? Doesn't that make us as bad as The Patron?"

"You have done nothing more than expose your people to a truth most would rather hide from. It is up to them what they will do with it."

Jack did not feel comforted by this.

"They will make the right decision. Have faith in your city."

The whistle blew across the chilled air of Cogrind and faded away. Shutters opened and the Arc-lamps that lined the street flickered off with the coming of the morning sun. It was time.

For several more minutes there was nothing but silence, punctuated only by Jack and Sallah breathing.

It didn't work. Jack thought, *Fine, we will start with disabling the Boilers while no one is inside. Maybe we can use Petty's office to find a way to the top floor of the Metronome Tow-* A scream pierced the silence. Another voice yelled for someone named John. Jack peered over the edge. A crowd was starting to gather underneath the display Sallah and Jack had left for the citizens of Cogrind.

It had taken them one hour and thirty-eight minutes to hang Petty's body from a lightning rod jutting out of the side of the top floor. It had taken them another two hours and twelve minutes to paint their message across the main entrance of the Conservatory. The work was precarious and they had to time the passing patrols, but as Sallah noted earlier, the Steel Watch rarely looked up. Each letter stood twelve feet in height. Three simple words painted in the same vibrant red as apprentice's aprons.:

WE ARE BROKEN

They were, and Jack would no longer allow them to ignore it. The murmurs and shouts below had grown louder now. More people were gathering at the foot of the Conservatory. Jack spied others peeking out of windows and cracked doors. Even they mustered the courage to come outside and witness the spectacle. A handful of Steel Watch had gathered at the Conservatory entrance, bewildered by the hanging body of the Master Tuner wrapped in a lavish red and gold coat and the words behind him. One was attempting to unlock the doors. Jack had already seen to that as well. It's hard to unlock a steel rod barring the doors. A sergeant sent one guard running down the street for reinforcements. The crowd was swelling and turning more unruly by the second. Calls for justice crashed with screams for protection from the Patron.

Shouts of "Bass Run!" crashed with a slow swell of "We are broken." in steady time.

Steel Watch reinforcements came rushing through the streets, towering over the rabble to bolster the beleaguered patrol. But they weren't organized and soon Watchmen became separated and were consumed into the swelling mob. Someone screamed. There was blood on a woman's dress as she fell back into the crowd.

That's when Jack started his second riot.

The Mob crashed into the guards and swallowed them whole. Their armor crushed beneath the swell of rioters. It was terrible to watch and Jack felt terrible for it. People were getting hurt. People were going to die. He felt sick to his stomach. This was his fault now. To make it worse, the situation was now out of his hands. It was all up to the whim of the Mob. Jack didn't know if he could go through with the rest of this.

Will there be anything worth saving after what I've done? my people are tearing themselves apart.

"We need to go," said Sallah.

Jack snapped out of his musings. "Right."

They made for the roof access of the Conservatory.

"More will die, Jack. Just like Moira, just like Barin, and just like the children. Our task is to make it mean something."

They stepped through the door and onto the platform as Jack set the coordinates.

"Do you read minds now?" asked Jack.

Sallah grinned. "I know you well enough to know you care about your own people. One of the few things we have in common."

The elevator slipped down below the fourteenth floor and

stopped at twelve. They ran through the hall towards Petty's office. A few apprentices on night shift gaped at them as they sprinted past. It didn't matter if they recognized them now. The plan was already in motion. Slamming the office door behind them, Jack quickly set the coordinates to a penthouse only a few blocks from Metronome Tower. The plan was to use the riot as a distraction to ghost themselves into the Tower. The guards would be occupied and with Jack's prowess, they would slip into a side entrance, capture the Patron and present him for judgement to the City.

But before he could finish setting the coordinates, Petty's office began to slip down from the building.

"We have a problem," said Jack. "I'm not controlling this platform."

Sallah grabbed Petty's desk chair and hurled it through the window."Then we jump."

They were at the tenth floor and dropping to the ninth.

"Now you're being suicidal," he replied.

"We either sit in this box and wait to be ambushed or we take our chances with the jump and the mob."

Jack heard the truth of her words. "Wait to get as low as possible. We go together," said Jack, looking at the mass of bodies churning against each other. "Hold on tight, but if we get separated, just keep on your feet and make for the western entrance of the Tower."

They were in between the fifth and fourth floor. They both stood in front of the window and watched the roil of fists and faces slip in and out of view from the passing windows, drawing them closer.

Jack grabbed Sallah's hand and blew out his breath. "I'll see you soon."

They ran and leaped out of the second floor. His body landed unevenly among unsuspecting heads and shoulders but soft enough to be alive. He managed to hold his grip on Sallah for a few seconds as he scrambled to find his footing and his bearings. But there were too many bodies, too many arms and legs and rage. They were pulled apart. She was gone.

"Sallah!" Jack shouted among the tumult. It took all his strength just to stay on his feet. Even then, the crush of bodies would lift his feet from the ground.

"Tower!" Jack shouted, "To the Tower!" He grabbed a woman by the collar and shouted the same right at her face.

The stranger took up Jack's call as well. Jack shouted at as many people as were near him.

They need direction. I got to get them moving. Jack soon heard more and more shouts for the Tower around him, others calling for the Patron to answer for the razing of Bass Run. The riot slowly stopped grinding into itself. The Mob was moving for the Tower.

It was hard to keep his footing or the air in his lungs. Shoulders, faces, and hands were all he could see and feel. He had to get out. The problem was figuring out which way "out" was. Jack just kept trying to move laterally from the slow march of the riot. If they were all headed towards the Tower, eventually he would hit the edge of the Mob and could make his way down the side streets. Squeezing in between the shoulders and feet was tiring and the progress was slow, but he was making progress. They were almost at Balcony Row and Jack could see the edge of the crush of people. A blast of trumpets sounded across the city from the Voxphones, louder than the Mob itself. A wall rose from the street twelve feet high, blocking off the entire city street and barring the mob's entry. Their progress was halted but only for a few moments.

"Tools to the front!" came the cries from the vanguard, the call washing to the back.

Within seconds toolbelts, hammers, and pry bars were being passed overhead. Some people had already spilled into the side streets. Jack took the opportunity to follow their path.

By the time he had managed to get past the other side of the barrier, one section of wall had already slammed back into the street with a thud that rattled his teeth. The crowd began pushing through the open section only to be met by a platoon of Watchmen, halberds pointed forward and marching towards the mob. One man flush with rage, charged them. He was cut down in an instant. Some tried to back away in fear but more came to the front screaming and wielding tools of their trades. Some were killed where they stood, but the mob found its spine again and the crowd pushed forward. Another section of wall slammed down revealing another platoon of guards.

The Patron will make this as slow and bloody as possible.

But his people were inventive and desperate. Some began scrambling up ladders on the side of buildings. Some had managed to remove the metal plates that made up the streets to shield themselves from the advancing guard. Jack ducked into a side street with a herd of others. He raced along the crooked streets until they too were blocked by a barricade. His wrench was in his hand before he knew it. He slid to his knees and began working on one of the four latches that held the wall up. Two others kneeled on either side of him, working the bolts with their own tools. One of them caught sight of Jack's arm. He wrenched the catch free with a clang loud enough to jolt him from his stare. Jack moved to the next catch closer to the man and locked eyes with him

I'm the most wanted man in Cogrind and you are working with me.

He heard the screams from the high street over the rooftops. A full battle was now raging with citizens bloodied in the chaos. Jack popped the next catch free with a mechanical strength. The wall slammed down in line with the rest of the street. None of the Steel Watch were waiting for them.

The Patron must be concentrating the Watch on the main street. It still won't be enough to contain them. So why not loose those damn snakes and stop the advance all together?

Some of the crowd overtook Jack as they sprinted down the alley towards Metronome Tower. Even more ran along the rooftops above his head. Some had disassembled the box vents and access doors and tipped them over the roofs onto the Watchmen below.

Of course. Get rid of the Watch and when no one is left to organize a defense, release the serpents and kill us all at the Patron's leisure.

He needed to get to the Tower. Now. Jack pushed forward ahead of the press, until the street emptied to the wide avenue that circled the Tower. People spilled in from streets and oozed over rooftops like oil from a blown gasket. The empty streets soon filled with people. All the shutters were closed tight on the luxury apartments and condominiums that lined the street above them.

Shutters won't save you from what's coming.

All the more reason he had to find The Patron quickly. Yes the elite bribed, browbeat, and cajoled their way to their lofty addresses, but they weren't at fault, not really. They were just a symptom of the sickness. The aristocracy would pay their tax in blood by the end of this day. All the more reason to get inside. He needed to protect everyone, or as many as he could anyway.

The gold-wrought doors of the Tower opened and out marched the Steel Watch in lockstep, four by four columns. They formed a half circle around the building, lowering their halberds. The crowd began throwing pipes and fixtures they had pulled from the streets antagonizing the guard, prodding them to break formation but they would not be goaded.

What are they waiting for?

A slow and rhythmic *BOOM* from the Tower's open doors answered his question. It was a replica of the Steel Watch armor. The movement was mechanical though. Its arms held an axe in each hand. The Mob gawked in silence as the Walker trudged towards them, barely clearing the Tower's sixteen-foot doorway. The doors slammed behind the Walker. Jack could feel the terror seep through the crowd. Its footsteps sounded like a sledgehammer against an anvil. Its arms hissed and puffed, blowing Arc steam in angry, streaming bursts from its limbs. The chassis were taken from the cranes found in the Proscenium. But the design was sloppy and the construction was haphazard. But it was big, and loud, and carrying axes with blades the height of a grown man. The rioters were silenced and began to back away. Jack had to get their spine back, better yet, their fury.

If they want to be sharp, we'll be blunt.

His eyes found a service panel to his left. Wrenching it open revealed a bank of levers, switches, and knobs. Jack didn't have to think about it. The instinct took over and he set about what he had planned in his mind's eye. The City was his. He could make it dance if he wanted. Right now he just needed to protect his people. He threw down the final lever and the plates of the streets in front of the rioters flipped straight up, forming a barricade and a momentary reprieve from the sight of the Walkers.

"Get the panels off the hinges!" Jack shouted to everyone within earshot, raising his mechanical arm to catch the city's attention,

"We're going to push them back!"

The word spread quickly across the frontline and the confusion from a moment ago became a familiar rhythm of working together. No one seemed to question where the order came from. They didn't seem to care. They had work to do. The street plates were twenty feet across and ten feet high of pure bronze. They would have crushed a dozen people under the weight. But there were not a dozen people under them. There were thousands to absorb the pressure from the front. Jack could feel in the soles of his boots the Walker getting closer. One of the other plates was already freed from its hinges, whining as it leaned against the crowd and slowly, with the crowd pushing back, turned upright. Other plates were soon freed and with it they formed a crescent shield against the guard.

"Counts of two! Push on two!" cried Jack over the shouts.

The word quickly spread across the people from the front line to the back.

"Ready. One!"

"Two!" the crowd thundered in response, pushing the plates against the guards, their call drowning out the sound of the Walker's approach. Jack clenched his teeth against the screeching grind but kept the steady rhythm going

"One!"

"Two!"

"One!"

"Two!"

It was working. The guards had figured out what was going on, but it was far too late. The Citizens were working as one. Jack heard shouts from the edge of the shield. They needed more people on the outside to pin them in.

Slowly the guards were corralled. But the Walker was not so easily contained. Jack saw the top of its chassis peer over the citizen's shield. Jack stopped pushing but still continued shouting the rhythm, trying to make his way to where he saw the Walker. It was too late. He saw the axe rise and fall with unrepentant strength. The blade cleaved the plate in half striking down six men. Without hesitation, men and women stepped into the fallen's positions and kept pushing as the two limp bodies were dragged towards the back.

"Get me up there," said Jack, climbing on top of a man wearing a leather apron. He clambered on to the thin and shifting edge of the plate. Half-running half stumbling, Jack made his way to the Walker as it lifted its axe again. He vaulted to the Walker's arm as the axe fell again. An exposed feed pipe struck him in the chest. He grabbed at it with his mechanical arm and squeezed.

It's not good for much, but I can certainly crush metal.

The arm raised again, turning Jack upside down, before the pressure from the crushed pipe proved too great and exploded. The arm fell limp knocking down a host of Watchmen and throwing Jack sprawling against the Tower steps. The Walker shuddered and tilted as the burst pipe

331

whipped and sprayed prismatic steam back and forth and with a final shudder, leaned and fell back. With all the confusion, none of the Watch had even noticed he was among them. Hopefully they wouldn't notice him long enough to get through the Tower's doors. Jack wasn't betting on it, but he had no choice and he was not going to get a better opportunity than this. He leaned against them, but before he could heave them open, the doors simply swung open, inviting him inside. Jack blinked back his surprise for just a moment and hurled himself through the doorway. A handful of Steel Watch saw the Tower open as well, but just as quickly as the doors had opened, they slammed shut and left Jack standing in the foyer, completely alone.

The cacophony outside was muted and muffled against the solid gold doors.

Though he could still hear the chant of: "One. Two!"

He felt . . . naked. When he was in that crush of people, his people, he felt strong, focused. But now it was only him, The Patron, and the elevator in between. He hurried across the velvet carpet towards the lift. The control console was ornate and simple to navigate. He pushed two knobs up to their highest catch, the door closed and he was taken to the top floor.

Why did the doors just open like that? Was it the Patron? Is he expecting me? Of course he is. We just raised the entire City against him. But why not let the Watch in as well? They would have had more than a decent chance of killing me.

The lift seemed to take pleasure in being as slow as possible.

What am I going to do when I get to him? Kill him? Talk to him? Beat him within a measure of his life?

Jack was tired of death. He had seen enough in a few

months to last him a lifetime. Barin, Moira, all those children like Sprocket, the Watch, Petty, the people outside struck down by those meant to protect them.

I need Sallah here.

He flexed his shoulder and felt the ache from the bruise of Sallah's fist. He had had this bruise for months now. She always managed to punch in the exact same spot. Jack grunted. *Maybe not. By the Paragon, I hope you're safe.* He did. He missed her. He missed annoying her. He missed learning from her. Most of all, he missed her company.

The lift doors opened to the top floor. It was empty. His own ragged breath was the only thing to shatter the silence.

"Focus on the task at hand," Jack said to himself.

That's what Sallah would have said, and she would have been right. He couldn't even hear the riot outside any longer. Jack took a deep breath and put one foot in front of the other. He walked down the hallway of engravings, The inventions displayed escorted him backwards through his people's history. Then he was at the doors to the Patron's chamber.

The Paragon held the first gear high above his head, but his featureless face stared back at Jack. And there was the cavity in the engraving in the Paragon's chest, in the shape of a whole note. Taking the sling from his back, he unwound the fabric and estimated the damage to the phonograph cylinder that Sallah had given him for safe keeping. It was cracked all the way through now, and shards of wax scattered around the cloth. This was not good but it was all he had, so he picked up the two pieces and squeezed them together as he slid them into the door. It was a perfect fit. Jack pushed until the end of the cylinder rested perfectly flush with the rest of the door. He waited. Nothing happened. Jack heaved a sigh of frustration.

Damn it, the cylinder has to be whole. I need to find a match or preferably a candle, two would be bette—

There was a click from inside the door. The cylinder started spinning. A happy little tune came from the walls, consistently skipping in two spots. Then the keyhole itself was spinning, then the Paragon's chest. The heavy deadbolt retreated with a satisfying click and the doors opened to the anteroom, and in turn, the anteroom doors swung apart to reveal the Patron's chambers. Jack walked in, his wrench already in his hand prepared for anything. There was movement above him, as he watched his phonograph cylinder sliding along a rail that wound around the office and descended into the floor. But the office was empty, nothing but the glass walls overlooking Cogrind and the ornate throne the Patron sat on the last time he was here. Jack desperately searched for any clue or possibility of where the Patron might be. The sound of a small *click* reached his ears. Jack whipped around prepared for a fight, but saw nothing but the throne. The sound had come from there. He slowly walked over, his eyes darting about, ready for an ambush. He studied the throne, but that is precisely what it was, just an oversized chair, from the gold wrought banding on the sides to the suede stained a deep red, all the way to the whole note at the top and center.

The whole note blinked at Jack.

Jack blinked back.

The whole note blinked twice.

Jack backed away. The throne was clicking more now, inner machinery whirring into life. The banding on the sides of the

Throne unfolded and extended, like arthritic fingers letting go of a cane. The fingers were multi-jointed and bent and splayed at unnatural angles, each one with a needle point tip made of diamond. The whole note extended from the chair, stretching and moving at the end of a polished gold tube with many joints of its own. From each side of the chair, the floor opened up as three long rows of phonographs, each with a cylinder much like Jack's, stair-stepped into place beside the throne. The fingers stretched straight and bent over the bank of phonographs like a maestro at a piano. The eye extended towards Jack as a voice came through the air, distant and scratchy.

"Hello Jack. It is so good to see you again."

Chapter 18

"Two!" Sallah shouted in time with the people around her.

The Watch were almost all corralled but the Walker had made it a struggle.

Sallah had watched Jack run along the edge of the barricade . She called to him but it was pointless. He was on the far side of the barrier, the Mob was too loud and he was too focused. Her heart dropped when he leaped onto the Walker and was lost from her view. The Walker had stuttered in its tracks and Sallah knew Jack was responsible. two others took Jack's lead. One was successful. The other was cut down. With two Walkers gone however, Corralling the guard was a simple and clever plan. She figured it was Jack who devised it.

Left to their own imaginings, this riot would've been a blood bath. The trick would come when the Patron would unleash the serpents. The people would destroy their own defense, then scatter and hunt the citizens, not as the insurmountable horde but as frightened individuals. She had no problem playing into the Patron's plans for the moment. Indeed it was necessary to contain the guard. They would be needed for the second wave. The real problem was just how

336

exposed they were. All of the attention was forward, towards the Tower. She needed something loud. She needed to get the attention of all, Steel Watch and citizens alike.

"Sallah!"

The voice boomed near and familiar. Charlie was there, a few rows behind her, covered in sweat.

She dragged herself to him. "Charlie! we need to get everyone's attention. There's worse coming."

"We've got the Watch. All that's left is to take the Tower."

Sallah shook her head. "Those things are coming. The same things that took Jack's arm. It's the only plan The Patron has left and we don't know what else the Patron has in the Tower. We have to organize these people. or at least get them somewhere defensible.

Charlie's eyes unfocused as he searched for an answer. "The Voxphone. It's made for city-wide announcements."

Sallah remembered the whistles each morning and the voice that blanketed the city two nights previous, goading Jack. "Where do we find it?"

"There are access points in different buildings. The closest that isn't the Tower is the Conservatory," Charlie shouted over the din.

Sallah didn't like leaving the fight. She had almost been trampled there this morning, but at this point most of the city should be deserted. "Let's go."

The decision was vastly easier than the process. The Mob had grown in size and fervor. Citizens had begun hoisting and hurling makeshift battering rams against the other doors of the Metronome Tower. Sallah and Charlie pulled and shoved their way through the shifting sea of humanity. More than once she lost her sense of direction but she would find

Charlie's bald head above the others and push in his direction. It was exhausting. It was winter yet she was sweating against all the body heat. The crowd seemed endless, shouts and shoulders and shoves. And the hate and anger and sadness on their faces. Sallah was scared, not the scared she felt on a hunt right before the adrenaline kicked in, but the child-like scared, helpless and without a solution. Because she was helpless. In an instant this crowd could turn on her, turn on themselves. These were not people, this was an unbridled force and she did her best to move against it. A vice-like hand grabbed her wrist. She wrenched free before noticing it was attached to Charlie. He was off his feet and practically sideways among a dense cluster of people. The same fear was in his eyes that she felt. She grabbed his outstretched hand.

I'm not letting go of this one.

She pulled in any direction that he wasn't. He found his footing again, and shoved a crack through the mob, pulling Sallah behind. It seemed an eternity but they finally emerged from the crowd. They made their way as fast as tired legs could take them down the Promenade. Eyes peered at them from behind shutter slats. Otherwise, Cogrind was deserted.

"Where's Moira?"

The question caught her in the gut. She stumbled for a moment before looking at Charlie. She couldn't bring herself to words. Charlie understood. She had watched what Charlie and Moira had. It was rare and good, like Agneth and Terran. Now it was gone. Just another person she couldn't keep from death. His eyes unfocused. Sallah could think of nothing to do but put an arm around his shoulder and shepherd him to the Conservatory. She had crawled out of the pain and anguish of tens of thousands of people, but the pain of this one man hurt her much worse.

He jerked up. "Jack?"

"Alive, at least he was the last time I saw him."

Charlie nodded, unblinking,

"He's not dead. He tried to save her. He couldn't. It was my fault. I didn't warn them fast enough. I am sorry." She meant it more than she showed. A force of habit. His breath began to calm, he stood upright, but his eyes still searched for understanding.

"How do I . . . " Charlie mumbled.

"You just keep going. It will still feel like this. You'll just feel . . . empty for a while." The words caught in Sallah's throat. "But you will think of her from time to time and it will hurt because the memories stopped when they should have kept going," Sallah felt the burning pressure from behind her eyes. She didn't care as tears rolled down her face. "And when it hurts, you can bury it and keep going, or you can keep remembering and wallow in the pain. But it doesn't matter, because whether you bury them or live in the memories, they will try to poison you. Their death poisons what they are to you." Her face was wet with tears and steady as truth. "I don't want Agneth to be poison to me. I won't let Agneth be poison. Because she was beautiful and wise and kind and loved me more than I had any hope to. Please don't let Moira be poison to you. Just remember who she was, not her death." She had felt that look in Charlie's eyes. She just wanted to help for once. To not be too late, for once.

The look in his eyes didn't change but the words were calmer.

"Follow me."

They hurdled over the slain bodies of civilians and Steel

Watch alike outside of the Conservatory. The doors were still barred, but Sallah broke through a tall window and clambered inside.

The access platform rose to Crowley's office as it stood beneath the gaze of the Metronome Tower. It was more than tall enough to see across the city and the riot at the foot of the Tower. The swell of people forming the Mob was incredible. It was like a floating ball of ants after a deluge, a densely packed crush of desperate arms and legs. Already the Steel Watch had retreated into the Tower. It was a small miracle to escape from the surge as they did.

"Only been in here twice myself," said Charlie, "But from what I remember, Crowley's Voxphone should be over there."

Crowley's office was nothing but polished metal and sweeping angles. Centered in the middle of the far wall was a dias on which sat an ornate podium. The body of the podium roiled and splashed in waving contours of music scales rendered in gold. It reminded Sallah of a mountain stream after the first thaw of the season. Charlie made for the podium. He pulled a metal bloom from where it rested and cranked on a handle at its base. He coughed into it. She jumped as his cough rumbled through the streets of Cogrind. Charlie raised his eyebrows and stared at Sallah. He had no idea what to say.

Frankly, neither did she. She slammed the Voxphone back into the Podium."You need to talk," she said, trying not to sound terrified of public speaking. "My accent is different from yours. They will trust your voice."

Charlie nodded at the logic of it. "You need to tell me what to say though." Charlie had clearly never done anything like this either. "I don't know what's coming and . . . well this was your idea."

Sallah found that palatable. "We need a way to control the confrontation. They need to be corralled so that there's only a few points of conflict. Then we need to get the Watch to the front, at those points. Move the barricades to form funnels into the Watch." She sighed at the impossibility. "I wish Jack was here." what surprised her more than the words, was that she meant it.

Charlie puffed out his chest. "Do you think Jack is the only hot rivet in the bucket? He didn't know the difference between a hammer and a half-penny before he met me."

It was a convincing enough lie for Sallah. Grabbing the Voxphone once again, he steadied himself. Something sparked in his eyes as he watched his people destroy the same things they had worked together to create. "Cogs!" Charlie's deep baritone thrummed through the city.

Even from this distance Sallah could see the constant churning lessen.

"My name is Charlie Maestoso. Some of you know me. Most of you don't," Charlie heaved a deep breath before continuing, "I'm broken. It was a bad weld. The pressure sheared my fingers off on my right hand. Everyone of you knows someone with a similar story, maybe the same story."

The crush of people was half a mile away and Charlie was doing his best to look each one in the eye.

"I was broken, without purpose, just like you, like all of us today."

A silent moment hung over the city.

"The Watch is not our enemy. They are fulfilling their duty, like we all have been tasked with at one time." Charlie turned to Sallah.

It was then Sallah realized the true weight of what she was doing. These people, the entirety of their society, rested on a plan she had concocted in about thirty seconds.

"They are not your enemy. The real enemy is coming and soon. We must ready ourselves or we will all die. Release the Steel Watch. Get them to the back of you."

Several seconds of indecision passed.

"They are tasked with protecting us. If they make a bad turn, then kill them, but for the love of the Paragon get them to the back now! If they wish to fulfill their duty, let them do it for all of our sake."

Sallah could hear the fire in his voice. She had known that feeling; the fire of necessity. The distant metal crescent slowly widened as a trickle of red overcoats and shining steel moved from the entrance, to the back of the Mob.

Charlie looked at Sallah again, still speaking into the Voxphone. "I will do what I can to prepare the city but for now you will listen to Sallah. Her voice will sound different from us, but her words will keep you all alive." Charlie handed the Voxphone and the city of Cogrind to Sallah.

She began directing the people into the avenues of defense. Platoons of Watch manning the front lines, the most able-bodied in supplementary positions. Some Tuners had even taken it upon themselves to try and repair the two broken Walkers, placing them as vanguard. This was not her forte. The most people she had ever commanded at once was six. That was just a simple raiding party, hidden in the dead of night. Attack, not defense. This was an army in the hundreds of thousands in broad daylight against an unknown number of metal monstrosities. As with all things, Sallah knew the answer lie in Nature.

She would make them a porcupine, slow but painful to attack. At the same time, Charlie was figuring out the range and capabilities of the podium. He had managed to create the preliminary barriers to stem the flow of attack but this was mostly through some educated guessing and trial and error. Sallah spotted the first serpent slither from an access hatch from the street. Charlie was still working to form the streets and buildings into an advantageous battlefield, or at the very least not a killing floor.

"They're here." Sallah realized she was still speaking into the Voxphone.

Charlie's body tensed as he began desperate combinations.

"You will defend each other or you will die. That is the only law now. You live as one, now fight as one. *Celeritate et Astu.*" It was an old blessing, one Sallah knew held no power here in the land of the unnatural, of the manufactured, but it was all that was left of her to give, and she gave it.

More of the serpents had emerged from below the streets, their wide diamond shaped heads licking the air for the scent of living flesh. They caught the scent as a mesh of writhing bodies made their way to the Tower. More and more poured from beneath the streets.

The serpents are blinded by the daylight, but it doesn't matter. They will be overrun, no matter what kind of barriers, there's too many. They are all going to die.

She was helpless to stop it. A shocking thud jerked her away from her thoughts. The sound came from the shops across the Promenade. She was looking into their interior as if the shop fronts weren't there. Because they weren't there. Charlie had slammed the front facing walls down onto the street, crushing a clutch of serpents.

"I found my new favorite lever." Charlie grinned.

Hope sparked in Sallah's chest. *If Charlie can weaponize the city, we can bleed their numbers and give the people a chance.*

Right on cue, Charlie forced two buildings together, squishing a writhing contingent. There was a crash outside the door. Sallah raced to it, jerking it open. There was nothing visible but she could hear them licking the air. The serpents had found them as well.

"Stay here and barricade the door!" Sallah commanded Charlie.

He stared back at her confused until he saw the look on her face. He understood. She slammed the doors behind her and ran down the hall. Thankfully, only three emerged from the shaft of the access platform. The hallway was too wide for her to gain an advantage. All that mattered was keeping them away from Charlie. That familiar chill ran down her spine as her breath quickened. No more feeling helpless or lost or late. This was something she knew. Her blades gleamed rose gold as she drew them from the sheaths. She positioned herself on the inside wall, waiting for the ambush. The first serpent rounded the corner and her blade bit through its neck. Another slipped into sight and Sallah brought down the blade between its closed eyes. A third lunged for her head. Sallah managed to blunt its bite but was barreled over by the force of its attack. She managed to regain her feet and roll away as the serpent bit into an ornate Arc-lamp on the wall. It screeched like grinding metal as the exposed Arc fused its head and body to the wall.

Good to know.

Still more came, bearing teeth and tongue. Her blades separated the metal like young flesh as she flayed another.

The hallway was silent for the moment, save for Sallah's deep breaths.

I need to block the access shaft.

Leaping over her kills, she made her way to the access. The building shook and for a moment she lost her footing. She made it to the shaft and peered down. The waiting serpent almost bit her in half. She fell back as it lunged up at her.

Its mouth snapped shut on empty air but its momentum slammed Sallah against the floor, pinning her arm to her side and sending her blades spinning from her hands. It was at least twice the size of the others. Its head was the same size as her whole body. Her blades could give it a good gash, but she couldn't kill it, not from here, not with one blow and not with empty hands. She struggled vainly against the weight. Its body weaved over her but made no move to lift its head for another strike. Its body struggled for purchase in the vertical shaft. No, the body was so large it was stuck.

The serpent's body moved and unraveled. The lobstered scales unraveled to form a conjoined neck, uncoiling to reveal a second head. It lolled drunkenly back and forth before its bile yellow eyes focused on her. She looked about frantically. She saw a work bench lined with Arc-welders. The canisters were the same type that fed Jack's arm. She closed her eyes and the tanks revealed they were brimming with lifeforce.

She stretched out her arm but the cart was out of reach. The head reared back and struck. Sallah didn't close her eyes. She would stare death in the face, like Barin, like Moira, like Agneth. The fangs came within a whisper of breaking her skin as a silver streak crossed right in front of her face. Tosi plunged his claws deep into the snake's eye, popping it from its socket. He landed, hackles raised and his long ears pinned to his neck, spitting savage fury. The snake jerked back, screeching like torn metal, its eye dangling from the optic nerve. The leverage changed as the larger head turned to face Tosi, and Sallah scrambled free, tipping the cart. Arc-tanks spilled. She grabbed one

Forgive me.

She prayed to the living essence inside. She turned to the snake that had pinned her. Shoving the Arc-tank into its mouth, she kicked its lower jaw with all that she had. It felt like she broke a toe, but it did the trick. Its teeth punctured the Arc-tank, as pressurized energy came spewing out. The head writhed in anguish, unable to escape the canister skewered on its fang. The head boiled out in color from metal to ash until disintegrating into slag. The smaller head jerked about impotently unable to move the massive bulk of its body. Sallah picked up one of her blades and severed its neck in one smooth motion. She turned to Tosi, his eyes still wide with the hunt.

"Where have you been?" Sallah said, angry and relieved.

Tosi did nothing but blink lazily at her and began rubbing against her leg.

"I missed you too." Though not as she intended, she had managed to block the access shaft. for the moment they were safe. She hustled back down the hallway. More relief as she saw Crowley's door had been untouched. She banged on the door. "Charlie it's me. I think we're okay."

A long silence was the only response.

"Charlie, are you okay?" Familiar fear crept inside her chest. She punched through the glass portion of the door.

Charlie had done a good job of barricading the door. climbing over the stacked furniture, she found Charlie where she had left him. He was turning and twisting every lever and knob at the podium in deep concentration.

"Charlie?"

He turned to her, his eyes dazed and flooded with terror.

"There's too many of them. We are being overrun."

Chapter 19

"What . . . are you?" asked Jack, unsure of what he was seeing.

The eye moved closer to him on its thin, gold, arm. The iris was made of lobstered metal, expanding and contracting, the same principle behind a daguerreotype lens.

"That is a very good question my boy, and despite the unique position of my being me, I don't believe I have a satisfactory answer for you. That is to say, one you would find satisfactory. Perhaps it would help your understanding if we started with who I am. My name is McKinley." Its words came in melodic cadence. Repeated words sounded identical. The intonation made no sense.

It was then Jack understood the bank of phonographs. "You recorded your words."

The eye squinted in approval. "Rather ingenious, if I do say so myself." It's pointed diamond fingers dancing along the rotating cylinders. "I love to talk, but it becomes rather difficult without a mouth. I had to transcribe the recordings many times, you see. I do apologize for the quality, but transcribing is no easy task when you spend most of your time as a chair." The eye began inspecting Jack's mechanical arm, closer than what was comfortable.

"My my," said McKinley, "What an ingenious design incorporated with proper materials. You should be very proud."

Jack couldn't keep the bitterness from his throat. "I'd be much prouder if I could get it to work."

"Are you trying to make a machine work, or are you trying to move your arm?"

"It's the same thing"

"If it were, you would have full control of your arm."

"How would you kno—" Jack cut himself off.

"I'm a bit of an expert on such things."

Jack thought about this for a moment before more pressing matters got the better of him.

"Where's the Patron, the Watch?" asked Jack.

The eye gestured to the pounded gold tiles above them. "Currently sequestered in his solarium. I've managed to separate him from his retinue, but it is only a matter of time before they overcome my barricades. I'm afraid time is short for many reasons."

Jack studied the whole note for a moment. "Are you the Paragon?"

The phonographs let out a sigh like violins going flat. "I will be forever amazed at people's need to simplify. I am what you believe to be the Paragon."

Jack felt more confused than when he started.

McKinley emitted another string-section exhale before continuing. "I was responsible for the design of Songcradle and the Arc-boilers. They were my life's work, and two of my gifts to our people. But I was not the only one responsible. There were Oremen, Smelters, Metalists, Tuners, Engineers,

Laborers, Artists, Healers, Musicians, Textilers, Tailors, Farmers and Cooks. We were the Paragon, Jack. Each one of us, responsible for the other. I designed the Arc-boilers, but we all built Cogrind. The Paragon is not a person, it is our people. It always has been."

Jack thought about this a moment. "You said you were responsible for designing the Boilers. How many people sacrificed themselves?"

McKinley nodded his eye. "You speak of the Patron and what he has done. You are worried that our history is built on the blood of innocents, but I assure you my boy, no one gave themselves unwillingly to the project. As a matter of fact, only one person was needed to power the Boilers. Well, most of one person anyway." The spindly fingers framed the chair.

"You were all that was needed?"

The eye nodded.

"How?"

McKinley let out a sound like trumpets laughing. "Ever the inventor, aren't you my boy. Who needs the why when you can figure out the how?"

For a moment the only sound in the room was the static crinkling of McKinley's fingers on the phonographs. "Before I was as you see me now, I was as human as you. Then I met someone who knew a great deal about life and the energy that made it all possible." His words were played more slowly now, the tone softer. "She taught me of the incredible potential in all of us, and as you might expect, my mind reeled at the possibilities." The recorded voice lapsed into silence once again. The lens unfocused from Jack's face.

The silence continued until Jack felt compelled to say

something. "What was her name? the one who taught you."

The lens snapped to attention.

Jack could hear gears and gyroscopes whirring in response.

"Dharra." His tone played soft and sorrowful. "She loved music. She did not care for me one bit until I played the violin for her."

Jack felt like he had been punched in the chest. Jack and Sallah's people were connected. More deeply than he could have imagined. This man, this machine, once loved a goddess. And from their love sprouted the city of Cogrind.

There was another silence before McKinley continued. "She showed me how she imparted fractions of her essence into living things, invigorating them with new life and connecting them to her life force, her very being. She made a garden and it flourished into the Greensea. I developed my own alternate methodologies. Anyway the upshot is this, my boy. I developed a method to partition off portions of my own life force and with it my memories, my knowledge, pieces of my very identity. I could store those portions in inanimate objects instead of living beings. I could give that essence protocols and directives. That essence can't learn or sense things, but it will tirelessly work towards its directive. twelve times I did this, one for each Boiler. My last gift to the City. There was no longer enough life force to sustain my body, so I developed this contraption to house the remainder. I am all that's left of McKinley now. So what am I Jack? I am an echo of someone who once was, a fraction of his essence, not dead but certainly not alive."

"I'm so sorry."

Another trumpet blast of laughter boomed from the phonographs.

"My boy, I chose this, freely and gladly. Millions of sons and daughters have lived better because of what I chose. My once beating heart has sheltered countless generations. I have committed regrettable and unforgivable actions in my time, though now I can't seem to recall what they were. Undoubtedly lost with the essence I have given. But I am proud of what I created here. Even if I have had to live the past five centuries as a chair. It is a rather nice chair, all things considered."

Jack tried to imagine what that would be like. To strip away your essence, your memories in calculated chunks, becoming less whole by design for the good of others. It didn't seem so unfathomable on reflection. It was basically the maxim for every citizen in Cogrind.

"The Patron," said Jack, "You gave him your technology?"

McKinley's lens shook as if it were attached to a skull. "No. I foresaw an abuse of my methods long ago, and so I worked to ensure they would fade away with me. Those memories were part of what I gave to the Boilers. No, someone else showed the Patron. Furthermore, the methods he uses are not the same as mine and as you have seen, bear vastly different results."

"The serpents, the Ichor."

"That's right. I gave myself freely, happily to the Boilers. The people the Patron used, those poor souls, they were terrified, angry, afraid . . . innocent. As a result, the Arc extracted was tainted with all those terrible emotions. The byproduct was the Ichor. The distillation of all that fear and pain, an entity that seeks to corrupt any life, but is not truly alive. It would then be a logical hypothesis that the Ichor combined with some of my mechanical menagerie. That was the Patron's intent and he succeeded to a horrible degree."

There was something that didn't quite click in Jack's mind. "Why didn't you stop him? You've been at his neck for the three years we've been installing the new Boilers."

McKinley's fingers froze in place above the turning records before playing his voice again. "As I told you, someone else showed the Patron. Someone much older and much more powerful than he is. I couldn't risk revealing myself. If he knew I existed, he would extract what little life force I have left. The same life force that lives in you."

"Am I . . . your descendant?" asked Jack.

"No. I'm afraid I only had one child, and they were born sickly, much like you. I was . . . not able to help my child. But I could help you."

Jack wanted to say a thousand things, but his thoughts couldn't stay still long enough to form a sentence.

McKinley continued. "Your father discovered me. A deep well of curiosity, your father. He even helped develop the Arc-tank, just like the one in your arm. He studied everything he could to help you, but found nothing. Every doctor and surgeon in the City was exhausted from his constant hounding to heal you. Eventually he turned to our history, our lost technology for a remedy. That led him to Songcradle, or should I say the Undercroft, and eventually me. Perhaps it was a mistake, to graft my life force to yours, but I knew your father's pain. So I did what I could. Your skull was half-formed and missing an eye, so I gave you mine. That is why you have white hair and mismatched eyes. It was a byproduct of the healing. Some of my physical characteristics when I had a body were passed to you."

Jack let the flood of information wash over him and found

353

himself feeling lesser. "So my knowledge, my skills in machinery and artifice . . . That's just you?" His head hung low. He was an imposter. Not a prodigy or savant, but a fraud. Just a boy given knowledge beyond all measure and entirely undeserving of such a prize.

"What use are tools without a hand to wield them? What use is knowledge without the desire to act? You may have been given a fraction of my knowledge, but I did not give you your spirit, your desire to help others, your willingness to sacrifice for those around you, bidden and unbidden. Over time, I do not doubt you will acquire much greater knowledge than was given to you, but the lives you have touched, the choices you have made, are completely your own, my boy."

Jack looked up. "What happened to my father?"

The diamond-tipped fingers rested on the spinning records for a moment, the crackle punctuating the silence before they started playing his voice again. "I asked for something, in return for helping you. To help stop the very threat that we all now face. He failed, but he bought the city time. I daresay he would have done it whether I could have helped you or not. He was much like you in that way."

"What was his name?" asked Jack.

The Eye did its best to smile. "Your full name is Jack Minuet Dowton the second. You inherited many things from him, including his name."

Jack had always felt adrift among the populous of Cogrind, almost vestigial. But now he felt anchored to this place, even if it was just knowing that he bore his father's name. "Who taught the Patron all this? Who killed my Father?"

"In his quiet moments, The Patron called it the Hunger," said McKinley, "But it is the same enemy we faced from the

Age of Flame."

It was an historical fact, The Age of Flame, but so little and so few had survived from that time five centuries ago, that most everything said was little more than hearsay of a legend.

The gyros whirred again as McKinley spoke. "The Age of Flame was a war, its devastation nearly complete. It almost consumed the world itself. Our first home, Songcradle, what you call the Undercroft, would have been destroyed, so out of desperation for our defense, I designed the Arc-boilers. I poured my essence into them. They generated the power needed to defend our home and even then, it was almost not enough. We thought we had destroyed it, but it was only waiting for the right time. The Flame rises again, and whether they know it or not, the City looks to you to save them."

But why me?

"So this is my destiny, then?"

The eye lowered itself until it was within a foot of Jack's face. "Destiny?" The records emitted a burst of brass section laughter. "No Jack. You can walk out that door, out of the city, and never give another thought to this place for as long as you live. It is not destiny that we speak now in this place. It was not fate for you to lose your arm and build another. You have a much greater ally than destiny my boy, and it is the very same reason why you won't walk out that door. You have conviction, complete and unyielding. You have the knowledge of what you must face and the courage to face it. That is what makes you our greatest hope. Not destiny, never destiny."

Silence draped the room, save for the ticking of a clock that overlooked the city.

"What must I do?" asked Jack. Fear gripped his heart, but

355

McKinley was right, he would do what he could to help. He stirred his people to a riot and burdened them with killing and death. It would be unconscionable for him to shirk what was to come next. If this is what it would take to fix all of it, then that's precisely what he would do.

"Good," said McKinley, "Our people are under attack as we speak. I have one last gift to give. You need to take me to the Conservatory."

Jack studied the chair, thoroughly attached to the floor.

"Much like your body," replied McKinley. "This is just an inconvenient shell."

The gold-wrought desk to Jack's right snapped in two and swung away in a half circle revealing a short pedestal. The pedestal was made of thin braided strands of iron, bronze, silver, gold, platinum, copper, and nickel, cradling an Arc-tank much like the one powering Jack's arm. It was the construction of the Arc-tank that caught Jack's attention, or rather of what it was made. It was the same rose gold hue of his wrench and Sallah's daggers, but the shape was knotted and scarred, like a tree trunk. Inside of it swam the last essence of the greatest mind the world had ever seen.

"It took some time to shape me into something compatible with your arm, but now I should fit quite well," said McKinley.

Jack studied the material expectant for an answer.

"Many and more questions and no time I'm afraid. Take me to the Conservatory and attach me to the Arc-chain. I will purge the entire system, eradicating the source of the Ichor from the boilers. Additionally, once I'm connected to the Arc-chain, the city will essentially become my body. I will give myself the directive to track and eradicate our snake problem as well. Like pulling leeches, but the leeches are very large and my fingers are buildings."

"But this is the last of your life force. You're going to die."

"My boy, I haven't been alive for five hundred years. This is merely a completion of plans set in motion long ago. The Patron is coming for you now. There is nothing more I can do. You must get to the Conservatory." The eye retracted back into the throne. "Thank you Jack. Oh, and one last thing. Take care of her, protect her, no matter where she may go. Without her, what we do today and every day after will mean nothing." The spindly fingers wrapped around the chair frame, the eye closed and became a whole note once again.

Jack was alone. The Arc-tank on the pedestal gave off that same, almost imperceptible hum as any other. Jack snapped off the catches from the Arc-tank on the back of his arm. It swung limply at his side. Carefully, Jack lifted the new Arc-tank from the pedestal. It was heavier than it should have been and cold to the touch. Jack thought back on Sean Lute when he held Jack's wrench. The descriptions were the same. He secured the catches on it and flicked open the feed nozzle. For a moment Jack waited as the system in his arm gained pressure. Tears came to his eyes.

He could feel it, his arm, as if it were the one he was born with. He looked down at the device surgically attached to his shoulder. He moved his hand, palm up, and flexed each finger individually. He touched his index finger to his thumb. It felt like metal but it was his metal, nothing more than a different texture of skin. He balled it into a fist. He could feel each click of the mechanisms in his arms, he could feel the pull of his tendons connect to the taut metal cables. He rotated his hand three-hundred and sixty degrees at the wrist. He even tried out the piston arm he designed. His fist shot forward from the elbow and retracted back like he was born to do it. It was his. It was always his arm, he just hadn't known it. The chair that was once McKinley lifted towards the ceiling.

Jack moved behind the piston on which the chair rode. Jack stole a look down to the street. To his amazement, he didn't see the chaos he created. He saw the order he sought. Citizens stood shoulder to shoulder, regimented and looking away from the Tower, Steel Watch in front, the Walkers, semi-functional and standing as vanguard. All but three streets had been blocked and barricaded with multiple street plates. Beyond that the streets were empty.

She's still alive.

The soft hiss met Jack's ears as the piston began to lower. Jack wanted a good look at him this time. The chair came into view from the vaulted ceiling and sitting upon it was the Patron, leader of Cogrind. He was fatter than before, his blood-red robes bulged with rolls where it used to billow. He was older too. Not the seraphic aura of composed benevolence that Jack had seen before. The man's face sagged, his eyes bulging from his head farther than the purple bags underneath them. His face was a sallow mosaic of white and yellow. Not that Jack had gotten a good look at him before, but this man looked like one foot was already in the casket. Petty's dead face flashed into his mind.

The Patron smiled at Jack.

"Young Jack Dowton," said the Patron, "Killer of mentors, destroyer of Cogrind."

Jack remained silent.

His voice was different from before, hateful and rasping. "How does it feel to have so much blood on your hands? To bring my people to such desperation?"

"Our."

The Patron's smile faltered for a moment.

"Our people."

"No, Jack." His voice changed to a deep thrum Jack could feel in his chest. "They are mine. Do you still think you are speaking to this bag of skin?" The patron's jaw went slack but words were still coming from him.

"You are the Flame," said Jack.

The Patron's head lolled to the side, but his eyes never wavered from Jack. "The Flame, The Fire, The Hunger. Your kind use these words because you cannot comprehend what I am. But it is not your function to understand."

"And what is our function?"

The Patron's jaw cracked and widened as his head jerked back. From his throat emerged a hooded cobra, a real one, a darting tongue and coal black eyes. "You are all fuel for my righteous engine."

Jack's wrench shot into his hand.

The Flame only laughed. "Do you think to end me here? Your friends already tried years ago, but you stopped them. My eternal thanks for that."

Jack held his wrench, ready to strike out before his curiosity got the better of him. "What are you talking about?"

"Why the day you earned your apprenticeship, Jack. Sean Lute built the new Arc-boilers to fail and Barin, as the Master Tuner covered his tracks. He would have killed hundreds, maybe thousands, including you. But it was worth it to stop me. Until you intervened, of course. You saved the day, didn't you?"

Jack swung at its head.

The Patron's body lurched forward. His speed was preternatural. He caught Jack mid-stride, pinning him to the glass wall overlooking the city. "After that, they decided to put all their hopes on you. Why sacrifice thousands when only one was needed? Lute just needed you to feel special, to praise your self-sacrifice and spend some of his considerable wealth when needed.. Barin needed to increase your knowledge and skill, to give you access to the Conservatory and Proscenium. The Headmistress just needed to keep you alive. They gave you access, resources . . . love. All of that, so you would sacrifice yourself at just the right time. So you could deliver the Paragon to the Proscenium. And die."

Jack's right arm was trapped to his side, but he had managed to wedge his left arm between the glass and Patron's chest. The body of what was the Patron weighed far more than it should have, closer to a ream of iron sheeting than a man's body. The glass wall would give before he could budge the Patron's body. Jack had to stifle a gag from the stench of the Patron.

The Cobra eyed Jack's wrench. "He must have believed in you a great deal to give you such a weapon. He was always short sighted. But it was never his to give. That belongs to me." The cobra weaved his head until he was a tongue flick distance from Jack's eye.

"Actually," said Jack, his breath straining under the weight, "I made a few tools myself." He unleashed his piston arm.

The Patron's body didn't budge from the strike, but the glass wall behind Jack shattered, and he fell. His vision was filled with his people fighting a horde of serpents. One of the Walkers had waded into the middle of them as it self-destructed, sending shards of the abominations spraying

360

into the air. Jack whipped his wrench against the building, grinding and hoping to catch a ledge. It did, slowing his descent, but his momentum was too great, sending his body flailing through the air. Blurs of street, sky, and building careened through Jack's vision. He tried to hold his wrench out again in a vain attempt to slow himself. The blurs of ground grew closer and closer. He reached for the side of the tower.

With a jerk he stopped in mid-air, sending a shower of pain through his body. He slammed against the wall. He was fifteen feet above the tower steps packed with people.

Looking up, he saw what he thought he would. The wrench stuck into the side of the building like a banded vine.

Are you trying to make a machine work, or are you trying to move your arm?

Jack had suspected this was the case with his wrench as well. It wasn't about commanding it or willing it, the secret lay in doing it, reaching into that same instinctive place in his mind that let him walk or wiggle his finger. Jack's mind went blank as he tried to reach that space. He dropped onto the heads and shoulders of his people as the wrench extended further. Not elegant, but at least he was getting the feel. Pulling his body across the mass of shoulders, he reached the edge of the front lines. The situation couldn't have been worse.

The carnage was constant. Almost all of the battalions of Steel Watch in their thick armor had already been killed. But the next citizen would step forward from the crush, weapon in hand, ready to defend the others. He had to leave them to save them. He just needed to get past a knot of the serpents to get there. Concentrating on his wrench was nearly impossible here in the middle of screams and bodies, but he went back to that place in his mind. He flung the wrench at the top of a barricade. The wrench head whipped out, clamped to the top edge and pulled Jack up, his momentum carried him over the top. He grabbed the edge before he toppled over to the coils of serpents below. One snapped at his dangling feet before Jack crushed its head in. He scurried to the top of the barricade and aimed his wrench for the top of a building. As before he let the wrench carry him through the air and onto the roof. He was on his way to the Conservatory.

He was going to fix all of this.

Chapter 20

Sallah didn't know what to do. Now more than ever she felt out of place in this city. Charlie was still furiously working the podium, attempting to stem the flow of serpents as best he could. Even Tosi was annoyed and confused as to why they were not hunting. But she didn't want to leave Charlie's side. If the serpents found another way to this floor, he would be vulnerable, and his work may be the only thing keeping this battle from being a massacre. The floor shuddered beneath her feet.

"That came from the Proscenium," said Charlie, holding the podium for balance. "Check it out now. If something happens to the Boilers, I won't have the power to keep this up."

Sallah hesitated for a moment.

Charlie threw a look back over his shoulder. "I'll be fine."

Sallah nodded. "Tosi, to me!"

Tosi was already trying to paw his way through the barricaded door. The pair sprinted down the curving hallway to double doors with the words *Proscenium Access* etched in the glass. On the other side, flights of stairs wound beneath her feet, each landing had a thick blast door to the interior of the building. She wrenched open the nearest door and stepped out onto the catwalk and the yawning expanse of the Orchestra Pit below her. At the center of the Proscenium, far below, she saw the fat-bellied boilers clinging to a platform that leaned drunkenly towards the abyss below. Braids of serpents bubbled up and writhed beneath her. It was hard to focus on what they were doing with the sheer mass of movement. They were chewing through the support beams and rending open pipes, disconnecting the Arc-boilers from the Proscenium itself. At the same time, some of the serpent's bodies would meld into what they chewed through, forming a platform of its own and closing off feed pipes. Everything was going to come down and there was nothing she could do. Jack had told her of the dangerous capabilities of these Boilers if they weren't treated just so. This was downright abuse.

She had to escape, out of this building and out of this city. She did everything that she could do to protect her people and if the serpents were going to destroy the Boilers, then the source of the Ichor would be cut off. That was what she wanted. That was her whole goal in coming to this wretched place.

Then why did she feel so guilty? Jack. Of course he was the answer, but for all she knew, he was already dead after he vanished behind the barricade of guards into the Metronome Tower. He was part of the acceptable losses though. Cogrind had destroyed at least a portion of these serpents. She could return home and prepare her people's defenses. Her people, her House mattered. Not some boy she barely knew.

I'm sorry Jack.

Glass showered her from above. Her blades were already in her hands. Looking up, she didn't see a fight. She saw Jack, leaping lithe as a monkey from pipe to girder to the catwalk where she stood.

He ran towards her and much to her surprise, Jack threw both arms around her. Straightening, he smiled at her. "We have a lot to discuss."

Sallah watched as he wiggled the fingers of his mechanical hand.

"A lot."

A support beam screamed as it tore through rivets, destroying a catwalk next to them, and clattering down into the abyss.

"I need to get to the Boilers. I can end this. I can stop all of them"

Sallah eyed the failing platform and the host of serpents between them. "Who would have guessed you would pick the suicidal option," said Sallah.

Jack smiled. "Please let me know when you find a different one."

Sallah couldn't help but smile as well. "I'll cut a path. Stay close to me." She jumped down from the walkway with Jack at her heels. She sliced down on two, severing their necks before they could rear back.

Jack slammed his wrench into another behind her. The supports gave way as the catwalk twisted in the air. She felt Jack grab her arm as he flung his wrench, wrapping around a pipe above them. She slipped from his grasp but she managed to catch herself on a pipe below. She plunged a blade into one yellow eye and removed the lower jaw of another. More were on her. Her blade pinned a snake's skull to the pipe, causing a rupture that melted the creature's head to slag. More threw themselves at her until their melted bodies plugged the spewing leak. A fang grazed her heel as a snake struck from the underside of the pipe. Spinning away, she lunged for an elbow joint and swung onto a lower catwalk. Jack was behind her now. She swept through a handful more of the beasts as Jack was pushed back by the onrushing serpents.

"Keep moving!" Sallah shouted.

He jumped onto a feeder pipe below just as the scaffolding holding the catwalk crumpled in. The metal screeched as the catwalk she was on gave way and toppled towards the Boiler platform. Sallah braced her feet against the railing and readied to jump. She waited as long as she could, then jumped into emptiness.

The Boiler platform was almost within reach, a whisper away. But her fingers only grasped air as she fell. Sallah pulled out her daggers and stabbed at the platform's main support. The blades punched into the smooth metal grinding her to a stop.

A catwalk crashed into the support below her and fell into the pit. Sallah dragged herself up one stab at a time. She reached a badly damaged support girder, gaining the attention of the serpents chewing through and replacing the supports.

She spotted Jack on a girder twenty feet away with a serpent bearing down on his heels. His footing gave out. His wrench shot forward and grabbed the lip of the Boiler platform. He swung towards her. She leaped for him, catching Jack around the shoulders. The wrench retracted and they rose to the platform. The serpents flung themselves into open air. Sallah locked her legs around Jack and stabbed at their attackers as they struck. She climbed onto the platform and pulled Jack after her. Tosi had already climbed onto the platform, distracting as best he could, a blur of spit, teeth and claws. Sallah cut through an overhead pipe creating a wall of steam on one side, burning her hand in exchange. Jack ran to the Boilers, unlatching the Paragon's Arc-tank from his arm. Sallah sliced through another pipe creating an alley of ruptured Arc and a moment's reprieve.

"Time for you to go," said Jack. He removed the Arc-tank from his arm. "Get back to your people and stay alive," he shouted over the hissing wreckage. The platform groaned as it strained to stay upright. "This isn't over. I need you to stay alive."

"Hurry it up and we can both get out of here!"

The platform began to shudder under their feet.

Jack gave her a grin. "Thank you Sallah. You saved us." Jack's wrench grabbed a pipe above his head as he wrenched it down. A curtain of glowing steam showered between them. There was nothing to be done.

She had lost another one. She fell back. She was numb. She couldn't hear the horrible screeching of metal. She couldn't feel the jagged metal edges cutting into her skin as she clawed her way to a dangling catwalk. She couldn't feel the weight of the blast door as she shouldered into it. She didn't feel the quaking beneath her feet as the building buckled from the inside, the energy imploding the Proscenium. She didn't feel the sun on her face as she escaped the Conservatory. She didn't feel the fogbank of Arc as it flooded the city behind her, melting away the serpents lacing the streets like frost on an early spring morning. She didn't hear the jubilation of survivors echoing through Cogrind. She didn't feel her lungs burning as she ran out of Stonehall and towards the Greensea.

All she felt was the distance between her and home.

Chapter 21

He didn't feel anything. The fear Jack felt just a moment ago was gone. He was bathed in a white nothingness. He had done what he needed. He fixed it. He didn't want to die. He was scared of what would come next, but this was nothing to be scared of. It was over. Now he was just waiting for death to take him. Or perhaps this was death, an unfeeling, peaceful awareness that goes on forever. Jack could live with that, so to speak.

He could sense them. Not from a dream that disappeared every sunrise. He could actually feel them. Her auburn hair that tickled his nose when she thought he was sleeping. He could feel him. The chapped lips beneath the stubble, kissing his forehead, and a dancing, joking voice in his ear. He could smell her. She smelled like damp earth and honeysuckle and home. He could smell him. He smelled like leather and lamp oil and safety.

He could be done. He could just be, with them, forever.

But there was someone missing. Sallah. She was not done. She still had to protect her people and she would have to do it alone. He hadn't kept his word. Jack hadn't protected her.

He put her in danger. She was still in danger. More so now than ever, because now she was alone.

Jack didn't want to leave, to feel pain and fear. He did not want to leave the love he had never experienced in life. But his work wasn't done. There was still more to fix. Sallah needed help.

Jack felt a pain creep into his fingertips and move up his arms. The white forever turned dim and gray, and then black. The pain crawled up to the crown of his head. There was a shallow surface of air in his lungs. His eyes were closed. He was lying down. His tongue was dry and stuck to the roof of his mouth. Jack's eyelids fluttered, fighting their own weight. His body racked in a coughing fit. His muscles ached at the sudden movement. Breathing left him exhausted. His eyes saw only colored blurs.

"All right Jack," said the familiar baritone.

Jack tried to smile. But his face hurt too.

"Al . . . Char," whispered Jack. "Water."

Charlie pressed a cool cup to Jack's lips. "Back from the dead for thirty seconds and you're already barking orders." Charlie stopped tipping the cup.

Jack let the cool water hit the back of his throat. They repeated the process several more times in silence.

Jack felt a bit of strength returning. "How long . . . "

"A little over three weeks. We had almost given you up for dead, but Claire was having none of it."

Jack grunted. "Headmistress?"

"Yes. I've taken to calling her Claire now. It would seem a little out of place to call her that during Council meetings," said Charlie.

Jack furrowed his brow. Words were hard to come by at the

moment. And if what the Patron said, no, what the Hunger said was true, he hadn't the strength to face such thoughts right now. But he would.

"Quite a few things have changed since you saved the city," continued Charlie. "We don't have a Patron for starters. We decided a Council would be smarter from here on."

Everything in his body was made of lead, but his mind was still agile enough for basic thoughts. "Dead?" Jack managed to whisper.

Charlie nodded his head. "Found his body. Or what was left of it. He was a mess of crushed bones. Nothing fell on him though as far as we could tell."

Images of the Patron's neck sprouting the head of a cobra flashed into Jack's mind. The Hunger had simply left his body like a suit.

"Council . . . You?" croaked Jack.

Charlie belted a laugh. "Thank you for your vote of confidence. The only reason I was invited onto the Council is because Cogrind is a dead city. We have no more power. The Arc-boilers are gone."

"Destroyed?"

"No. Gone. We've been sifting through the rubble in the Proscenium for weeks with no sign of them. Like they were never there. So we started looking for alternative power sources. I brought up some ideas I had on hot water."

"Steam," corrected Jack.

Charlie laughed again. "They are going ahead with the plan, my plan to power the whole city." Charlie couldn't keep the pride out of his voice.

Jack gave him the best smile he could muster.

"So far it's just me, Claire, and Sean Lute. We are still

looking for a member or two to represent Bass Run. We've just now begun construction. I think we got a little too used to having Arc. Rebuilding has been slow."

"How . . . am I . . . alive?" asked Jack.

"Damned if I know mate. We had started the salvage operation at the Conservatory the day after the attack. We had figured the serpents had just done enough damage to the Boilers to overload the whole system, but if that were the case, there would be nothing but a Cogrind-sized crater in the earth. They found you in . . . well, they said a cocoon. At first they thought it was some sort of egg left from the serpents. They tried to smash it open. Instead the cocoon pulled back, turned into your wrench, and there you were. Busted up, burned, and dehydrated, but still alive. I don't know what you did, but you did an incredible job of it."

Jack couldn't remember anything like that. He remembered Sallah reaching for him. Then the prismatic steam of the Arc blinded him. Then the white nothingness.

So that is what the Hunger wanted. The Arc-boilers. The energy they produce, its righteous engine. The Serpents could fuse into the metal, providing both structure and transportation. That's how it disappeared the first day I saw them. It fused into the feed pipe it ripped open. Or perhaps it wants what's left of the Paragon. No, not the Paragon. Mckinley. We are the Paragon.

"Wrench," said Jack.

Charlie leaned over and tapped his mechanical arm. "Right there. you never let go of it."

Jack looked down at his left arm. The feeling was gone from it, just like before. "Damn." mumbled Jack. Perhaps it was stupid to be disappointed. He had helped save his home. He was ready to die for the cause. But he was alive, and now that he was, he wanted to feel complete again. But he couldn't feel the phantom pains either. His eyes were still blurry. His fingers had probably fused together at this point. Yet, his fingers released the wrench, just as he thought it would. Then they closed around the grip, just as he wanted. Jack flexed his fingers back and forth. The feeling had left him, but the gift had not. Tilting his head, he searched for the Arc-tank that powered it, but none was to be found. Somehow, someway, *he* was powering it now.

"I'm sorry," said Jack. His eyes started to burn.

Charlie reached for the cup of water, but Jack rolled his head away in refusal.

"For what mate? Not tidying up after the revolution?"

Charlie's broad smile only made Jack feel worse.

"Moira."

Charlie's smile faded. He placed a hand on Jack's chest, as it heaved softly in quiet sobs.

For a long while they mourned together. No words passed between them. There was nothing left to say when you lose something so precious. Three friends from the slums of Stonehall. Now, they were just two, and neither would be here without the third.

"She would be proud of us. She would be proud of you," said Charlie. "Though, she'd be shooing me off right now due to my horrendous bedside manner. Moira gave me a reason to get sober. She gave me a second, third, by cogs, a dozen chances to make something of myself. Now I get to help rebuild our home. Doesn't feel like home without her here though, does it? . . . Just glad I didn't lose you too."

Jack was scared he was going to lose Charlie too. Not to the violence of weeks previous, but that Charlie would just drift

373

away from him, a piece of his life he couldn't reach in time. But he was here, beside Jack. He wasn't going anywhere. Jack allowed the silence to surround them. Until Jack realized he was missing someone.

"Where's Sallah?" said Jack, still flexing his metal fingers.

"Last time I saw her she was on her way to the Proscenium. A little while after that the whole building felt like it was coming down. I made it out, but I didn't see her. I'm sorry."

Jack tried to sit up. He felt weak and everything felt bruised, but he managed it. "She's not dead, too smart, too quick. I have to find her." He tipped the cup to his own lips this time. Even the cup felt heavy.

"Why?"

"It's not over. We didn't win. We survived. What happened here is going to happen to her home."

Charlie folded his arms across his chest. "We got plenty of work here mate. We still need a Master Tuner after all. And since I'm not a total fool, I have already put your name forward. I think you might be a bit of a lock for the position, considering everything."

Jack let the idea wash over him. The respectful nods of the Luthiers as he strode across the Proscenium. Knowing each and every screw, nut, and bolt in the Conservatory. The one everyone would look to compose the groundwork for every new project in Cogrind. The Mainspring to the Greatest Machine. "This job first. Then the next."

Charlie rubbed the back of his own neck. "And how do you plan on finding a smart, quick, ghost of a woman who's been trained her entire life to remain hidden and cover her tracks?"

Jack hadn't the foggiest idea. She first appeared before

him in the dungeons below the Metronome Tower, the most secure and patrolled property in Cogrind. Sallah had always seemed impossibly adept. He had no idea if he was even capable of finding her, let alone help with the battle to come at all. But he remembered Mckinley's words.

Take care of her, protect her, no matter where she may go. Without her, what we do today and every day after will mean nothing.

A pair of bright green eyes peered over the foot of the bed. Tosi jumped up and sat on Jack's chest, staring at him wide-eyed and expectant.

Jack smiled and reached forward as Tosi allowed him exactly one pet before strutting to the foot of the bed. "I think it's time we took you home."

—

Three more weeks passed as Jack managed a full recovery. The constant ache in his back from the weight of his arm dissipated with the winter cold. Spring began to creep into the corners of Cogrind, warming hearts and minds exhausted from loss. Jack had spent the weeks convalescing into designing standardized blueprints for prosthetics. The basics of his design were sound and now quite thoroughly field tested. The trick lay in applying the design universals to unique amputations and reducing the size and weight of the prosthetic. Fingers, toes, feet, hands, and everything else had to be accounted for. Jack was not going to let a failure of imagination prohibit his gift to the city. After two weeks, he completed his task, designing unique blueprints and even wrote a lengthy addendum detailing specific foibles with each prosthetic type. Though they would have no Arc to power them, Charlie's steam idea had taken root in Jack's mind. Arc-tanks could easily be retrofitted to bear steam pressure and frankly were over-designed for it, adding a level of safety to their operation.

The last week of his recovery felt wholly unnecessary. When Charlie would leave on Council business, Jack would make his way out of his shack and walk the worn path of Stonehall. He walked along the moat, stopping at the pipework that he, Moira, and Charlie had worked so hard on eight months ago. It stopped only twenty yards from Moira's front door. Jack would climb the ramshackle stairs to Moira's old shack. The tubs of water now cold and milky, the smell of lye still clinging to the air. Jack would cross the half-stone, half-metal bridge and turn south. He never bothered looking at the time.

He helped any person or project he could find in Bass Run, still decimated from the razing, and still the lowest priority for reconstruction. His arm would catch eyes, but he ignored them. It was just the first prototype after all. The prosthetics they would receive would be better, lighter, beautiful. Instead of Mouse, he had earned a new nickname in those weeks. It was whispered wherever he went, just at the edge of his hearing—the Broken Prince. Cogrind slowly recovered, but it was different now. The Stacks would no longer sing, Balcony Row was a terraced hospital, silk and lace used as tourniquets and gauze. Jack was grateful for it, but the Patron's words still haunted his thoughts. What he said about Claire, Sean Lute . . . and Barin. There was one last thing for him to fix before he left.

—

"We are still cleaning up scrap all over Balcony Row. Most of the main streets still need repair or replacement. I hardly think we need to start experimenting with steam boilers now. We finish clean up first." Sean Lute's voice echoed across the vaulted ceiling of Metronome Tower's first floor.

Behind the half-circle table sat Charlie, Claire and Lute. They held all meetings on the first floor, so that anyone could watch the decisions being made and how the citizen's labor would be directed. It was a far cry from private sessions of the Chorus and the lofted Patron before, but even now the entry doors remained closed, the hall empty, save for the Council.

"We still have more than enough labor to do both. At some point we must begin looking to the future. I understand this will be most taxing on manufacturing to sta—"

The entry doors swept open in front of them. Jack strode towards the Council, a warm, spring breeze in his wake.

Charlie smiled broadly. "Good to see you up and about mate."

Jack smiled back. "It is good to see you too. Well then, I have great news. I have come to dissolve this Council." His words echoed across the ornate space. Jack's smile did not abate.

Charlie's smile turned to puzzlement, but trust in his best friend kept him silent. Claire was scandalized, while Sean Lute smiled with his tobacco stained teeth.

"And on whose authority?" replied Sean.

Jack strode directly in front of him. "Mine. Which should more than suffice." His wrench slid from his forearm into his hand with an echoing CLANG.

"You would threaten us at a time like this?" admonished Claire.

Jack turned to her, unblinking. "Unfortunately violence is the only language some in power understand." He turned back to Sean. "I have heard such awful rumors about the quality of construction of the new Arc-boilers from someone who *was* in a position of great authority on the matter." He leaned into Sean's ear. "It would be a capital offense of the highest order if that was found to be true."

Sean Lute's smile fell. Jack stared at him.

"And how exactly do you expect this city to right itself Mr. Dowton? To rebuild?" asked Claire.

Jack turned to Claire as he slowly walked backwards towards the open double doors. "By remembering the Paragon's first gift to us, the Chord."

The sound of footsteps and murmurs bled from the street as citizens began stepping into the great hall. Unsure and hushed whispers filled the air.

"Cogs for the Greatest Machine?" scoffed Sean Lute. "That is how we got into this mess in the first place."

"That is not the Chord. It never was," said Jack. "Though few in power tried to make it such over the years." He turned away from them to the crowd gathered behind him. "Each one of us possesses a unique voice, a unique song, a part to play. Individually beautiful, but greater when joined in harmony. As such, we have a duty to add our songs to the Great Symphony of Cogrind. All will contribute. All will be heard. I welcome you all as the first members of the Council of the Broken."

The whispers among the crowd grew louder.

"Like me, each one of you has given a piece of themselves to the city. So in turn, each of you will have a piece of the city given to you."

Claire, Sean, and Charlie began to register that each one of the citizens standing in front of them were amputees.

"You are free to reject the position of course, but know that it will always be available to you, as well as rooms to stay here in the Tower and wages to match your position. Additionally, if you so choose, you will be fitted with prosthetics." Jack extended his mechanical arm towards Sean. "Provided, with thanks and for free, by Lute and Sons." He turned back to Sean "So you see, Sean you will be far too busy rebuilding what was lost to worry with the affairs of the city."

Sean looked like he had been hit over the head by a rather large hurdy gurdy, before managing to stammer. "Y-y-yes of course." Without another word Sean Lute swept from his chair and walked briskly out of the Metronome Tower.

"Headmistress Claire. You are to be removed as well," said Jack.

Claire was crestfallen, compounding failures weighing her shoulders down.

"And appointed as the new Principal of Surgery for all of Cogrind."

Claire clasped her hand over her mouth as her eyes moved from Jack to the crowd beyond.

"You are the only one to have performed such a surgery, pioneering techniques that will be necessary to make our citizenry whole again. As your father taught you, so will you teach others."

Tears welled behind her half-moon glasses as Claire rounded the desk and embraced Jack. She had deceived him, lied to him. He would never trust her again. But she could heal many. Jack figured that was a suitable punishment for a woman that only wanted to protect and to heal in the first place.

She released Jack as he whispered in her ear. "Just make it right."

Charlie had already begun to stand from his chair as he prepared to exit the Tower as well.

"Where are you going?" asked Jack

"You dissolved the council mate. I know when to take my exit," said Charlie.

"Charlie, you will stay exactly where you are. You qualify, after all." Jack couldn't keep the grin from his face. "Besides, I needed to come up with a punishment fit for a drunk who's burned a dozen chances at respectability." He turned back to the Crowd.

"Ladies and Gentlemen, I present to you the first Conductor of the Council of the Broken. Although I'm willing to bet he prefers being called Charlie."

Charlie stood gaped-mouth looking over the crowd of people in front of him. He rushed towards Jack and pulled him aside. "I don't know how to do this . . . governing," he whispered.

"Well you better figure it out mate, because I just made an incredible speech." His smile broadened. He took the back of Charlie's neck into his hand and touched their foreheads together. "Just do what would make Moira proud. You'll be brilliant." Turning to the crowd, Jack addressed them one last time. "There are more orphans today than before the revolt. I suggest that to be your first issue you all address." He made his way through the gathered crowd. He tried to meet as many eyes as he could as he passed, respectfully nodding to each one, as was fitting for their new stations. He could feel their eyes on the back of his head.

"Right, well let's get everyone settled in and fed," said Charlie. "Then we can begin to figure out some arrangements . . ."

Jack let the warmth of the sun wash over him as he stepped out onto Balcony Row. Even now, people were finishing the last of the major cleanups and some had even started rebuilding walls and reglazing windows. He didn't know when he would see this place again. He hoped it was soon. But he was leaving, probably for a very long time. Feeling something curl around his leg, Jack looked down. Tosi was weaving between his feet, eager to begin the journey.

"Lead the way, cat. Let's go find my sister."

About the Author

You can connect with me on:

🌐 https://dshardin.co

📘 https://www.facebook.com/profile.php?id=61567616669108

🔗 https://www.instagram.com/d.s.hardin